PARALLEL PASSAGES

A Historical Novel

Ann Miller

Ann Miller

Larry & Peggy,
Peace. Love. Joy—may you
always have all three.

Ann

PARALLEL

PASSAGES

Copyright© 2016 by Ann Miller

This is a work of fiction. All characters, names, incidents, organizations and dialogue in this novel are either products of the author's imagination being used fictitiously, or are a matter of historical record.

ISBN - 13:978-1522792772
ISBN - 10: 1522792775

ACKNOWLEDGMENTS

Virginia Williams, 105 years of age, phoned me every few weeks for 3 years to find out how my book was coming along. I might have quit but for the fact I didn't want to disappoint Virginia. Thank you, Virginia. My son, Andrew, edited, "fleshed" out a few of the characters, designed the cover and supported and encouraged me throughout the 3 years of research and writing. Thank you, Andrew. Jerry Jackson and Linda Radosevich did a wonderful job editing my manuscript and Susan Lanning, who has published several books, helped me format Parallel Passages.

Thank you.

AUTHOR'S NOTE

Parallel Passages follows two families, a black family and a white family, who begin together on a tobacco plantation in Virginia. There is a connection between them and their descendents living in the Civil Rights Movement of the Sixties.

Because this is a historical novel I am attempting to keep it as historically accurate as possible. Therefore, I have used the word 'nigger' in Part I, the Slavery Period, in Part II, the Civil War Period and in Part III, the Civil Rights Movement of the Sixties. This word was used by both white people and African Americans during the 1800's and by some whites during the Civil Rights movement. I do not mean this in a derogatory way. If I offend any of my readers, I hereby apologize. Some of the dialect used by slaves is included as well.

A few of the characters in the book actually existed. Harriet Tubman was a famous conductor of the Underground Railroad and a spy for the Union during the Civil War. William Still took accurate records of slaves who escaped through the Philadelphia Underground Railroad.

Elizabeth Van Lew and her Mother were Civil War spies for the Union, as was Mary Elizabeth Bowser. Rose O'Neal Greenhow was a spy for the Confederates. Clara Barton was a nurse for the Union. And, of course, there were President Lincoln, President Jefferson Davis, General Grant, General Lee, and Colonel James Montgomery.

In the Civil Rights Movement there were President John F. Kennedy, Attorney General Robert Kennedy, President Johnson, the Rev. Martin Luther King, Jr., 'Bull' Connor, Governor George Wallace, Malcolm X, Stokely Carmichael and Imperial Wizard Robert Shelton. Just a few of the others involved were James Farmer, Medgar Evers, Michael Schwerner, James Chaney and Andrew Goodman, John Lewis, Huey Newton, Bobby Seale and Eldridge Cleaver.

PART I

THE SLAVERY PERIOD

"If you hear the dogs, keep going, if you see the torches in the woods, keep going. If there is shouting after you, keep going. Don't ever stop. Keep going. If you want a taste of freedom, keep going."

Harriet Tubman

Chapter 1

1840

Joe glanced at Tom as they followed the path along the river to their favorite fishing spot. It was good that their Master gave them Sundays off from working in the fields. Only a few Masters did that. They could fish on Sundays and add to the small amount of food the Master gave them each month.

"What dat noise, Joe? Dar an animal in dem bushes."

"I's takes er look." Joe laid his fishing pole down by the river and cautiously approached the bushes behind him. He, too, could hear a rustling, and leaned down for a better look. "Thar er man in here. Yer come out whar us ken sees yer."

A dirty, raggedy young Negro man about their age crawled out. He was shaking. "I's Ben. Please, don't tells on me. I's jes goes ter Canada. Does yer hab food? I's mighty hungry."

Tom and Joe looked at each other. "Yer ken hab our food. We hab chicken and corn cakes. W'en yer las eats?"

The man's eyes brightened. He grabbed the food as soon as Joe retrieved it and began to gnaw on the chicken leg. "I's been runnin' from dem patrollers an deir dogs fer seben days. Mas'r posted er reward fer me. Him sells de wife and chil'n down south. I's not goin' ter wait til' him sells me. Iffen him cotch me now him beats me. Him bery mean. I's got ter gets ter Canada." The man looked up at them and Joe and Tom could see fear in his eyes.

Joe noticed Ben's shirt was ripped and just barely hanging on his back. He hesitated, thinking that he only owned two shirts that were supposed to last all year. But then, poor Ben had none and how could he reach Canada with no shirt? "Here, Ben, yer shirt be torn. Yer ken hab mine. I's hab anudder shirt." Joe took off his shirt and handed it to Ben.

3

"Thank yer." The man stood up. Far in the distance, a howl was barely audible. His nostrils sucked in air and his eyes widened. "I's goes now."

Joe and Tom watched him walk quickly along the river. The stars had just come out and they could see him headed toward the North Star, known as the drinking gourd by the slaves. "Yer eber wants ter foller de drinking gourd, Joe?"

"I's 'spects I's will some day. I's thinks 'bout it. I's heerd er Negro ken owns land in Canada an builds er farm. I's wants ter do dat."

"W'en yer goes ken I's goes too? I's sees de hoo doo doctor fust an gits some pertection from dose patrollers an deir dogs. Dose dogs tear de niggers in ter pieces. I's feered ob dem."

It was two days later and Joe was walking down the road near the plantation. A white man on a horse came toward him. Behind the horse was a Negro being pulled by a chain. Two dogs were following. The Negro had his head down, but Joe recognized the shirt.

Bella leaned her plump body partially out of the rickety chair and wiped her daughter's forehead with a cool, wet rag. Charlotte, her face twisted in pain, lay on her mattress. It had been pulled down from the small loft where she normally slept and placed on the dirt floor in front of the fireplace. The baby was near coming. Bella was a root doctor and midwife to both the slaves and the whites on the plantation. She wanted to be with her daughter during the labor and delivery. Too bad the Mistress was having a baby too. The Master wanted her to stay with his wife so Bella could use her root medicines to help the Mistress with her pain and bring the baby out.

"Charlotte, de Mas'r says I's mus stays wid de missis. Dineh stays wid yer 'til I's comes back. I's gib her somefin for yer pain. 'Spects I's be back before de baby comes."

"I's tries ter wait til yer gits here." Charlotte glanced up at her Mama and tried to smile.

As Bella puffed and panted up the hill to the Big House the large red ball was just coming up over the sycamore and oak trees in the distance, painting the Big House with its 4 white pillars a pale pink color. She glanced back at the log cabin she shared with George and Charlotte. Because she managed the Big House, their cabin was almost as big as the overseer's house, and nearest to the hill and the path leading to the Big House. She frowned as she looked at the other five slave cabins which were for the field hands. They were smaller, all rectangular in shape, and were neatly laid out in two rows. Joe, their son, lived in a cabin in the second row and was crowded in with with other field hands. She couldn't see his cabin from there but knew he and the other field hands were already working in the field.

Bella adjusted her red kerchief on her curly black hair, hitched up her long brown skirt, and scrambled along the dirt path through the oak trees and up the hill to the back door of the Big House. The cook smiled at her as she came in through the kitchen. "Mas'r bin lookin' fer yer. Yer ter go right up ter de Missis' room. I's gits de food ready so yer ken take it up wid yer since yer goin' ter hab er long wait."

Bella took out some herbs from a bag she carried. After putting them in a cup with boiled water she carried it on the tray with her food up the long spiral staircase. "That you, Bella? Please hurry! I'm in a lot of pain." The mistress sat up in bed. "Is this what you gave me before John was born? I remember it helped with the pain." After drinking the hot mixture, she laid back, her long blond hair spread out over her pillow. Bella pulled back the blanket and examined her.

"It 'pears der baby not ready ter comes, Missis Lillian."

"Then I'll take a rest until it's time. There's a chair for you in that corner." The mistress casually gestured to her right. Bella sat in the chair and ate her food. She tried to settle down for a long wait, but all she could think about was her daughter. Mrs. Ramsey looked over at Bella and frowned. "Quit moving about and sighing so much. I'm trying to rest."

5

Early morning the following day, Bella placed a baby girl into the arms of the Mistress. "Go let Charles in, Bella. He's been quite patient, waiting to see his new daughter."

"Lilian, she's beautiful. Just like you." Charles leaned over and gave his wife a kiss. "Let's name her Margaret, after your Mother." Lillian looked up at Charles and smiled happily.

"Scuse me, Mas'r, but ken I's goes? Charlotte goin' ter hab er baby too, an I's wants ter hep her."

Charles glanced at Bella and absentmindedly replied, "Oh, you can go. We'll get a granny midwife to look after Lillian and the baby."

Bella ran as fast as her plump legs would carry her, out the Big House and down the dirt path to her cabin. Dineh came out to meet her. "O, Lor! Bella, Charlotte done tuck sick. De baby bin turn de wrong way an I's neber seen sich er thing before. I's bin so consarned. She bin in sich dre'ful pain tryin ter gits dat baby out."

Bella ran to her daughter, and knelt beside her. "I's here, Charlotte. Mama's here now. I's turns de baby so it comes out right." Bella reached in and turned the baby so she was able to help the baby out. She smiled at Charlotte. "Yer hab er baby girl, Charlotte." Bella cut the cord and then wrapped the baby in a blanket and placed her into Charlotte's waiting arms.

"What yer wants ter name her?"

"Rose," Charlotte gasped weakly. Bella wiped Charlotte's forehead and noticed that Charlotte was having trouble breathing. She'd lost a lot of blood. Charlotte was trying to say something, and Bella had to lean close to hear her. "Mama, don't lets dem makes Rose er field hand. Yer gits dem ter makes her er house girl."

"I's will, Charlotte. I's trains her ter be er house girl an' den they be wanting her fer dat job." Bella remembered how she'd tried to get Charlotte into the Big House to work with her, but the Master had said he had enough house girls. He sent Charlotte to the field to carry water when she was seven. At twelve, Charlotte became a field hand. That is a hard life, working in the hot sun from sunrise to sunset. Bella turned away and wiped her eyes. The fields kill the soul of all but the strongest. At thirteen a white overseer forced Charlotte into an unused shed a few times, and now she had a baby. "Yes, Charlotte, I's be making sartin Rose be er house girl."

Charlotte seemed to relax upon hearing that. She smiled down at her daughter and whispered, "Yer life not be hard like mine, Rose. Yer hab food an yer won't gits de lash. Mebbe, we'n yer most grown, yer can foller de drinking gourd ter de North."

"Lets me puts on one ob dem purty cloths yer makes fer her so yer ken sees it." Bella dressed Rose in a blue dress, remembering how Charlotte was so excited about having a baby. She would work all day long in the tobacco field, come back to the cabin, and sew baby clothes out of the pieces of cloth the mistress had given Bella.

Bella held Rose up so Charlotte could see her in the dress. Charlotte smiled at her Mama and her new daughter. She lay back on the pillow and closed her eyes. She did not open them again.

George and their son, Joe, built a wooden casket for Charlotte. Bella helped wrap Charlotte in a cloth with her hands placed across her chest. A metal plate was placed on top of her hands so the spirits in the coffin couldn't return home. The coffin was nailed shut. Charlotte's funeral was arranged for that Sunday night.

The Master walked into his wife's dressing room, followed by their four year old son, John. He sat in an easy chair, watching his wife at her dressing table. He frowned as he saw her staring at herself in the mirror, leaning over various brushes and containers for powder and makeup. Lillian was still beautiful after having two children, but, unfortunately, she knew it. "Lillian, I've given Bella and George permission to use our horse and wagon for Charlotte's funeral Sunday night. I've also given permission for all the slaves from the plantation to attend, and a few slaves from a neighboring plantation have permission from their Master as well."

Lily paused, her hairbrush in midair. "Why, Charles?"

"Bella has been good to us. She's been a midwife for little John and now for Margaret. And she manages our household." Charles paused for a moment. "Have you ever seen a slave funeral?".

Lillian, eyes wide with wonder, glanced sideways at Charles. "Why ever would I care to do such a strange thing?"

"It's rather interesting. I hid out and watched one when I was a child. They line up two abreast in a long line. The horse and wagon, with the wooden casket, follows behind the procession. Some of the mourners hold lanterns to help them find their way in the dark. The funeral procession goes deep into the woods. It stops at a large hole that's been dug under a spreading oak tree. Maybe we could ride down there sometime and you could see it."

"Why do you have such a strange fascination with our slaves?"

Charles looked away and cleared his throat. "The casket is put into the ground, with the feet facing east so the dead wouldn't have to turn around when Gabriel blows his trumpet in the eastern sunrise. Then each slave tosses a little dirt onto the casket. Items belonging to Charlotte or whatever she might need, such as seashells, broken dishes and a broken vase, will be placed on top of the grave."

"Charles. You didn't answer my question, did you?"

"Well, I've become curious about our slaves' lives, their exotic ways and traditions since I heard certain rumors from some of the slave sellers about the hidden, wild, and... passionate lives that our slaves may lead and how their men have certain opportunities..."

"I hope you aren't suggesting we behave like our ignorant slaves!"

Charles wiped sweat from his brow and continued. "A pipe is driven into the ground so that the living can talk to the deceased through the tube. I'm not certain what the broken dishes mean, but they are put on top of the grave. Perhaps this is something from their African forefathers."

8

Lillian yawned, "Not tonight dear. I have no interest in this now."

John shook his head and mumbled to himself, "I thought not," and got up."I won't bore you any longer, my dear. Go back to brushing your hair."

Little John followed him out of the room."Papa, could I see a slave funeral some day?"

The master smiled. "I think that would be a good idea. When you're older you'll be running the plantation with me. It will help you work with our slaves if you know something about them."

Joe watched his Mama wipe the tears from her eyes. His sister, Charlotte, had always liked the singing and the getting together that happened at funerals. And there were a lot of them, especially babies, and the women who died while having them. Just like his sister. Then there were those who died from something the overseers liked to call malaria or pneumonia. He thought it more likely that their bodies were tired and used up. There was only so much work you could whip out of someone. Nobody really knew what brought death to the slave quarters, but it was always there. His sister's death didn't need to happen and wouldn't have if his Mama had been there to help with bringing the baby out. It was their Master who caused his sister to die. How he hated him. And how he missed Charlotte.

Since the Masters didn't like them getting together in groups, Church and funerals were about the only times they could sing, dance, drink and talk together. The masters were nervous. They were afraid slaves would plan escapes if they gathered together and might even plot to murder them. He did know that the "promised land" of Canada was talked about at Church and funerals, but had never heard talk of killing the Master. He'd like to run away and be done with all this misery. And he would—some day.

Singing, dancing and talking. The funeral lasted most of the night. George, who had always been close to his daughter, was quiet and not joining in the singing. Bella thought with fondness how he'd always helped her through the bad times. Their first child died in childbirth. Their second child, Harry, was sold to pay the Master's gambling debts. Now they'd lost Charlotte. She worried about George because he'd been so silent about Charlotte having a baby by that overseer and now about Charlotte's death. Only Joe was left. Bella remembered so many years ago when she and George got married at the Big House. Even though a slave marriage wasn't legal in the eyes of the law, when they jumped over the broom it meant to them and to everyone else that they were married. Bella knew that only one of them being sold down south or death could ever separate her and George. Yet that could happen. No one was ever safe as a slave.

Bella noticed her Joe in a group with other young men. They were muttering to each other in low voices. She raised her hand to her mouth and closed her eyes. No. Not Joe. He couldn't. Not after what she'd already lost. When they walked back to the slave quarters in the early morning hours Bella took Joe aside. "It 'pears yer an' yer friends wuz talking serious at de funeral. I's heard somefin ob it an' am consarned."

"Dey seys dat my sister still be livin' iffen yer warn't er slave an hab ter takes care ob der Missis 'stead ob yer own chile. Dey sez only way dat happen is us'n hab our own land. Our own country an no white folks. Two ob dem wants ter follow de drinking gourd ter Canada. Dey wants me ter go wid dem."

Bella's eyes widened; her nostrils flared. "Stop dat now, will ye! Don't yer listen ter sich talk. I kaint bear it if yer goes. I's hab only yer left out ob 4 chil'en. Dey hab dogs for trackin' niggers an iffen dey cotch yer de Mas'r beats yer. He ken sells yer ter de soul drivers an yer be toted downriver, whar dey kills niggers wid hard work and starvin'."

"Mebbe I's stays fer now, but some day I's follow dey drinking gourd ter freedom, whar I's ken hab er farm an keeps any monies I's earns wid carpentry an not hab ter give it ter de Mas'r."

Chapter 2

1845

"Dat be yer, Joe?"

"It be me, Reuben. Tom wid yer?" Two men stepped out from behind trees, holding cloth bags over their shoulders. Joe joined them and he was carrying a bag as well.

"I's hab some pepper ter rubs on our feet so dose dogs kaint foller us. Iffen we leaves now we ken gits fur away before dey finds us be gone. Dey dancin' an' drinkin' an' singin' as dey always does on Sattidy night. Sunday is Church an' no one thar tells dat us be gone. De overseer kaint knows us be gone til us not in de tobaccy fields at sunup. By then us be fur away."

"Dat don't matter. De paterollers an deir dogs be all 'roun, lookin fer dose dat runs so dey ken gits de reward." Reuben looked down at his feet.

"Look thar yander, Reuben." Joe pointed upward. "Thar be de drinking gourd dat takes us ter Canada whar us ken be free. We follers dat an stays near de ribber so dose dogs kaint foller us."

Tom put his hand on Joe's arm. "I's trusts yer, Joe." He gestured to Reuben. "We both knows yer been run'n round de woods fetch'n roots fer yer mama an' sneak'n off since yer was small."

Joe looked sheepishly back at Tom with a grin, "I's don't sneak off at night. Well, not much. Overseer don't know noth'n."

Tom laughed, "Yer know how much worry yer gib your mama at night! Yer know! Jes don't lose us."

Joe straightened up, his face serious. "I's won't."

Joe started along the James river, the other two following. Tom had a lantern, but they didn't dare use it for fear someone might see the light. They stumbled along the shore with only the

11

light of a half moon and the stars, walking as fast as they could and occasionally looking behind in fear. Part of the time they walked in the river so the dogs would lose their scent. At other times they used the pepper on their feet. When daylight came Joe crawled up under some low bushes and Tom and Reuben followed.

"I's thinks I's ken goes furder, Joe."

"No, Reuben, us goes at night an hides an sleeps in de day w'en de paterollers are eberwhar. I's reckerlects us been walkin fer elebin days. Us sho hab er lot furder ter goes ter follow dat drinking gourd. Us be out ob corn cakes an needs more den dose berries. Both ob yer looks fer berries an gits water an I's makes er trap an' cotch er rabbit. Be bery quiet 'cuz us heard dogs yestidy."

Joe gathered some sticks and made a trap which he put nearby and then sat under a tree to wait for Reuben and Tom. "Joe, looks what I's hab. It were on er tree." Reuben held up a poster, and Joe, who could read a little, was able to see it was describing the three of them. He read: THREE RUNAWAY SLAVES FROM RAMSEY PLANTATION JOE, TALL, MUSCULAR, ABOUT 26 REUBEN, A MULATTO, SHORT TOM, VERY BLACK WITH SCAR ON CHIN $100 REWARD

"Us gots ter be bery keerful. Dey knows us be follerin' de drinking gourd so dey be lookin fer us dis way. Now, I's thinks I's heard somefin." Joe left and soon returned with a rabbit. "Reuben, makes er small fire dat kaint be seen bery far."

The rabbit was soon cooked and each of them quickly devoured the small amount of meat. Reuben sighed and looked at Joe. "Iffen us finds er station ob de Underground Railroad likes dey talks 'bout, den dey heps us.

"I's knows, Reuben. We jist needs ter keeps goin' an keeps lookin."

Tom looked at the other two, then down at his bag. He settled and rested his head in his hand. There was a long silence. He glanced at Reuben and quietly cleared his throat. He pulled a small pouch out of his bag and held it up for Joe and Reuben to see. "Yer sees dis? It be made fer me by er hoo doo doctor an it keeps me safe from dem paterollers an deir dogs."

"What in it?" Reuben held out his hand.

"Lodestone in it. I's spects dat iffen yer stays wid me den yer both be safe. I's sartin ob it."

"I's don't knows 'bout dose conjurers, Tom. I's hopes it heps yer an Reuben an me though." Joe looked up at the sky. "It be dark soon an us needs ter sleeps before den." The three men stretched out beneath the trees.

Suddenly Reuben sat up and looked around. "I's heard dogs an dey sounds likes dey close. Us not near de ribber an' dey ken picks up our scent. What us do, Joe?" Reuben's eyes were wide with terror and Tom was looking around for a safe place to hide.

Joe pointed. "De ribber down dat way. Us runs." The three took off, running as fast as they could. The barking was getting louder and louder. Reuben stumbled and almost fell, but Joe reached out and grabbed him and they kept on running. Joe could hear Reuben panting and could see him struggling to keep up. "Hurry, Reuben. Us ken makes it. It not much furder."

Joe could see the river and Tom had almost reached it, but Reuben was panting heavily and slowing down. Joe glanced behind him and saw 3 dogs rapidly approaching. Reuben would never make it and he couldn't leave him behind. Sweat beaded on Joe's forehead. He winced and forced himself to slow down. His own promise echoed in his ears, "I's won't, I's won't lose you." Joe looked around and saw a tree with a couple low branches. "Here. Gets on ter de tree." Joe helped Reuben reach the lowest branch and then found another tree and climbed up as fast as he could. The dogs reached the trees and stood under the tree Reuben was in, barking loudly. Reuben looked down, terrified, and then lost his grip, falling right onto the 3 dogs. Joe watched in horror as the dogs attacked Reuben, ripping him apart as he lay on the ground, screaming. At last there was no sound. The dogs then left Reuben's body and stood, barking, under the tree that Joe was in. It was a short wait and two men appeared on horseback.

"Well, look what we got. This must be two of the niggers that were on the poster. Where's the other one?" The men dismounted and tied up their dogs. "Get down from the tree, you."

One leaned over Reuben and told the other, "This un's still breathing so we might get the full reward for him if he doesn't die before we reach the plantation." One of the men held a gun on Joe as he climbed down. Another tied Joe's hands together. They threw Reuben's body over the back of a horse and had Joe get on the other one. A patroller got behind Reuben, the other behind Joe, and they headed back toward the Ramsey plantation, the dogs following behind.

A day later the horsemen pulled up in front of the plantation. The one dumped Reuben's body on the grass between the slave quarters and the Big House and the other kept the gun on Joe as he dismounted. A slave ran to the Big House and told the Master. Bella was working in the House, overheard, and came running out and down the path.

"Joe! Joe! Yer be hurts?" Bella looked Joe over and sighed with relief. Then, frightened, she looked pleadingly at the Master. "Mas'r, Joe neber does this agin. Him be er good slave an works hard." Joe just stood with his head down, saying nothing.

The Master paid the two men on horseback the reward money and sent them on their way. "I'm sorry, Bella. I always said I'd never beat any of my slaves unless they tried to run away. When they run they need to learn a lesson. I also need to show the others what will happen if they try this. Go back to the house." The Master waited until Bella was out of sight and then directed a slave to tie Joe's arms around a tree. By this time a slave had fetched the overseer from the fields and the Master told the overseer to give Joe 100 lashes. Then he directed slaves to move Reuben to a shed because there wasn't much they could do for him.

Bella waited until the Master returned to the Big House. "Please, Mas'r, lets me takes care ob Joe. I's ken puts medicines on his sores an' mebbe hep Reuben." Bella looked at the Master and Mistress, tears running down her cheeks.

"Oh, Charles, you've punished Joe enough. Let his Mama take care of him. She's done so much for us; and this is her only son." Lillian looked up at her husband with a pleading look.

"Bella, you have my permission. Have a couple of slaves untie him and take him to your cabin. And see what you can do for Reuben, although I don't think he'll make it. Those dogs really tore him to pieces."

Bella rushed out of the Big House and found two slaves to untie and move Joe to a mattress in front of their fireplace. George was taking care of the Master's horses and someone rushed to the stables and told him so he was at the cabin when Joe was brought in. They made Joe as comfortable as possible and Bella went to pick the roots she needed for medicine to dress Joe's blisters and relieve the pain. At least the Master didn't have the overseer pour red pepper and salt into the open blisters as she knew some slave owners did to runaways. Still, it was bad enough. Joe's entire back was a mass of open, bleeding sores. Bella applied the bruised leaves of the passionflower to Joe's blisters, which would relieve the pain. She gave him poke root tea, which also helped with the pain. As soon as she saw that Joe was resting peacefully she left George and little Rose to watch him while she went down to the shed to check on Reuben.

Reuben had lost a lot of blood from his open wounds and was unconscious. Bella tried to stop the bleeding and put the leaves of the passionflower on him, but realized it was only a matter of time before he was gone. She left a friend to watch over him as there was nothing further she could do, and went back to Joe.

It was four days later and Joe was back working in the fields. Suffering burning pain with every movement of his body, Joe swung the tools in his arms, struggling and stumbling through the field. These wounds felt like they'd never heal, but he knew they would. The more he swung at the dirt, the more his wounds stung. Hobbling across the field, he imagined himself walking to freedom. He knew his bloody hands scrapped the soil once more, but his eyes were set on the horizon. The scars were healing over, leaving their permanent marks. Yet, Joe had other stronger marks staying with him. The marks of his time away from the plantation. For now, he couldn't sneak out at night. However, he often dreamed of Tom running ahead of him, glancing back, on his way

15

to freedom. Tom hadn't been caught and the slaves were all hoping he'd reach Canaan. It was talked about in Church that Sunday. Joe told what he and Reuben and Tom had been through; and mentioned that next time he'd try to learn where a station of the Underground Railroad was because it was too hard to do it on your own. Bella wanted him to say he wouldn't try it again, but Joe said he would be free someday. He'd follow the drinking gourd, but not for a while. His good friend, Reuben, had died and the funeral was that Sunday night.

Chapter 3

1846

"Lets me looks at yer, Rose." Bella glanced at Rose, who was wearing the new dress Bella had made for her, and smiled her approval. "I's be larning yer 'bout workin' in de Big House since yer wuz 3 yar old. Yer larns fast. Yer knows how ter listen ter de white people an nebber talks back ter dem. I's larns yer how ter sets de table, cleans de silver, an' cleans de furniture. Yer be 'roun de House w'en de mas'r an missis be out. It 'pears yer ready ter meet de missis. I's asked de missis iffen I's ken sees her an her say yes."

Bella took Rose's hand and they walked up the dirt path to the back door of the Big House. Mistress Lillian had a house girl bring them up to her dressing room. "Hello, Bella. Is this your granddaughter, Rose? She was born right after my Margaret, wasn't she?" Bella nodded. "What did you want to see me about?"

"Missis Lillian, I's larned Rose 'bout de Big House an I's knows her be er good house girl. Ken her works more wid me an yer ken sees how her be?" Bella paused because, at that moment, Margaret walked into her Mother's room and spotted Rose.

"Mama, whose that little slave girl? What is your name, slave girl? How old are you?"

"I's Rose, Miss. I's six."

"I'm six too." Margaret turned to her Mother. "Mama, I want Rose to be my very own slave. She can help me dress and pick up my toys and bring me food from the kitchen. Please Mama!"

Lillian looked at her daughter and then at Rose. "Well, I suppose we could try it and see how it works out." She turned to Bella. "You want Rose to be a house girl and Margaret seems to want someone her own age as her slave. Bring her with you tomorrow morning."

"Thank yer, Missis Lillian. Us be here." Rose nodded shyly at the Missis and Margaret, and they left the Big House.

"I's tole yer Mama, Rose, dat I's gits yer in de Big House. Yer needs ter do whatebber Miz Margaret tells yer an don't eber fights wid her eben iffen her be mean an says bad things ter yer. Yer knows what I's says, Rose?"

"Yes, Grandma Bella, I's knows. I's does eberyt'ing Miz Margaret tells me."

"Come here, little girl," Margaret commanded. Rose shyly approached Margaret, who was sitting on the floor holding a doll. "You see the things in my room?" Rose nodded. "You are not to touch them unless I say you can. Since I may want to play dolls with you sometime, you must bring your own doll because I don't want you touching mine."

For the rest of the day Margaret ordered Rose to pick up anything that was dropped, run down to the kitchen to get food for her, go on a walk with her while holding an umbrella over her head to protect her from the sun, and help her get dressed for bed. It was a long first day for Rose, and when she returned home she didn't say much.

"What de matter, Rose?" asked Bella, after seeing the look on Rose' face.

"Miss Margaret wants me ter bring er doll an I's don't hab one."

Bella smiled. "Us ken makes one wid de cloths de missis gib me." Soon Rose and Bella were searching through a bag of material, picking out cloth for the face, lips, body and 2 buttons for the eyes. "Dis brown be good for de face, Rose. An yer hab found buttons for de eyes." Eventually a rag doll with a cheery red lipped smile emerged from the pile. "I's makes er purty dress fer yer doll dat yer ken takes off iffen yer wants." A little later she said, "Here yer be." Bella handed the doll to Rose who hugged it and gave

Bella a big smile. She had never really had time to play before. Every moment, even her secret time with Joe, had involved some work task that needed to be done. She was nervous she would not be good at playing dolls and Margaret would get upset. But at least she had done one thing that Margaret wanted; she had her very own doll. And the cheerful expression on the doll's face stirred something in her. She thought carefully and decided to call her doll Lucey.

The next morning when Rose walked into Margaret's bedroom Margaret looked up from where she was playing. "Let me see your doll, Rose. Oh, she's pretty. What's her name?"

"I's calls her Lucey."

"My doll is Fanny. Maybe they can play together."

"How yer likes workin at de Big House?" Joe crouched down so he was eye level with Rose.

"It not like yer an me sneak'n off Sunday nights in de forest, findin roots, Joe. No birds, no swimin' hole. Always I hab ter be fo Miz Margaret or I's be in trouble. Mos times I's likes it, but sometimes Miz Margaret be mean. I's jes does what I's tole."

Joe smiled. "Dat whats us'n hab ter do til us'n goes ter Canaan an be free."

"What it mean ter be free, Joe?"

Joe sat on the packed dirt floor in front of the fireplace and pulled Rose onto his lap. "Free mean not hab'n ter sneak away. Free mean de white people kaint tells yer what ter do, an w'en yer earns monies yer gits ter keep it. Free mean yer ken buys land an builds yer own house. An w'en yer be married dose white people kaint sells yer or yer wife ter anudder plantation. I's be free someday, Rose."

"Yer not runs away an gits beats wid de whip agin, Joe?"

Go Down Moses, an Swing Low, Sweet Chariot? An de song dat say O Canaan, sweet Canaan, I am bound for the land of Canaan? Dose songs 'bout going North in ter Canada whar us ken be free. De white people don't knows what dose words means an yer don't tells dem, Rose."

"I's don't tells, Joe, but I's don't wants yer ter goes ter Canaan. I's wants yer ter stays here wid me."

"Rose, w'en I's goes ter Canada I's works on carpentry likes Papa teach me. Den I's buys er farm an builds er house on it. W'en yer be big yer comes ter Canada an lives wid me on de farm."

" Den I's be er slave fer yer an not Miz Margaret."

"No, Rose, us both be free. Dar no slaves in Canada. Yer ken goes ter school an larns ter read an write an yer ken works an keeps yer monies. W'en I's leaves , Rose, yer knows I's goes ter hab er farm fer both ob us. Always 'member dat."

Chapter 4

1847

Bella and George watched as a rugged looking white man walked up the path to the Big House, leaving his horse tied to a tree near the slave quarters. A little later this man came down the path with the Master. They walked to the second row of slave cabins. Soon they returned and the stranger was leading Joe, who had his hands tied together.

"What yer doin wid my Joe, Mas'r?"

"Bella, I'm selling Joe to settle some debts. I can get good money for him because he's young, big, and strong. I don't know that Joe might try to run again, so I've decided to sell him."

Rose ran to Joe and put her arms around his waist. "You kaint sells my uncle." Rose turned and looked up at the Master.

"Oh yes I can. He's mine and I can do whatever I want with him. This slave trader is taking him down south. Say your good-byes quickly so he can be on his way." The Master glanced sheepishly at Bella and George and then turned and walked rapidly up the path to the Big House.

Bella, George and Rose hugged Joe. He leaned over to Rose and said in a low voice, "Jes 'member what I's says, Rose. I's sees yer someday in Canaan. Goodbye, Mama an Papa. Us'n not always be slaves. Mebbe I's sees yer agin w'en us'n all be free."

Bella started sobbing. "Yer de las ob my four chil'en. Dey says befer dat dey leaves me one. Why yer tries ter run away? Dat why de Mas'r sells yer."

Joe looked Bella in the eye, a determined expression on his face. "Mama, I's goin' ter be free. Dey ken sells me ter er slave owner down south but I's runs agin. I's goin' ter reach Canaan an be er free man."

Just then the slave driver approached Joe, proceeded to chain him, mounted his horse, and led Joe away. George put his arm around the sobbing Bella and helped her back to their cabin.

Rose stood and watched Joe until she could no longer see him. "I's sees yer in Canaan, Joe. I's will."

Rose sat in the corner of Margaret's bedroom and listened as the new tutor was teaching Margaret something called the alphabet. The tutor explained to Margaret that she needed to learn this in order to read. Rose had heard in Church on more than one occasion that it was something special if you can read so she silently repeated the letters as Margaret said them to the tutor. After the lesson Rose waited until the tutor and Margaret left the room, opened the book they'd been studying, and turned the pages. Margaret came in just then and caught her. "What are you doing with my book, Rose?"

"I's jes sees how yer larns ter read. I's wants ter larn."

"You can't learn, Rose. My Papa told me there was a slave named Gabriel here in Virginia that was going to kill a lot of whites so they hanged him. Then they made a law that no slave could learn to read and they couldn't get together in groups either."

Rose hung her head and looked so unhappy that Margaret thought for a moment and then said, "I could teach you. It's not like you'd have a tutor. Sit in the corner when I have my lesson like you did today. After the lesson, we'll play teacher and student, and I'll practice my reading while I teach you."

"Thank you, Margaret!" Rose beamed, her eyes wandering over the books, but her hands still not daring to touch them again.

Joe stumbled along after the slave trader's horse, trying to keep up. The sun had been directly over them when they'd started out from the Ramsey Plantation and now it was starting to set on the horizon. "Is that you, Patrick?" the slave trader called out. Soon Joe was pulled along to where another white man was standing, his horse tied to a nearby tree. Next to him was a Negro woman whom Joe recognized. It was Liza from the plantation next to theirs. He noticed her hands were tied and she was looking at the ground. The slave trader dismounted and greeted the man named Patrick.

"Look what I have here, Will. She's a 'fancy girl'. She's either a Mulatto who is half white, half Negro and very light skinned, or she could be a Muldoon, with only one quarter Negro blood in her. Don't think you've seen one of these before, have you, brother? You're new to the trade. Plantation owners like 'em because they can make 'em do things their wives won't do. They do it all." Patrick leered at Liza. "At least they do it if they know what's good for 'em. We'll get a good price for this one in New Orleans. I only paid $300 for her because her owner didn't know what she was worth. We maybe can get $1000 for her in New Orleans." Patrick slapped his brother on the back.

"Well, Patrick, this here's Joe, and he's big and strong. He ran away 'bout a year ago so he's like a lot of them we get cheap. The plantation owner doesn't trust Joe anymore, and sold him as a lesson to his other slaves on what will happen if they run off."

"Hmm...," Patrick said, tilting his head and looking Joe up and down. "Don't say anything about him running. The buyers in New Orleans don't need to know that. I think we can still get a good price for him, though not as much as my fancy girl here."

"Let's find a place in these here woods to camp. Tomorrow we go to Richmond and pick up the five we got held in the slave pen. Here's a clear space with trees where we can chain these two 'til morning." The trader, Patrick, chained Liza to one tree while his brother, Will, chained Joe to another. They walked away to collect wood for their fire and make their camp.

"Liza, I's Joe from de Ramsey Plantation. I's sorry ter sees yer here."

"Oh Joe, I's din't knows yer at fust. Did yer hears what dey plans ter do wid us? I's don't thinks I's ken bar it." Liza lowered her head and started to cry.

"Dar now, Liza. Mebbe us both gits er good Mas'r dat treats us good an don't do dose dre'ful things ter yer dat dey talks 'bout."

Liza and Joe talked quietly, but were so exhausted from their long walk that they soon lay down beneath their respective trees. A little later they were given water and corn meal and then they settled down for the night. Just as the sun rose in the sky Joe and Liza were given more corn meal and water, and chained together. A long chain went from them to Will, and they were forced to follow, stumbling along, behind his horse. Patrick rode on ahead to Richmond.

Patrick met them at a slave pen. "Will, I received a letter from a plantation owner nearby who saw our ad in the paper. He wants to sell three to five of his slaves. We need to change our plans and leave these two with the others in the slave pen for two days and visit this here slave owner. We could head out to New Orleans with twelve slaves instead of seven."

Will looked over at Joe and Liza. "It will only cost 25 cents a night for Joe and 25 cents for the girl. We'll make a lot more if we can buy five slaves, and we can be back here in two days. Let's see the pen owner and leave right away."

Liza was taken into one part of the slave pen and Joe to another. He saw there were Negroes owned by other slave traders who were being held there. Joe approached one of the men. "What it likes here?"

The man leaned against a wall and studied Joe. "Not too bad. Dey hab er kitchen. Der be er courtyard wid er high wall whar us ken walks. Iffen us gits sick thar an infirmary. Dey gib us lot ob vittles. I's sartin dey wants ter keeps us well so dey gits er good price in de auction."

Joe looked around him and shook his head. He paced back and forth examining the joints of wooden beams in the ceiling and doors.

"If a man wants ter be free what him have ter do?"

"Iron bars, high walls, an too many slave drivers. Nobody runs from here."

Joe sat down, but his eyes still scanned the beams and boards.

Two days later the slave traders appeared and formed a coffle by chaining the eight men by pairs in two rows of four, with the four women walking behind. Joe was in the last row and he noticed that Liza was trying to follow closely behind him. Trader Patrick pulled the coffle along behind his horse while Will rode his horse on the side or behind the group. Will told them before they started out that they would be walking for seven weeks, and they'd better keep up because he had a whip to use on those who lagged behind. He cracked the whip against a nearby tree to show them he meant what he said.

Joe figured they'd been walking fourteen days. He noticed one woman was not keeping up and Will had struck her two times with his whip. She was older than the rest of them and looked like she'd not done hard work in a field. Perhaps she was a house servant. Toward the middle of the day she just went over to the side of the path and sat under a tree, crying. Patrick stopped the coffle and Will rode back to her. The slave trader told her to get up or she would be left behind to starve to death. She tried to stand, but her legs gave out from under her. When Will got off his horse to take a look, he shook his head at Patrick. "This un's got a fever. She can't make it any further."

"We'll have to leave her, Will. We can't stick around to wait for her to get well."

Joe spoke up. "Me Mama larn me 'bout roots. She be er root doctor an midwife. I's ken finds roots ter bring down de fever. She mebbe ken walks de next day."

"What you think, Patrick? We could camp out here until tomorrow and just lose half a day, but maybe we'd have this here nigger to sell. If we go and leave her behind we lose the money we paid for her."

"Alright, Will, you go with Joe to find the roots. I'll prepare camp and watch 'em."

Joe was unchained and led Will into the woods to look for the healing roots. I's stronger dan de trader, Joe thought to himself.

25

I's ken hits him an runs. What happens ter de older woman and ter Liza iffen I's leaves though? I's orter heps dem. Mebbe it be better ter runs w'en I reaches de new plantation. Den I's plans it. I's jes kaint leaves Liza. Joe kept his head down, searching for the plants he needed.

Joe soon found boneset, slippery elm and passion flower. He made the boneset into a tonic, which he gave to the woman. He stayed by her and gave her the tonic during the night and by morning her fever seemed to have gone and she appeared much stronger. "Joe, I'm freeing you from your chains so you can help this here nigger walk. I'll be watching you though," said Will, cracking his whip over Joe's head. The traders fed them corn meal and water and they resumed their journey. Joe had made extra boneset tonic and also slippery elm tonic. He was given permission to give the woman the root medicine when they stopped to eat.

Two evenings later as they camped by a river, Joe applied a wet cloth to the woman's forehead. The fever had come back and the tonics were no longer working. Joe didn't know what else to do. "Dar now, Joe. Thank yer fer yer hep. Yer er good man. I's ready ter goes ter Glory. I's sees de chil'en an husband what gone 'fore me. Tell dose soul traders dey done lose thar monies on dis woman." She smiled at Joe.

Joe crouched by the woman at sunrise. She didn't seem to be aware of him or of her surroundings. Will and Patrick walked over and Joe looked up at them sadly. "Her don't knows us an I's kaint hep her wid dose roots no more."

"We'll have to leave her behind. Let's go."

Joe piled some leaves under the woman's head to make a pillow and left some corn meal and water beside her in case she woke up and was hungry and thirsty. Patrick then handcuffed and chained him with the rest of the men. He looked back and sighed. He'd wanted to make her well like his Mama did with the sick slaves and the white people, but maybe he still didn't know enough about root medicine. Maybe, though, she was just too ill for the root medicine to work when she had to keep on walking and couldn't rest.

Will went into a town a week later to get supplies, and was gone a long time. Patrick seemed worried. Then a rumbling noise was heard and Will rode up to their encampment with his horse pulling a covered wagon. "Look what I have. I had a chance to buy six slaves from eight to ten years old for not much money, but I don't think they could walk for four weeks. A man sold me the wagon real cheap. This way we can buy more supplies and put them in the wagon, and the children can take turns riding when they are tired."

Six little black faces peered out from the back of the wagon. "What are you doing, brother? Now we can only travel by roads. We can't use the paths that make our trip shorter. And children cause trouble. How are we going to look after them and the rest of the coffle?" Patrick glowered at his brother.

"These are almost old enough to pick cotton. I only paid 100 dollars apiece and we can get at least 300 or 400 dollars for them in New Orleans. And I can sell the wagon there and get our money back."

Patrick relented after hearing about the money they could make and he and Will began placing the children in with their other slaves for the night. Joe had heard some children are raised from babies to be sold and are kept from their Mamas. They don't become so upset when sold. He was certain, though, that some were pulled right out of their Mamas' arms and sold. A little girl about Rose's age was sitting on a log, sobbing. During the night more than one child was crying. Joe and a few of the others didn't get much sleep.

The next day, after they'd had their cornmeal and water and started out, Joe noticed the women walking and talking with the children. The little girl was holding a woman's hand and had stopped crying. Later in the day the children began to take turns riding in the wagon. When they camped that night they seemed to be more comfortable and there was less crying.. Seeing the little girl reminded Joe of Rose and how much he missed her. He wondered if he'd ever see his little niece again.

Liza sat down next to Joe when they were camped a few nights later. "Joe, I's hab er bad pain. Ken yer finds medicines fer it?" She pointed to her middle.

"I's hab ter lets de traders know so one ken goes wid me ter finds de roots." Liza nodded. Joe called out to the traders and Will walked over. He agreed to go with Joe and they quickly walked further into the woods before the sun went down.

Joe found poke root, which his Mama had taught him was good for pain. He also brought back passionflower which had to be applied topically. Liza seemed much better after she'd taken the poke root tonic and Joe was relieved. He asked if he could stay by her during the night because she might need more medicine. That was granted, so Joe lay down beside Liza. Liza snuggled up next to him. "I's feels safe w'en yer wid me, Joe." He reached over and kissed her and they fell asleep in each other's arms.

In the morning Joe looked over at Liza and saw that she'd been bleeding between her legs during the night. "Liza, what wrong wid yer?"

"I's goin' ter hab me masr's baby. Dat why him done sells me. He din't wants de missus ter knows. I 'spects I's lose de baby." Liza began to cry and Joe took her into his arms.

"I's takes care ob yer."

Joe told the traders that Liza had lost her baby and was bleeding badly. He asked permission to go to the river and get more water so he could clean off the blood. Will walked with him and they drew enough water for everyone. Joe had one of the women clean Liza and apply the passionflower on her stomach and between her legs. He gave her poke root tonic for the pain.

Will looked down on Joe, who was kneeling by Liza. "How's she doing, Joe? We need to start traveling."

"Liza kaint goes til de bleeding stops. De only way her ken goes tomorrow is ter ride in de wagon. Her kaint walks. Her be bery weak fer er few days."

Will and Patrick talked amongst themselves and then Will spoke up. "Why can't we just put her in the wagon now and you can give her medicine along the way? We're losing money by these here women being sick and having to rest an extra day."

Joe, upset, looked up at Will. "Yer says Liza goin' ter brings yer lots ob monies. Yer wants ter hab her dies before us in Orleans? Liza bery sick an weak. Her not goin' ter ride in de wagon wid all de bumps on de road dis day. I's needs ter takes care ob her here an stops de bleeding an den her be able ter goes in de wagon." Although the traders grumbled, not liking another day lost, they knew they had no choice.

The next day Liza's bleeding had stopped and a bed was made for her in the wagon. Joe walked alongside so he could give her medication when she needed it. The children had to walk for longer periods and only one child could ride in the wagon at a time.

Two days later Liza was strong enough to walk. Joe was allowed to help her keep up with the wagon. As they walked the children gathered around Joe to listen to his stories. Joe had never learned to read other than just a few words, but he would listen to the stories told by other slaves and the stories his niece, Rose, read to him. He was able to remember them and could repeat the stories, using a lot of expression. The children especially enjoyed the stories of Br'er Rabbit and he was asked to tell them more than once along the way.

Another four weeks had passed and Joe could see they were approaching a town the traders told them was New Orleans. It was the end of a long, weary journey, lasting seven weeks. Joe was relieved the sores on their feet could now heal, and they would be in one place to get more regular meals. Care would be there if one of them was sick. But what would happen to them now? They would face the auction block and he and Liza would most likely be sold to different plantation owners. He dreaded to think about Liza and what her life would be like as a fancy girl. There was no way he could protect her from that and keep her safe, as he had tried to do on their long walk.

A mournful howling floated in the air. Patrick's horse ducked out of sight ahead as they approached a small farm. Wondering if this was an opportunity, Joe glanced toward Liza and the children while viewing the nearby woods. No. None of them could leave. Gripping his whip, Will frowned and stared right through Joe. His spine tingled. "Nobody think about movin'. Nobody!" barked Will.

Moments later, Patrick's horse dove back out of the bushes. "Had me a good talk with that farmer," grumbled Patrick. "He had his dog tethered to a post out in the sun. That's cruel! You know I can't stand to see a dog chained up like that."

On their last night together they encamped by a river. Joe and Liza slept in each other's arms. The children huddled around them, knowing that the next day they would be separated. In the morning, Patrick took the men down to the river. The ones with beards were told to shave and the eight men had to get into the river and clean themselves. Joe took his clothes off, jumped in and swam until Patrick told him to get out. He quickly washed his clothes and put them on wet, knowing that they'd be dry soon enough. Then Will took the women and children to the river while Patrick watched the men at the campsite.

Later that morning the coffle walked into the town of New Orleans. "Stays by me, Joe. I's skeered." Joe put his arm around Liza as they followed the wagon. The children pressed close to them, a little girl clinging to Joe. They were led into a large building surrounded by high walls. The men were taken one direction while the women and children went in another. Liza looked terrified as she glanced back at Joe and was led away.

Chapter 5

1848

"Mama, look! Bella made dresses for my Fanny and Rose's Lucey." Margaret came up to her Mother who was sitting at her mirror, examining her face, and held out her doll.

"Not now, Margaret, go play with your doll. I'm busy." Margaret walked dejectedly to the door. She went into her room and angrily threw her doll with the new dress onto her bed.

"Mama's gone out. Let's look in her room." Margaret led Rose into the large dressing room and she gazed in wonder at the fine things around her. A canopied bed so large, so well carved it could be a gentleman's carriage. Blue quilts softer than the moss of the forest. Paintings like the views from a hill top. Full length curtains flooded the room with blue that continued into the blue quilt on the bed. Rose cleaned and polished other areas of the house, but this room was the exclusive work of Grandma Bella, at the Mistresses' request. The details and finery were as clear a warning to Rose as the stripes on a snake. Everything told Rose she shouldn't be here. Margaret wandered over to the dresser, Rose following reluctantly. When Margaret opened the carved jewelry box they both stared at the necklaces of many colors and sizes.

"Please, let us go, Margaret," Rose whispered.

Margaret looked incensed. "You dare not tell me where I can go. You go where I say or I'll tell Papa!"

Margaret withdrew a necklace of blue stones that sparkled in the sunlight coming in through the window. "Isn't this beautiful? I want it." She turned to Rose. "I know. You can steal it for me. Then when Mama asks I can say I didn't take it."

"What if your Mama asks me?"

31

"You can say you didn't take it. Then she'll think one of the other house slaves took it." Rose, looking at the ground, slowly shook her head. "I's kaint. Dat's stealing. God wouldn't like it."

Margaret's face became red and she stomped her foot. "You're my slave and you have to do as I say. Take this necklace and put it in my room under my pillow."

Rose again shook her head. Margaret grabbed the necklace and stomped out of the room, leaving Rose to close the door and follow. Margaret placed the necklace under her pillow, grabbed a book, and didn't talk to Rose the rest of the day.

The next morning the Mistress was waiting for her. "Rose, I was missing a necklace last night and asked around. Margaret finally admitted you took it. I can put up with some things from slaves, but not stealing. I'm getting another slave for Margaret and you are to report to the field from now on." She looked at Rose and shook her head. "I expected more of you. Go now."

"What de matter, Rose? It de middle ob de day. Is yer sick?" Bella bent down, folding Rose in her plump arms. Rose, crying softly, told Bella what happened. "De Mistress won't believe yer over her daughter. I's 'fraid yer goin' ter hafter works in de fields, Rose. I's so sorry." Bella looked out towards the tall oak in the wood and whispered, "I's so sorry, Charlotte."

It was Sunday and Rose had worked in the fields, carrying water to the slaves, for five days. She was stiff and sore and her hands were rubbed raw from carrying the pails. At least today she could stay home and rest. She was angry at Margaret for stealing and lying because she could never again be a house maid. This would be her life from now on, or until she could join her uncle Joe on his farm in Canada when she was big. She knew why he wanted to leave. Field work was like dying slowly every day.

Margaret wandered around the house, no one to play with, nothing to do. She'd asked her Mother to give Rose another chance, but her Mother said no, she could never trust Rose again. If I tell Mother it was me... No, she'll get really angry. I can't do that. She has that older girl as my slave, but she's no fun. Not like Rose. I thought Mother would get angry with Rose, but not tell her she couldn't be my slave. She picked up her doll, Fanny. It's no fun playing dolls by myself.

By the next Sunday Rose felt a little better—still sore, but not quite as exhausted. Her hands were blistered and hurt, but Bella put passionflower on them for the pain.

"Mother, I have something to tell you." Margaret stood at her Mother's door, head hanging down.

"What is it, Margaret?" Lillian glanced up at her daughter, then continued brushing her hair.

Margaret hesitated, a look of fear on her face.

Impatiently, Lillian asked, "What do you want to tell me?"

"I was the one who took your necklace, not Rose." She waited anxiously.

"Margaret, what are you saying? You took the necklace and then blamed Rose?" Lillian looked down at her daughter, frowning. Why would you do that?"

"I don't know. Mother. Punish me any way you want, but let Rose come back. It wasn't her fault." Margaret hung her head. "I'm sorry."

On Monday, Mrs. Ramsey called Rose to the Big House and told her she was to be Margaret's slave. When Rose went upstairs to Margaret's room, Margaret glanced up from the floor where she was playing with her doll. "Oh, there you are, Rose. Get your doll." Rose took her doll, Lucey, from the corner and sat beside Margaret, saying nothing. She looked at Margaret, thinking, because of you I spent two weeks in the field, and I can't say anything to you about what you did or I'll get into trouble. I wish I was white and then I'd tell you what you are—a thief and a liar! I hate you! She clenched her hands into fists behind her back.

"Tomorrow is the auction and we want you to look good. We're taking you down to the river to get clean and we have clothes for you to put on." Will and Patrick chained the eight men and walked

33

them to the river. Patrick held a gun on them after Will unchained them so they could clean themselves. When they were back in the slave pen Will handed out hats, coats, trousers, shirts, and shoes.

"My feet don't fits in des here shoes."

"Joe, you're just going to put them on or I'll have to cut off your toes to make room." Will laughed at his joke, but Joe tried a little harder to push his feet into the shoes.

Early that next morning Will and Patrick brought the men, women and children into a long building and lined them up against a wall, the tallest man first and down to the shortest. Then the women were also arranged by height, and finally the children. The women were dressed in frocks of calico and kerchiefs on their heads. "Niggers, you are going to be sold, and we want you to look good and bring us a good price. Joe, you know a lot of songs, so you can sing. You all can dance and show that you are healthy." Patrick then looked Liza over. They'd bought her a colorful, revealing dress. Liza looked about to cry and was cowering against the wall. "You, Liza, I want you to look like you would be happy to please. Show off that good body of yours and that pretty face. If you don't sing and dance and try to get us a good price for you I'll beat you with the paddle."

Joe had seen a slave beaten with a paddle in the slave pen the day before. One of the slaves told him that the paddle was used instead of the lash because it didn't leave the marks for the buyers to see. It was thick wood that had been bored full of auger holes. The slave had been stripped naked. Joe turned away as he saw the man's blood begin to pour out of the holes in the paddle. Now trader Patrick was threatening to do this to Liza if she didn't act happier. Joe was frightened for her.

"Here come the plantation owners to look you over." Patrick then motioned for Joe to sing and had the women move around as if they were dancing and enjoying themselves. Joe was relieved to see that Liza was moving and pretending to look happy.

Joe stopped singing as soon as he found himself being prodded and his arms pinched. He was told to turn around, walk back and forth, and open his mouth to show his teeth. One man asked him to take off his shirt. "Trader, this man's been beaten. He's a runaway."

"No, he had a master who used to beat his slaves to show them whose boss. Joe would never run away. He's a faithful slave and a hard worker. He worked on a tobacco plantation up North in Virginia, but his master had to sell him to pay some debts." Will then pointed at Joe's arms. "Can you see how strong he is?"

Two other men, upon hearing Will, came over to examine Joe. Patrick slapped his brother on the back and murmured, "Good talk, Will, you're finally learning."

Once again Joe was poked and prodded. A man asked Joe, "Do you think you could work hard and fast in a cotton field?"

"Yassuh, I's er good worker. See dat woman, Mas'r? Her be my woman an iffen yer takes us bofe, we works hard fer yer. Liza be er house servant in Virginia."

The man laughed and walked away. "I don't need no fancy girl." Liza had heard Joe and the man and looked fearful. She knew now what would happen to her. Joe wished he could go over and talk to her, but there were four white men near her, making her bend over, walk around, and show her teeth. One old man was stroking her arm and staring at her breasts. Joe wanted to go over and hit him, but he knew that would make it worse for both of them. Another man took Liza into a room and examined her privately. Joe thought to himself, Someday I's be free, but I's not goin' ter hab Liza wid me, I's knows dat now.

At ten o' clock it was time for the auction to begin. There were approximately 100 slaves to be auctioned off, belonging to five slave traders. The plantation owners, in their black coats, wide brimmed hats, some sucking on their cigars, gathered near the auction block and examined their catalogs which listed the chattles from chattle number 1 to chattle number 100. The slaves, many with anxious and frightened faces, stepped up on the auction block one by one. Men were auctioned off first, the strong healthy ones bringing from $600 to $800. The bidding for Joe, chattle number five, looked like it would only go up to $700 because of the beating marks on his back marking him as a runaway. Then a stern looking man bid $800 and Joe was sold to him. The man kept Joe with him while he continued to bid on other slaves.

Mr. Butler, the auctioneer, finally put Liza, on the raised platform. He mentioned that Liza was a good worker, trained as a house girl, and a strong and healthy mulatto who would, he was certain, have other talents. In rapid voice, he started the bidding at $600, and immediately two men bid against each other. The bids rose higher and higher. Joe looked at the 2 men, trying to see if one looked like he'd be a kind master. A portly man seemed determined to win, but finally shook his head when the bidding became too high for him. The auctioneer pointed. "Sold to Mr. Hill for $1000." A thin, well-dressed man in his forties grabbed Liza off the platform. Joe was certain he had a wife and children on his plantation and that Liza would be a house girl who would have additional duties to perform. Liza looked sadly at Joe as she was led away. He wasn't even given a chance to say good-bye. Soon all the women had been sold, the price being usually $500 or $600. A few of them were begging their new owners to buy their children too. They were led away sobbing at being separated from their husbands and their children. Next the children were put on the platform one by one and were sold for about $300 each. As they were led off by their new masters, two looked back at Joe with frightened expressions on their faces. The little girl who reminded Joe of Rose was crying. Joe could only hope they would be treated kindly.

It was finally over and Joe, as he was led away, tried not to show the anger he felt at being treated much like a horse being examined before a sale.

His new master led Joe down to the dock to take the steamboat up the Mississippi River. "If you work hard for me and don't try to run away I'll never beat you. My cotton plantation is in Tennessee." They walked up the plank and Joe was taken to a large room on the lower deck where male slaves were kept chained and left by their masters. The women were sitting nearby and a guard was posted. Joe was told to sit down and was then chained to a post.

After his master left, Joe looked around and discovered that three men, one child and two women were from the coffle he'd been in. One of the women moved and he saw Liza crouched behind her. "Liza. I's so glads ter sees yer. Iffen I's could jes be close ter yer." He strained at his chain.

"Oh, Joe, I's wishes yer could. I's so skeered."

A little later Joe's new master and another man walked in their direction. "Let me show you what I bought today. He looks like he'll be a good addition to my plantation. Maybe he'll help me bring in the first and biggest crop to market." The men looked down on Joe.

"Mas'r, please. Can yer moves me over ter whar dat woman is? Her be my woman an I's wants ter be by her iffen yer lets me." Joe pleadingly looked up at his new master.

The master laughed. "I remember her from the auction. I heard you try to persuade someone to buy you both. Yes, I'll move you so you can spend some time with your woman before we dock." He proceeded to unchain Joe, move him away from the men and chain him next to Liza. As the two men walked away he could hear his master say, "Now that I've done something for him that he wanted he'll be more willing to do as I say when we are on my plantation."

Liza moved close to Joe and he put his arms around her. "Liza, I's wishes de Mas'r buys bofe of us. I loves yer an wants ter marry yer. I's goin' ter follow de drinking gourd an w'en I's in Canada I's works an den I's finds yer an buys yer. Den yer be free an we ken marry. I's wants us ter hab er farm an raise our chil'un ter be free so dey ken neber be sold from us."

"Dat sound good, Joe. I's waits fer yer ter do dat." She and Joe wrapped their arms around each other and tried to sleep. It had been a hard day. A little later Liza's new master came down to check on her. He unchained her but warned her to stay there because a guard was on duty.

Something woke Joe. A Negro woman, who had been huddled by herself in the corner, crying for her children, quietly rose and walked by the guard who had fallen asleep. Joe watched but she didn't return, and he fell asleep again. The next morning, the woman's master realized she was gone and a search of the boat began. A man on the upper deck mentioned that he'd been walking on the deck late at night and heard a splash. Joe, when he learned about it, knew what happened. He'd heard the woman moaning that she didn't want to live without her children. In despair, she had jumped overboard. Her master was complaining about the loss of the money he'd paid for her.

The boat chugged slowly up the Mississippi River, stopping at ports, letting off plantation owners and their slaves, and taking on logs, supplies, more plantation owners, and slaves. Joe learned they were no longer in Louisiana, but were going through Arkansas. Soon they would reach Memphis, Tennessee, where his new Master had his plantation. Joe knew that after they left the boat he would never see his Liza again. He shuddered at what he knew her fate would be, and held her closer.

Joe looked up as a well-dressed white man approached him and the rest of the slaves being held in the lower deck. The man smiled at them as he came closer. "Hello. My name is Brother Daniels. I brought thee some water because I thought thee might be thirsty." The man began to pass a container of water around the group. "I am a member of the Society of Friends. We believe there should be no slavery and that thee should be as free as I am. If thee might try to follow the Drinking Gourd north someday, I just want to tell thee that I live in Cincinnati, Ohio. If thee is ever there and asks for me, someone will take thee to me and thee will be safe." The man suddenly looked toward the entrance to the lower deck. "Someone is coming. I'd better go." He turned and left quickly.

Joe's new master came in, frowning. "Who was that, Joe, and what did he want with you niggers?"

"I's don't know, Mas'r. I's 'spects him jes curious ter see what us'n niggers looks like."

Later three white men came into the lower deck. They appeared to look them over and one bent to examine the leg chains. They glanced around the room and left without saying anything.

Bang! Crash! A sudden jolt caused the Negroes in the lower deck to be thrown against each other. They could hear people on the upper deck shouting. There was no noise from the paddle wheel. "I's wonders what happened. Why us stopped?"

"I's not chained, Joe. I's goin' ter goes ter de upper deck an finds out. De guard is on de upper deck."

"Be keerful, Liza. Yer master be bery angry iffen him catches yer."

Liza sneaked quietly to the upper deck and hid behind a barrel. She heard one of the deck hands explain to the Captain that something was blocking the narrows so the boat couldn't get through. A few of the passengers were milling around, listening. One of the three men who had come below pointed to shore. "There are some men in that boat that could maybe help your deck hands with the snag. Look, they're coming this way."

The boat pulled alongside the steamboat and one of the men called out, "What's the trouble?"

"There seems to be something blocking the narrows."

"Let us aboard and perhaps we can rig up a way to help you through. We know the river here."

A ladder was let down and six rough looking men climbed aboard. Liza saw the three men who had come below earlier surround the Captain and the two deck hands who were with him. One of the three men held a blunderbuss on them. "We are now in charge of this ship. If anyone moves we'll shoot." He motioned to the six who had just climbed aboard. "Five of you, go round up the passengers and lock them in the Captain's room. Step forward those of you who own the slaves in lower deck." Four men stepped forward. "Go down and unlock the slaves and bring them up here. Henry, you go with them."

Two gentlemen were standing near the barrel that Liza was hiding behind. "I thought the army and vigilante groups took care of the pirates on the Mississippi and Ohio Rivers back in the 1830's."

"Some are still on the river, and I think we have a few on this boat. I wonder what will happen to us." The two men looked at each other, frightened expressions on their faces.

Liza waited until the rest of the slaves were brought to upper deck and slipped in next to Joe. "Joe, us be captured by pirates. Us goin' ter be killed."

"Quiet you," a pirate yelled. He then walked over to the cowering Negroes and appeared to look them up and down, finally stopping by Joe. "You! You are very big. Are you strong?"

"Yassuh. I's bery strong. I's ken lifts an carries big loads."

The pirate looked over the side where a ship was fast approaching. "There's our sloop. I want you and you," pointing to Joe and another large Negro, "to help load our plunder onto the sloop. The passengers don't seem to be in any shape to do much. If you Negroes help us it will go better for you. Now, Jack, take these miserable slave owners and put them in with the rest of the passengers. The Negroes can be locked in a smaller room." A pirate stepped up to do his Captain's bidding, a blunderbuss in his hand and a shiny dagger fastened to his hip with a scarf.

Joe and the other Negro man worked with the pirates, gathering up the plunder picked out by a pirate, who seemed to be in charge. Joe noticed the pirate chose food, drink, clothing, bedding, a medicine chest, mattresses, some jewelry from the lady passengers, wood, tools, and all the pieces of eight and pounds and shillings collected from the passengers and ship's crew. Some of the plunder had to be carried down a ladder, but a lot of it was tossed over the side and onto the deck of the pirate ship.

When they were finished a pirate approached Joe. " I'm the quartermaster on the sloop. You worked very   hard today. What's your name and where are you going?"

"I's Joe, an de new mas'r takes me ter er cotton plantation in Tennessee."

"I know you're strong, Joe. What else can you do?"

"I's er carpenter an I's knows some 'bout root doctoring."

"A carpenter! We need a carpenter. We also need someone who can help when one of my men gets injured in an engagement

or gets sick. Joe, you're going with us and you will learn to be a
pirate. You'll work hard, but it's better work than picking cotton
and we all get a share of what we take."

"What happens ter de other Negroes? My woman, Liza, is
wid dem an I's fears her be treated bery bad by her new mas'r."

The quartermaster looked thoughtful. "Well, Joe, if you
promise to be a hard working pirate and serve me faithfully I can
take your woman further up the river. I'll leave her on the shore
and she can maybe make it to the North, where I hear you slaves
can be free."

Joe's face broke into a big smile. "Thank you, Mas'r. I's
serves yer faithfully iffen yer does dat. Her an me hopes ter meets
agin in de North."

The quartermaster frowned. "That won't be for a long time,
Joe. We always need a carpenter to do repair work on the sloop.
You'll be a pirate for a few years."

Then the quartermaster called his crew together. "This is
Joe, who is a carpenter and a root doctor and is now with us.
Damage the steamboat so she can't follow us, and let the Negroes
leave the boat except for Joe's woman, Liza, who will be going
with us further north. We'll keep the slave owners locked up and it
will take them a while to get out. That will give the Negroes time
to get away. Now, let's get outa' here!"

On some errand to the master's office Joe remembered seeing a
model of a grand ocean sloop. Every edge polished. Holes for
cannons placed evenly. The best of what wood could do. Here
every edge had been chewed by some varmint. Cannons stuck out
of odd holes. The thing looked more a piece of worm eaten
hardtack than a ship. Even the rails had extra little cannons or guns
clamped to them somehow. The hull was all oakum caulk, tar and
plywood. It seemed to sink along in the direction they wanted it to
go.

"What's that look fer? Don't snub my ship." Joe looked
down to see a squinting, angry little man staring up at him through

a mat of curly gray hair. "I'm the master gunner and the cannons you see are under my care."

"To be fair, Sir, we do need to double shore up the deck on account of the extra weight of those infernal cannons. You still owe me from when I was below and that monster gun of yours fell through the deck and landed partly on my foot," broke in a thin man in a worn, striped shirt.

The master gunner kept his gaze on Joe. "Bah! First rule of the river—he with the most cannons wins. Those extra guns are the only things keeping us from the hang man's noose. That and the tiller. See that, boy?" He pointed to a man intently pushing a sharp, wobbly, wooden triangle around at the stern. Joe guessed it connected to a rudder or something. "We could see the buttons on the navy men's shirts. The buttons! But Ezra here pulled hard and whoosh, 90 degrees into the backwaters, then out behind 'em. Navy can't turn like that with their nice wheel." The master gunner gave a grunt in Joe's direction and left.

The man in the striped shirt tried to laugh off the tension. He leaned toward Joe and murmured. "Never know when Calvin's gonna' appear. Man's so scrawny he steps behind the mast and disappears."

"Only one mast?" asked Joe.

"Only need one. She's light and fast," bragged the friendly sailor. He leaned in again with a smile, "or she would be without all these guns."

The friendly pirate, who just went by Ralph, showed Joe around. He saw men Ralph identified as sailors working on the rigging, getting the sloop ready to sail. "Ah, yes. The men are rigging up the new ship-made top sail. Want to see if it'll give us more of a push of speed out of here. You'll be keeping the ship together, but I'll be making her move. I'm the only sail maker on this crew. Those three skinny triangular ones aft or front are all jibs 'sept the last which is a stay sail. They're easy enough to deal with. But this one," Ralph pointed up at a squarish sail with one sloping side running from the back of the mast to well over the back end of the ship. He shook his head and patted the mast. "This one is trouble. The rigging can barely hold the weight of this mainsail. I'd advise you to watch yourself around her and don't you dare hurt her. There's not a man within three hundred miles of here who can fix her properly, not even me."

"Joe, the captain's in charge when we're on an engagement, but the quartermaster is the one you'll have to obey the rest of the time. He's fair enough, but don't cross 'im and do what he tells you to the letter. His job is to maintain order and he does, if you know what I mean. He also keeps records, fights with us, and figures what plunder to take. So he's everyone's friend." Ralph grinned. "Boatswain supervises maintenance and supplies, but between you and me, I don't think he does much else."

"Not much else, do I?" rasped a husky deep voice coming from below deck. "Look who else isn't at his work. You expect those mangy pirates to get the rigging right while you're standing around? MOVE!"

"Sir!" shouted Ralph, and leaped forward and up into the jibs like a squirrel.

"Get to work," growled the portly man as he waddled up a ladder and flopped onto the deck. "Can't tell he was ever a professional master sailor before we captured him, can you? You pay him no mind. You're the carpenter. You just maintain that hull, that mast and the yards, there, those things holding up the sails. Anyway, the mate is the one who's really supposed to be showing you around, he knows the rigging and ship as well as anyone. I'm going to be inventorying the...uh...new food provisions in my bunk if you want me for anything. But do watch out for the master gunner. Been sifting gun powder lately, maybe he breathed too much of it in."

Everyone was working frantically. Eventually, he was passed along to an office in the stern of the ship. The quartermaster, a foreboding figure in a black coat, was sitting behind a desk, examining a map. "Hello, Joe, welcome aboard. I'm George Morgan, and I'm in charge of this sloop. We need a carpenter because we lost the last one in an engagement. Sign the pirate oath here. Can you read?" Joe shook his head. "I'll read it to you and then you can make your mark on it." The quartermaster looked down at a paper and began to read.

"The pirate code tells what will happen to you if you disobey. You will be marooned if you try to run away, marooned or shot if you stole, and you'd receive Moses' Law, which is forty stripes lacking one on the bare back, if you strike someone. If you don't keep your arms clean and fit for an engagement, you will be cut off from your share." The quartermaster glanced up at Joe. "If you lose a joint during an engagement you shall have four hundred pieces of eight and eight hundred if it's a limb. You'll receive one share and a quarter of the plunder. Joe, do you understand what I read?" Joe nodded. "Put your mark here." Joe leaned over the paper and placed his X. This man had a plain flat face, dark hair and nothing that would make him stand out. His voice was neither high nor low. Joe had never really taken Reuben seriously when he talked about hoodoo, but there was something about this man...When he looked at you, a cold wind blew down your spine and you felt you had no hope of escape. Joe glanced down at his X and winced. What was he really giving up for Liza's sake? The office was inviting and well lit. The desk was almost too tidy. The man's plain outward appearance was usual. But that dark coat and the unmoving eyes spoke of a certain hidden resolve or influence Joe had only seen in his Father. Joe heard the quartermaster quietly slide a long metal object from below the desk. "Now you must swear an oath of allegiance on this sword," he commanded.

Somewhere on the ship a voice shouted, "Cast off."

Liza sat on deck, watching Joe pound new planks into the floor and the bulwarks where the rotten ones had been removed. She noticed Joe looked worried. "What wrong, Joe?"

"Des planks." Joe's brow was furrowed. "None ob dis make sense. How I's make 'em curve an fit?"

Liza leaned over and squeezed his shoulder, her eyes wide. Rough looking men with piercing eyes watched them through the rigging. A voice called out, "We'll let your woman go, now fix the ship!"

"What de men going ter do wid us iffen yer kaint fix de ship, Joe?"

Joe looked longingly across the water to the dark woods. "I's don't know, Liza."

"Hah!" came Calvin's obnoxious voice from behind. Joe almost fell over. "Ain't seen no carpentry like this, 'ave ye boy?", hissed the master gunner, grinning from ear to ear. "I don't think you know what your doing. Wait 'til the quartermaster hears about this!"

Joe stared back at the master gunner and wanted to twist his neck. Then his eyes dropped down to the boards. Wait. Twist? He could just about figure how these boards would fit.

Leaning in close to Joe the master gunner yelled to the crew, "Let's let 'er off at this careenage."

Hold on, thought Joe, What's a careenage?

The sloop turned abruptly toward the bank, the sail grew a little and flapped to life. The entire sloop lurched with new speed. Liza watched the bank and dug her fingers into Joe. "Us'n gonna' crash, Joe!"

Everyone fell forward, all except the master gunner, who just stood there with a grin. The master gunner eyed Joe again and yelled once more to the crew, "Unbolt the guns and store them on the port side below deck." Within minutes Joe couldn't work let alone stand. The deck was steadily tilting more and more on one side toward the shallow water below. Pirates grunted, heaving cannons below deck. Joe winced at the thuds. He knew the ship was taking a beating.

Soon Joe was standing on a wet sandy bank with a pile of wet wood, water sloshing around his ankles.

"We ain't careened in over a year. See to it you replace these here rotten planks on the hull bottom," laughed the master gunner. "An don't go askin' us. We never had time to pay attention to all that stuff an' we don't care. We're always stuck moving guns.

Just knock them planks in somehow, boy. You a carpenter, aint' ya?"

I's a carpenter what don't know what I's doin', thought Joe. He didn't even know that a ship's bow took such an impossible curve inward like this below the waterline, let alone how he'd keep it that shape. Joe walked back and forth, thinking.

"Aint you done yet?", the crew kept yelling.

Joe swallowed hard. Time to pretend to do things again. He could bend the planks near the upper decks for the upper hull, but this looked impossible. He wished his Papa was here. Joe scratched his head and closed his eyes, mumbling into his worn hands. Now Papa, I ben sneak'n in and out ob woods, an I's knows you ain't approved ob it. But I's knows one thing—that I ain't neber seen a long leaf pine bend dat way. Papa, you would say I's jes need a strong will, but I's sorely needs somethin' else. Yer taught me all I's knows 'bout de carpentry, but dis scares me. What skill yer ever taught me that show me how ter bend in de new planks?

"Carpenter, here's a barrel of drinking water for yeh. Looks like you're getting dizzy from the heat, boy. Look out below!" called a pirate.

Joe saw the barrel hit the water in slow motion. The splash from it hitting seemed to cool his burning brain. He now knew how he, a plantation Negro, could manage as a ship's carpenter. We had no cooper at the plantation. Papa an I's had ter make de barrels ourselves, recalled Joe. But he couldn't be like the last carpenter and do it all on his own. He called down a couple of men from above. They'd hab to larn dis too.

Joe smiled and calmly instructed the men. "Now, yer hold dat plank here an yer bend it an keep bending it...Stop! Don't break it! I's mean bend it when it gives. It'll give soon as I's settle it on dis flame an douse it wid de river water." Joe grinned as he took a rough ax out of his pants. "We gonna steam bend an shape us some real big barrel staves."

The quartermaster approached them on deck. "Joe, you're a good carpenter. We'll complete our bargain with you and let Liza of at the start of the Ohio River. We're almost there now so, Liza, you need to get your bag."

Liza stood up. "Thank yer fer taking me up de ribber. Thank yer fer de clothes yer gib me." Liza glanced down at her nice dress that had come off the steamboat the pirates had plundered. She left to collect her bag, but looked back longingly at Joe.

A little later Joe and Liza watched as the pirate ship came in closer and closer to shore. "Liza, yer needs ter finds out whar be Cincinnati, Ohio. Dat where dat Mas'r Daniels be. Him say him hep slaves. Iffen yer meets someone what says 'thee' in Cincinnati, asks him ter shows yer ter Mas'r Daniels an yer be safe. Here be er piece of eight de quartermaster gib me. I's loves yer, Liza." Joe took Liza in his arms.

"I's loves yer too, Joe. I's waits fer yer in Canada."

Joe sadly watched his Liza disembark. Soon he heard "Cast off." It was time to learn to be a pirate.

Chapter 6

1849

"You and I are nine years old today, Rose. Here's a present for you." Margaret handed Rose a wrapped package. When Rose opened it she cried out with delight. "When we walk down by the river you are always looking at the birds and wondering what they are so I bought you this book on birds. Now when we go to the river you can look them up and tell me about them."

"Oh, Margaret, this is a wonderful gift," exclaimed Rose. "Can we go for a walk now and see if we can find some of the birds in this book?"

"Yes. My lessons are done so Mother won't care that I'm gone. Let's take a picnic down there." Margaret went to the kitchen, Rose following, and told the cook to pack some chicken and corn cakes for their lunch. Rose took the opportunity, as she always did, to do all the helpful little things she had to do as Margaret's slave. She grabbed Margaret's hat and umbrella, took a fan in case Margaret was hot, then gathered up her brushes, paints and canvas. They ran out the back door, down the hill and past the slave quarters, until they reached the river. Margaret found a comfortable spot on the grassy slope, under a cottonwood tree, where she sat and opened the basket with the food. Rose was too excited to eat. She wandered around, gazing at the trees, trying to spot birds.

"There's one, Margaret." She turned the pages quickly. "Oh, it's a cardinal. See the bright red color?" Rose looked in her book and thought to herself, it does what it wants. It even stays behind in winter if it pleases. Yet, many of these birds also travel miles and miles from here if they wish. She turned away for a moment, longing to feel the wind carrying her high into the air, to see where all the other towns were, and trace the open roads with a freedom she'd never known. Beyond the reach of glaring eyes; beyond the reach of endless orders. To be so high that no one would be looking over her shoulder but God. The world as seen from high above. What really lay beyond the plantation? Where was her uncle Joe trying to go?

Rose pointed to her left. "Over there in that tree is a yellow breasted chat. Listen to it sing 'cheer cheer cheer.' It also sings 'whit chew whit chew'." So this one chooses to say whatever it pleases whenever it pleases. I thought so. I think I'd like to be a bird. "Oh, I've heard the yellow breasted chat in the trees and wondered what bird sang like that."

Margaret could see Rose's face was beaming and knew she'd chosen the right gift for her.

"Sit down, Rose. Let's eat and then we'll look for more birds."

While they were eating, Rose glanced at Margaret. Should I ask her now? She's kept the secret of my learning to read and treats me better since last year. Sometimes it's almost like we're friends. No, she thought. Negroes and whites can't really be friends. She is nicer though. And she just has to say no if she doesn't want to do it. "Margaret," she hesitated as Margaret looked up. "There's something I want to ask you. Would you loan me some of your books? There's a few in the quarters who want to learn to read. I think I can teach them a little. They can write the alphabet in the dirt, but need books to practice reading."

"Are you sure you want to do this, Rose? You know it's against the law. You and the others could get beaten and maybe some of them sold down South if you are caught. I don't want you and the other slaves to get into trouble with my Father for such a foolish thing as books. Besides, Mother says reading makes you squint and gives you wrinkles so people shouldn't read much. Why would slaves want to read? They don't need to know how to read and write to work in the field. Besides, they might talk."

49

"No one will talk. They all know how to keep a secret from white people. It will help some of them someday if they can read and write."

Margaret clasped her hands around her knees, a thoughtful expression on her face. "Would you let me teach with you? I'd like to help. We'd learn a lot teaching them. I'd never tell Father. It would be fun." Margret clapped her hands together and smiled at Rose.

Rose hesitated and silently groaned to herself. "I'd like to teach with you, but you know this may go on for a very long time. If you get tired of it and want to quit, just tell me. Will you?" Margaret nodded absently. Was Margaret understanding the reality of this? Rose wondered if she had spoken firmly enough.

"Oh, Rose, we have a problem. You know my brother, John, is always trying to catch us at something so he can tell Father. He might follow us or wander down to the slave quarters looking for us."

"Yes, you're right. He'd do that." Rose looked thoughtful. "We'll have to watch out for him. Let me tell our idea to the people at Church on Sunday. I think I should tell them first. Is that alright?" Margaret looked disappointed but agreed.

"Now may we look for the birds in my book?" The girls spent the next couple of hours happily wandering along the river, checking the bushes and trees for birds.

Bella frowned. " I's don't knows, Rose. Yer be askin' fer trouble I's afeared. Dey neber goin' ter wants dat white girl ter teach dem. Dey wonders 'bout yer. Yer sounds like white people since yer be wid Margaret mos time."

"I know, Mama, but we'd like to try."

George helped Bella set up for Church in their home on Sunday by putting out what chairs they had for the older people. They came from their slave cabins, awkwardly carrying their chairs or holding blankets to sit on. The children and a few of the younger men and women sat on the dirt floor. Once everyone was settled an older member said a prayer. Then George led the congregation in singing "Amazing Grace" and "Swing Low, Sweet Chariot". George clapped his hands and the others joined in. Rose's nerves were tingling. Her grandfather's quiet will and passion seemed to move and sway the whole congregation with him. Rose felt she needed whatever it was he had. The singing went on, cries of pain, great release, pleading with God and praising Him, all rolled into one beat.

Although Bella couldn't read, she knew several Bible stories, and could speak with fervor. She'd been to many church services at the white Methodist church because the Negroes always had their service after the white people had left the church. Her sermon that day was about the Israelites being set free and leaving Egypt for the Promised Land, a favorite story and one that was often repeated. There was a lot of nodding and shouting as Bella told the story. After the sermon George led them in singing, "Go Down, Moses" and "Follow the Drinking Gourd".

Bella stood up and announced, "My granddaughter, Rose, wants ter talks wid yer." She sat down and motioned to Rose, who began to speak.

"You know it's against the law for slaves to learn to read. What I'm going to say must be kept a secret from the white people or we'd be in trouble. Does everyone agree to never tell any of what I am going to say to the white people?" She glanced around the room and saw everyone nodding so she continued. "I learned to read and write because my mistress, Margaret, lets me sit in and listen to her tutor. After she has her session we look at her book and practice reading and writing. We've been learning to read for three years. I know that some of you would also like to learn to read. Mistress Margaret and I would like to teach whoever wants to learn. We would do that here for an hour after Church. Margaret is willing to loan us the books she first used with her tutor and would like to help me teach. How many would like to take lessons from Margaret and me?"

No one spoke up and Rose could see hesitation in their faces. "You might be worried about having a white person teaching you, but Margaret is kind and a good teacher. She would never tell anyone." Rose bit her lip, wondering if she was doing the right thing. "If she comes next Sunday and it doesn't work out, we won't continue the lessons. Now, how many would like to learn to read?"

Bella stood up and looked around the room. "I's always wants ter larn ter read. George an I's goin' ter be in it. Let's try it." George nodded and looked out at everyone. Many in the room nodded their assent.

A few weeks later Rose and Margaret were giving a reading lesson when the guard at the door called out. "Master John coming." They'd practiced before so everyone knew just what to do. The women put the books under their skirts and the men sat on them. George immediately got up and started them singing "Swing Low, Sweet Chariot." John came in the door and waited until the song was finished. "What are you doing? I thought you had your Church service earlier."

"We likes ter sing an we sings after Church." Bella looked at John and smiled. "Would yer likes ter joins us? Margaret is here wid Rose."

"No thanks." John frowned at Margaret and quickly left. The guard reported he was walking up the hill to the Big House.

" My brother may try again if he suspects something. Do any of you want to quit? It will be alright with us if you do." All the people in the room shook their heads. Margaret looked at Rose and nodded. "I guess we go on."

Later that evening John burst into Margaret's room. Rose and Margaret were sitting on Margaret's bed, talking. "I know you're up to something, Margaret, and I'm going to catch you and tell Father. Then he won't think you're so wonderful. He gave me responsibilities. Can't you see I'm trying to make this plantation more efficient for Father? How can I do that with you constantly interfering with the slaves?" John glared at them and left, slamming the door.

Chapter 7

1851

Margaret and Rose collected the books from the children and said good-bye to them one Sunday afternoon.

"Rose? Rose! Wherever do you go when your eyes open up like that? Pay more attention! I was just saying they're all so pleased to be learning to read and write, are they not? Have I not taught well?"

Rose exhaled and narrowed her eyes. "Bella and George sit at home nights and read together by the light of the fireplace." She was the one who persuaded the adults to try the class and they're all happy they did. "Thank you, Margaret. I couldn't have done it without you."

"You're welcome." Margaret smiled. "Remember when we had that close call with John coming down here? Everyone pretended they were there to sing. Brother is not interested in religion. He left as soon as someone invited him to stay. He has not returned since." Margaret snorted, amused at the memory. "The only religion he has is Father, this plantation, and his twisted sense of honor. You saw his black eye? Another 'lady' to avenge no doubt. Yet I do still see him and his wretched friends in Church every few Sundays. He spies on you slaves, you know. And he never talks to me," she added bitterly.

"You're not fond of your brother?", Rose asked cautiously. Margaret resenting her brother did not surprise her. Margaret blatantly telling her this personal information was a shock. Information was dangerous for Negroes. Backing away, Rose hoped to restore some kind of prudent distance. Margaret excelled at making her feel uncomfortable. She just knew Margaret couldn't keep her mouth shut once she began. More broken master/slave taboos would follow, and surely, more trouble.

Margaret glanced at Rose and noticed she was backing away. "What's the matter?"

Rose looked down at her feet. "I don't think you should be talking to me about this."

"Why not? We are as close as sisters! No secrets. Nothing separates us after all."

Rose balled her fists and took a deep breath. I can't speak with complete freedom to you, even now, she thought. I cannot always be frank. Do you not understand I am still a slave? We certainly are not sisters. These things do separate us. Of course this makes me bound up tight! Do you think you know the real me?" Rose was shouting at Margaret within her mind. Then her eyes widened in realization as she thought, I do not even know the real me. Who am I besides Margaret's slave?

"Weren't you wanting to paint today, Margaret?" Margaret's paintings of flowers, gardens, buildings and other impersonal objects were hopelessly boring. They were also remarkably safer discussions to have than Margaret's relationship with her brother.

"Oh yes! I want to make a special painting for Mother and Father and I want your help."

"It would be my pleasure." Rose sighed, relieved.

A little while later, Margaret and Rose sat under a tree near the front of the Big House, trying to decide how to fit everything on the canvas. There was the mansion with the flower gardens in front, the semi-circular area for the horses and carriages to drive up and leave off their passengers, and the dark green tobacco fields stretching a little way from the side of the house down to the river. "You might include some Negroes working in the fields," Rose advised. "And don't forget the magnificent four white columns in the front of the house and the smokestacks."

"I don't know if I can get it all in.. Perhaps I should just leave out the tobacco field and the Negroes."

Rose shook her head. "It won't be a tobacco plantation if you don't include the field and some Negroes. It will just be a big house."

"Oh, I guess you're right. I'll try to fit it in somehow. I have a rough idea how it will look so now I can finish it in my room."

"Take a look at my painting, Rose. It's all done and I'm going to give it to Mother and Father tonight."

Rose approached, examining the large canvas on Margaret's easel. "It's nice, Margaret, but where are the Negroes you had in the fields?"

"Oh, I showed the painting to Mother and she wanted me to take them out. She thought they spoiled the beauty of the painting."

Rose paused, thinking of what to say. "I'm just wondering how you can paint a tobacco field on a plantation without Negroes working in the field."

Margaret grimaced, her face turning pink. "I know, but the painting is for my Mother and Father and my Mother didn't want it in. What could I do?"

Rose pursed her lips, lost in thought. Someday we hope there won't be slaves working in the fields. Uncle said we'll have a place to call our own, far from the whites. Maybe this is a painting of the future. I hope I see it.

Later that day, Rose managed to coerce Margaret into some of the more remote wooded areas. She breathed easier out here, almost happy for a moment. Margaret decided they should run back through the slave quarters. Rose hurried along behind her, being careful to let her win the race.

Margaret turned toward Rose, smiling. "You're so pretty. You'll have the favor of any boy you want."

Rose grabbed at her cloak. "What do you mean?"

"Just then, as we passed the slave quarters, Adam saw you and cut his foot with the scythe."

"Oh dear!" gasped Rose. She turned away. "I just don't like being around boys."

"Why not? Mama says you're becoming very beautiful, just like your Mother."

At this, Rose stepped away from Margaret. Without looking back she called out in a wavering voice, "Don't you think... we should get back to your room, Margaret?"

"Guess what, Rose. Mother and Father have decided to have a grand ball and invite the neighboring plantation owners and their families. I met a boy about our age from the Graydon plantation two years ago. He rode in with his Father on the way to another plantation. If he comes we'll have someone to walk with down by the river. He'll probably like finding birds with us."

Rose hugged her knees as they sat on the floor. "He won't want me around, Margaret. I'll stay at home so you and he can get better acquainted. What's his name?"

"I think his name is James. You should join us! Well, at least you'll enjoy watching the ball. All the women will be in beautiful gowns with their petticoats." Margaret waltzed around the room, a dreamy smile on her face. Stiffening up her expression and body she danced until she tripped over the bed and added, "and the men will be in their fancy coats and ruffled shirts, bowing and asking the women to dance." Rose muffled a laugh into her apron. She stepped over and helped Margaret up. Margaret popped up undeterred and surprised Rose by swinging her arms around like a conductor. "Father is hiring an orchestra and the dances will be fun to watch. It will be in a month to give time to get the invitations to the plantation owners and make all the arrangements. I'm so excited."

"I-I can see that," smiled Rose.

"I've never been to a ball before. In just a few years I'll have my coming out ball and this will give me an idea of what to expect. Aren't you excited?"

Rose gave a polite smile, "Of course, Margaret." But all she could think was more polishing, more preparations. No relief. Rose turned to the window and scanned the distant woods where she kept her best memories. She'd seen many birds in that wood, far from this house, doing what they wanted, flying where they pleased. That was freedom.

Three weeks later Margaret came running toward Rose who was walking up the path to the Big House. "Rose, come to my bedroom. I have something to show you." There on Margaret's bed were two beautiful gowns, identical except for color. "Mother had our seamstress make them for the Ball. Yours is the green one and mine is blue. Let's try them on."

Margaret threw on her gown, snapping at Rose to hurry up. Rose carefully picked up the gown, looked at it and paused. There would be trouble if she made the tiniest mark on these fancy new clothes. How could she hope to keep this gown clean next to her working clothes in their little cabin with its dirt floors? Another burden. What was the real motive for the mistress giving her a gown like Margaret's? What did the Ramseys expect in return for this gift other than the usual shadowing of Margaret? Rose dressed and followed Margaret into her Mother's dressing room, smiling politely.

"Oh, Margaret and Rose, you both look so pretty. Margaret, that blue dress matches your eyes and goes so well with your blond hair. Rose, your skin is so light and your hair is straight. In that dress you're so much prettier, you could even pass as a white girl. You are both lovely." Rose smiled again, gritting her teeth.

When Margaret was alone in her room she wondered about what her Mother had said. Why did it matter that Rose had light skin? Why would Rose want to pass as a white girl when she had such a good life belonging to her? What really mattered was that Rose took care of her. She hoped they'd always be together.

Mr. Ramsey called them out of the room and smiled. Gazing at them intently, he put his large hands on Margaret's shoulders.

"Dear daughter, there is a small restriction I must place on you now that you are clearly becoming a beautiful young lady, and I trust you will be obedient to your Father's instruction."

Rose noted a strange glance from Mr. Ramsey that she did not understand, but she unconsciously stepped back from Margaret and Mr. Ramsey.

"John tells me you're spending too much time in the slave quarters and woods. You must now keep near the house and garden. I don't want you near the Negro men; their appetites are dangerous."

This struck Rose like a slap in the face. What would it be like to be white? She envied Margaret. They were so close, but their lives were so different. What if she'd been born Margaret and had her lovely bedroom with its comfortable, pretty bed and the large window overlooking the flower garden and the oak and sycamore trees in the front of the house? She'd own all those beautiful dresses and her three dolls. She'd live in this lovely, big house with its wooden winding staircase, the heavy rose colored curtains covering the windows that went from the ceiling to the floor. Most fascinating of all, she'd have the library with its huge number of books that she could never get through in a lifetime. She'd sit at the window looking out on the back of the house, with the flowers, the large oak and cottonwood trees and the barely visible bend in the river. She'd sit there for hours, devouring one book after another. But the biggest difference was respect, just the basic respect. It was like a chasm between her life and Margaret's, which could never be crossed. If she just had that one thing her days would not weigh her down. And if she was Margaret, she'd let all the slaves free. Compared to her Margaret had so much power, but she was so blind. Margaret was kinder now, but still so oblivious sometimes. Now, Rose reasoned, she didn't believe what Margaret's brother had said, that Negroes were inferior to whites and couldn't learn as much. What would John say if he knew she could read better than Margaret?

If I was Margaret I'd have nasty John for a brother and my Mother and Father would be the cold, dull Mistress and the unkind

Master. My Bella and George are warm and kind, but always want me to stay in the cabin all night. At least when Uncle Joe was here we took what chances we could. Ever since Joe was sold, everyone seems to be trying to keep me out of the woods.

An odd hollow, crunching sound came through Margaret's window. Heavy, slick, metal trimmed wheels were gouging the bright crushed clam shells on the ground. Carriages were pulling into the white circular road. Margaret and Rose sat in the window seat of Margaret's bedroom on the second floor and watched as the slaves helped people alight from their carriages. The front doors below were alive with laughter. Food and drink were waiting for the guests as some had driven great distances to attend. Margaret pointed to a boy alighting from one of the carriages, followed by a Negro boy. "Look, I think that's James and the Negro must be his slave. Let's go down and meet them."

Margaret and Rose shyly approached the boys. "Hello. I'm Margaret and this is Rose, my slave. Are you James?"

"Yes, I'm James and this is Henry. Henry?"

Henry looked at Rose. He absently tapped on a metallic object in his pocket. "S-Sorry, James," Henry stuttered.

"Another tune? Henry here claims he sees in music sometimes." James elbowed Henry in the ribs.

"It's early yet. We have some food we can take down to the river. Rose can show you her bird book," Margaret directed, clasping her hands together.

Rose raised a skeptical eyebrow at Henry. "I hope those tunes don't trip you on the path," she whispered, as they silently followed Margaret and James.

Henry smiled, twitching his fingers and flipping the harmonica around in his pocket. He settled into a walking rhythm behind Rose, a small black cloth bag drumming his back as he walked in step with her.

"I-I could n-never lose sight of your m-melody, Miss," Henry answered with a half smile.

Rose rolled her eyes and shook her head.

"Rose, are you coming?" called Margaret, ahead of them.

Rose walked faster, looking carefully over her shoulder at Henry, and keeping a wary eye on James ahead of her.

They sat down under a tree and James asked, "May I see your book, Rose?" Rose clasped the treasure in her hands as she watched James reach out. After a moment, she dropped the item into his open palms. He slowly turned the pages. "Look at those bird pictures, Henry. They almost look alive. Have you seen a lot of these birds here?"

"Margaret and I identified quite a few. We spend a lot of time down here by the river. Margaret sketches and paints landscapes while I look for birds. She's really good."

Rose drew close to Margaret and whispered in her ear. "Perhaps we should return to the house. We don't really know these boys."

"Nonsense, Rose! That's why we're here! Why don't you try getting to know them? Ask Henry or James something," Margaret whispered.

Rose watched Henry's hand drumming on the harmonica in his pocket. Henry looked at her, humming a slow, happy tune, and smiled. She glanced shyly at him. "Do you like to look at birds, Henry?"

"I don't know that I've really noticed what they look like, but I wouldn't mind learning. Maybe you can show James and me. I've heard a few though. Here." From his rumpled black bag Henry produced a small, lumpy mess. It approximated a banjo. Made from an old firewood fretboard and a gourd resonator, it buzzed as he wrested with its pegs. He plucked and rubbed a rusty string. "Wawww, Waw, Waw!" cried the gourd.

"A laughing gull!" giggled Rose.

"Why don't you play a few songs for us?" suggested James.

Henry played and Margaret accompanied him when she knew the song. When he'd finished, James and Rose clapped. "Henry, you can really play; Margaret, you have a beautiful voice. I didn't know the two of you were so talented." James smiled and clapped again.

"Henry's... instrument is out of tune," noted Margaret.

"I think it sounds lovely," Rose snapped, then added carefully, "But of course the instrument needs some fine tuning."

Margaret turned to Henry. "Yes, we must ask Father if you can use the tuning fork set."

After the concert and when they'd finished eating, the four began to walk along the riverside, sighting and identifying a few birds, Margaret and Rose trying to be careful of their new gowns. Suddenly Henry stopped, "Do you hear that noise? It certainly isn't a bird. It sounds more like a moan."

James leaned over and listened. "Step back. I think it's under those bushes." He looked around and wrestled Henry's banjo away from him. James carefully approached the bush and crouched down, holding the banjo over his shoulder like a club. Henry glared at him. The moaning quieted down. There was a moment of deep silence as James peered into the bush. "Oh, it's a Negro and I think he's hurt. Henry, come here and help."

The two boys carefully pulled the man out from the bushes and discovered he had cuts and bruises all over his body and appeared to be unconscious. James looked at Henry as if sending him a message. "I think he's a runaway slave. We can't let any of the adults know. They'll turn him over to the patrollers." Henry returned a knowing glance to James.

Margaret looked back and forth between them. "Isn't there someone else who should be doing this? Isn't he considered a fugitive?" she asked weakly, looking over her shoulder.

"Look at the condition he's in, Margaret!" exclaimed James.

Margaret hesitated. "I guess Rose can find some cloth for bandages and a pail for water so you can wash him. I'll get some food because he'll probably be hungry when he wakes up. Rose, be careful my brother doesn't see you, although he'll probably be with a girl and not interested in us."

Soon James and Henry were busy washing and dressing the man's wounds. James removed the man's shirt and the girls gasped. His back was shredded and bloodied from lashings and pieces of shirt were stuck into the skin. Margaret turned her head away. James growled. "This is what happens to slaves who have cruel masters. Henry and I have seen it before, haven't we?" Henry nodded.

"I've seen it too. My uncle Joe was beaten like that." Rose looked at Margaret who turned away.

The Negro stirred and tried to sit up. James addressed him in a very matter of fact manner. "You need to rest. Here, have some water and food. I don't imagine you've had much to eat lately." The man looked up at James and shook his head. As he began to devour the chicken and corn cakes and drink the water life seemed to come back into him.

After he'd finished he looked at the four of them. "Thanks yer. I's been runnin' from de paterollers and deir dogs fer three days. My mas'r beats me an I's kaint takes it no more. I's goin' ter gits ter Canaan or dies tryin' ". He suddenly looked frightened. "Yer don't tells yer peoples, will yer?"

Henry looked at the man, a soft expression on his face. "No, we won't tell anyone." James looked down at the man. "I'm James, this is Henry, and the girls are Margaret and Rose. We'll try to help you get on your way to Canada. What's your name?"

"I's Joshua."

"Margaret, do you have an empty barn or a place we can put him in for the night? My parents and Henry and I have been invited to stay tomorrow and tomorrow night so maybe we'll have time to plan how to help him." James tilted his head and looked at Margaret.

"You can put him in our old barn. No one goes there anymore."

The boys lifted Joshua up and, getting on each side, supported him as they followed Margaret to the abandoned barn. They made a bed of straw and laid Joshua on it after Rose had returned with a blanket. "Margaret, could I get some poke root from the woods? Uncle Joe taught me. Poke root tonic helps with pain. "

"Of course, Rose. Go!"

Rose ran swiftly, despite her dress, through the thick woods. She knew every rabbit trail and every gap in the trees. Even so, it had rained. New grass and wildflowers obscured the wild herb patches. She knew it was near. Aha! There were the leaves hidden among the taller plants. Rose dug the herbs up with her fingers and returned via a deer track. Henry helped Joshua sit up and drink the tonic.

"We'll leave you now, Joshua, before our parents wonder where we are. We'll check on you after the Ball. Henry and I better clean up." James looked down ruefully at his shirt which had dirt, straw and a few spots of blood on it. "Mother always says I can never keep clean."

It was the next morning and the four were in the shed, watching while Joshua ate the breakfast Margaret had brought for him. "Joshua, you're a lot stronger, but still too weak to walk to Canada. There's a Society of Friends community about a half day by horseback and I'm certain they'd help you. Brother Holloway has helped Henry and I deliver packages before."

"Deliver packages? How will this nonsense help anything?" Margaret asked. Rose couldn't help but give James a knowing smile.

"The Holloways are known for helping runaways reach the North," James continued, his hand on Joshua's shoulder. "I only hope they haven't become too well known. But even if they're still station masters, how do we get you there? Henry and I go home tomorrow morning. We can't leave you here. Any ideas?" James looked worriedly at the others.

"James!" Rose said, unable to hold it in any longer, "Margaret could ask her Father if she can borrow a carriage so we can show you and Henry around the plantation and the next town. You could ask your Father for permission to go. We could pack a picnic lunch and say we'll be gone until late afternoon. You know how to drive a carriage, don't you?" James nodded.

Margaret, mouth gaping, looked at Rose with new eyes. "Well... I suppose we'd better make the arrangements then. Let's meet back here soon."

"Father, Rose and I would like to take James and his Negro around the plantation and to see the town. Could we use a carriage? James knows how to drive."

"Margaret is getting entirely too friendly with the Negroes Father! First Rose and now she's friends not only with James, that odd Graydon boy, but his Negro. One shouldn't get friendly with niggers. It will addle her mind and ruin the slaves. They're property." John, a smug expression on his face, looked over at Margaret.

"Be quiet, John. I'm tired of the way you're always finding fault with your sister." Their Father turned to Margaret. "Are you certain James can handle the horse? He's only about twelve, I believe."

"James said that if you have any question about his managing the horse and carriage to ask his Father. I guess his Father trained him and lets him drive the carriage when they are going anywhere."

"Alright then, be back before dark. Be careful."

James drove the carriage near the door of the barn and Joshua was quickly loaded in and covered with a blanket. Henry sat up with James and the girls climbed in the carriage, the picnic basket between them. They headed out at a leisurely trot, knowing they couldn't go fast as they were a heavy load for the horse.

Three hours later James slowed the horse, pulled to the side of the road, and stopped. "I think we'd better let the horse graze and drink and we'll have our picnic lunch. Joshua, you'll have to stay in the carriage, but we'll bring you some food."

"But can we really afford to do this?" Rose asked, looking around her and crossing her arms.

"We have no choice. This horse must rest."

Margaret gratefully climbed down from the carriage and brushed off some of the dust from the road. They spread out a blanket and, after bringing Joshua a plate, settled down to eat.

"What are you doing?" Two men on horseback rode up, both holding rifles, and glanced down at the four.

James stood up. "The girls are showing us the area because we aren't from here. We're just having a picnic and then we are going to see the town."

"We're patrolling for runaways. Have you passed a nigger looking like this one?" The man leaned down from his horse, and handed James a poster that named Joshua and described him.

"No, we haven't passed any Negroes coming this way," James quickly and calmly dismissed the paper. One of the men squinted out from under his hat, staring James directly in the eye. James drew in a sharp breath, then shrugged and returned a wide-eyed look. He stepped forward. "Don't they hide in the woods? They wouldn't be on the road, would they?"

The one man looked at the other. "I don't think the nigger could have come this far. From what I heard he'd been beaten and has been running about 3 days now. Let's go further back this way."

As they rode off, the four looked at each other. Rose cringed. "That was close! We're lucky they didn't have dogs trained to sniff out runaways. Perhaps we'd better be on our way. At least the patrollers are going the opposite direction."

James helped Margaret up and Henry assisted Rose. They put the picnic basket and blanket in the carriage where they found Joshua curled up, grasping one side of the cart. Margaret touched his shoulder gently. "It's alright, Joshua, they're gone. We don't have far to go now. Isn't that so James?" Margaret called forward as they lurched back into motion. James nodded, his eyes firmly set on the horizon.

Time slowly trotted by. Margaret shifted in her seat, then moved again. Rested her head in her arms one way, then the other. She stared blankly at the front wheels of the cart as they turned endlessly. Rose was running her fingers through her hair over and over again. Henry lay hunched over in the front seat. There was a thump and some stones clattered down the old wooden boards then out the back of the cart. Henry took out a harmonica and started a basic beat with it. The beat matched the sound of the clattering stones. The others put their heads up and smiled. The cart seemed to be moving faster now. A steep valley lay ahead. Suddenly Henry stopped playing. Rose was leaning over the side of the cart, gazing down into a ravine by the side of their cart. "Most impressive view, Henry. Look! Why have you stopped playing?"

Henry puffed out his cheeks and rubbed his stomach. He was looking a little green.

"I don't like high places, Rose."

"But you can see an entire town there and see where all the roads go and everything. You can even see the river at the bottom. And look. There's a bridge. You're missing quite a view."

Henry winced. "N-no bridges, no towns, no roads, no rushing rivers, n-no h-heights."

"Don't you wonder what the land looks like, where everything is, what a whole town looks like?"

"Yes," Henry answered, "But maps don't make me nervous or sick"

When they reached town James said, "You stay here. I'll find someone who can give us directions to the Society of Friends community." James had Henry take the reins.

A little while later James returned with a white haired man who introduced himself as Brother Holloway. "Thee are welcome, my friends. I understand thee has a package for me and my wife. If thee will follow me to my home, thee would be able to deliver the package."

The two carriages soon pulled up to a small white frame home with a lovely front garden. The smell of magnolia blossoms permeated the air. Brother Holloway glanced around and then motioned for them to bring Joshua into the house. There they were introduced to Sister Holloway who welcomed Joshua and assured him that he would be safe and that they would help him on his journey. "Thee sit down and have some food and drink before thee start thy long ride back."

"Please." Rose looked at Margaret, James and Henry. "We should go."

James sighed, "Perhaps Rose is right."

"Leave and miss this meal?" Margaret touched James' hand. "Don't worry, I can be very persuasive with Father."

Henry started imitating a military bugle call on his harmonica at the table. Mr. Holloway glanced at him and smiled.

"Must you do that before every meal, Henry?" James smiled nervously. "It seems the matter is decided."

Soon the four and Joshua were enjoying a delicious meal with the warm, friendly couple. "I'm glad thee made it here without running into the patrollers whom, I believe, are looking for thee, Joshua."

"Oh, two of the patrollers rode up while we were having a picnic and showed us a poster telling about Joshua, but he was in the carriage and they didn't look in there. James convinced them we were just four children on a picnic." Margaret looked at James with admiration.

"Thee are lucky. Thee probably hasn't heard of the Fugitive Slave Law passed last year. It means that people even in the free states have to assist slave catchers if there are runaway slaves in their area. Slave catchers have immunity when in the free states to do their job. It's illegal to assist any runaway. Slave traders are coming into the North and capturing even the free Negroes, claiming they are runaways and then selling them down South. We now must help runaways into Canada because they are no longer safe in the North of the United States." Brother Holloway saw Joshua's wide stare. "Don't thee worry, Joshua. We'll take thee to the next station on the Underground Railroad and thee will be helped until thee is in Canada where no Patroller can reach thee."

"Thank you, Brother and Sister Holloway. We'd better leave as it will be getting dark by the time we reach the plantation." James and the others stood up and said their good-byes to the couple and to Joshua.

Joshua stood up. "I's thanks yer fer yer hep."

"That's alright, Joshua. Maybe I'll see you in Canada sometime." Henry smiled and shook Joshua's hand.

"It's dark and we've been worried." Margaret's Father and James' Father were waiting for them as they rode in. Both looked upset and angry.

"I'm sorry, Father. We went further than we'd planned and then James couldn't make the horse go too fast as the horse was tired. We all watched the road." Margaret apologized to her Father as he helped her out of the carriage. "We did have a lantern for when it got dark and we were almost home by then."

"James, you should know better than to keep these lovely girls out so late. Now, you and Henry get some sleep. We are starting for home early in the morning."

James' father took him aside, "I worry about you and especially Henry. He can be a little too bold for a slave and..."

They glanced at Henry to see him dreamily humming a tune at the stars.

"He's certainly absent minded," James added.

Mr. Graydon lowered his voice and continued, "Look, son, I know you're caught up with these abolitionist pamphlets of yours, but don't involve the Ramsey girl in your ideologies."

"Respectfully, I must say, Father, that if I'm able to rescue our farm then I should use my abilities to help those in bondage. And, indeed, I did introduce many of my own successful technological innovations to our farm, such as the new indigo crop varieties."

"Yes, those new varieties you tested on my finest shirts. They are now pink. Yet I must admit some of your innovations, and certainly your hard work, saved our plantation when I was sick. But you don't have to save everyone. I've told you before," Mr. Graydon lowered his voice another degree, "you know I don't like keeping slaves, but what else is there?"

"It seems the time may come when men must change their hearts, their actions, and their plantations, Father. Don't worry. As I have kept our plantation out of trouble, I can keep Miss Ramsey from trouble as well."

Margaret and Rose met the boys at dawn to say good-bye. James took Margaret's hands in his. "Henry and I had a wonderful time with you and Rose. We want to come back often. Maybe I can persuade my Mother and Father to visit your Mother and Father next year sometime. Would that be alright with you, Margaret?" Margaret nodded shyly.

"How about you, Rose? Can I visit you?"

"Yes, Henry, I'd like to see you again. We can look for more birds and you can play more songs for us if you like."

Margaret and Rose waved good-bye as the carriage left the circular drive. They slowly walked back to Margaret's room where they reminisced about their first experience with boys. "We didn't see much of the beautiful ball." Margaret sighed.

"We must admit, though, that Henry and James gave us a night we'll never forget." Rose smiled dreamily.
"Mr. Morgan, may I talk with you?" Joe stood at the quartermaster's door, hat in hand.

"Come in, Joe, and sit down."

Joe sat and stared down at his feet. "Mr. Morgan, I've been a pirate for three years and I've learned a lot. Jack has taught me to be a sailor and has even helped me learn to read and to speak better. I like doing the carpenter work and you've shared one and a quarter of the plunder from each engagement with me as you said you would. I've always wanted to have my own farm and I'm asking you to release me so that I can go to Canada and try to find Liza and buy a farm with the money I have." Joe finally looked up at the quartermaster.

"Joe, you're the best carpenter we've ever had. You repair the sloop's hull when the rats gnaw through it and keep the entire ship in excellent condition. You're a good root doctor. You saw off limbs injured in battle and use roots to help with the pain. You've helped to cut down on the number of pirates dying from sickness and injuries. You've learned how to do most of the jobs on the ship. You know the rigging and the sails and can steer her. You can use a pistol, a blunderbuss and a cutlass. You're a member of the boarding party and you're good at tossing the grappling hook and climbing up the side of the captured ship. You don't want to kill, I understand that. So you make yourself useful in battle by

69

pulling aside to safety the injured pirates and stopping their bleeding. You've suggested a few ways of capturing a ship so that often we don't even have to fire our big guns. You are one of the most valuable members of my crew." The quartermaster shook his head. "No, Joe, I can't release you. I can never release you."

"Just think of all of your people you're helping. Ever since the time you were captured I've let the Negroes go to shore first so they can start toward Canada and then I release the slaveholders and the rest of the passengers. You're not just helping the crew and me, but you're helping your people."

The quartermaster looked thoughtful. "Joe, I hate to do this, but I'm going to have to chain you at night when we are in port and have someone watch you closely when we are on shore. I think you might try to run and I just can't lose you as a member of my crew. That's all, Joe."

A call was heard from on deck. "They've spotted a ship. Get armed and ready to board."

Joe felt the familiar rush of excitement as he strapped three pistols over his chest and grabbed the grappling hook. Pirates in charge of the ten big guns fired at the sails and the rigging in order to damage the ship, but not sink it. The sloop then pulled alongside and the boarding party threw their grappling hooks and climbed up the sides of the captured ship. A few of the captured crew tried to fight off the pirates with knives and pistols. Two men were lying on the deck, bleeding. Joe saw that one was Jack, who had taught him so much on the sloop. Pirates and crew fighting with cutlasses, daggers and knives were practically on top of him. Joe crouched over and ran to Jack, taking him under both arms, and pulling him to a safer part of the ship, away from the action. He knelt down to take a look. "Joe, it's about time you showed up. Got anything for bleeding and pain?"

"I can take care of this, Jack. Just be quiet."

Later, back on the sloop, his shoulder patched and having had a root tonic for the pain, Jack looked up at Joe. "Thank you, Joe. I don't know what the rest of us pirates would do without you."

Joe walked along the deck that night, thinking. He had to admit he enjoyed the excitement of capturing a ship. He was getting wealthy from his one and a quarter share of the plunder. But what was he able to spend it on when he was on the sloop most of the time? The pirates were almost like a family. Jack had taught him reading and writing and how to talk like white people as well as how to handle the sloop. It was good to be able to save lives with his surgeon skills and root medicines. Perhaps he should just accept the pirate life and forget about farming. Even if Liza had escaped to the North she had probably found someone else by now. Joe looked up at the star studded sky, immediately focusing his eyes on the big dipper, the slaves' drinking gourd leading to Canaan. And yet…

Henry grabbed his black bag containing his banjo and harmonica and set off down the road. This would be his first time playing for people, other than when he played for James, Margaret and Rose. The Negroes at the next plantation had asked him to play for their Saturday night of partying and he'd accepted. Now he was wondering, was he really good enough? James thought so, but maybe he was just saying that. If he did well, maybe some day he could earn money with his playing. As he trudged down the road Henry dreamed about entertaining a large audience and collecting so much money he could buy a good banjo.He heard a horse galloping behind him and moved over to the side of the road. The horse stopped and the white man astride asked, "What are you doing out here? Who do you belong to?"

"Graydon Plantation, Sir," replied Henry. He wasn't worried. The Graydons were well known in this area.

"That so," smiled the Patroller. "Show me your papers and prove it."

"I-I," Henry couldn't speak. Papers? What papers? He didn't bring papers with him. Beads of sweat formed on his forehead.

"I'm tired of waiting; I'm taking you in!"

71

"Wait! Ask the Graydons! Wait!"

"You ordering me, boy? What kind of uppity slave are you? Uppity slaves need to be taught a lesson. No papers; then you belong to me."

Wham! The Patroller made a sharp movement; Henry's world went black.

Crawling over the hills like a bright round beetle, the sun failed to light the valley of the Graydons' plantation below. James shivered as the chill crept in through the frills of his fine shirt. He sat in the tool shed, candle by his side, staring intently at yellow brown paper. In dark, curly letters that looked like leaves, on the opposite side of the pamphlet, were the words: "Doctor Erasmus H. Greenwood's Little Agricultural Miracle Catalog for the Future Advancement of Mankind." His fingers brushed over a diagram of something that looked like an oddly shaped turning plow covered with cogs, wheels and cranks. It was fascinating. He'd been taken by schemers before, but this! This one would change the plantation. Ha! Surely such a design will impress Henry. Maybe we can use this on the new indigo field. Where is he?

"Edward! Edward! You seen Henry?" James called out to an old, bent slave in a rocking chair. "I need to remind him to ready the cart this morning so we can pick up those new hoes from the blacksmith." The thick, dark, humid morning absorbed most light and sound. The old man's soft voice mixed with the hissing of insects and was almost lost.

"Haven't strummed wit him in a long time, Mas'r. He think he be ready ter play on him own. Fact, he be invited ter de next plantation over by some other Negroes to play fer dem. Yer mean yer didn't gib him his papers?"

"Oh no!" James broke into a run.

Henry was in town, laying on the bloodstained, wooden floor of a jail cell. The small interior was littered with leaflets and depictions of menacing Negro-like creatures. A man twice Henry's size stood over him. His face and body were fat, burnt red, and droopy. His massive frame sweated through a thick padded coat he wore despite the heat and humidity. "I've been reading and learning

72

all about the tactics of your kind for years, Nigger," spat the man. "Uppity, conniving animals must be kept under control at all costs." There was a loud twang. The man was ripping his banjo to pieces. The giant grunted as he ripped and then tightened Henry's old banjo strings into knots around his wrists. Henry's wrist began to seep blood. He then bound Henry's legs. "Your white-hatin', nigger music will only cause you pain, Nigger! Remember that. I hope these strings cut you good. We know all your uppity tricks. You crawl around down there like you should and polish the floor." He shoved an oily rag into Henry's mouth and pushed his face into the floorboards. "We're good at breaking niggers here... and killing them."

"I think I'll put my feet up and rest now." A creaky stool moaned under his weight. Henry heard the man's shoes slap the wall in the corner. "I've read that some think slaves catch disease from bad smells." He placed his filthy, scratchy stocking feet on Henry's back and rubbed them into Henry's fresh whip cuts. "Lets see what this does, shall we?"

Henry had yelled when the beatings began. He had cried for help, begged until the giant had smashed him into silence. Henry heard the cough of fine gentlemen on the street. They leaned up against the outer wall of the jail. The quick tip-taps of ladies' shoes in the dirt as they passed the jail window. Carriages of people, pedestrians, men leading animals all crowded the street on the other side of these walls. At one point he had actually managed to scream out the small window, "Help! H-He's killing me!" No one looked up. How could the entire world ignore him? He was going to die in pain and these fine townspeople, strolling in their frilly coats, didn't even blink. His life really didn't matter. A life wasted on silly music. He'd not spent time making friends in the quarters and had foolishly come to trust a white boy, who, in reality was just another master. His life was ending and James wasn't here. The giant again raised the blunt end of a bull whip handle above his head like a club.

"Henry! Stop man! Stop!" shouted James. He ran into the cell, leaped up, and grasped the man's arm. The giant raised his arm slightly and James' feet lifted off the ground. James held onto the huge arm and dangled there as if it were the limb of a tree. The man's small, cold eyes fixed on James' face. James exhaled all the air from his gut and gulped.

The human tree lowered his arm while maintaining eye contact. "A patroller said he had an uppity look to him, you know, since he had the instrument and all. We can't oblige that. You know what evils their black minds create when they're idle. And him traveling without his papers too! So we set him straight. You Graydons oughta' learn how to manage your slaves better. That'll be fifty cents." James jumped out of the cell, threw some coins at the man sleeping behind a desk, and dove back to Henry's side.

"Henry! Henry! I've come to take you out of here! Quick!" Henry sobbed and didn't move from the floor. James could hardly recognize him. Tears and blood ran down his swollen face. Yet more blood came from his wrists. James cut the strings loose, releasing Henry, then quietly lifted Henry's bleeding, contorted body up into a standing position. He placed Henry's arm around his shoulders, and carefully supported him to the carriage.

Henry sat next to James in the carriage on the way back to the plantation. "Didn't you think to ask permission? Why not take your papers like the other slaves?" Henry gripped the seat and stared at the plantation fence line. You really are a slave, Henry, nothing else, Henry thought to himself.

Chapter 8

1853

Margaret and Rose were sprawled out on the floor, reading, when there was a knock on Margaret's door. Quickly Rose hid her book under her dress before Margaret said, "Come in." Margaret's Father peeked into the room. Margaret smiled at Rose with relief. At least it wasn't her nosy brother.

"Margaret, I need to borrow Rose for awhile."

Margaret nodded. "Come back here when you're done, Rose."

It was an hour later when Rose entered the room. Margaret glanced up from her book. "Rose, what's wrong? You're shaking. Do you have a fever?"

Rose shook her head. "May I go home now? I'm tired."

"Of course you can. I'll see you in the morning. I hope you'll feel better by then."

The next evening Margaret's Father again appeared at the door and asked Rose to accompany him. Rose, a fearful expression on her face, stood up slowly and walked toward the door.

For the next three months Rose left with Margaret's Father once or twice a week and would then return to Margaret's room an hour later, very subdued. Margaret was becoming worried because Rose appeared to be changing. At first it was difficult to be sure. Rose was normally fairly reserved, but this was different. She didn't laugh or even smile as often and was much quieter.

"I guess Father is having you work as his secretary. He must have found out you can read and write. He doesn't appear to be upset about it so that's good." Rose put her head down and didn't respond.

"Here Rose, Mother bought me some new dresses. You can have these 3 older ones. Try them on so we can see if they fit. I think we are about the same size."

Rose took off her dress and began to put a blue plaid one over her head. "Let me help you, Rose. It seems to be stuck." Margaret pulled, but the dress wouldn't go on. She gave Rose a puzzled look. "I'm certain we are about the same size so my dress should fit you. Have you gained weight?" She looked at Rose's stomach. "You have, Rose. You are much bigger around the waist." Margaret looked at Rose again, a surprised expression on her face. "You're going to have a baby, aren't you?" Rose nodded. "Who is the father? Is it one of those two good looking field hands? I thought that you really liked Henry and I like James, but I guess you found someone else in the quarters. Tell me. Who is he?" Rose shook her head. "I thought we told each other everything. I won't tell anybody."

"I can't tell you, Margaret. I just can't. Please don't ask."

"Alright, Rose. You'll tell me eventually. It's exciting. We'll be able to dress it, take it for walks and teach it to talk. I hope it's a girl. They are more fun to dress and play with than boys. Do you know when you are going to have it?"

"Grandma Bella thinks I've had the baby in me three months. She knows a lot about this. She's a midwife. She delivered both you and me."

"Mother still has my baby clothes and John's. I'm certain she'll give them to you. There's a cradle and baby blankets. I'll help you take care of the baby, Rose. Now you better go home and rest. Any time you get tired let me know and you can go home." Margaret gave Rose a hug. "I'll see you tomorrow."

That evening Margaret glanced at her Mother, Father and brother as they sat at the table, eating. "Rose is   going to have a baby." Her Father looked up, startled, then quickly put his head down and continued to eat.

"My goodness, she's only 13 years old, the same age as you, Margaret. That's rather young to have a baby. Who is the Father, dear?"

"I don't know. Rose won't tell me."

John smirked. "She probably doesn't know herself. You know how the niggers sleep with everybody they can."

Margaret glanced at her Father who was busily shoveling food into his mouth. Suddenly she knew.

"Father, it's you! You came and took Rose from my room every week. It's your baby! Father, how could you?" Margaret started crying and ran from the room.

"Charles, I know you sleep with slaves, but you should know better than to take a servant girl, especially Margaret's Rose. Don't you go near Rose again or any other servant girl or you will regret it." Lillian glared at her husband. "I don't know if Margaret will ever forgive you for this."

The next morning Margaret motioned for Rose to sit next to her. "I know who the Father is, and I am so sorry. It's my Father, isn't it?" Rose put her head down and stared at the floor. "When I announced at the table last night that you were going to have a baby, Father looked up and his expression gave him away. All those times he came to my room to get you I thought you were helping him with some papers." Margaret shook her head. "Mother said to tell you that Father is never to touch you again. If he tries you are to tell me so I can let her know. Your baby will be well looked after. We are both so sorry."

"I wanted to tell you, Margaret, but I couldn't. Grandma Bella says this happens all the time. One of her babies who was taken from her and sold down south was fathered by a white overseer. And my Father was a white overseer as well."

"It just isn't right." Margaret clenched her fists and looked as though she'd like to hit someone.

"What about Henry? I really like him. Will he want to be with me after I've had a baby?"

"Of course he will. In that last letter James said that they can hardly wait to see us again and are planning to come early next year. You'll have your baby by then. If you don't want to explain what happened I'll tell James and he can tell Henry. You aren't to blame. Henry will understand. Now, what are you going to name your baby?"

"Samuel if it's a boy and Rebecca if it's a girl. Do you like those names, Margaret?"

"Five years, Jack. I've been a pirate five long years. The quartermaster is still putting me in chains when we're at port. Might as well be a slave."

Jack, who was at the wheel, looked over at Joe. "We need you. And everyone of these men will tell you, despite its faults, life on ship is fairer than life on shore. I started with the Navy in Sumatra, and I just couldn't leave the water. But Navy life is insufferably strict so I stay here. Even the master-gunner hates life ashore and he complains about this ship more than anyone".

"You low down swab! I heard that! Why I outta-", came a crusty yell from below. Jack continued, steadily speaking over the man's yells. "The quartermaster depends on you more than anyone. I know you want to go north and find your Liza, but do you think she'd still be waiting after five years? She was really beautiful. Some man would have taken her as his wife by now. Besides, how could you abandon your shipmates after all we've provided for you? The pirate life isn't a bad one. You'll get more out of life with us than with anyone on land. You belong with us, Joe. Maybe if you could accept that you are a pirate the quartermaster will unchain you."

"I know she'll most likely be married even if she made it to Canada, but I want to find out for certain. I think about her all the time. I imagine her in my arms, her head on my shoulder, telling me that I make her feel safe." Joe sighed as he stared out at the unending water.

"Jack, hand me the spy glass. I see something port side. It looks like a ship." Joe looked through the spyglass. "It is a ship and I think it's military. Sound the alarm! It's gaining on us."

Upon hearing the alarm the captain rushed up to use the spyglass. "We can't outrun it and it's heavily armed. We'll fight to our death. Get your arms. Prepare for battle."

Joe strapped on his pistols. Their sloop shook. Shots were hitting its port side. The few big guns on the sloop were returning fire, but it was only a matter of time before an army would be climbing over the side. Joe and the rest of the pirates knew what would happen. The captain and quartermaster would hang. The rest of them, if not hanged, would spend their lives in prison. Joe looked at the pirates and at the army men and thought to himself, This isn't my battle. He removed the three pistols, grabbed his pieces of eight and put a few of them in a pouch which he tied around his neck. The rest he placed in a pocket of his trousers. He quietly walked to the starboard side and jumped into the river.

Joe swam, then rested and swam some more. He was thankful for growing up by a river. He and his friends would sometimes go swimming at night after working all day in the burning hot tobacco fields. He remembered those rare good times when he'd had the chance to sneak away and teach little Rose to swim. She loved getting on his shoulders and diving into the river. Joe smiled at the recollection.

Eventually Joe reached shore, climbed onto the river bank and stretched out on the sand to catch his breath. I must be in Tennessee. The pirate captain never went up the Ohio River anymore. Military ships and vigilante groups hunted pirates in those waters. I need to follow the Mississippi to the Ohio and then follow the Ohio. I know that much. I wish I could find someone in the Underground Railroad. I need help. I'll have to stay near the river so I can jump in if I hear dogs. Joe shivered at the memory of Reuben being torn to shreds by the patrollers' dogs. I'll sleep under bushes during the day and follow the drinking gourd at night. Someone said it could take more than a year to walk from New Orleans to Canada, but I'm part of the way there now. Here's a large bush. I'll just crawl under it and try to sleep.

It's good to feel the dirt beneath my feet, thought Joe. He looked up and saw the Drinking Gourd high in the night sky, beckoning him. Maps he'd seen on the sloop showed that he had to pass through Tennessee, a little of Illinois, through Indiana and then into Ohio. He'd studied the maps, always with the hope that someday he'd be free to find his way north.

He'd been walking for three weeks now and had found only berries and ground nuts to eat. There's a farm up ahead that's not far from the river. Should I risk sneaking up and trying to grab a chicken? There would be a farm dog, but maybe it's tied up. Joe walked close to the farmhouse and then crouched down to get even closer. A dog started barking. Joe ran, crouched over, to the building that looked like a chicken house. As he crawled inside the chickens began to squawk.

"What's that noise for?" a man shouted, heading for the chicken house. "I'm trying to sleep. What the…? You get out of there, you chicken thief!" He put the rifle to his shoulder and pulled the trigger. He missed. Joe grabbed a chicken and ran as fast as he could toward the river. He traveled several miles to put distance between him and the angry farmer. I'm not going to try that again, no matter how good the chicken tastes, thought Joe, as he sat next to a small fire. He had just cooked the chicken and was now devouring it.

Joe could see slivers of town through the woods. A distant tapping on metal echoed through the valley. Dogs kept barking. The loudest animals of all were the donkeys that would not shut their mouths. Hee-haw! Hee-haw! The unmistakable rumbling and squeaking of wagon wheels. Various odors and hues of smoke spread out through the woods. I wish I could go into town and buy some food and clothes with my pieces of eight, but I don't dare try it. What good is all this money doing me? I haven't had a good meal in a long time. At least when I was pirate we ate good, except for the one time we couldn't go to a port because they were looking for us. The rats we had to eat didn't taste that bad. I wish I had one now.

Joe thought he must be getting close to the Ohio River. While he'd vowed he'd never risk grabbing another chicken he'd only eaten the chicken and one rabbit plus some roots and berries in two months. He was hungry. There were holes in the bottoms of his shoes. He was feeling desperate. The last two days and nights he'd been encamped at the edge of a wood, watching an isolated farmhouse. He'd noticed that an older man and woman lived there. The man left early in the morning for the fields, taking his dog with him. The woman fed the animals and hung clothes on the line. That's what interested Joe. The man looked about his size. Here she comes and she's hanging her wash on the line. Joe couldn't believe his luck. The woman hung up what looked like pantaloons and two shirts. As soon as she went into the house Joe rushed up and grabbed the clothes. He ran as fast as he could to the chicken house and took a chicken. When he reached the river he ran a ways before stopping to put on his new clothes. It was risky to have a fire in the day when patrollers might pass by, but Joe couldn't wait. He cooked his chicken and ate it; then crawled under a bush close to the river and fell asleep.

There was a full moon when Joe started out and the drinking gourd shown bright in the sky. He felt much better in his new clothes and with a full stomach. Joe remembered there was a town called Cairo near the junction of the Mississippi and Ohio Rivers. A slave who had been on a boat the pirates captured told Joe he was caught near there because slave catchers knew runaways followed the Ohio to freedom. He mentioned there were a lot of patrollers and dogs along the Ohio. This could be the most dangerous part of his journey. He would have to walk in the river sometimes so dogs couldn't follow his scent. He remembered the church people singing "Wade in the River".

Joe finally reached the junction of the Mississippi and Ohio Rivers and began to follow the Ohio. Often he could hear dogs in the distance. Reuben's screams echoed in his mind. He wished he could find a station where he could be safe but was afraid to go into a town. There were no lanterns in windows or people saying "thee" near the river.

It was October and getting cold at night. Joe wore two shirts, but they didn't stop the biting wind. He wished he had a coat and longed for another chicken. There were no isolated farmhouses nearby. It was now daylight and time to find a bush and hide until nightfall.

What was that? Joe sat up suddenly. Loud barking and it was getting louder. He must get to the river. Joe jumped up and ran as fast as he could. When he reached the river he discovered reeds along the shore. He walked out amongst them, got down, and floated on his back so he wasn't visible from land. As soon as the dogs approached he lay still, scarcely daring to breathe. The dogs could neither see nor smell him. They seemed to stay a long time on the shore. When the patrollers joined them, both they and the dogs went up and down the river. Finally the patrollers rode away, the dogs following.

It was some time later before Joe felt safe enough to come out and crawl under a bush. They wouldn't be back because they'd already covered the area. He tried to sleep, but was wet and cold and couldn't stop shivering. He stayed under the bush the rest of that day and all night, curled up, trying to keep warm.

I'm so hot. I must get to the river for some water. I can't stand up. Need water. I'll crawl. With great effort Joe pulled himself along the ground until he reached the Ohio. He took a drink and had started back towards the bush when he collapsed in the open.

The two men walked along the river, fishing poles in hands. "Yer knows our wives aren't goin' ter likes us sneaking off at dawn ter goes fishing an not goin' ter church wid dem."

"I's knows, Jim, but us habn't been fishin' in er month an de fishin' better at dawn dan late Sunday afternoon. Dey forgives us w'en us gib dem all dose fishes us cotch."

"Up here whar thar be er lot ob reeds. I's done caught fish in thar." Jim suddenly stopped. "What dat on de shore?" He started running and when he reached Joe he crouched down beside him.

"Him breathing, but him be burning up wid fever. Look like him be er freedom seeker, Abram."

"You stays wid him an I's goes ter gets de horse an cart."

Soon Jim and Abram were lifting Joe into the cart. "Us takes him ter my house, Jim. I's hab de room."

Jim took Joe's arms and Abram the legs and they carried him into Abram's home and put him into a bed. A woman stood by, silently watching. "Flora, dis here man us found by de ribber. Him burning up wid fever."

Flora bent over Joe and felt his forehead. "I's goes ter gits Jinny. Her hab root medicines ter bring de fever down."

Jim frowned. "Mebbe us should gits de doctor. Him mebbe bery sick."

"Jim, yer knows de doctor jes lets de blood run out him. Iffen yer gits er doctor de white people finds out an gib dis here freedom seeker ter de patrollers. Jinny cures him wid her root medicines an us sends him ter de next station. Jes put er cold rag on de forehead until I's returns wid Jinny."

Soon Jinny, a bent over, wizened, old black woman, was examining Joe. "We needs ter brings his fever down an wakes him so I's ken gits de boneset tonic in him." Jim, Abram and Flora wrapped Joe in a wet blanket while Jinny prepared her tonic. Soon Joe began to stir and mumble something none could understand.

"Sit him up.", Jinny directed Jim and Abram. She looked at Joe. "Yer must open yer mouth an drinks dis. It heps yer gits well." She held the tonic to his mouth and he finally opened it and drank the liquid. After they laid him down Jinny looked at the three of them. "I's stays wid him tonight an gibs him de tonic. Him might not makes it ter de morning."

When Abram and Flora stepped into the room the next morning they found the exhausted root doctor who told them the man had survived the night and was now breathing normally. Jinny told Flora how to care for the man and left for home while Abram went to his carpentry shop.

That night Joe was awake and able to talk, although still very ill. Jim and his wife, Cloe, came to visit. They told Joe they were free Negroes, Abram working as a carpenter and Jim as a farmer. Jinny stopped in to check on Joe and gave Flora more medicine for him. Joe was very grateful, but too weak to talk long so Jinny gave him some tonic and they left him to go back to sleep. To Joe, all these events passed as dreams he could barely recall.

It was a week later and Joe was able to eat with Abram and Flora and could walk around a little. He was still very weak and had a slight fever. Jinny came daily to give Joe the tonic.

"Abram, I must be on my way north. I can't let you and Flora care for me any longer."

"Jinny says yer kaint goes ter de north til yer be well. Us knows er underground railroad station dat us takes yer ter w'en yer ken travel. Yer says yer er carpenter. W'en yer better yer ken hep me in my shop an dat pays fer yer food."

Joe brightened at the thought of being able to pay for his lodging. "I can go with you tomorrow. I can sit in your shop and work and not get tired."

"I's checks wid Jinny an iffen her say yer ken goes I's takes yer. I's er lot of work an yer ken be er big hep."

Jim burst into the room, a frightened expression on his face. "Abram, us must takes Joe right now ter de station. Two slave catchers are in town an dey be asking all de Negroes ter show dem their papers. Iffen dey finds Joe dey takes him down south an sells him."

"But Joe still not over de sickness."

"Him kaint stays here. Iffen him caught dey ken takes us too. I hear dey axt free Negroes fer their papers an den tears dem up. Dey goes ter court an seys de free Negro er runaway slave. De judge signs de papers dat gib de free Negro ter de slave catcher. De slave catcher takes de free Negro down south an sells him. Iffen him found wid us, de slave catcher mos likely takes us ter court an sells us down south. I's afeard for Flora an Cloe an Jinny too."

"You must take me now. I don't want to put any of you in danger. You've been so good to me."

"I's hab de cart outside an it be full of vegetables. Us loads yer in de cart, Joe, an den us puts vegetables over yer. Us done dis before." Jim looked at Abram and smiled.

"Dat true, Joe. Us takes yer ter er conductor er half day ride from here. Him always gits de passengers ter de next station on their way North.

Joe wrapped himself in a blanket and Jim and Abram covered him with vegetables. Flora waved good-bye and they rode off. Four hours later they reached the home of an abolitionist, Brother Henson. Abram and Jim helped Joe into the house and put him into bed. They were relieved to see, despite the bumpy ride and his weakened condition, he had survived the journey quite well. Joe thanked the two who had saved his life. Jim and Abram said good-bye to Joe and Brother Henson. Joe heard them talking as they rode away. "Him looks well. I's hopes him stays well an gits ter Canada."

Bella bent over Rose and gently pulled. The labor had been long and difficult, but finally Rose heard her baby's cry. Bella held up the infant for Rose to see. "Yer hab er boy, Rose." She handed the baby to her.

Rose's whole body shivered with relief. Even in her pain she had noted the flowers and wild wheat at the edge of the woods as she walked to their shack. What was it, her last thought before going into labor; how was the verse worded exactly? The wheat plant dies so the seed may sprout and live. Perhaps it wasn't her time yet. She didn't have to die, like her mother, for her baby to live.

Rose looked down at her newborn son and smiled. "Your name is Samuel and you are going to be free someday."

Chapter 9

1854

"They're coming! They're coming!" Margaret hopped around the room. "I see their carriage. Look, Rose."

Rose peered out the window, squinting and intensely examining the figures below. "I wonder what James and Henry will think of us after not seeing us for three years." She turned to Margaret. "You will explain to James so he can tell Henry about my baby?"

"Of course I will, but you don't have to worry. You're beautiful. And he'll love Sam just as we do."

"I hope so."

Soon the four of them were walking by the river, remembering the runaway they helped the first time they met. It was late in the day when they returned to the mansion to eat and play games. Rose noticed that Margaret took James aside and had a talk with him before they all retired for the night.

The next day the four of them were enjoying a picnic lunch by the river. "This chicken is very good. I wonder, did you read poetry to it?" James smacked his lips.

Margaret burst out laughing, "Why should we do that?"

"I thought you would have seen the latest issue of 'Fine Animal Science Weekly'. They say it is an undisputed fact that reading poetry to chickens grants them a deep soulful flavor," answered James in mock seriousness.

"At least you are beginning to understand how amusing you sound sometimes," Margaret replied, laughing.

"I'm only educating you..." began James.

"And I love it when you do. You broaden my view. You stretch my mind."

"And the truth," quipped Rose, "is that some pamphlets make grand claims in order to sell. It's a clever strategy."

Henry turned to Rose. "W-Would you go for a walk with me?" Rose nodded and Henry helped her up. The other two waved good-bye and James continued to devour the chicken.

"You don't think it was rude to leave them, do you?"

Henry smiled at her. "No, I d-don't, since James asked me to take you away. He wants to t-talk with Margaret alone. I think he wants to tell her how f-f-fond he is of her. A-And probably explain more strange ideas about animal husbandry. I-I want to see you alone for the same reason."

"I doubt you want to talk of animal husbandry," Rose smiled.

"N-No, that's not what I mean," Henry smiled back as he produced a banjo from a small bag by his side. Rose looked shocked and could not help but stare down at the deep old scars on his wrists. "Henry, I didn't think you still played ever since..."

"You see, Rose," Henry paused in thought, "You help bring me back, allow me to heal." He strummed the banjo and sang the words, "I'm fond of you too. Can I hope that you feel the same?"

Rose looked up at Henry. "Did James tell you about my baby?"

"It makes no difference as to how I feel. I c-can't wait to meet little Sam. James t-told me he's 6 months old..."

Rose brightened. "I want you to meet him. Yes, I do feel the same, Henry."

They melted into each other's arms and there was no conversation for several minutes. Finally Henry lifted his head and said, "I w-wonder if Margaret and James are like we are right now."

"You and James are friends, but are you...?" Rose stopped herself. She bit her lip.

"You mean are w-we equal as friends?" asked Henry. He exhaled loudly and looked up at the stars. "I-I live in the music in my head. James and I grew up a little d-differently than most young masters and slaves. Besides, I don't notice people."

"You don't notice anything," Rose remarked, poking him in the ribs.

"I notice how to take care of myself, after being in j-jail," Henry growled, rubbing his wrists. "The fact is, r-regardless of how much we try we will never be treated like them. And they c-can never truly understand us."

"At least you can speak more frankly with James. I detest most not being able to say quite everything." Rose drew the words out of her mouth slowly, like she was gagging. This was more difficult to admit than she had thought.

"Y-Y-You can say what you like around me. But Margaret will have to change soon, r-regardless, or she and James cannot be."

"What do you mean?"

"I thought you noticed everything. James does not do anything halfway, Rose. D-D-Despite his faults I do admire that about him. Margaret will have to decide where she stands. She will have to decide soon."

"I should tell you now," Rose paused, studying Henry's face. "I don't take risks. Taking risks never helped my Uncle Joe."

Later the four friends sat under a large oak tree by the river, Margaret in James' arms and Rose's head on Henry's shoulder. A gentle, happy twanging drifted up from Henry's latest banjo-like creation. "Margaret and Rose, we have something we want to ask you and we want you to think about it before you answer. Henry and I have become actively involved in the Underground Railroad. I suspect my Father knows, but he doesn't say anything when I borrow the carriage and am gone during the night. He's always felt uncomfortable about having slaves, but doesn't know how he could manage the plantation without them. Our slaves have nice quarters, plenty of food, and land for their vegetable gardens as well as more than just the one set of winter and summer clothes."

"Yet we must acknowledge t-that we are not free," Henry added, looking at James.

James coughed, "Right. But he's also giving them their freedom in his will. He knows I won't have slaves. This is what we want you to consider. There's too much distance from the station near us to the one that is past your plantation. We thought of using that isolated barn you have where we hid Joshua as an Underground station."

"I don't know, James. My Father isn't like your Father. Slaves are property to him and my brother. He would be very upset with me if he ever found out I taught Rose to read and helped teach other slaves. How could we possibly hide a station from them?"

"You'd have to be very careful. There could be some danger involved as well if the patrollers find out you are hiding runaways. Henry and I haven't had any problems, but something could always go wrong. This is an illegal activity and you could be fined $1000.00 if you're caught. Your Father would probably be very angry, Margaret, and he may find out, especially with your brother poking around like he does."

"We want you both to consider the possible dangers before you decide."

James handed Margaret a book. "Uncle Tom's Cabin was written by Harriet Beecher Stowe two years ago. She's an abolitionist who knows slaves and how they truly suffer. The book is changing people's minds about slavery. Please, would you and Rose both read it before you give us your answer? You can send a message to us and we'll set everything up if you let us use the barn." James bit his lip in thought for a moment and continued. "If you don't think you should be involved we'll respect that. Just let us know."

Henry gave him an approving nod.

Rose reached out and took the book from Margaret. She leafed through it, pursing her lips and mumbling. "I've heard of this book, Margaret." She placed it carefully into Margaret's lap, looked up at James and shook her head. "I hear running is always harder than one thinks."

It was a sad parting the next morning. James and Margaret went one direction along the river; Rose and Henry the other. "Rose, I think Sam and I are going to be g-great friends. I want you and me, Rose, to be m-m-more than friends."

"I do too, Henry."

James looked down at Margaret and cupped her face in his hands. "You are wonderful, Margaret. I'm so fortunate that you love me. It's hard to leave you. Henry feels the same way about Rose. I'm going to get Father's permission to come here in a few months. We won't let three years pass by this time."

"Do you really think he'll let you come? I can't bear it if I don't see you soon."

"Father depends on Henry and me a lot at the plantation, but he'll let us come here more often—especially if he knows how you and I feel about each other. He and Mother were young once too."

A few days later Margaret and Rose were sitting in Margaret's room playing with baby Samuel. "Margaret, we've both read Uncle Tom's Cabin. What do you think about it?"

"The whippings bothered me the most. I can't forget the welts on the back of the runaway we rescued. His shirt was actually stuck way into his skin. Oh Rose! I forgot! Father ordered someone in your family to be beaten for running away."

"Yes, my Uncle Joe. Then he was sold down south." There was a brief silence. Rose tensed her shoulders and did not look at Margaret.

"I think we need to have a station to help people like Joe reach Canada."

"No, Margaret, we can't. Your Father would find out some way. Probably your brother would discover what we were doing. It's too risky for you."

"It's more dangerous for you. Father would sell you down south. He'd know that would punish both of us. I couldn't lose you, Rose. We'd better tell James and Henry 'no' only..."

"How art thee feeling, Joe?" Sister Henson shifted back and forth on her feet, holding a damp cloth as if ready to dab his forehead. She had done this so many times for days on end that it had become almost a habit. Brother and Sister Henson examined Joe as he took a piece of chicken from a plate, and analyzed every move he made with concern.

Brother Henson moved over to Joe and placed his hand on Joe's shoulder. "Thee has been here three months and the doctor seems to think thee are well enough to continue thy journey. We shall miss thee, Joe. We love the table thee built for us. It's strong and thee has finished it so beautifully. Thee truly art an excellent carpenter. If it was only safe for thee here I know we could keep thee busy as a carpenter."

"Thank you, Brother and Sister Henson. You have been so kind. I must be on my way now since the doctor has said I can go. I need to get to Canada and look for Liza."

Brother Henson laid out his hands on the table, drawing an imaginary map with his fingers as he spoke. "We can take thee by carriage to the next station. Thee are in Louisville, Kentucky, so are close to Ohio. There are many abolitionists, Friends, and free Negroes in Ohio who will help thee on thy journey. I shall take thee to Cincinnati where the Society of Friends will help thee."

In Cincinnati, Joe was taken at night to a home and introduced to Brother Daniels. "Aren't you the man who visited the slaves on a boat captured by Pirates?"

Brother Daniels looked surprised. "Why yes, I am."

"I was a chained slave on that lower deck. Liza, the woman I love, was there with me. She was going to Canada and I told her to ask for you in Cincinnati. Did she come here?"

"I'm sorry, Joe. I don't remember anyone by that name." Noticing Joe's crestfallen look he added, "Thee must remember there are many underground stations all over the northern states and thy Liza could have passed through any of them."

"We need to get thee to Canada so thee can look for thy Liza. The best way is to follow the Ohio River until thee reaches Beaver, Ohio. That is the start of the Beaver and Erie Canal, which thee can follow all the way to Lake Erie. It is 136 miles, but when thee reaches Lake Erie thee can take a boat across to Canada. Thee must be careful because slave catchers are looking for runaways along the Ohio, the Canals, and on the shores of Lake Erie."

Joe took the food Sister Daniels prepared for him, thanked Brother and Sister Daniels, and began the long journey north. He traveled over hills, through woods and meadows, by farms and towns, staying as close to the Ohio as he could. Joe was thankful Brother Daniels had taken one of his pieces of eight and bought him a coat, shoes and a blanket because the March weather in Ohio was cold and the wind seemed to go right through him. He wondered if he would ever reach Canada without freezing.

Finally, Joe saw the beginning of the canal at Beaver, Ohio. He could follow the towpath the 3 horses or the oxen took along the side of the canal, pulling the packet boats filled with passengers and the line boats which carried freight. Joe thought it would be good if he could buy a ticket and travel down the canal. Despite those chains, I was as free as I'd ever been before on that pirate ship. I miss being on the water. However, Joe watched them from a distance and calculated that these boats only went four miles per hour. He'd also been told it would be too dangerous to take a boat.

Joe soon found the station in Beaver. That night he had a meal and a bed to sleep in. He waited until the next night and started out again. Each night he raced along the canal until day break, his desire to reach Canada pushing him forward despite his exhaustion.

"Rufus, look what I found under this bush. He's probably a runaway and they give good rewards for catching them and handing them over to a slave catcher or a Federal Marshal. Grab him!" Joe heard them talking. He kicked out at the closest one to him, knocking him down. Springing up, he grabbed the other, pitching him into the canal. He started running as fast as he could, the little man whom he'd kicked in close pursuit. Joe turned around suddenly to face his pursuer, and punched him in the face. Wrestling on the ground, the little man was no match for Joe's large, muscular physique. Joe picked him up, threw him into the canal, and ran as fast as he could to put distance between them.

Joe left the Beaver Division of the Canal at New Castle, where he found the next station. "From what you've told us, Joe, we think you should stay a few days. The two men who chased you may have reported you to a Federal Marshal or slave catchers who could be looking for you along the canal."

Three days passed slowly. When it appeared that no one had reported him, Joe was told it was safe to continue. Again, Joe was fortified with food before he left the warmth and kindness of his host and hostess to face the frigid night's journey. He'd gone 31 miles and now was in the Shenango Division of the Canal, which was 61 miles long.

Four uneventful days later Joe reached a safe house in Meadville, where he stayed with free Negroes who had been to Canada and had decided to move back and settle in Ohio. Meadville had a large Negro community. They urged Joe to stay because there was a lot of work for a carpenter. Joe explained that he had to go to Canada and was directed to continue to follow the canal 45 miles through the Conneaut Division until he reached Lake Erie.

There it is, thought Joe. I'm at Lake Erie and it's so big I can't even see across it. How am I going to reach Canada on the other side? A constant breeze blew out from the lake. Joe moved his eyes back and forth over the water's surface. In the distance he saw a terrifying sight, the white slivers of cresting waves. Though far out, he knew they were huge; he'd never seen waves that big before. The shore wind blew the blood from his face and sent shivers down his spine. These waves are keeping me from my freedom and perhaps from Liza as well. Dejectedly, he sat down on a log and stared across the immense expanse of water. A Negro approached Joe. "Are you a freedom seeker, wanting to reach Canada?" Joe looked up, startled. He had always considered himself strong, but this man had the largest arms he'd ever seen. It looked very funny, especially since the rest of the man seemed so small. "My name is Albert. I live in a village by the lake. We help many freedom seekers reach Canada. You can stay with me until we can take you across."

Joe drooled as he turned the gourd dipper in the milky mussel stew Albert scratched together. He sat as close as he could to the rusty stove in his shack, crouched under a blanket. The wind was shaking the timbers around them. A large driftwood cross hung on the wall, knocking against the rough boards. Jars and bottles filled with specimens of goggle-eyed fish and slimy mussels rattled on the floor. Albert sat near Joe and leaned into his ear to speak over the din. "We're free in this village. Negroes here are relatively safe; there's good work here too. But unless you have no other choice, during the day stay away from the lake shore! Slave catchers look for fugitives along the shores, and they check the Negroes who board the steamboats that dock here. Even I take chances when down there sometimes. We usually row freedom seekers across in the evening. I'll take you tonight if you want to go."

"Joe, if your Liza came up the Ohio River she would probably be in Ontario. There are several towns where fugitives have settled. You may want to start at London, which is west of where we land. Someone in London will help you learn more about the towns to visit. I do a lot of trade on the Canadian side; folks up there are friendly."

That evening Joe and Albert approached the rowboat as it bucked and rocked on the shore. "I don't know, Joe. A storm might be coming in. The waves are getting higher. Maybe we should wait until tomorrow night." Albert looked up at the sky and at the waves and hesitated. "I've been out in rough weather before with this boat. If you want to risk it I'll take you now." Joe nodded.

Soon it was evident they'd made a mistake. The waves rose higher and higher and began to splash water into the boat. Joe kept busy bailing while Albert groaned as he tried to row against the pounding waves. They made little progress. The boat began to fill with water and Joe couldn't bail fast enough. Lightening was all around them. Was this how it was going to end-so close to Canada, never to have reached it? Hours later they pulled the boat onto the shore and collapsed on the sand. The storm had eased up during the last hour and Albert decided he could safely make it back home. They said their good-byes and Joe helped push the boat back into the water.

Joe, dazed, glanced around him. In the moonlight he could see the white capped waves on Lake Erie, the sand he was standing on and the smudge of dark green from the trees near the shore. Was he really in Canada after all these years? Could it be true that no slave catcher, slave owner or pirate could capture him and make him work for no money? Was he free to walk the streets of a town without worry? Could he walk into a store and buy what he needed like any white person? Would he be able to work as a carpenter and keep what he earned? Would it be possible to buy a farm some day? Was he now able to start looking for Liza?

I'm free, Joe thought to himself. For the rest of my life I'll live as a free man. I'm finally free!

Rose pulled open the curtains and then yanked the blanket off Margaret. "It's one o' clock and your Mother is wondering why you didn't come downstairs to eat. I couldn't tell her you've had too much to drink the last three nights and I've had to undress you, and put you to bed. What is wrong with you, Margaret?"

"Oh, don't yell. My head hurts." Margaret grimaced and sat up slowly, clasping her head in her hands. "I don't like drinking so much, but Robert likes to drink and says his future wife needs to drink with him. I have to go to town with him. He drives his horses too fast and I don't like that he beats them. They have marks on their backs."

"I don't understand why you've agreed to marry Robert when I always thought you loved James."

"Of all people, I thought you would have figured it out, Rose! My Father and Robert's Father are so set on us marrying because then the two adjoining plantations will eventually be one. They think Robert and my brother, John, can manage the plantations together. Robert likes the idea and I don't appear to have any say in it." Margaret looked up at Rose from her bed. "You have to agree that Robert is handsomer than James and is a gentleman. He's always telling me how beautiful I am and compliments me on my dresses. James hardly ever did that."

"When are you going to tell James?"

"I already sent him a letter. Robert has been here three days and now Father, Mother, John and I are invited to their plantation for a few days. Since it's official that Robert and I are to be married I saw no reason to keep this from James. I'm certain he'll find someone else." Margaret busied herself with dressing and avoided looking at Rose. "Robert thinks you should stay here when we go to his plantation. He's noticed how we are always together and says he and I need to spend time by ourselves, getting acquainted. We leave tomorrow."

"Whatever you wish, Miss."

Margaret glanced up at the many columned mansion belonging to Robert's parents. It was much bigger than theirs. Inside she gazed at the double winding staircase with its rose carpet, the green velvet curtains gracing the large windows, and the many paintings hung near the entrance and along the wall to the second floor. The curtains were drawn, a dim green light filled the building. A clock ticked away in the eerie quiet.

"Shall we start with the library?"

"Ah!" Margaret gasped in surprise. He had gone somewhere and reappeared suddenly by her side. "Oh, yes. Of course, Robert. A library! How impressive!"

Robert showed her his Father's immense library where the two largest walls held books that reached floor to ceiling. A carved wooden desk and chair with a reading lamp was positioned in the back of the room. Across the room from the desk was a large window with a view of a beautiful garden and a couple of large oak trees. A comfortable chair was by the window so one could sit there and read while occasionally looking out onto the garden. Margaret sighed, thinking how much Rose would have loved to be in this room, sitting on that chair with a book chosen from one of the shelves.

"I heard you like picnics so why don't we have a picnic down by the river where it's private? Mother and Father would like us to plan our wedding so we could do it there. I'll have cook prepare a picnic basket for us."

As they started to walk to the river Robert noticed a slave passing by and called out to him. "Sammy, did you catch my horse from the pasture this morning?"

"No suh, Mas'r Robert. Dat horse half wild. Him gib me er chase. I's needs some hep ter cotch him."

"Come here, Sammy. I doubt if you even went to the pasture and tried to catch him. Take off your clothes and put your arms around that tree." Robert flexed the whip he always carried with him. He waited until the slave had done his bidding, then tied the slave's hands together on the other side of the tree. Margaret saw the terrified look on the slave's face, his dark skin on his back quivering, his head tucked into his tense shoulders. She turned away, but could hear every strike of the whip and Robert announcing the number. "I'm stopping at 50, Sammy, but if you don't do what I say, next time it will be 100. Now, get another slave and go catch that horse." Robert turned to Margaret. "Let's have that picnic."

As they walked to the river Margaret hardly heard what Robert was saying. She had just witnessed her future husband beating a slave. She couldn't marry this man. She must tell him when they were having the picnic and then tell her Father. Her Father would be upset, but she would remain firm. Margaret realized that Robert was cruel. He beat his slaves and his horses. He drank too much. James was a kind and much better man. She knew that now. It wasn't important she be told how beautiful she was or how pretty her dress looked on her. That was how her Mother was treated and then her Father slept with Negro women. James admired her mind as well as her body They could read books together and talk about them. She was much more to him than just being beautiful. Why hadn't she seen that before? Her Mother had such a dull life. Sewing and supervising the house slaves was basically all she did. She was certain that Robert would regard her as his property once they were married and she would end up just like her Mother. No, she resolved, she wouldn't do it. She would never marry Robert.

Robert spread the blanket out and helped her sit down. "Before we eat, Robert, there is something I need to tell you." Robert looked up. "I cannot marry you. I'm in love with another man, and I don't think we are suited for each other. I'm going to tell my Father when we get back to the house."

Margaret saw the same angry expression on Robert's face that she saw when he was yelling at the slave. "Oh yes, you'll marry me. I prefer not to be married, but Father reminded me of my duty to produce a heir and that combining the plantations would be good for us. If I have to marry it might as well be to a beautiful woman, and you are beautiful, Margaret. Let's have no more talk of this."

"You don't understand, Robert. I will not marry you." Margaret started to rise, but Robert grabbed her arm and pulled her down beside him.

"I'll soon teach you to be a good wife. Wives, slaves and horses need to be taught to obey." He grabbed the bodice of her dress and ripped it open, gripping a firm breast in his hand. She was pushed down on the blanket and Robert began to pull up her dress with one hand while holding her down with the other. Margaret struggled and was able to lift one hand and claw him in the face, drawing blood. Robert's face turned blood red. He slammed his fist into her face and began to pound her on the arms and chest. She yelled as loud as she could. "Go ahead and scream. No one will hear you. When I'm through with you we'll go back to the house and you won't mention this to anyone. If you refuse to marry me I'll come to your plantation some time and cut your beautiful face to pieces. Do you understand me?" Robert shook the sobbing Margaret by the shoulders.

Suddenly a punch in his face sent Robert sprawling. "I understand you, Robert. Now you understand this. If you ever come near my sister again I'll kill you." Robert stood and charged into John, who began to hit him hard in the face and stomach. Margaret watched, trembling. All of a sudden Robert slumped to the ground and didn't move. John leaned over and said, "He's still breathing, but he's unconscious. He won't bother you anymore."

He paused and looked at Margaret. "We don't want him following us to the house. He's so angry he could get a gun. We need to tie him up." John looked around him.

"We could make my underclothing into strips."

"That will work." John turned away while Margaret took off an undergarment and they began to rip it into strips and tie Robert's hands and feet. "I have an idea. Do you see all the red ants? Let's put some of your chicken from the picnic basket on him. Red ants like meat and they bite. I think he deserves a lesson for what he did to you." Margaret smiled and helped John tear the chicken into little pieces and cover Robert's face and body.

John picked up the blanket and gently placed it around Margaret's shoulders. She pulled it tight so the ripped bodice wouldn't show. John put his arm around her and slowly helped her up the path to the house. "What am I going to tell Father and Mother? I don't want them to see me like this."

"They need to see what he's done to you. I'll do the talking. This has to be settled right away and we need to leave for home." Margaret looked up at her brother, surprised at seeing him so firm and in charge.

Robert's Father and Mother and their Father and Mother were sitting together, talking, when John and Margaret walked into the parlor. "Margaret! What's happened to you?" Lillian rose and came toward her daughter.

"Robert attacked her. That's what happened to her. She can never marry that man. He's cruel. We need to take her home, Father."

Robert's Father stood up. "Is this true, Margaret?" She nodded. He looked at her. "I'm so sorry."

"The marriage will not take place. We are leaving now. I don't want to see Robert at our plantation again." Margaret's Father came over and put his arm around her.

"We understand." Robert's Mother stood, wringing her hands. "I don't know what is wrong with him. He's always had such a terrible temper. Of course he won't come to your plantation. We are so very sorry."

That evening, after Rose had cleaned Margaret and given her poke root tea for the pain, there was a knock at the door. Rose opened it. "May I come in?"

"Of course, John."

"I'll leave you alone." Rose quietly left the room and shut the door behind her.

"Thank you again for saving me. I'm wondering how you happened to be there when I needed you."

"I saw Robert beating that slave in front of you and I know how you hate to see a slave beaten. I thought there might be trouble so I followed you. I was staying well behind, but heard you scream." John paused. "I know I tease you and Rose unmercifully sometimes, but you are my sister and I don't want anything to happen to you. I want you to know that I'll always try to protect you."

Margaret reached over and gave John a hug. "I love you, John, and I'm glad you're my brother. Now you need to leave because I am very tired."

"How does this sound, Rose? 'Dear James, I'm not going to marry Robert. I still love you. I would like to see you again if you can forgive me.' I don't know what else to say. Do you think he'll come to see me? Do you think he still loves me? Maybe he's found someone else."

"I know he still loves you. I think he'll ride for here as soon as he receives your letter. I just hope Henry comes too."

A few days later James and Henry rode up to the mansion. James dismounted and took Margaret into his arms. "When I got your letter saying you were marrying someone else..." James paused and looked down at his feet. "I just couldn't bear it. Someday I want to marry you." James took Margaret's face in his hands and looked into her eyes. "I love you, Margaret. Could I hope that you love me too?"

"Thank you for agreeing to use the empty barn." James looked down at Margaret who was nestled against him. "Jim and his wife and daughter are settled in there and you've given them food and blankets. They'll leave tonight for the next station. Jim told me they were going to sell him down south and he didn't want to be separated from his family so they decided to follow the drinking gourd."

Rose spoke up. "The slave you brought us two weeks ago told us a little about himself. He came from a rice plantation in Georgia where they had to stand in water all day. Babies died because their mothers didn't get enough to eat and many people died from disease. He'd worked on a cotton plantation before that and had to be in the field from dawn until dark, but he said the rice plantations were worse. He was so thin and weak he could hardly walk. We kept him in the barn and fed him for three days until he was strong enough to go on."

"James and I are asking a lot of you and Margaret. We want you to know you can quit at any time. We don't want anything to happen to either of you."

"No we don't. And now, since we have only a limited time to be together, I propose that Margaret and I go in this direction and you go in the other."

Henry waited until Margaret and James had walked away, arm in arm. "S-Sit here, Rose. T-T-There's something I want to ask you." Henry hesitated and then took Rose's hands in his. "W-We've said we love each other and have talked about spending our lives together. James and his Father would never sell m-me, but if something happened to them I could someday be sold as part of th-th-their estate. I could never be certain things will remain as they are now. The same is true for you and Sam. We'll never be secure as long as we're slaves. W-W-Would you and Sam go with me to Canada?"

Rose paused a moment, then looked down at the ground. I want to go with him, she thought to herself, and I would if it was just the two of us. But I have Sam to think of now. What if we were caught? I could be sold down south or Sam might be. The Master would probably sell one of us just to punish me for running away. James would take Henry back so he'd be alright, but Sam and I...No, I can't risk it.

She looked up into Henry's eyes. "I love you, Henry, but I couldn't leave Margaret and my Grandma Bella and George. I'm needed here. As long as Margaret is alive I'll be safe here and I'll never be sold. And they've promised they'll never sell Sam. You have a good life with James, helping him run his Father's plantation. I don't see why you have to leave. Don't go. Please stay with us. We can marry like we've planned and Sam and I can move to the Graydon plantation if James' Father would by us. I can still be close enough to see Margaret and my Grandma Bella. Please, Henry."

Henry gently pushed Rose away from him. "I'm sorry, Rose. I-I've made up my mind. I've told this to James and he w-w-won't try to stop me. He was going to arrange for the three of us to leave. I have to help James on the plantation for a while, but I'll be l-l-leaving next year."

Rose stood up, tears in her eyes. "Good-bye Henry." She turned and ran up the hill to the Big House.

The next day Rose stayed upstairs in Margaret's room while James and Margaret said their goodbyes. She sat on the window seat and tearfully watched as James and the man she loved rode away.

Chapter 10

1855

Joe glanced around the small town of Port Dover, where Albert had rowed ashore and let him off. He'd slept under a tree the night before. Now was the time to find out if he was really free. There was a grocery. He entered and looked around him. There were two white people who seemed to be shopping. He picked up food supplies and approached the man behind the counter. Lowering his head, he asked, "May I buy these?"

"If you have money you can. Don't recognize you. Are you new to Port Dover?"

Joe handed over the money. "Yes, I'm looking for a Negro woman named Liza. Do you know her?" The man shook his head. "Could you give me directions to London?"

"Yes, it's 72 miles from here, going that direction." The man pointed. Joe thanked him and started out on his journey to find his Liza..

Edward had somehow dragged himself and his strange, homemade rocking chair near to the front steps of the Greydon mansion. He strummed a few large pieces of rope hanging on a long stick nailed to his chair. The bass notes throbbed in the air. He clapped his one good foot on the ground in time. Henry sat on the mansion's front steps. Swaying, he strummed the rough strings on an old board. The board was attached to a half rotted bucket. The sound was shrill and grating. He sang softly into the bucket of his make-shift banjo.

"Crying, pulled from my Mama's arms at the age of five,
Father sold down south before I was born, don't know if he's alive,

Master Graydon bought me then, James treats me like a brother,
but if they die or something changes, I'll be passed on to another.
Rose, quiet and beautiful, if we run we will suffer,
Rose, quiet, sweet and noble, we stay, we suffer too,
Rose, quiet and always truthful, Sam will also suffer,
Rose, quiet, wise and youthful, what will we ever do?
If my family will suffer, I don't want a family at all,
Memories of your beauty in that green dress at the ball,
First time James and I saw you two our heart felt the call.
With blood upon your dress you helped us save a runaway,
No matter what, I'll not forget you till my dying day!
Rose, quiet and beautiful, if we run we suffer,
Rose, quiet, sweet and noble, we stay we suffer too,
Rose, quiet and always truthful, Sam will also suffer,
Rose, quiet, wise and youthful, what will we do?
Virginia can be a prison, Virginia is a curse,
But if they catch you running, your fate will be far worse.
They'd sell Sam far away,
They'd lust over your skin,
They'd make you be a fancy girl,
and that would be the end.
Rose, quiet, wise and youthful, what will we do?
Rose, quiet, wise and youthful, what will we do?"

Edward put a hand on Henry's strings and stopped him in
mid strum. Reaching over he grabbed Henry's shirt and yanked
Henry's ear close to his mouth. He slapped Henry on the back of
the head. "Don't yer eber talk ob run'n when near de big house!"
Edward wheezed. "Yer should know better! Thought that jail
knocked some sense inter yer! Listen. Don't think yer problems be
so important. Yer er slave dat watch us out in de field fer de Mas'r.
I's knows yer hate it, but it better dan dey field work. Yer problems
not so big." Edward hissed harshly at him and paused. James hung
his head. Edward coughed and looked severely at him. "Yer want
ter end yer suffering, Henry? Work de field till yer be struck by er
sythe in de foot an become sick, old, an dy'n. Yer even think about

drag'n this Rose an Sam ob yours into another life somewhere, yer only bring deeper suffering yer not yet know."

Something resembling James approached him. The figure had blue hands, a reddish purple body, and was covered in what looked like either grass or thick green hair.

"Henry, what are you doing just sitting there? James sat down on the steps next to Henry and looked at him. "What's wrong?"The indigo harvest waits for no one. I need your help. That new harvester/fermenter machine I ordered keeps spraying everyone and turning them purple."

"Could you ever leave Graydon plantation, James?"

"Henry, look at the land in front of you." James pointed straight ahead. "See the rolling hills beyond the river? They are such a bright green that even from this distance it almost hurts your eyes. Then there's the winding James River where we swim and fish and have picnics under the cottonwood trees nearby. The woods have trees like the mighty oak, the sycamore, walnut, birch, pecan and maple. We can pick berries and find nuts. Then, above the woods you see the meadow and the path leading to the front of my Father's and Mother's mansion and to the stone steps where we're sitting. Look to the side of the steps and there are all the multicolored flowers Mother had planted. Behind the mansion you and I have our garden where we've had good times growing our own vegetables for the family since we were little. On both sides down to the river are the tobacco fields where you and I supervise the work and watch the tobacco being planted and grow into big leafy plants that bring in money to help keep the plantation going. I love this land, Henry. I love to feel the rich black earth in my hand and watch the soil, sun and rain make things grow. I do hate slavery, and when this plantation eventually becomes mine I shall give all the slaves their freedom and try to run the plantation with those free Negroes who will stay with me and work for wages." James shook his head. "No, Henry, I can never leave. It's different for you though. You don't belong to this land and don't love it as I do." James took in a deep breath and walked away for a moment, looking out at the rolling hills.

Henry turned to Edward and whispered in his ear while pretending to look at his banjo. "Why does he not understand, Edward, even now? His situation is completely different. We're trapped. It's not a question of 'belonging', it's respect, and freedom. No matter what small changes are made on the plantation, he should realize I'll never truly have that here."

"Not possible fer him ter know," grunted Edward.

Henry took a deep breath, got up, and walked up to James' side. "I'm trying to decide whether to go to Canada without Rose and Sam, because she won't leave Margaret, Bella and George." Henry squinted and looked James in the eyes. "What would you do if you were me?"

James scratched his head and sighed. "That's a tough decision. I know you love Rose, and Sam too, so it would be really hard to leave them behind. But if you stay and something happened to Father and me, you could be sold down south, and that would be a terrible life. Even if you married Rose, she or Sam could be sold. And I know you hate supervising slaves. If you go to Canada you might find someone to love there and if you married and had children you'd know they'd be with you and you'd all be free."

"But it's only been a month and I miss her so. How could I go North by myself and leave her behind? And she won't change her mind."

"I've been trying to work this out myself. You are family, Henry. Though we can't quite treat you that way. And I don't want you to leave. But if I'm to be true to any of the principles I've read from the abolitionist writings, I should let you escape. He paused. "I don't think you should go alone if you do go."

"I know. You're afraid I'll get caught by patrollers again. Become like the bloodied runaways that die in our arms. It's true, I could be sold down south. But I'm more careful now. I should go." Henry grit his teeth.

"It'd be easier with my help," murmured James, as he looked down at his feet.

"But you can't help me forget her," replied Henry.

James cleared his throat, "You'll have to choose. I'll leave you to think about it some more. I'm fed up with that harvester anyway. Just know that whatever you decide, I'll go along with your decision."

Henry looked up and smiled. "Thank you, James." Henry waved at James, "Save that machine's purple excretia for me! Patrollers take Negroes, but I've never heard of them hunting a big purple beet!" James threw a wad of indigo at Henry's face and left him to mull over his options.

Margaret ran into her room and found Rose dusting the furniture. "Rose, hurry! James and Henry just rode in. Henry asked if you'll meet him down by the river. He wants to talk to you."

Rose patted her hair and looked down at her dress. "Do I look alright?" Margaret nodded and Rose left for the river, wondering what Henry wanted to say to her after their last unhappy meeting.

Henry came to meet her and reached for her hand. "Rose, this has been the longest month of my life. It has taught me that I can't live without you. I'd rather be a slave with you than a free man without you. Just promise me if there is any danger of any of us being sold down south that you and Sam will leave with me immediately."

"Oh yes!" Rose flew into Henry's arms and it was a while before they joined Margaret and Henry. Soon the four were talking about the station and the refugees James and Henry had brought with them who were now settled in the barn.

"It's been a few months and Rose and I are happy we agreed to help. When the runaways tell us what they've gone through-- beaten, separated from their families, worked from dawn to dusk and having very little to eat or wear--we just want to help them on their way to a better life."

James looked at Rose and Henry. "Margaret and I have been talking. Any time you want to take Sam and start on the

Underground Railroad, we won't stop you. We'll do what we can to help you on your way. It's best for all of you. You need to leave." James patted Henry on the shoulder and furrowed his brow. His lips tightend into a straight line. "Just please, be careful. I don't like you all leaving on your own but-."

Henry pulled Rose closer to him. "Thank you, but we've decided to stay here for now." Jame's eyes widened, his mouth partly open. Henry looked down at Rose. "I need to go back to the plantation to finish some jobs for James and his Father. James is going to stay here. I don't know why." He smiled at James and Margaret. "I'll join the three of you in a few days. Then we can have some more time together, Rose. I'll miss you."

Three days later a slave ran up to the Quarters, panting heavily. "Bella, dey cotch er fugitive 'bout two day from here. De slave catchers beat him 'til him tole who him belongs ter an whar him been hidin'. It wuz on dis plantation an him tole 'bout Rose an Margaret. Dey takes him ter de owner an den dey comes here wid de federal marshal."

Soon James, Margaret, and Rose were sitting with Bella and George in their cabin. Bella looked worried. "Us in de quarters knows 'bout what yer does wid de barn, but dis be trouble. Rose, yer can be beaten an sold South. Margaret, yer Father ken have ter pay $1000, an him might sells Rose ter punish both ob yer. I know," Bella began to break down, "I's seen it all before," she sobbed. George stared at them all in silence. He held Bella's hand. "Why they all taken from me, George! Why!" cried Bella.

James looked at Rose. "You and Sam need to go at once. You're no longer safe here."

"Yes, my Father will sell you, Rose, to punish us. He knows what you mean to me."

"You're right. I have to wait here for Henry though. He should arrive tomorrow. He was only going to be away four days."

"No! Not tomorrow! Go now, Rose!" Margaret snapped.

"Not without Henry!"

"James, I don't like Rose leaving me. Now that I'm involved in the Underground Railroad I'll find it hard to live in a slave state. Maybe we can go with them to Canada and start a new life there. What do you think?" Margaret paused and watched James' face. He was turning pale. His arms outstretched, he looked back and forth between Margaret and Rose.

"That's a big decision, Margaret. I hate to leave Father and Mother. Father depends on me to help manage the plantation. If Henry and I both leave there is only my sister with Mother and Father. I don't see how I can go."

"Just think about how it will be without Henry and Rose. The situation in the South is getting worse. There's more tension between the South and the North. Do you want our children to grow up in a slave state? Your Father will understand. He knows you hate slavery."

"I've told him enough times. Now..." James answered reluctantly, standing and gripping the sides of his head. He turned and looked down at Margaret. "I have to take action. I'll send a message to Father and Mother and we'll join Rose and Henry. If it doesn't work out for us or if Father really needs me we can always come back?"

"Yes. Absolutely," she answered quickly, standing and putting her hand on his shoulder.

"James, why don't you and Margaret go to the next station tonight? I'll wait for Henry. He doesn't know the way. You know how distracted and lost he gets. If you take the carriage you could bring Sam with you. I can ride with Henry on his horse and we'll meet you in two days."

That evening Rose, Bella and George said sad good-byes. Rose hugged Sam tightly and whispered, "I hate to let you go, but Margaret and James will take good care of you. I'll see you soon. You are going to grow up free, my little one." She handed Sam over to James and wiped tears from her eyes. "I've never been parted from him before. This will be a hard two days, but I know it's for the best."

Rose waited for Henry the next day but he didn't appear. The following morning three men rode in and walked up the hill to the Big House. Rose hid on the porch near the sitting room where she could hear. The master at first sounded astonished at what they were telling him and then became very angry.

"You mean to say that my daughter was involved in helping slaves escape? I don't believe it!"

John leaned toward his Father. "If Margaret and Rose did this, Father, they need to be severely punished."

Rose decided she'd heard enough and ran down the hill to their cabin. When she told Bella and George they wanted her to take a horse and leave immediately. "No, I'll wait for Henry. I can hide in the loft. When they find out that Margaret, James and Sam are missing they'll assume I'm with them. It's good I sent Sam on ahead because he might have cried and given us away."

Soon the master and his son, John, with the federal marshal, looked through the isolated barn where they found a blanket and three dishes. They walked down to the quarters and went through each cabin, questioning the slaves who insisted they knew nothing.

"Bella, yours is the last cabin. Tell us where your Rose is." The master, John, and the marshal glanced around the two rooms in the cabin.

"I's don't knows, Mas'r."

"If she comes back here, you're to let me know. You understand?"

"Oh, yassuh, I's understands."

Bella waited a few moments after they left and told Rose, "Yer ken comes down, Rose. Dey gone."

Rose climbed down the ladder from the loft and brushed off the straw from her dress. "I wish Henry would get here so we could start for the next station. At least they are done with the search so it should be safe now." She hugged Bella and brushed a tear from her eye. "I'm going to miss you and George."

John entered his Father's study. "Father, Rose is still here. I stayed behind and listened at the door. She was hiding in the loft.

She'll know where Margaret and James are. I'm certain she'll tell us if you beat her."

"Good work, John. We'll get it out of her." Mr. Ramsey scowled and slammed his hand down on the table. "Let's go."

Rose and Bella looked up in surprise as Mr. Ramsey and his son barged into the room. "We caught you and you're going to tell us where my daughter and James are."

"Please, Mas'r, James an Margaret jes done takes de carriage and goes fer er ride. Dey takes Sam fer er ride wid dem. Dey comes back soon I's 'spect, ter brings Sam ter his mama."

"Don't believe her, Father. They've left. I checked in Margaret's room and some of her things are gone. I don't know why Rose is still here, but I'm certain we can beat it all out of her."

"Rose, tell us where they are going or I'll have to beat you."

Rose straightened up to her full height. "I have nothing to say."

A slave was directed to strip Rose of her clothes and tie her arms around a tree near the quarters. The master looked down at her. "Rose, this is your last chance to tell me where Margaret is or I'll have the overseer beat you until you do tell." When Rose didn't reply the master told a slave, "Get the overseer."

Soon the overseer rode in from the fields and alighted from his horse, holding his long bull whip in his hand. "You are to beat her until she tells you where my daughter is. No one is to take her down until I say she can be taken down, or you will be beaten." The master turned and strode up the hill to the Big House. John stayed behind to watch. One, two, three, four—the overseer expertly landed his whip on Rose's back—fifty, fifty-one, fifty-two.

Bella was sobbing. "Tell them, Rose, tell them."

Rose looked over at her Grandmother. "I can't," she gasped. "Sam'll be free now." Her eyes rolled back and refocused. Now she seemed to be staring out at the birds, wildflowers and wild wheat grass at the edge of the woods.

John glanced away and murmured, "I never thought she'd go this long. I can't watch anymore." He slowly walked up the hill, never looking back.

When the overseer reached 100 he paused. Everyone could see Rose was unconscious, her head hanging down and blood streaming from the deep cuts going from her neck down to her ankles. "No use beating her anymore. I'll report to the master. Remember, he said no one is to take her down."

As soon as the overseer left for the Big House, Bella, sobbing, ran up to Rose. She tried to get her to take some water, but Rose was unable to respond. Bella then washed off some of the blood and applied passionflower on the deep cuts for the pain. Two of the slaves helped Bella cover Rose with a blanket to keep the flies off the wounds. Bella sat on the ground near Rose, where she remained the rest of the day and evening, washing the wounds and applying more passionflower, all the while talking to Rose and telling her how much she loved her.

It was late evening when Henry came galloping up on his horse, reined him in, jumped off, and ran to Rose. A slave near the entrance of the plantation had told him what had happened. "Rose, my love, can you hear me? Oh Rose! If I'd only gotten here sooner. We could have been out of here and on our way to Canada." He looked around at the Negroes standing nearby. "Why is Rose still tied to this tree?"

"De Mas'r done sez him beats us iffen her be taken down."

"Now you can tell him Henry took her down. Come here and help me." Two Negroes, relieved that they now had someone who would take the blame, assisted Henry in untying the rope from Rose's hands and gently lowering her to the ground. Henry took her head in his hands.

"Rose, darling, please open your eyes. We'll be free now. You and I can join Margaret and James and Sam and leave for the promised land. We'll have a real wedding in Canada, not just jumping over a broom. You and I will be married and we'll raise Sam and have more children. Please, Rose, I need you. Please wake up."

Rose slowly opened her eyes and smiled. "Henry." She shuddered and was gone. A breeze blew across the wildflowers and carried with it a new procession of birds. "Twee-dee-lee-twee!," the mournful farewell of a painted bunting finch reached their ears as it passed overhead. It circled them twice then soared north, passing the old oak near Charlotte's grave.

Henry and the two other Negroes dug a hole and placed Rose in it. The word spread through the quarters and several gathered for a brief funeral service. After it was over, Bella tearfully told Henry that Rose had wakened briefly that afternoon. She had said to tell Henry where he was to go to reach the next station. Henry said good-bye to Bella, George and the people gathered around, and rode away, his head hanging low.

Chapter 11

1855

London, Ontario, was much bigger than Joe had imagined. The owner of the hotel where he'd stayed last night said there were about 12,000 people, with three hundred and fifty being colored persons, in the town. He'd also told Joe about the Methodist Church that was just for colored people. Since today was Sunday Joe decided to attend. Perhaps they could tell him if there is a Liza in London or give him directions on where he should go.

Joe entered the church and sat down. Some members looked in his direction and smiled. A few of the hymns were familiar to him and the minister talked about the love of God and how people should love their neighbors. Joe remembered a verse the minister in Virginia used to like to preach about: *"He that knoweth his Master's will and doeth it not, shall be beaten with many stripes."* Joe was thankful he would never hear that verse quoted to him again.

After the service the congregation gathered in front of the church, talking to each other. The minister and a few others welcomed him and he was asked where he was from and how long he'd been in Canada. When he said he was from a plantation in Virginia a man who was facing the other direction turned and stared at him.

"Joe, is that you? It's me, Tom. You made it to Canada! We both followed the drinking gourd and are free men today." He gave Joe a hug.

Joe looked at Tom, a big smile on his face. "I never thought I'd see you again."

"Where's Reuben? Did he come with you?"

"Reuben's dead, Tom. The patrollers' dogs got him."

114

"I told you and Reuben to stay close to me because the hoo doo doctor gave me powerful medicine. If you'd stayed near me that night..." Tom shook his head. "Joe, I have a home not far from here. Why don't you stay with me and my wife until you can get settled? She didn't come today because one of our children isn't feeling good."

It was two weeks later before Joe left London. Tom sold him a six year old sorrel mare and taught him to ride and to care for the horse. In Chatham, Joe learned there were about four thousand persons, about eight hundred being colored. He discovered colored people building and painting houses, running shops, farming, and working in the mills. They had separate churches and schools. Even here the whites seemed not to want them around. He remembered the hushed conversations he'd had with friends in Virginia- at funerals and weddings. The whites had caused them so much pain for so long. Some of his friends were convinced, barring a revolution, new communities had to be formed without whites in free lands.

He had dreams of such a safe haven for years. Certain it was the only way; he had even thought out plans for such a community.

At the time he wasn't willing to fully trust whites either. He doubted whites would ever treat them fairly. Joe wasn't sure he agreed with that now. His ideas had changed. Negroes and whites had worked together on the pirate ship. Somehow, it all seemed to work. We had the same tasks. We were all in the same boat. Joe smiled to himself. Wouldn't the whites and colored learn to get along better if they worshiped together and the children attended the same schools?

Liza wasn't here in Chatham either. Joe backtracked to London and then rode a short distance to Queen's Bush. Queen's Bush was a wilderness. It was mainly settled by Negroes in about 1846, and was about as separate from the whites as the Negroes could live. Since then no whites had rushed out to join them, though opportunity was there. Joe learned he and Liza could buy and clear from fifty to one hundred acres. The soil was good; the

115

timber was hard wood. He'd have to talk with her about where they should live when he found her. Now it was time to move on.

Later, Joe arrived in Hamilton. He'd learned to ask grocery store owners and attend the colored churches. At the second grocery store, the owner paused and then replied, "Yes, there is a colored woman named Liza who works as a domestic for a wealthy couple. They own a large business and live just outside of town. Liza comes to this store to buy their groceries. I don't know where she lives, but I can give you the address of the couple she works for."

"You know the address!" Joe repeated slowly, raising his palms, as if slowing down the force of the information as it hit him.

"Yes"

"And her name is Liza?"

"Yes. You look overly excited. Care to buy some of Doctor Erasmus H Greenwood's Humor Calming Elixer?," The store owner held up a bottle to the light, "Says here it contains the four esential ingredients the body needs: blood, yellow bile, black bile and phlegm. Great when mixed with morning oats apparently."

Joe's eyes shone as he gently clasped the man's arm. "If you can tell me where Liza works, I'll buy 10 bottles."

Joe could hardly believe his ears. Could this really be his Liza? The grocery store owner didn't know if she was married. He reported she was light skinned and young. It sounded like it could be Liza, but he couldn't just go to the door and ask for her. He'd have to wait nearby until she was finished for the day. Joe sat under a tree near the road in front of the house and waited all afternoon. It was early evening when he saw a young, slender colored woman walk down the path toward the road. He rose to meet her.

"Hello, Liza." The woman looked at him, no recognition showing on her face. She held up her hands and backed away. "Liza, it's me, Joe. Don't you remember me?" Joes great shoulders tensed as he cautiously stepped forward and called to her.

"Joe, is it really you, after all these years? Tears streamed down her face and she went into his open arms. "I've waited, but I'd almost given up hope." He held her tight and kissed her.

"Liza, I've searched for you and now that I've found you I'll never let you go. Will you marry me?"

"Yes, Joe, yes!"

Margaret rushed out of the safe house when she heard the galloping sound of a horse. She looked up at Henry. "Where's Rose?"

James put his arms around the sobbing Margaret. "I should have stayed. Mother and I could have reasoned with Father and he wouldn't have beaten her. I'll never forgive him, or myself, for leaving her there alone."

"From what I understand, it was your brother who told your Father that Rose was still there and suggested she be beaten until she talked. You and Rose have told James and me that John has always tried to cause trouble for the two of you, but this…" Henry faltered. "You can't blame yourself. If I'd gotten there the day I said I would, we would've been out of there. Something came up and I was a day later. It's my fault." Henry looked down at the floor.

James looked at Henry and Margaret. "Neither of you can blame yourselves. We had no idea this would happen. If there is any blame to be laid it is with your Father and brother, Margaret. I had no idea they could do such a thing."

"I'll never forgive either of them. Sam has lost his Mother and I've lost my friend."

Henry looked at James and Margaret. "I promised Rose that when we got married Sam would be my son. The three of us will take care of Sam. He won't lack for love. She wanted him to be a free Negro and he will be. It's time for us to go to Canada."

"Liza, would you mind going with me to the town of London? I have a friend there. I have money and we can buy land and farm it. My friend, Tom, will help us find some good land. Some of the white people don't want us there, but we're protected by the law. It's like that in all the towns that have both white people and colored. In London, though, we can attend any church and there's Baptist and Methodist churches for colored people. There's a school organized by a Rev. M. M. Dillon under the patronage of the English Colonial Church and Society. It seems like a good place to farm and raise a family."

Liza snuggled up to Joe. "It sounds lovely. Let's go."

"Margaret, your Father has posters up advertising for the return of Sam, his slave. He's saying we kidnapped him so there's a reward for the return of you, me and Henry. We can't travel together now or we'd be recognized."

"Oh, James, what will we do? I don't want us to be separated."

"I've been thinking. Let's darken your hair and you travel with Sam as his Mother. He's light skinned. Henry, you and I can travel on business to Maryland, you going as my slave."

"Where will we meet?"

"We'll meet at a station in Maryland. The station master here has gotten word that Harriet Tubman will be leading a group from Maryland into Canada. Henry can go with her and we can go by carriage and meet him in St. Catharines."

"Isn't there a way we can stay together?"

"It's just for a little while, my darling." James took her in his arms. "Soon we'll be in Canada and we can get married."

Two days later Mr. and Mrs. Jones, with whom they were staying, took Margaret and Sam to the steamship. Mrs. Jones, a motherly, gray haired woman, hugged Margaret and stroked Sam's hair. "Now, give Aunt Mary my love. She will be so happy to see her niece and meet little Thomas. Good-bye dear." The two waited until Margaret and Sam boarded and the ship left the dock.

118

"They are safe on the ship," Mr. Jones announced to the worried young men left behind. "Now we need to get you on your way to Maryland. James, your horse is well rested and you have a carriage, but someone might know that you left with your horse and carriage. Henry has his horse. It might be better if you both ride and leave the carriage behind." James nodded. Soon they had the directions to the next station and were on their way.

After a long, wearying journey they reached the station in Maryland and were reunited with Margaret and Sam. "Oh James, can't we go together the rest of the way?"

"I'm afraid not, Margaret. The slave catchers and federal marshals are still looking for two men, one woman and a baby. We know that Harriet Tubman takes her passengers to her home in St. Catharines. You and I can take Sam as our baby in a carriage the rest of the way and meet Henry there. Henry, you'll be safe with 'Moses', as Harriet Tubman is called. She's never lost a passenger yet." Henry smiled and softly hummed, "Go down Moses" to himself.

Finally word reached the station. Harriet Tubman was in the woods outside town and would meet any that night who would like to be her passengers to Canada. That was what Henry had been waiting for. Margaret, James and Sam had already left for St. Catharines. Henry was lonely and anxious to join his friends. Reaching the meeting place he discovered a plain, unimposing woman and six people, including one infant. The very average woman wore a large, bland, black dress. A simple scarf covered the top of a very forgettable, round face. An old ugly shawl covered her shoulders. Her mouth was perfectly straight. Her expression was neither a frown nor a smile. Yet her eyes cut through him. They were unwavering and strong. A sharp, worn, crease in her forehead emphasized these eyes and added to the intensity of her gaze. Could this woman actually be their conductor, the Moses he'd heard so much about?

Henry's hand moved to his pocket to nervously twirl his harmonica.

"What be in yer pocket?" the old woman scolded.

"Only a harmonica. See?" Henry pulled it out as the woman quickly stepped back.

The harmonica caught the light. She raised her head and glanced into his hand. Relaxing, she gave a curt smile. "Fine, my child. Fine. Yer can't always know what folks hab in thar pockets. Must deliver de packages safely, mustn't we?" Henry noted her other hand withdrew from something within the inner folds of her long, dusty, shawl.

She spoke in a firm voice, stating that they must be very quiet and telling the infant's parents that she would have to give the infant a sedative when he started to cry. She held up a gun and said that there was no going back once they started out. If anyone tried to leave she had her gun and she would use it. Now Henry had no doubt she was 'Moses'. He knew he could trust her with his life.

"Let me carry your baby for you a ways so you can rest." Henry had noticed the man and his wife passing the baby back and forth, but both looked tired.

The man hesitated and glanced at his exhausted wife. "Us ken takes care ob him."

"I know, but I'm missing my son, Sam, who is about your boy's age. I'd love to be able to hold a baby."

The woman gave Henry a grateful look and handed over the boy. "This be our boy, George. Thank ye." The baby settled into Henry's arms and they continued their journey.

The next day Moses gathered the group together down by the river. "Us in er dangerous area. Lots of patrollers and dogs. Us now travels in de water fer er ways." The river bottom had slippery rocks and deep holes that tripped them. When one man fell in, the current started pulling him downstream and the others had to quickly grab him. The six trudged after Moses, who seemed undisturbed by the current or the rocks.

"I's din't think it be dis bad," grumbled a man named Charly. "I's ken hear dem dogs." He looked around fearfully.

Finally Moses said it was safe to climb back on the river bank. They sat and ate a lunch the couple at the last station had made for them. All were feeling much better when they resumed their journey.

Suddenly Moses swayed and fell to the ground. Henry, who was behind her, tried to catch her, but was only able to ease her fall. The group soon discovered she was unconscious. Charly looked around him. "Us out in de woods an hab no idea whar us be. Our conductor be out ob her head. Us goin' ter die out here or dos patrollers an deir dogs git us. Dose dogs tears us apart." The man rubbed his head and Henry could see he was trembling.

"Don't worry. I heard Moses does this sometimes. She was hit on the head by an overseer when she was young. She'll be alright soon and will take us the rest of the way."

"O, Lor! I's neber should hab comes. Me Mas'r not dat bad. Him be better than dying out here. I's goin ter goes back ter de las town and finds a federal marshal ter takes me back ter me mas'r. Iffen I's goes back him mos likely not beats me."

Henry casually bent over Moses and picked up her gun. Turning, he pointed the gun at Charly's chest. "You aren't going anywhere. Don't you remember Moses warning us? The patrollers and federal marshals beat runaways until they tell all they know about the Underground. You'd be putting us and other conductors, stationmasters and passengers in danger. Moses said, 'Dead men tell no tales'. Sit down!" Henry growled at Charly and he meekly sat on the ground. Eventually Moses sat up. Henry handed her the gun. She raised herself and, saying nothing about what had just happened, resumed her journey, the six following.

Harriet Tubman led them from Baltimore to Philadelphia, where she introduced them to William Stills, whom she called the 'Father of the Underground Railroad.' He first talked with the man and his wife who had the baby and then it was Henry's turn to be interviewed.

"Henry, Philadelphia is one of the central stations of the Underground Railroad. I keep records of everyone passing through here. Sometimes I've been able to locate someone or contact those left behind and let them know their family member is safe. I need to know about you, where you are going, and if you have any aliases." Henry told William Stills about himself, Rose, Margaret, James and little Sam. He said that he and James would like to set up a school for Negroes in Ontario, but weren't certain where that would be as yet.

After Henry had finished he asked, "Mr. Stills, my Rose died before she could make it to freedom. She had an Uncle Joe who asked her to escape and meet him some day in Canada. His dream was to own a farm. I'd like to find him and introduce him to Rose's son, Sam. Could you help me do that?"

"There are quite a few towns in Ontario where Negroes have settled. You may have to visit each of these towns. You could look for a good place to build your school while you search for Rose's uncle. If he is in one of the towns the people there will let you know. I'll help all I can." Henry thanked him and left.
Moses led them to New York. When they reached Niagara Falls Henry saw they had to cross a suspension bridge that was only 3 feet in width. When it was his turn to cross he felt the bridge moving from side to side and up and down in the wind. He reached the middle of the bridge, looked down at the rushing water so far below him and froze. He couldn't move.

"Henry, yer needs ter cross so de rest ob us ken gits ter Canada. Yer forced me ter goes wen I's goin' ter turn back. Now yer goin' ter goes or I's goin' ter push yer." Charly put his hand on Henry's shoulder. Henry looked around at Charly. He slowly faced Canada, breathed deeply, and started to move. Eventually he made it across and sighed with relief.

"Thank you, Charly."

They were there. They were in Canada and they were free. Harriet Tubman led them to her house in St. Catharines. James and Margaret, with Sam, rushed to meet him.

Henry was overcome. They had made it to freedom. He only wished Rose could be here with him. He vowed he would make a good life for Sam and would tell him about his Mother and her courage—how she had saved them and how her greatest wish for her son was that he'd grow up to be free.

PART II

THE CIVIL WAR

"Peace does not appear as distant as it did. I hope it will come soon, and come to stay; and so come as to be worth the keeping in all future time."

Abraham Lincoln
August 26, 1863
Letter to James Conkling

Chapter 12

1860

Margaret stood at her cast iron stove in the little kitchen and smiled to herself. Never would she have believed it if someone had told her a few years ago that she'd be cooking the evening meal in a log cabin that she had helped her husband and Henry build. The three of them had spent about a year clearing their land after they arrived in Hamilton, Ontario. She'd even had blisters on her hands. Her Mother would've been shocked. Margaret smiled in remembrance, then looked down at her black skirt and white blouse, partially covered with a long blue apron. Quite a change from the fancy dresses she used to wear. She'd sold a couple of those dresses and could no longer fit into the one she'd kept. Having their two children had put some weight on around the middle. James didn't seem to mind and still told her she was beautiful.

Margaret suddenly noticed little Rose had opened a sack of wheat set on the floor. She raked her tiny hands through the grain, laughed, and threw the grain into the air. "Rose! Stop that! Ah!" Flecks of grain hit the stove, burst into flame and landed on the floor.

James entered and stamped out the sparks on the floor. "Rose! Margaret! Are you alright? Careful! One of these days this place will burn down!"

"We have good wheat harvests. Paid for your bed and your brother's, but not so much that we can afford to burn the house down, little one!" Margaret swept up the blonde, blue eyed Rose from the floor.

James gave them both a hug. "Mind your back, dear."

"My back is still strong. Helped you and Henry clear all the brush and trees from the two properties—until I was going to have a baby and you made me stop.

"I still feel bad you had to sell all your jewelry so we could purchase the land."

"I don't mind. The jewelry doesn't exactly go with these clothes." Margaret looked down at her skirt, blouse and apron and smiled. "We've accomplished a lot in these five years haven't we, James? Remember the first year-1855? It was so cold! We had to sleep in the main room, next to the fireplace. I must admit, I thought about going back to Virginia a lot.

"Me too!"

"You and Henry made our bed and the huge wooden table and chairs that winter."

"No shortage of wood here."

"Then spring came and it started to feel like home. I wove that carpet." Margaret continued. "No one was whipped into working or held against their will. Slaves didn't build this place. That's why this rough cabin is better than any Virginia mansion." Margaret bent down to the floor. She swept up some grain with her fingers, held her head high and threw the grain playfully at James, "Isn't that right, Rose?".

"Well! Think I'll retreat and correct a few more papers." James held up a pile of cursive practice sheets. "Of the nine regular white and negro students in our school Sam's only six and writes so beautifully with his ink. I caught Edmund trying to drink it, and he's eight now."

Margaret followed James into the main room and watched as he sat down at a small table and began grading papers. Wouldn't Mother and Father be shocked to know I prefer our log home to the fancy mansion? Margaret smiled. She looked around the main room with its roaring fireplace, the pictures on the wall, the new sofa, the small rug and the green curtains she had sewn for their one window. It was a cheerful, comfortable room and she had played a part in making it so. She sighed a sigh of contentment.

Margaret watched blonde, blue eyed Rose sit in a corner with her brother, who was intently building a house and horse pens with his building blocks. Oh dear, Rose is getting tired and has started to whimper. "Where Sam? I wants my Sam."

"Sam and Henry will be here soon, Rose. Go to your Father. He'll hold you."

James glanced up, smiling. "Come here, Rose. Would you like to help me grade papers? Here's a pencil and a piece of paper." Rose immediately began to smile and walk toward her Father, holding her rag doll with one arm and reaching her other arm up to her Father. Margaret had made the rag doll much the same as the one Bella made Rose when they were little. It brought back fond memories.

There was a knock at the door and Ben got up to let Henry and his best friend, Sam, in. Rose, upon seeing Sam, climbed down from her Father's lap and ran to Sam. She tugged on his trouser leg until Sam said, "Alright, Rose, I'll pick you up." Sam had been enthralled with Rose since her birth and was excited when they named her Rose after his Mother. The two had a special bond. "Hello, Henry. I read the newspaper today and it tells about Abraham Lincoln being elected President. We have a lot to talk about after we eat."

Margaret stopped any further conversation. "The food is ready. Let's come to the table." Soon the three adults and three children were sitting around the rough wooden table, bowing their heads while James said a prayer. Ben quickly grabbed a piece of chicken before it was passed around and received a frown from his Mother and Father. Embarrassed, he placed it on his plate and waited until everyone had been served before picking it up again.

Knock. Knock. Who could be knocking at this hour? Margaret frowned. "James, would you get the door, please?" James opened the door and they all looked up at a tall, well-built Negro man standing there.

"I'm sorry to be calling so late, but I just arrived from my home in London. My name is Joe Harper, and I'm looking for Mr. and Mrs. Graydon."

"I'm James Graydon. How may we help you?"

"I grew up on the Ramsey plantation in Virginia, but eventually escaped from slavery to Canada." Joe turned his head toward the table as Margaret let out a gasp. "My Mother and Father, Bella and George, still live on the plantation, and I wrote them to find out how they and my niece, Rose, were doing. Someone wrote back for Bella, saying that Bella and George were well, but I should contact Mr. and Mrs. Graydon in Hamilton, Ontario, to meet Rose's son, Sam. The letter said nothing about Rose."

"Come in, Mr. Harper, and join us for supper. You are most welcome."

Introductions were made. Joe was provided with a plate and food was passed around the table to him. Margaret then related the story of Rose. Sam asked, "Did you know my Mother?"

"Yes, I did, Sam. She was about your age when I knew her, and a bright and pretty girl she was. She was always asking questions like "Why is the sky blue? How do clouds make rain?" Since I couldn't read I'd make up the answers. I learned to read finally and hoped to answer her questions when she came to Canada." Joe looked into Sam's eyes. "You see, Sam, I told Rose I would get to Canada and buy a farm and she was to join me when she got older. Then we would both be free." He shook his head, a sad expression on his face. "Now she'll never see my farm and meet my children." He put his hand on Sam's shoulder. "I hope that now Rose's son can meet and get to know his cousins. I'd like to invite all of you to visit us in London to meet my wife, Liza, and my children. It 's only 72 miles from here."

After the children left the table talk turned to Abraham Lincoln being elected President. "I remember in Lincoln's nomination acceptance speech for the United States Senate he criticized Steven Douglas, the Supreme Court and President Buchanan for promoting slavery. The Supreme Court had actually declared that Negroes were not citizens. Lincoln had said then, 'A house divided against itself cannot stand.'"

"Yes, James," spoke up Henry. "In the Lincoln Douglas debates he said he doesn't want slavery to expand into the territories. That really made the South angry. What do you think about all this, Joe?"

"Of course I'd like to see Lincoln free the slaves, but I think that will take time because the South is determined to keep their free labor. I'm just glad I no longer live there and am now a citizen of Canada. No one can make me work without pay or take my wife and children away and sell them." He pounded the table for emphasis.

"You're right about that, Joe. Margaret and I came here with Henry and Sam so they could both be free and our children could grow up in a land where they wouldn't see so much prejudice. The school Henry and I now run has both Negroes and whites and they play and study together. Oh, there's some prejudice in the town, but for the most part we all get along."

James leaned over toward Joe. "We'd love to have you stay here if you don't have to go back to your farm right away."

"Thank you. I'd like that. I notice you're building onto your house. I'm a carpenter and would be glad to help."

Henry spoke up. "That would be wonderful. We're building a bedroom for little Rose. It will certainly go more quickly if there are three of us working on it. Sam and I would be very happy if you stay with us as we have more room. That way you and Sam can spend some time together as well. It's getting late. Perhaps we should say good-night."

Chapter 13

1861

Rose O' Neal Greenhow, well known for her beauty and social standing in Washington society, stepped outside the doorway of her mansion, carrying a tray of drinks. "It's a warm July evening, gentlemen, and I thought you might like a cool drink."

"Thank you, Rose," replied Massachusetts senator, Henry Wilson, as the three gentlemen stood up when she approached.

"Oh, it's much cooler out here. I think the party will go on without me for a little while. I'll just sit over here and have my drink." '

Rose sat in a nearby chair and looked out into the night, slowly sipping her drink. She also listened to the politician, the Union general, and the Union colonel discuss plans for the first battle with the Confederacy. Eventually these plans managed to reach General Beauregard, which helped him win the Battle of Bull Run. Union General George McClellan later commented, "It's almost as if the rebels knew the orders even before some of our Union commanders."

The August evening was warm so James and Henry had brought their chairs out in front of the house where they could catch the slight breeze and enjoy the star studded sky. The heavy scent of the several flowers Margaret had planted wafted toward them.

"Henry, I've always wondered how you were able to stop your problem with speaking."

Henry smiled and stretched his legs out in front of him. "It was Rose and her love for me. She helped me become more comfortable when I was with other people besides you. And

Canada has made me more comfortable as well. I still am interested in what happens in the U.S., but I'm glad to be living here, free, in Canada."

"Speaking of the U.S., I wonder what President Lincoln will do now. Since he was elected, first South Carolina and then 5 more states seceded." James turned toward Henry. "And now they've formed the Confederate States of America with Jefferson Davis as president."

"That's not the worst of it. General Beauregard opened fire on Fort Sumter and they captured the fort. Then, after President Lincoln was sworn in, four more states seceded. We are at war."

"Yes, Henry, and on July 21st, when we had our first real battle at Bull Run, the Confederacy routed our Union forces, sending them fleeing all the way back to Washington. Apparently, soldiers fled in panic, with Confederates shooting after them. And to make matters worse, there were hundreds of sightseers, some with picnic baskets, who had arrived from Washington in carriages to watch what they thought would be a Union victory. They were fortunate they didn't get shot, but they certainly moved quickly, trying to get out of there."

Margaret pulled up a chair and joined them. "The children are finally asleep. What are you two talking about?"

"The fact that the North and South are at war. Congress has called for 500,000 men. Margaret, I'm thinking of volunteering." Both Margaret and Henry stared at James.

"Why, James? We aren't even in the US any more. It's not our war." Margaret leaned toward James. "You and Henry have so much to do here with the farm and your school. And the children and I would miss you so." Margaret, a catch in her voice, added, "Please don't go."

"What do you think, Henry?"

"I think it's up to you. I can carry on the farm work and the school if you need to go."

"Margaret, it is my war. I still think of Virginia as home and I miss it. My Father is getting older and may need for me to return and help with the plantation. If that happens I want to return to a Union where all the slaves are free. This is my opportunity to help make that happen."

Margaret put her apron to her eyes and ran into the house. James and Henry sat in silence. Moments later Margaret rejoined them. "If this is important to you, James, then you should go. I'm certain Henry and I can manage." She looked at Henry and he nodded.

"Thank you, Margaret. I won't go until after the harvest. Everyone is saying the war won't last long so I'll be back before you can miss me."

The end of October finally came and the harvest was finished. James packed his bag, said his good-byes, and left to join the Union Army.

Elizabeth van Lew opened her Mother's bedroom door and poked her head in. "Mother, may I come in?"

"Of course, dear. What news have you?"

"General Winder has finally given permission for us to visit the Northern prisoners and give them books, food and whatever we may wish. There are so many prisoners since the Battle of Bull Run and they are in such a wretched state. The ladies of Richmond are sewing and knitting for the Confederacy and they aren't happy that I want to help the Northern prisoners. Do you still want to go with me when I visit Libby Prison?"

"Yes dear, when shall we go?"

"It's nice that Libby Prison is just down the hill from us so we don't have far to walk. Thank you, Ben and Thomas, for carrying the food baskets and books for us. You don't need to wait here." The two Negro men started up the hill after seeing the guard let Elizabeth and her Mother into the prison. This was their third visit and they immediately started walking around the prison, distributing food to the malnourished men and giving out books to those who asked for them. As they approached a window Elizabeth glanced out and noticed a Confederate troop marching by. She asked a soldier, "Do the troops come by here often?"

"Oh, all the time, Miss van Lew."

Elizabeth looked around and saw there were no guards nearby. She motioned for three soldiers to come closer. In a low voice she asked, "Would you like to help the Union win the war?" They nodded.

"I just realized that if you soldiers watch out the windows and report the troop movements to me when I come with the food and books, I can pass them on to a Union officer." She looked out the window again. "There are two roads out of town and we can even let the Union troops know which direction they are headed as well as the number of men." She clapped her hands and smiled. "You can be spies with Mother and me. Are you willing to do that?"

"We certainly are. It will give us something to do and we'll be helping the Union." The soldier who spoke up looked at the other two. "We can pass the word along to others and we can take turns at the windows. But how do we get the message to you? It isn't often that the guards aren't around."

Elizabeth's Mother spoke up. "You can return the books to us with messages in them."

"Good idea, Mother. They might check the books but perhaps you could lightly underline something or write a number. We'll figure something out. Thank you for volunteering. You do know that if we are caught you could be hanged."

"That doesn't matter, Miss. We are Union soldiers and it's our duty to serve the Union, from wherever we are."

John entered the room and sat down at the table with his Mother and Father. They waited while a slave dished up their plates and then began to eat. "John, didn't you escort Elizabeth Wells to a Ball some time ago?"

"Yes, Mother, why do you ask?"

"Elizabeth's Father just rode by yesterday on his way to the Graydon plantation and mentioned that Robert Jones had proposed to Elizabeth and she accepted."

"What? She can't marry him! He's the one who almost raped Margaret. He's a cruel, vicious man!" John rose suddenly from the table. "I must warn her."

John rode up to the Wells plantation, dismounted, and handed the reins of his horse to a slave. He knocked on the door, asked to see Elizabeth, and was taken into the parlor to wait. John paced up and down the room, wondering what he should say. He'd always planned to marry Elizabeth someday when he felt he was ready to marry. Now she'd chosen someone else—and a terrible man whom John knew would treat her badly. Would she believe him when he told her what Robert had done to Margaret? How about his own feelings for her? Even if she broke the engagement with Robert, Elizabeth was a beautiful woman and some other man would come along soon enough. Perhaps it was time to...

Elizabeth entered the room. John noticed how her blue gown matched her large blue eyes. His eyes were drawn involuntarily to her low neckline showing the rise of her bosom. He saw that Elizabeth was smiling. She obviously was aware where his eyes had taken him.

"Hello John. Are you just traveling by? Would you like a drink?"

"No thank you, Elizabeth. I've come to see you. I have something to tell you about Robert, your fiance', that I think you should know. Could we sit down and talk?"

Elizabeth sat in a chair across from him, clasped her hands in her lap and waited quietly while John related the story of what had happened to Margaret. When he'd finished she looked at him. "That was a long time ago. He could have changed since then. We are engaged and both our families are happy about it. Why should I break off the engagement just because of what you've said?"

John leaned forward. "I'm concerned about you marrying Robert because I think I know what he's like and I don't think he's changed." He hesitated and looked into Elizabeth's eyes. "But there's another reason. I love you and want to marry you. I know I should have spoken long ago because I've loved you for years. I guess your becoming engaged made me wake up and realize what a fool I've been. If you do decide to break off the engagement would you let me court you properly? I promise if you begin to love me I'll ask your Father for your hand in marriage and will marry you and take care of you the rest of our lives together."

Elizabeth walked over to the sofa and sat next to John, turning toward him. "I've loved you for years as well, John, but you were seen with girls from all over the area. I had no idea you loved me and so it seemed time to accept another man into my life and forget about you."

John smiled and put his arms around Elizabeth. "Does this mean you'll break off the engagement with Robert and let me court you?"

"Yes! Yes, my darling!"

After a few moments, Elizabeth gradually pulled away. "You'll have to do something though. My Father is in his library and you'll need to have a little talk with him. He's going to be very confused about all of this."

While John was in the library with Mr. Wells, a slave announced the arrival of Mr. Robert Jones. Elizabeth stood and told the slave to bring Robert into the parlor. She sighed. Might as well get this over with now. "Come in, Robert, and have a seat. I've something I need to tell you." She waited until Robert, looking puzzled, had sat down. "I can't marry you, Robert. I love someone else. I'm breaking off our engagement."

Robert came over to her, a menacing look in his eyes. "You can't do this, Elizabeth. Our parents want this, I want this, and I'm certain you want this. Forget this other fellow, because I WILL marry you." He grabbed her shoulders and roughly pulled her to him. "Who is this other man that you are not going to marry? Do I know him?"

Elizabeth attempted, unsuccessfully, to pull away from Robert's grasp. "Yes, you know him. His name is John Ramsey."

This time Robert pulled away, staring at her. "John Ramsey!" Robert spat out the name. "Mr. John Ramsey stood between me and a woman I was going to marry once before. He's not going to get away with it again." He grabbed Elizabeth's arms so tightly she cried out. "You'd better understand this, Elizabeth. I'm going to marry you or something will happen to that Mr. Ramsey, because if I can't have you no one will—certainly not John Ramsey!"

Robert was so intent on Elizabeth he failed to notice Mr. Wells and John standing in the doorway. "Now you listen to me, Robert Jones. My daughter has told you the engagement is off and I don't like what you just said and the way I saw you treating her. I want you off this plantation and I don't want to see you here again. Do you understand me?" He waited until Robert reluctantly nodded. "Now leave!" He and John moved aside to let Robert leave the room and they all waited until they heard him ride away.

"That man has a terrible temper. You'd better stay out of his way, John. I think I'll be far happier with you married to my daughter than if she was married to that man."

Chapter 14

1862

"It's cold outside, but of course that's to be expected. It's January in Canada." Henry came in the door, and stomped some snow off his boots, then turned to see Margaret kneeling over a pail, vomiting.

"What's wrong, Margaret?" He came into the kitchen and leaned over her. "You were sick when I was here two days ago. Do you have influenza?"

Margaret lifted her head and tried to rise. Henry helped her up. "Henry, I'm going to have a baby."

"What? When?"

"The baby should be born in July. I knew before James left, but I didn't tell him because he thought he needed to fight for the Union. I didn't want to interfere with his going. Besides, he doesn't think the war will last more than a few months so he'll probably be home before the baby comes. Don't you write him about this!"

"I won't, but it doesn't seem right not letting him know he is going to be a Father again. What will you do if he doesn't get back in time?"

"I've heard there's a good midwife in town."

"Henry, I just received another letter from James. Let me read it to you." Henry came into the room and sat down, looking at Margaret with anticipation.

July 15, 1862

Dearest Margaret,

I miss you and the children and Henry and Sam so much. I long to hold you in my arms, hug Ben and take little Rose onto my lap.

When I enlisted I was given an enlistment uniform allowance of 1 hat, 2 caps, 1 cap cover, 2 coats, 3 trousers, 3 shirts, 1 blouse, 3 drawers, 2 pair shoes, 2 pair stockings, 1 tie, 1 great coat, 1 wool blanket, and 1 ground sheet. These are to last a year and are already seeing a lot of wear. I certainly appreciate the ground sheet and blanket.

No one joining the army could be prepared for the horror that is war. Both the blues and the grays are experiencing terrible loss of life. I'm writing you and Henry of some of the battles. The Confederates are winning some and we are winning some. At this point the war could go either way. From what I've heard, the Rebels have good leadership in Robert E. Lee, though he is, of course, a fiendish swine. Here's a little of our battles thus far:

I heard General Grant captured Fort Henry and Fort Donelson in Tennessee in February, and earned the nickname"Unconditional Surrender" Grant. Then, in March, the Confederate Ironclad 'Merrimac' sank two of our wooden ships and it was a draw with our ship, the Ironclad 'Monitor'. I guess we found out wooden ships can't last against an ironclad ship. In March, our Army of the Potomac with General McClellan advanced from Washington down the Potomac River toward the Confederate Capital of Richmond, Virginia. However, our Peninsular Campaign ended in failure, with General McClellan retreating from General Robert E. Lee's smaller Army of Northern Virginia. We failed to reach Richmond. If General McClellan hadn't retreated I wonder if we could have taken Richmond. A lot of the men are wondering the same thing.

I was with General Grant at Shiloh on the Tennessee River in April when the Confederates surprised us. It was the bloodiest battle so far. I learned later that the Union had 13,000 killed and wounded and the Confederates lost 10,000 men. Bodies were strewn all over the land, gray and blue often lying side by side, sometimes falling on top of each other, their guns or swords beside them. Blood was everywhere. I thought it ironic that the battle took place by a small church named Shiloh, which means "place of peace" in Hebrew. After it was over, I searched everywhere, hoping to find wounded. I managed to locate two men, but one died while we lifted him out, the other in surgery later. Most of the time I just wandered in a daze, collecting weapons and supplies from the dead. The grays also scavenge this way. It made me physically ill. Some of the dead were only boys, ages 14 through 17. They're not much older than those boys from Church who help us during the harvest. I picture the Mothers of these boys weeping and wailing when they receive the news.

On April 24, 17 of our ships took New Orleans, so now we have the South's greatest seaport. I hope Jefferson Davis choked on the news. That man has a lot for which he must answer. We can stop supplies coming in and perhaps starve the grays into surrendering after we get more of the seaports. June 25 was the beginning of a Seven Day Battle when Lee attacked us near Richmond. There were heavy losses and General McClellan began a withdrawal back toward Washington.

I miss your cooking, Margaret. Our rations are fresh or salted beef, salt pork, flour, sugar, salt, vinegar, dried fruit and dried vegetables,which are usually beans. It's not often we have fresh vegetables. I miss our garden. Most of the time we subsist on hardtack. As you know it's just flour water and salt made into a thick cracker. The army has found it to be most resistant to roaches and mice in the camps, but weevils, unfortunately, like it. We generally dunk the hardtack in coffee or soak it in water and then fry it in bacon fat. After a few months all the food here seems to taste the same. We, fortunately, do have plenty of coffee.

Tell Henry it makes me feel so much better that he is there to look after you. This war is lasting longer than I thought it would and I have no idea when it will end. I think of you all the time, Margaret, and our life together in Canada. Coming home to you is what gives me hope in my darkest hours.
Fondest Regards,
James

Margaret, tears in her eyes, put the letter down on her lap and looked at Henry, sitting on a nearby chair and staring at the floor. "I pray daily that James will be safe and come home to us. I didn't realize the war would be this terrible. I guess this means that James won't make it back for the birth of our baby. I'll need your help, Henry."

It was a warm day in late July when Henry and Sam arrived for their supper. "Henry, it's time. Go fetch the midwife."

Henry, a stricken look on his face, soon returned with Mary, the midwife, who took charge at once. "Henry, please boil the water and then can you look after the children while I'm with Margaret?"

It was several hours later and the children were all asleep, when Henry heard the welcomed cry. Soon Mary appeared and said he could come in. There was Margaret, lying in bed smiling, the baby in her arms. "It's a boy, Henry. I think I'll name him Robert James."

"I've asked Mary to join us for the Sunday meal. She did such a wonderful job delivering Robert James. I think she likes you, Henry."

"I'm not interested in another woman. Rose is my only love."

"Rose is dead and it's time you found someone else. Mary is a beautiful woman who is kind and intelligent. She told me her parents were free Negroes living in New York, but they came over to Canada when she was ten years old because the Fugitive Slave Law meant no Negro was safe. Her Mother's cousin, a free Negro, was captured by a slave trader who tore up her papers and took her down south to be sold. That's when they decided to move to Canada. After going through school here Mary took training to become a midwife. I think you should at least get to know her. Rose would want you to be happy."

James put on his slouch cap and prepared to go to battle. It was September 17 and a fog drenched dawn at Antietam, Maryland. James couldn't see his opponents. He knew they were out there though, waiting for him. General McClellan gave the order to attack and attack they did. The fighting was fierce and blood was everywhere. Noise from cannons and guns was overpowering. A rebel came at him with a bowie knife and he could feel a sharp pain in his left arm. A Union soldier shot the rebel in the back. James saw another coming his way but had time to shoot. One of his friends fell nearby, but there wasn't time to stop and check on him. The battle stopped for no man.

When the two sides decided to end it for the night James was taken to the field hospital where he waited to be seen. He'd lost some blood because there had been no time to stop and bind his wound. Someone hastily wrapped a tourniquet around his arm and then he was left alone. He saw a field doctor leaning over boards laid across a pair of barrels. Tubs placed under the boards caught the blood from the man stretched out on the boards. The doctor stood with a saw in his hand and James heard him say, "We're out of Chloroform. Give him some whiskey."

"No! No! Don't saw off my leg!" The soldier started screaming and struggled to get up as six orderlies, three on each side, held him and another forced some whiskey down his throat. The doctor applied a tourniquet, then wiped off a scalpel and a saw on his bloody apron and began to amputate. He saw the doctor cut through the flesh with a scalpel. When he began to use the capital saw on the bone James looked away, but the man's screams penetrated his whole being. Minutes later the leg was off, the doctor threw the limb onto a pile of other arms and legs, and then sewed up the major veins and arteries with sutures. The soldier was immediately removed so another could take his place. Men were lying in the dirt, under nearby trees and around the makeshift operating table. A pile of bloodied legs and arms grew higher and higher near them. The flies were thick around the pile of appendages and around the men lying nearby. Screams of pain and moans filled the air. James was scared. Are they going to say my arm can't be saved and saw it off? What will happen to me then?

A nurse came up to him. "What's your name, Colonel?"

"I'm Colonel James Graydon."

"I'm Clara Barton. Let me take a look at this arm." She bent over, cut the sleeve off his coat and off the light blue flannel shirt underneath, wiped away some of the blood and then straightened up. "You're lucky, Colonel, it's not deep. I can take care of this for you and then you can return to your troop."

The next day, James and many of the Union soldiers returned to the battle field to bury their thousands of fallen comrades and do what they could for the thousands of wounded soldiers. The Confederate soldiers did the same. James saw Clara Barton was out there, taking care of the wounded Union soldiers. James had heard stories of her courage, nursing the wounded even when a battle was raging. He was glad she'd been there yesterday to help him. He didn't think he'd mention being injured to Margaret when he wrote. Why worry her?

When it was over, Lee ended his northern invasion and headed back to Virginia with his army. James was happy to see them go.

John glanced up as his Father stomped into the room. "Another two slaves have run away. They hear rumors that Lincoln has set all the slaves free so they try to run away to the North. Some of the Union soldiers are helping them escape. When will this war be over, John? We won the first Battle of Bull Run and then, at the end of August, General Stonewall Jackson defeated the Union at the second Battle of Bull Run. I don't like it that battles are taking place in Virginia, too close to our plantation."

John looked at his Mother, sitting in the corner sewing, and then at his Father who was settling into his chair with a glass of whiskey. "I need to talk with both of you. I've decided to join the Confederacy."

John's Mother clapped her hands together. "No, John, you can't. What if something happened to you? I've lost Margaret. I can't lose my son as well."

"You can't leave, John. You know we've lost slaves who have run away and I don't have enough help to run the plantation as it is. I need you here." John's Father frowned as he poured and drank another glass of whiskey.

He's been drinking a lot more lately, John thought to himself. I wonder if he feels guilty about Rose like I do. I know it'll be hard on both of them when I leave, but I need to do this. "I have to go. The Confederacy has had a conscription law since April and all white men from 18 to 35 have to join. President Jefferson Davis is requesting more men so we can win this war. You know what this means to the South. On September 22, the North's President Lincoln issued what he calls the 'Emancipation Proclamation',which he says frees all the the slaves held by the Confederates. It says our slaves can enlist in the Union Army. The slaves are hearing about this and many from the plantations, including ours, are leaving to join their Army. If we win we'll have our own country and the North can't tell us what to do anymore. If we lose, then Lincoln will free all our slaves and life as it is now will disappear forever. I can't see how this plantation would survive without slaves. We've won some important battles even though the North has more men and more guns. If President Davis thinks we can win this war if we have more men then I need to join."

"What does Elizabeth think of your joining, John? I suppose you've told her."

"Yes, Mother, I told her. She doesn't want me to go, but she understands why I'm going. I hope you do as well."

"John, I see you are determined. I don't know how we'll get along without you, but I know how important it is to Virginia and to our plantation to win this." John's Father poured himself another drink.

"The Confederacy isn't going to lose this war. I'll be home soon."

"Henry, I've received a letter from James."
December 12, 1862
Dearest Margaret,

I hope you're receiving my letters. I did receive one from you, but it is very hard for the mail to reach us as we are always on the move. You are continually in my thoughts and I know I am in yours. I dream of the day when we can be together again, and I will never leave you from that day forward. I miss Ben, Rose, Henry and Sam too.

On August 29 and 30, we had a Second Battle of Bull Run, where we were defeated again, this time by General Stonewall Jackson. I thought Shiloh was the bloodiest battle with the most killed and wounded, but Antietam in Maryland, on September 17, has turned out to be the bloodiest yet. We learned that someone gave General McClellan a copy of Lee's plans, which had been found wrapped around some cigars near an abandoned Confederate camp. Can you imagine carelessly leaving your battle plans wrapped around cigars in a deserted camp? I thought General Lee was smarter than that. However, he didn't have to worry because General McClellan thought it might be a trap and didn't act on the information for 16 hours. General McClellan, with many more men, finally stopped General Robert E. Lee, but not without a huge cost in life.

A big surprise though, was that President Lincoln replaced General McClellan with General Burnside as the new Commander of the Army of the Potomac. I did read in the newspaper that when General McClellan sent a dispatch asking for more horses, President Lincoln responded by saying "I just read your dispatch about sore-tongued and fatigued horses. Will you pardon me for asking what the horses of your army have done since the Battle of Antietam that fatigues them anything?" He apparently grew impatient with General McClellan's slowness to follow up on the success at Antietam, telling him, "If you don't want to use the army, I should like to borrow it for a while." Two weeks after the letter about the horses General McClellan was relieved of command.

Did you hear that we have a balloon corps? A Professor Thaddeus Lowe and his crew make reconnaissance flights and then send the information to Union officials. The pace of progress greatly impresses me these days! I imagine they can see a lot from up there. Wouldn't it be exciting to be able to look down on the landscape from above? Perhaps they are seeing a piece of what God sees.

From your letter I gather all is well with you. Has Joe visited from London? Is Henry able to teach and keep up on all the chores? I hated to leave him with everything. Tell him I'll try help him a lot more when I return.

Fondest Regards,

James

Henry, frowning, looking at Margaret. "Do you really think it's right to keep him unaware that you two have a baby boy?"

"I can't tell him now, when he's so far away. He'd wonder why I didn't tell him when the baby was born or even before that." She threw her hands up in the air. "When he comes home he'll be so happy to see us he won't be angry that I kept the news of Robert James from him. At least I hope he won't."

Henry sat down on the sofa and Mary walked over and sat next to him. Henry moved further away and looked down at the floor. Mary turned toward him. "Henry, Margaret has told me about Rose. I've had evening meals with you and Margaret and the children almost every Sunday for more than four months and I've come to really care about you and Sam. You almost run away when I come near you. I understand your loyalty to Rose, and I'm certainly not asking you to stop loving her, but perhaps you could open yourself up to maybe loving someone else as well. I don't think Rose would mind if you did."

"I have started caring for you, Mary, but then I'd think about Rose and how much she gave up for us. I'm raising her son as my own, and I thought that would be enough, but now I'm realizing that perhaps it isn't enough." He turned to look at Mary and took her hands in his. "Margaret thinks Rose wouldn't mind and I know she'd want me to be happy. If you think we could let this develop slowly...?"

145

"Oh yes, Henry. Sam already seems to like me and you and I need to spend some time together to get to know each other."

Chapter 15

1863
January through June

Betty Van Lew and her Mother slowly walked down the hill from
their mansion to Libby Prison, carrying books and baskets of food.
A guard waved them in and commented to another guard, "Here
comes 'Crazy Bet', talking to herself as usual. Don't know why she
wants to help them Union soldiers, but she's harmless and she
always brings food for us too." As Betty walked around the prison,
prisoners, gaunt and dressed in rags, came up to her with friendly
words, returning books and empty food baskets.

After they returned to the Mansion, Betty and her Mother
looked through the two books and the baskets. "Betty dear, this
book has some faint lines on some of the pages. You might want to
take a look at it. I understand a little of how we gather information,
but can you explain it more fully, please?"

"I suppose if you're determined to commit treason with me
you'd better know what they'd hang you for. I had some questions
hidden in a basket of food on our last visit and it seems that the
prisoners have answered them. They see so much from the
windows of their prison and have been able to accurately estimate
the strength of the troops and supply trains that pass by and even
the probable destination by the roads which the Confederates take
to leave town. They overhear information between surgeons in the
hospital and between prison guards and that helps. New prisoners
bring in information too. Now I'll put a cipher dispatch in with our
seamstress' dress goods and she can take it to the second station,
our farm below Richmond. Since the dispatch portion is written in
ink that can be seen only if milk is applied, it will just look like a
little note of instruction to our farm manager. He'll pass it onto our

next station and finally it will reach the Union Army. Often I tear up the dispatch into pieces and have more than one courier take the pieces to the next station. Then, if one is caught, the piece won't mean anything."

"Betty, do you ever think about the way our life used to be years ago—the balls and receptions and garden parties and the visitors to our estate? Chief Justice Marshall, the Adamses, the Lees, the Carringtons, and Fredrika Bremer, the Swedish novelist, have all been our guests."

"Don't forget Jenny Lind, who sang in our great parlor and Edgar Allan Poe, who read "The Raven" to us. Yes, Mother, I certainly remember those good times. I used to love riding in our coach drawn by the six beautiful white horses when we went to some of the resorts." Betty sighed and leaned back in her chair. "And now our neighbors think we're traitors to the Confederacy and will walk on the other side of the street when they see us coming. No one comes to our door." She looked at her Mother. "I talked you into this and you've lost all your friends because of me. I'm so sorry."

"Betty, I volunteered. You and I both were educated up North and we know slavery is wrong. We know, too, that it's important to help preserve the Union. You and I happen to be right in the Confederacy capitol and can furnish valuable information to the Union soldiers. I miss my friends, yes, but we have a job to do."

Betty reached over and held her Mother's hands. "Thank you, Mother. I don't know what I'd do without you."

Henry put his arm around Mary and she leaned into him, sighing with contentment. Margaret took a chair across from the sofa after the children had settled, playing together with their toys.

"I'd like to talk with the two of you," Henry said quietly. "As you know Lincoln has passed the Emancipation Proclamation, which frees all the slaves in the Confederate states but not those in the North. Hopefully, that will happen if the North wins the War.

Lincoln has also called for the enlistment of Negro men in the Union Army. Margaret, you know how we tried to help slaves escape by having a station of the Underground Railroad. Now I think I can help even more by joining the Union Army. I know it will be hard on you both if I leave, but Sam can take care of the animals and help with the farm and we can find someone to run the school while James and I are gone. The war has already lasted two years—I don't think it will last much longer."

Mary turned her head toward Henry, a sad look in her eyes. "Henry, we've just declared our love for each other. I don't want you to leave. We hear reports of the large number of soldiers that are being killed in those battles. I don't want to lose you. I want to spend the rest of my life with you and Sam."

"I agree with Mary, Henry. Why do you need to leave too? Isn't one from our family enough?"

"You know about Frederick Douglass, the slave who escaped North and gave speeches against slavery and published a newspaper called The North Star? He's encouraging Negroes to join the Army because he believes it will help Negroes get full citizenship. Even though I no longer live in the United States I want all Negroes to be as free as I am. I'm sorry. This is something I have to do. Both James and I will return soon, when the war ends, but I need to do what I can to free all the slaves. I'm going. I'll pack my bags and leave tomorrow."

Sam, sitting on the other side of the room with Ben and Rose, suddenly stood and walked toward the door. "Someone just rode up. I'll go see who it is." Soon Sam cried out, "It's Joe and he's brought George with him." Sam ran to the carriage and greeted his great uncle and his cousin. "Go in, Joe. George and I can take care of the horses." The two started to lead the horses to the barn while Joe entered the cabin.

"Welcome, Joe. It's so good to see you." Margaret and Mary rose to give Joe a hug and Henry and Joe shook hands. "Sit down, Joe, and I'll get you coffee and something to eat. I imagine you're hungry after your long journey." Margaret went to the kitchen, baby Robert James riding on her hip.

"Thank you, Margaret. Yes, I'm a little hungry and tired. I received your letter, Henry, saying you're going to join the Union Army, and I decided to come and say good-bye. Margaret and Mary, if you need any help while Henry and James are gone, you can call on me."

"Joe, did you think about what I asked in the letter—about you and me joining the Union Army together?" Margaret, Mary and Henry all looked at Joe.

"Henry, the United States wasn't good to me. I was treated as less than human and all I got was pain and humiliation. Compare that to what I have now. I'm a citizen of Canada and I don't have to fear that I or my wife and children will be sold down south. What money I earn is mine, not a slave owner's. Liza and I have been able to buy and clear our land and build a home and a barn. Our farm is making money for us. We can attend the Church of our choice and our children go to school and are learning to read and write, opportunities I never had as a child in Virginia. No, Henry, I have no desire to leave Canada and fight for the Union. My family and I are happy here and will never return to the United States."

"Our experiences were very different, Joe. I was a slave, but belonged to James, and he treated me as an equal, or close to an equal. I never found my parents, but I want friends in Virginia and slaves in other states to know the freedoms we have here. I hope you see how important that is."

Joe folded his arms and straightened his back. He looked Margaret, Mary and Henry in the eyes in turn. "Liza and I want to invite you to visit us in London before Henry goes off to war. I stopped at your neighbor's farm on the way here and he's prepared to feed your animals while you're gone. I propose we leave tomorrow for London and that you spend two weeks visiting us. Sam's cousins will enjoy seeing him and Ben and Rose. Margaret, Liza is really looking forward to seeing you and Mary. Henry, you can leave for the Army from London."

Margaret's eyes brightened. "Oh, I think that's a wonderful idea! I haven't seen Liza in such a long time. And she's never seen

Robert James and he's already eight months old." Just then Sam and George walked in. Margaret looked at them and at Ben and Rose. "Children, how would you like to visit Liza and Joe and their children in London?" She smiled as the the four began to jump up and down and all began talking at once. "I guess that means a 'Yes' from the children. Let's start packing."

John entered the Confederate camp and walked to an officer's tent. He heard noises from within the tent, cleared his throat and said, "Private John Ramsey reporting for duty." The tent flap opened and an officer bent down to get out. When the officer stood up John's mouth gaped open.

"What's the matter, Private Ramsey, are you surprised to see me?" Captain Robert Jones sneered. "It's going to be a pleasure to be your superior. Let's start with you standing at attention. That's better. Now I want you, as a new private, to learn guard duty. You will march around the camp with your rifle for 4 hours tonight as a picket. You can stay here for awhile because my boots need polishing and my clothes need to be washed."

Much later, John joined his friend, Lewis, who was busy preparing his three day rations. Lewis looked up and saw John's unhappy expression. "What's wrong? I expected you earlier. Did you report to an officer?"

"Yes, and Captain Robert Jones hates me because of things that happened in the past. I'm afraid he'll try to get revenge while I'm under his command."

"President Davis, Rose O' Neal Greenhow has arrived."

"Send her in."

President Jefferson Davis stood up and went to greet his guest. "It is so nice to meet you at last, Mrs. Greenhow. You've done so much for the Confederacy and have been imprisoned twice because of it. The way you sent one cryptic note inside of a woman's bun of hair showed great imagination. You have helped us win battles with your spying. I now have another mission for you if you would accept it."

"I will do whatever you ask of me, President Davis."

"With your beauty and your social graces I think you would be the ideal person to travel to Britain and France as a propagandist for the Confederate cause. We need to convince these countries in Europe to accept the Confederate States of America as a separate country, needing their aid with guns and ships. I think you may be able to help with that. Will you travel to Europe for the Confederacy?"

"Yes, President Davis, I will."

Mrs. Greenhow approached President Davis's Desk. Glancing down, she saw a shiny, gilded cherub. It sat within a Parisian candelabra, next to a fine Italian glass bottle holding expensive-looking Spanish wine. She smiled and added, "Anything for the Confederacy."

Henry turned to the soldier next to him. "That looks like Harriet Tubman over there, but it couldn't be. Why would she be with the Union Army?"

"It is her. She was a cook and a nurse for the Army before she was recruited by Union officers to be a spy. I hear she recruited a group of former slaves and they go through swamps and up rivers to scout the locations of rebel camps and report on the movement of Confederate troops. They also look for slaves to enlist in the Army."

"I wonder if she'd remember me. I was one of the many she led to Canada. Excuse me, Tom, I think I'll talk to her." Henry walked over to Harriet. "I don't know if you remember me. My name is Henry. I was on one of your trips from Maryland to Canada."

Harriet looked up at him and smiled. "Of course. Yer de man who were fraid ter walk across de Niagara Falls Bridge." She saw his sheepish look. "I's also member dat yer carried a young chile fer his parents an dat yer held a gun on a Negro who was going ter turn back when I's fell asleep. It be good ter see yer, Henry. I's seem ter recall dat yer be bery bright and ken read an write. Colonel James Montgomery jes asked me ter go on a special mission wid him an I's ken use a man I's ken trust on dat mission. Will yer join us?"

"I'd like to, Miss Tubman, but I'm assigned to the Massachusetts 54th Regiment, under the command of Colonel Robert Gould Shaw. You'd have to get his permission, or one of his officers."

On the evening of June 1, Henry stood by Miss Tubman's side, watching as 300 men boarded the three small U.S. Navy gunboats. Harriet and Henry boarded the John Adams. The gunboat, Sentinel, ran aground shortly after leaving Beaufort, South Carolina, but two remaining gunboats, the Harriet A. Weed and the John Adams, arrived at the mouth of the Combahee River at 3 AM. Henry watched Colonel Montgomery land a small detachment there and saw fleeing Confederates riding to the nearby village of Green Pond to sound the alarm. Another company landed 2 miles above and deployed in position. When the two ships reached the Nichols Plantation the gunboat, Harriet A. Weed, anchored and the John Adams, with the remainder of the 2nd South Carolina and Harriet and Henry, continued upriver to Combahee Ferry, where they set the bridge on fire. "No banjo tonight, but that sure is a beautiful camp fire," remarked Henry.

Harriet smacked her fist in her palm, her face set firm,"Now de Grays hab ter run thro de riber." Captain Brayton, of the 3rd Rhode Island, continued from Combahee Ferry, proceeding up the left riverbank to the Middleton plantation. He was under orders to confiscate all property and lay waste to what couldn't be carried off.

In the summer, because of epidemic diseases in the low country, such as malaria, smallpox and typhoid fever, the Confederate officers had pulled back most of their troops from the rivers and swamps. The Confederates had received a false alarm before this raid, so didn't respond immediately. By the time they did, the Union troops were headed back across the causeway. Henry was amazed at how quickly the John Adams, with its superior firepower, forced the Confederates from the causeway and into the woods. Meanwhile, Montgomery's troops had torched nearby plantations—the houses, mills, and outbuildings, leaving the plantations as smoking ruins. They took rice and cotton as well as potatoes, corn and livestock.

Word spread amongst the slaves working in the fields that the ships and troops were there to liberate them. Soon hundreds of slaves stood on the shore, begging to be taken on board. After the small boats were more than full and ready to return to the ships, the slaves on shore held onto the sides of the boats to prevent them from leaving, almost capsizing the boats. They were afraid the gunboats would go off and leave them. Oarsmen had to pound the oars on their hands until they relinquished their hold. Eventually, the small boats made several trips back and forth to pick up the slaves who wanted to leave. Harriet and Henry laughed at the sight of a woman carrying a pail of rice, still smoking from the fire, on her head, holding it with one hand while digging her other hand into the rice pot, eating. A child was hanging on behind, two more had hold of her dress, and down her back.

When the Union ships returned to Beaufort the next day Harriet Tubman, Henry and some soldiers took the new freedmen to stay at the Baptist Church before they were transported to a resettlement camp.

Henry sat by the water near their base camp, staring out at the setting sun, his head resting in his hands. A stiff blue figure with a tall hat marched up to him. "What's the meaning of this, soldier? You should be proud of what we accomplished, son." It was an old white officer with an intimidatingly ridiculous mustache.

"N-No S-Sir! I-I mean, yes I am." Henry stood up quickly. "I just regret that we couldn't rescue everyone, Sir!"

"You see that lady over there?" The captain pointed to Harriet Tubman. Harriet caught their gaze and smiled.

"Yes Sir!"

"Because of her planning and intelligence, and Montgomery's raid, of course, our officers tallied the total freed slaves on this mission to be 750 persons."

Henry's mouth opened, "Seven hundred and-"

"Yes. Many of those new men have joined the Union Army. Keep your heart in the cause, Soldier!"

"Yes Sir!"

Harriet and Henry said good-bye to each other. "Thank yer, Henry, fer yer help." She tipped her head with an amused smile. " I's guess yer needs ter return to the 54th Massachusetts."

John wrinkled his nose and glanced over at his friend, Lewis, lying next to him. "The stench in here is terrible. Sibley tents are designed for twelve men and we've had to squeeze twenty in here. No one has been able to take a bath. I can't remember when I last had one. If I was home I'd have a bath and lie down in my soft clean bed in my own bedroom, with a nice, clean blanket over me. I'd sleep. Oh, would I sleep!"

"Tents aren't all we're short of. We're low on food and clothing and guns. My shirt is in rags and my shoes are worn thin. Look at the hole in the bottoms of both shoes." Lewis held up his shoes for John's inspection. "A lot of our soldiers don't even have shoes anymore, and they're wearing anything they can find off the dead bodies. Our rations have gotten less and less and we're raiding abandoned camps and farms wherever the fighting takes us. The only reason I have a Springfield musket is that I took one off a dead Union soldier. This does not befit a southern gentleman. We have to resort to going on the battle field after the fighting is over, looking for clothes and weapons. I'm tired and hungry all the time and my feet hurt."

"Yes, and soldiers are dying, not just from the battles, but even more from all sorts of diseases—smallpox, malaria, typhoid, pneumonia and other diseases I'd never even heard of. Just about everyone gets diarrhea and soldiers are crowding by us every night to get outside because of it."

"Did you ever think it would be like this when you joined, John?"

"No, I thought I'd be helping us get out of a Government that always tells the South what to do and we'd then be able to keep our slaves and life as we know it—or used to know it. President Davis kept saying the war wouldn't last long. Now I see soldiers running away all the time and I can understand why they do."

"Would you ever run away?"

"I've thought about it, but just couldn't bear the shame. I'd love to be back home, helping my Father run the plantation. If I'm shot I don't know what he'll do. I have no brothers, only one sister, and she's living in Canada. I didn't realize how much the land means to me."

"You have every reason to run. Captain Robert Jones treats you worse than anyone in camp. Everyone notices it. Someone should report him to his superior officer."

"It wouldn't do any good. He told me he's told his officer that I am lazy and insubordinate and that he needs to teach me what it means to be a good soldier." John paused a moment. "He also told me if I deserted he'd have me hunted down and hanged. We'd better try to get some sleep, despite the coughing, snoring and the smell. Reveille will be at five AM as usual."

"Lewis and John," a voice called from inside the tent. "Come and help me. George died during the night and I need help getting him out."

"Oh, poor George. He's been sick for several days. Someone said he had dysentery. I know his stomach hurt bad and he had diarrhea. Come on, John. Let's get him out and bury him. At least that will make a little more room in the tent."

June 20, 1863
Dearest Margaret,

I received your letter, saying that Henry has joined the Union Army now that they are accepting Negro soldiers. I can understand why he did, but I worry about how you and Mary are managing. Sam is a good worker, but he's only a boy. I just hope the war will be over soon. It doesn't look too good though. In May, we were defeated at Chancellorsville in Virginia by Lee's much smaller army. General Lee is a brilliant tactician. The Confederate army did manage to shoot their own General Stonewall Jackson whom they mistook as a Union officer. That's a huge loss to them and may help us as General Jackson was a great fighter. President Lincoln has replaced General Hooker with General Meade, the 5th man to command the army in less than a year. What the North needs is a General like Robert E. Lee.

The North is so desperate for men that the U.S. Congress enacted a draft in March. All citizens, aged 20 to 45, are now required to serve. There is a provision, though, that exempts those who pay $300 or provide a substitute. Many poor Northerners are complaining. It hardly seems fair that rich men don't have to fight because they can pay to get out of the draft.

You asked in your last letter if I have any reading material, knowing how much I like to read. Besides the newspapers, the U.S. Christian Commission has distributed Bibles. There's also portable libraries, each with 70 to 125 books. We don't have much else, but at least we can read. That is a welcome relief when we aren't in battle and have nothing to do in camp but play games and read.

How are you, dearest Margaret, and how are Ben and Rose? Tell Ben and Sam that there's a new game we play when we are in camp. It's called baseball and I'll teach it to them when I get home. It's been two years since I've seen them and Rose. I won't recognize them when I return. I miss you and think of you every day and at night before I retire. I pray that soon I'll be holding you in my arms.

Fondest Regards,
James

Margaret folded the letter after she read it to Mary. "We read such awful things in the newspaper about the battles and the numbers of men who are killed, maimed, gone missing or captured. I read that more are dying of diseases than in battle. I am so worried about James and Henry."

It was early evening and John, who was relaxing in front of the campfire, looked up as Lewis approached. "Lewis, we've finished cooking our three days of rations for the march tomorrow so how about a game of checkers before we go to sleep?"

Lewis glanced down at his feet. "I can't, John. Three Union soldiers hid near the camp earlier and bargained with me and another soldier. They traded money and coffee for tobacco so I'm spending the money on a night with one of the camp followers." He held up a bottle. "I want a woman. Haven't had one for a long, long time. John, if you'd like one too, my woman can find you one because I still have some money."

"No, Lewis. I'll just write my fiance' and hope I'll be home with her soon. I'm tired anyway. Besides, they're saying that men are catching a disease from these camp followers."

Lewis looked at John, a determined look on his face. "I don't care. I need a woman and I'm going to have one." He walked off, not looking back.

Today was June 24 and they'd been marching from Virginia since the June 15. They'd marched 18 to 21 miles a day from Virginia through W. Virginia, crossed the Potomac River and were now in Maryland. John could hardly breathe because the dust rising from the marching column got into his eyes, nose and mouth and went down his collar, shirt, and trousers, which rubbed against his skin whenever he moved his arms or legs. He was happy to stop for the night, but then the rains came. His clothing, shoes and blankets were soaked, the food was wet, and wood for cooking and for heat could not be lit. Arms and ammo were wet and needed to be cleaned and dried, but there was nothing with which to dry them. John couldn't remember a time when he was so miserable. Despite the cold and wet, the sore and bleeding feet, aching muscles and the lack of food, both he and Lewis were so exhausted they finally fell asleep.

They were now on a forced march, doing eighteen miles in the hot sun with little water. A lot of men fell out of the ranks with sunstroke, some died. "John, we are a long way back from Captain Robert Jones. He wouldn't know if we dropped out of the ranks and sat by the side of the road. The soldiers would just think we had sunstroke. We could wait until they were all out of sight and then find our way home. I'm certain Captain Jones will put you in the front in each battle and I don't like your chances of survival. I don't like mine either."

"I can't say I'm not tempted. I'm beginning to think I'll never see my fiance' or Father and Mother again. I started something, though, and am determined to see it to the finish, whatever that may be." He turned toward Lewis. "You do it. I'll pretend to help you to the side of the road and leave you there. One of us should survive this terrible war."

Lewis sighed. "No, if you're going to continue, I will too."

As they marched through Pennsylvania , John could see that the people looked frightened and angry. He noticed the small farms seemed to be laid out in squares of six to two hundred acres. There isn't as much woodland as we have in Virginia. Seeing the farms makes me miss Virginia even more. The houses are large here. Stores are closed, probably out of fear of us. There's a few good looking girls, but none as beautiful as Elizabeth. I wonder what she's doing now. Does she think of me as much as I think of her? Will I see her again? John looked around him and smiled. We've burned a few fences, wagons, railroads and bridges along the way and gathered all the horses, bees, and cherries we can find. Union soldiers destroyed our land so I'm glad we can finally destroy some of theirs.

Chapter 16

1863
July through December

"She's just arrived." Betty went into the hall and reappeared with a slender Negro girl. "Mother, this is Mary Elizabeth Bowser."

"It's nice to see you again, Mary. Thank you for coming such a distance to help us in our work."

"I'd like an opportunity to repay Miss van Lew and you for sending me to school up North. I feel honored that you've chosen me for this important mission and I'll do my best."

"Let's start on your training, Mary. I have someone who will place you as a nanny and a waitress in Jefferson Davis' home. People never pay attention to Negroes who work in a mansion so you'll be able to listen in on conversations and perhaps even read battle plans. Once you are in there you can have no direct contact with Mother and me. It would be too dangerous because some people already suspect us as being spies. We'll have ways that you can send messages to me and I can pass them on to the first of my five stations. The messages will eventually reach the Union Army."

Henry gave a self satisfied smile. He was back at the 54th Massachusetts Regiment, still feeling good after helping Harriet Tubman rescue 750 slaves. That many all at once! When they were a part of the Underground Railroad, they only helped a few escape. Never had he imagined he could be a part of an operation that rescued 750 at one time! Some of the men had even followed him and joined the 54th.

Today they'd heard good news from Colonel Robert Gould Shaw. The soldiers had become discouraged, wondering if they'd ever get a chance to fight. They'd finally received permission after weeks of doing nothing but physical labor because white officers didn't think former slaves would be any good on the battlefield. He really respected Colonel Shaw, who had fought to get shoes for the men and had turned down his pay, along with the men, when they learned that white soldiers were paid $13 and they would only receive $7 a month. Then he'd pushed until he was given permission for them to fight. Now, after their rigorous training they would finally get an opportunity to show the white officers and soldiers what they could do.

When they reached Darien, Georgia, Henry was surprised. The little town was almost deserted. He was standing near Colonel Shaw and Colonel James Montgomery and could hear them talking. Colonel Montgomery was ordering Colonel Shaw to have the 54th loot and burn the town, along with his men, the 2nd South Carolina Volunteers. Colonel Shaw was objecting as the town was undefended, to which Colonel Montgomery responded, "You carry out my orders or I'll put you on report. Then your troops will come under my command." He ordered his 2nd South Carolina Volunteers to loot, which they immediately began to do and seemed to enjoy. Colonel Shaw then ordered the 54th to take only what they could use back at camp. He reluctantly ordered them to burn the town. Henry had never seen the Colonel so angry.

After they were back at camp Henry and his friend, Ned, were sitting, leaning against a tree, relaxing. "Ned, I was with Harriet Tubman and Colonel Montgomery when they freed 750 slaves. Colonel Montgomery did destroy plantation buildings and crops along the river, but I never thought much about it. Seeing what happened today, though...The men weren't there, probably out fighting us, and we burned to the ground the homes of those poor women and children. Colonel Shaw didn't want to do it and I can see why. I don't think so much of Colonel James Montgomery after seeing him in action today. I hope we don't have to join with him and his 2nd South Carolina Volunteers again."

"If Colonel Shaw has anything to say about it., we won't."

The old Negro servant entered the library of Miss van Lew's mansion, dusting around the room. Finally he reached the ornamented iron fireplace where he spent some time dusting a couchant lion, which appeared to raise up slightly, like a box cover. The servant reached into the shallow cavity, drawing out a cipher letter. Back in his room he slipped the message into a slit in his thick soled shoes and plodded slowly toward the van Lew farm outside town, a journey he'd taken many times before.

Bella and George entered the mansion's parlor, where the Master and Mistress had retired after their evening meal. The Master, stretched out on the sofa, was snoring, an empty bottle of whiskey on the floor beside him. The Mistress sat on a chair sewing, an unhappy expression on her face. She looked up. "What is it, Bella and George?"

George looked anxiously at Bella and she nodded encouragement. "Mistress, us'n hab only six other Negroes here on de plantation. De rest done runs off ter de North. Der not enough Negroes ter tend de fields. Dem six wants money or dey runs too. What's yer wants ter do wid dem?"

The Mistress raised her hands in the air and sighed. "What can we do? I have almost no money and just a little jewelry left, which I hid from the soldiers. I suppose I'd better try to sell the jewelry. The Union soldiers and then the Confederate soldiers took all our horses and cows and chickens except for the one horse and 2 cows and a few chickens and pigs you hid in the deserted old barn. That was the barn Margaret and Rose used for their Underground Station, I understand. How did you know to do that, George?"

"A Negro from anuder plantation tole me his Mas'r done hide his animals in de woods and saved dem dat way. Dis barn a ways from de Big House so I's thought us'n better do dat too."

162

"Thank you. Do you have any ideas how we can persuade the six Negroes to stay without money to pay them?"

Bella spoke up. "George an' I's hab an idee, Missus. Since us'n kain't raise tobacco no more yer could gib some land ter dem Negroes ter farm if dey stays here and heps in de Big House an makes er large garden fer de Big House." She paused and they both looked at the Mistress expectantly.

The Mistress glanced at her husband and shook her head. "As you can see the Master is in no condition to make decisions so I must. At least if those Negroes make a large garden for us we won't starve. That's what's important now. I hope the war is over soon and John can come back and take over for his Father. Until then..." She looked at George and Bella. "I'll need the two of you to manage the Negroes and help me decide what needs to be done on the plantation. You've worked here for years, George, and you've done just about everything outside, including taking care of the animals. You can manage the Negroes who do the gardening and other outside jobs. Bella, you already manage the household, so you can have one or two of the Negroes to help you with the cooking and cleaning. We can close off some of the rooms. We'll just have to keep on this way until John returns."

"I'm so tired." Lewis sat down next to John and looked at his plate of meager rations. "How can we keep fighting on so little food? We don't even have time to raid the farms around Gettysburg because we're always fighting. It's July 2 today and there's been two days of continual battle already. I can't believe we didn't arrive until noon today. I thought we could march faster than this."

"We can, but not under such heavy shelling! And how did everyone keep fighting this long? I think everything started around 2 PM, but I gather it didn't stop until 8 PM."

"We don't seem to be getting anywhere. I don't understand. On that first day we drove the Union soldiers right through Gettysburg to that place they call Cemetery Hill"

"What?"

"Yes, after the battle there were all those bodies just piled up there in a heap. Apparently it's called Cemetery Hill. Seems appropriately named after seeing all the dead lying on the hill after the battle. I don't know. At least those who fought said it looked like we were winning."

Lewis dipped his head. "Then, today, an officer told me we fought in several places around the town and gained some ground, but the Union soldiers still held their positions on Cemetery Hill and Culp's Hill."

"I couldn't even hear the orders the officers were shouting at us. Noise of the battle was deafening-- cannon and muskets going off. And the smoke made it hard to see. I was using my musket and then my bowie knife when we were fighting in close quarters. I had one soldier on top of me, but someone came up and shot him. Was that you?"

"Could have been; they were coming at us so fast I don't remember how many I shot."

"I just pushed him off, got up, and kept fighting, covered with his blood." John looked down at his trousers and shook his head. "I'm still covered with his blood." John shivered and then stood up, glancing down at Lewis, a serious expression on his face. "Tomorrow is going to be another day of fierce fighting so we'd better get some sleep."

"You go ahead, John. I have to clean my musket. It's going to have to kill a lot of Union soldiers tomorrow." Lewis stroked his rifle.

John paused. "Lewis, it appears we were right. Captain Robert Jones does seem to like putting me in the front charge. If I don't survive the fighting tomorrow and you do, would you look for me after the battle and take three letters out of my knapsack? One is to my Mother and Father, one is to my sister in Canada, and one is to my fiance'. I'd like you to mail them for me." Lewis nodded. "I hope we'll see each other here tomorrow night, Lewis." He turned and walked slowly toward his blanket.

John and Lewis watched as cannons from both sides fired upon each other along the battle lines. John estimated that their side had around 150 cannons. Smoke and flames were everywhere. Slowly, though, the Union cannons ceased fire. Maybe the Union's cannon batteries had been knocked out. That was what their officers seemed to think. It was now two o'clock and they'd been waiting in the hot sun, sweating, for two hours. John was feeling weak and dizzy. Finally, the order came for Pickett's Virginia division to lead the charge up Cemetery Ridge. John and Lewis joined the long line of nine brigades marching over open fields to reach the Union line. As they marched the Union's cannons started firing at them. They hadn't been knocked out after all. John estimated their line to be about one mile across as they walked across the field toward the Union soldiers, who were up a small ridge and behind a stone wall, waiting for them. What are we doing? They can shoot us down as we approach and they're protected behind that wall.

As the Pickett's men came within 300 feet gunshot rained down on them and John saw men falling over to his right and to his left. The firing was coming from the right and left flank as well as the center, where they were heading. John kept marching, trying to shoot at the heads raised above the wall. The man next to him toppled over onto him, almost knocking him down. John slowly lowered the man to the ground and then caught up to the line. Thoughts raced through him. I'm never going to see Margaret to apologize about Rose. How could anyone of us survive this onslaught? Out of the corner of his eye he could see some of the soldiers leaving the line and heading away from the fighting. I should do that too. I hope Lewis leaves the field so he'll be able to come back and get those letters. I'm almost to the wall. There's not many of us. If I can just get over it I can shoot a few soldiers before I die.

John climbed the wall and fell onto the other side. He landed on a Union soldier. A terrible pain passed through him. Looking down at his leg he saw blood coming out of an open wound. Wouldn't be long now.

Colonel James Graydon walked around the area the next morning, checking the ground for wounded Union men. He could see some men writhing and hear moans and screams. Vultures were circling overhead. The stench of the dead, lying there in the hot sun, their bodies blackened, swollen and oily from internal gases, was overpowering. Months ago looking at their faces with their tongues bloated and sticking out and their eyes bulging would have made him ill. Now he was more annoyed by the swarms of flies buzzing around him. There were a few Rebels, but not too many. Most never made it over the wall. James saw a lot of them run away as they came close to the stone wall and he couldn't blame them. The Confederates must have lost at least half of their men in that stupid charge. Here's a Rebel lying across a Union soldier. James looked down and reached out his arm, intending to move the rebel so he could check on the Union man. He stopped, looked, then looked again. It couldn't be. He bent over and peered at the man's face. "John?" James crouched down. It was John, and he was still alive, but barely. "John, can you hear me? It's James, Margaret's husband." James carefully rolled John off the dead Union soldier and onto his back.

John opened his eyes. "James...Get letters from... knapsack." He sighed with relief when James extracted the bloodied letters. "Send them...to Mother and Father and... Margaret and... fiance'. Tell Margaret...sorry about Rose...please forgive me--I love her and...always have." John was exhausted from the effort of talking and his breath was becoming shallower. James grabbed a coat from the dead soldier and tightened it around the wound in John's leg, even though he knew it was too late. He took John's hand.

"I'll tell her, John. I know she'll forgive you. She loves you too." John looked up at James, tried to say something. There was a gurgle in his throat and he was gone. James covered John with the coat, then looked around. I can't leave him here. There's a tree not far away. I'll bury him under the tree.

"What are you doing with that Rebel soldier, James?" Ned approached his friend and looked on curiously as John grabbed the dead man's arms and began to drag him.

"This happens to be my wife's brother and I just can't leave him here. I'm going to bury him under that tree over there." He motioned with his head and then continued to drag John.

"Here, let me help you. I never mentioned it but my Father has slaves and was furious when I joined the Union Army. He thinks I'm a traitor to the South and wouldn't even speak to me when I left. I think this war has separated a lot of families. I don't know if he'll even let me come home when the war's over." Ned grabbed John's legs and, together, they carried John to the tree and began to dig.

"I know what you mean. My Father has slaves, but he understands. Our neighbors in Virginia though, and Margaret's family, think we're all traitors. Guess it's good Margaret and I are living in Canada."

Henry listened to the unending rhythm of the ocean waves and the shrieks of the seagulls as he rested with the 54th Massachusetts Regiment on a South Carolina beach. Colonel Robert Gould Shaw had volunteered the 54th to lead the charge on Fort Wagner and they would soon be marching toward the Fort. His friend, Will, sat beside him, arms around his knees, staring at the water. "Will, the 54th will finally take part in a real battle, and, in fact, we'll lead the attack on the Fort."

"The Fort looks well defended." Will paused and looked over at Henry. "I wonder how many of us will be killed. I know we're ready. It's a chance to do what we've been training for since last May, and it's now July 18. That's long enough. We'll finally be able to show the white people we can do more than build railroads and do heavy labor around the camps. He looked over at the hundreds of Negro soldiers resting along the beach and sighed. "We are almost like family and I wonder who in this family won't be returning to their tents tonight."

"I wonder too, Will. I wonder too."

Colonel Robert Gould Shaw dismounted from his horse and passed through the soldiers until he reached the front. He gave the order to march. The men followed behind him, and as they drew closer to the fort he gave the order to quick step and then a double quick step. They were almost running now. Cannon and gunshot fire began to rain down upon them when they were beneath the fort. Bodies flew up in the air and fell to the ground. Some just fell over. Still they continued to climb upward toward the fort. Henry could see Colonel Shaw at the front, urging the men on. They surged over the sharpened wooden stakes that surrounded the fort and through the water-filled ditch. Colonel Shaw waved his sword and shouted, "Forward, 54th" and then was hit. He tried to move forward and then was shot two more times before he fell. A command urged everyone forward. Henry saw the soldier carrying the American flag stumble and fall, but Sergeant William Carney grabbed it and continued up the slope. He gained the crest, knelt, and held the flag while the battle raged around him. Henry tried to shoot at the rebels firing the cannons, but they were too far away and too hard to see with all the smoke from the cannons and muskets. He and some others climbed onto the fort and did battle with their sabers before ordered to retreat. Henry had reached the beach again before he felt a sharp pain in his arm, looked down and saw blood running down his side. Will ran to him and wrapped the arm as well as he could before helping him walk down the beach to safety.

Henry woke up in a makeshift field hospital, lying on some boards. A doctor was leaning over him with a knife. Henry's eyes filled with terror. He knew what was coming. "We're giving you some chloroform, soldier. Your arm has to come off."

"Please, can't you save my arm? I'm a farmer and I need that arm."

"Sorry, soldier, you got a lot of sand in the wound from walking down that beach. The man who brought you in stopped the bleeding and saved your life, but the wound is infected. The arm has to go." Henry watched the doctor apply a tourniquet around his arm. Then the chloroform took effect and Henry faded into darkness. He didn't see the doctor cut the flesh with a scalpel, saw through the bone, toss his arm onto a pile of other arms and legs and then sew up the major veins and arteries with sutures. Some things are better to have missed. Will saw it all though, and felt sorry for his friend.

James sat under a tree, pencil in hand and a thoughtful expression on his face. Should I tell Margaret that her brother died on July 3 or should I wait until I'm home and can hand her the letter he wrote her? Yes, I think it might come easier if she could read the letter. I'll just write her a little about what's going on here. She's always so honest with me though. I hate hiding this from her. He put his head down and began to write.

December 5, 1863

Dear Margaret,

    The Siege of Vicksburg lasted from May 18 to July 4, when the Confederates finally surrendered their garrison. General Grant had given them 3 hours every day to bury their dead and take care of their wounded. I hear Rebels were deserting Vicksburg all the time. They had no reinforcements or supplies coming in. so must have been very hungry. Winning Vicksburg gave us command of the Mississippi River, which is a big win.

    Did you hear about the race riots in New York? Apparently they lasted from July 13 through the 16. It started because some of the poor working class, mostly Irish, were upset that rich people could get out of the draft by paying $300. Then it turned into a race riot when people started blaming the Negroes for causing the war. Some people were killed and buildings, including an orphanage for Negro children, were burned to the ground. I don't think the rich should be able to buy their way out of being shot at either. The draft should be for everyone of a certain age.

    I heard the 54th Regiment was involved in an attack on Fort Wagner in South Carolina in July? Half the men in the 54th died in the battle. I think you wrote me that Henry was in the 54th. Have you heard from him? Please let me know. Apparently the men of the 54th gained a lot of respect because of their courageous fighting.

I suppose you read in the Harper's Weekly about the address President Lincoln gave at the ceremony dedicating the Gettysburg battlefield as a National Cemetery on November 19. I was impressed with his words. He started his two minute speech with "Fourscore and seven years ago our fathers brought forth on this continent a new nation, conceived in Liberty, and dedicated to the proposition that all men are created equal." I liked his ending: "...that we here highly resolve that these dead shall not have died in vain-that this nation, under God, shall have a new birth of freedom-and that government of the people, by the people, for the people shall not perish from the earth."

That's why I'm here, Margaret. Sometimes I forget the reason I joined up in the heat of the battle and in the boredom of camp life and in missing you and the children. But I'm here for a purpose—to preserve the Union. And I'll stay here until that purpose is accomplished. When that day comes, I will return and take you in my arms, never to leave you again. I promise you that, Margaret.

There is some good news. In November, Union forces under General Grant defeated the siege army of General Bragg in Chattanooga, Tennessee. They stormed up the face of Missionary Ridge without orders and chased the Rebels away from what was thought to be an impregnable position. One Union soldier cried, "My God, come and see 'em run!"

I miss you so much and long to hold you. Hopefully, this terrible war won't last much longer.

Fondest regards,

James

Chapter 17

1864

Elizabeth sat across from her Mother. She looks so much older and more frail. I wonder how she'll bear what I have to tell her now.

"Mother, I have some bad news. John has been conscripted, despite his ill health, and ordered to report to Camp Lee. He deserted and was being concealed in the outskirts of Richmond."

"Oh, Elizabeth, not my only son!" Mrs. van Lew burst into tears and put her head down into her hands. "What can we do?"

"Unfortunately, 109 prisoners escaped from Libby Prison through a tunnel so vigilance has been redoubled. We've hidden a few of the men in our small parlor with its blanketed windows. I went to General Winder and he was unable to get John declared unfit for service, but did get him in his own regiment so John won't have to go to battle."

Mrs. van Lew began to sob, tears rolling down her cheeks. Elizabeth knelt beside her and put her arms around her Mother's shoulders. "Please don't worry, Mother. We'll keep John safe and away from the fighting."

Mrs. Van Lew looked up, wiped her eyes, and patted Elizabeth's hand. "I know you will, dear, but it's not just that. It's this awful war. I know we're almost out of money because our fortune has gone to feed and take care of the Union soldiers in Libby Prison and in other prisons. When the war started we were paying $6.65 for our groceries. Then it rose $68 per month in 1863 and now it is $400 per month with the terrible inflation. And we are trying to feed the prisoners as well as ourselves and our servants!"

"Yesterday when we walked to the store, did you see that my once very dear friend spat upon me and called me a name? I've tried not to let the threats of prison, of fire and of death worry me, but it does. People who were once our friends shake their fingers in our face, call us names and make threats. When will it end?"

Elizabeth hugged her Mother. "I don't know, Mother, I don't know. I'm so sorry I brought this on you."

Rose O'Neal Greenhow turned sideways to see her reflection in the mirror. Yes, the dress is beautiful. Women will envy me when they see my fancy dress from Paris and learn that I actually was received into the court of Napoleon III and had an audience with Queen Victoria. My memoirs have been well received and made me a lot of money. She smiled as she looked down at the pile of gold coins on the nearby table. Too bad I couldn't get Britain and France to recognize the Confederate States of America as a country. I know they were sympathetic to our cause, but when the Confederacy started losing some of the battles they decided they couldn't support us. President Davis is going to be very disappointed. It's time to go home now though. I've been in Europe a year. I won't be able to return to Washington because that detective, Pinkerton, will try to put me in prison again. He put me in twice, but couldn't keep me there. I have too much on certain Union politicians. They certainly won't want to sleep with me anymore. She smiled to herself. I think, though, I'll go to Virginia. I'll ask President Davis to find me a house near his home.

Joe opened the message just delivered by a young boy. "Liza, listen to this. 'Joe, could you pick me up at the train station? Please come alone. Henry.'"

"George, bring the carriage, please. I'll be back with Henry in time for supper."

Joe saw just a few men on the platform when he arrived. There he is. Oh no, what's happened? He walked up to Henry. "Hi Henry, welcome home. It's so good to see you." Joe tried to look just in Henry's face and not at his body.

"Good to see you, too. And, yes, I lost my arm in battle. I'm used to people staring." His face was grim as he picked up his bag and followed Joe to the carriage.

"The family is looking forward to seeing you. Liza is getting supper ready."

Next morning Henry climbed into the carriage next to Joe and they set off for Hamilton. "Mary is going to be so happy to see you." He glanced over at Henry and smiled.

"I'm not going to see her. I want you to take me directly to my home. I want to see Sam, but none of the others."

"Oh. Uh. You must want to rest more before you meet them then?"

"Mary needs a complete man, not a broken one with an arm missing."

"You do need rest, you're speaking nonsense!" Joe turned toward Henry. He'd forgotten the road.

"Why, I can't even completely dress myself. How am I going to do farm work with only one arm?"

"We all help each other, Henry. It's what we are supposed to do. And Mary loves you."

"I don't want her marrying me out of pity."

" You're just tired, that's all. You've been through a lot."

"I'd like you to drop me off at my house and then go by Margaret's and tell her and Mary that I'm home, but I don't want to see them." In as steady a voice as he could manage, he continued. "Also, please tell Mary that I'm not going to marry her and she should find someone else. She's so pretty and intelligent and wonderful that I'm certain it won't take her very long. Can't even play music anymore. Nor can I hear it in my head. All I hear is cannon fire."

"Of course I'm going to see him! I don't care that he's lost an arm. He's the man I love." Mary stood up and headed for the door. Joe barred her exit with his long arm.

"I know, Mary, but give him time to adjust and then go to him. He's not ready to receive you now and it could just make the situation worse."

"I agree with Joe, Mary. You need to wait even though it's hard." Margaret went to Mary and put her arms around her. "We'll help him understand that he's the same Henry he always was and that loss of an arm doesn't change that."

"It's now the middle of April. Over a month has gone by, Margaret, and Henry still refuses to see us. He won't come here to eat and has Sam bring food to him. Sam says he just sits in a chair, staring out the window and rarely talks. Apparently he has occasional nightmares where he wakes up screaming. I'm going over there tomorrow and see him whether he likes it or not." Mary sat down, a determined look on her face.

The next morning Henry sat in his chair, staring out the window. Looks like its clouding up in the distance. Wait, that's no cloud—it's smoke from a fire. "Sam, come here quickly!" When Sam came into the room, Henry exclaimed, "There's a fire coming this way. We need to get out of here! Hitch up the horse and carriage and also the horse and wagon. We'll take the seeds for planting and as many animals as we can. Tie the two cows and my horse to the back of the wagon and put a few chickens in the cages. Now, hurry!" Sam ran out the door toward the barn, a terrified expression on his face. Henry gathered a few clothes and personal items of his and Sam's and threw them in a bag. He then ran to the barn and began helping Sam tie the animals to the wagon. "I'll finish this. Take the carriage to warn women and children to get ready to leave. And tell them to hurry!"

Soon Henry and Sam were helping the frightened women and children into the carriage. "Where are we going, Papa?"

"We'll go to our friends, the Joneses, in town. I don't think the fire will reach that far. That way you and I and Ben can help fight the fire. You two follow me with the wagon." Sam and Ben nodded, looking solemn. Henry glanced back. The fire was moving fast toward them. They needed to get out of there now!

Two weeks later Henry and Sam drove Margaret and Mary back to their farms. Margaret gasped when she saw the scorched trees and then the charred logs, the remainder of what was once their home. She could see that nothing was left of Henry's home as well. Both she and Mary burst into tears. Henry and Sam looked grim, then Sam spoke up. "At least we're all alive and houses can be rebuilt."

Mary turned to Sam and hugged him. "You're right. Thank you, Sam, for reminding us of that. And thank you, Henry and Sam, for saving our lives. We are all together and that's what's important." She smiled as Henry came to her and put his good arm around her shoulders.

Margaret watched Henry with Mary. At least the fire brought the two of them back together. Henry learned he could still do a lot with just one arm, and Sam is such a big help to him.

"Margaret, I'm taking you and Mary and the children to Joe and Liza's in London. When the house is finished I'll come and get you." Margaret started to object, then apparently thought better of it. "Sam and I may have to stay with you awhile until our house is built."

"Alright, we'll get our things from the Joneses' house. It will be good to see Joe and Liza again. Children, we're going to visit Joe and Liza." She smiled as Rose began jumping up and down.

Joe returned with Henry and Ben and Sam and work on the barn and house began. The woods in the back of their property had survived the fire and they began cutting logs. It wasn't long at all until the barn was finished and the log house, with its three bedrooms, took shape. Soon it was ready for occupancy. Henry turned to his neighbors. "Thank you. We'll never forget this. I hope some day we can repay you for your kindness."

After they'd left, Henry said, "I guess its time to get the family and see how they like their new home."

"Oh Henry, it's beautiful, and the rooms are bigger than they were in the old house." Margaret and Mary checked the bedrooms and kitchen, exclaiming at the furniture. "Where did you get the beds, the dressers and the sofa?"

"Joe built most of it and the neighbors contributed some. We'll have to put off building my and Sam's house until we get the planting done. Hope it's alright if we stay here with you for awhile. Sam and I can sleep in the main room."

Margaret shook her head. "No, Henry, we can double up in the bedrooms. Rose can come in with me and you, Sam, Ben and Robert James can share the other two rooms. She turned to him. "Thank you for all you've done. You saved our lives and you rebuilt our home. We can never repay you!"

They were at Cold Harbor, Virginia, after engaging in two inconclusive battles. "Ned, I don't know how we'll be able to take the offensive here. I'm beginning to wonder what General Grant is trying to do. The Rebels are well fortified. Remember our agreement. If one of us doesn't show up in camp the other will look for him. If he dies his letters will be sent to his family."

"I remember, James. We'll look after each other until this War is over and we're on our way home."

James sat at the small table, a pencil in his hand, and stared at the blank paper. I don't know what to write. All I see is blood and death and I don't want to just write about that. I've been gone so long Margaret and the children seem almost like a distant memory. He bent his head and began to write.

June 10, 1864

Dear Margaret,

We've had some good news. In March, President Lincoln appointed General Grant to command all the armies of the United States. He seems to be a good commander like the Rebels' General Robert E. Lee. He's made some mistakes, but he's better than the other Generals we've had. Perhaps he can lead us to victory and end this terrible war.

You said in your last letter that Henry is home. Was he sent home because he had an injury? I'm so glad to hear he's now out of the War and am looking forward to getting home as well and helping him with the farm work.

In May, General Grant began to lead our Army on an advance toward Richmond. We had battles at the Wilderness and at Spotsylvania, both inconclusive, but costing a lot of lives. An oak tree caught in the cross fire at Spotsylvania was reduced from a full sized oak tree to a stump about 2 feet in size.

The battle of Cold Harbor, Virginia, in June, cost us 7000 casualties in twenty minutes of fighting. The Rebels were too well fortified. The worst loss, to me, in that battle, was of my friend, Ned, from Maryland. He's been fighting by my side since we entered the Army about the same time. I searched the battlefield after the fighting was over and couldn't find him so I can only hope that he's been taken prisoner and is in one of the Confederate prisons and is alright.

Even though these last battles weren't successful, I'm feeling more positive that the Union may soon win this war. Then I'll be home and we'll all be together again.
Fondest Regards,
James

Ned marched along with the rest of the captives, Rebel soldiers pointing rifles at them and urging them forward. He knew they'd finally reached Richmond. Now they'd stopped at a 3 story brick building where armed guards opened the doors and let them in. The large area inside was filled with prisoners standing, sitting and lying on the dirt floor. Ned could see doors opened to some sparsely furnished rooms and wondered how many prisoners were crowded into each of them. After the soldiers left a prisoner approached him. "What's your name, Captain?"

"I'm Captain Ned McDowell. What prison is this?"

"I'm Captain John White. You're in Libby Prison, Ned, and consider yourself very lucky. We have a woman angel who brings us food and books and other supplies. Townspeople and the guards call her "Crazy Bet" because she talks to herself and holds her head to one side, but if she's crazy she's a good kind of crazy. She lives up the hill and she and her Mother have been helping Union prisoners survive since the beginning of the War. Prisoners in other prisons don't have a Miss Elizabeth van Lew to look after them and many are starving. We have one prisoner who escaped from Castle Thunder Prison here in Richmond, was captured and put in here. He says great numbers of prisoners are dying there every day and Captain Alexander, who is in charge of the prison, has been accused of extreme brutality. He thinks this prison is heaven compared to Castle Thunder." Captain White shook his head.

"Why do the guards allow this Miss van Lew in?"

Captain White smiled. "She has permission from John H. Winder, who is Commander in charge of all the prisons. Also, she brings the guards food too, and they are just about as hungry as we are. Food is scarce all over the south because both the Confederate and Union soldiers took all the farm animals and stripped the crops so there's hardly anything left. You must have seen that as you marched through."

"Yes I did. Most of the battles have been in the south so their citizens have suffered the most, I imagine."

"When Miss van Lew and her Mother come tomorrow she'll want to interview you and some of the other new prisoners. She'll talk to you when the guards aren't around. They don't bother watching her very often anymore. Tell her everything you can about the battles you were in because it may help her assist the Union. Please keep that to yourself though."

When Ned looked puzzled, Captain White just said, "Miss van Lew will explain."

Ned watched a woman about his Mother's age and a frail, bent over older woman walked into the prison and began to greet the prisoners. He could see the older woman passing out fruit and bread from a large basket and the woman who was Miss van Lew was handing out a few books and collecting some in return. He saw Captain White talk to her and point to him. Soon she managed to break away from the crowd of men around her and work her way over to him.

"Hello, Captain McDowell. I'm Elizabeth van Lew. May I talk with you a few minutes?"

"Yes, Miss van Lew. Captain White said you might want to talk with me about the battles I was in."

"Yes, but first I must explain why." Ned sat quietly as Miss van Lew explained about spying on the Confederates and how he could help. His eyes brightened when he heard how he could still be useful to the Union, even while in prison.

"I'll be glad to do anything I can to help us win the War." Ned told her about the Wilderness and Spotslyvania battles and how he and others thought General Grant made a mistake at Cold Harbor, fighting against such well fortified soldiers. He looked down at his feet. "I don't understand, Miss van Lew. We lost so many men in such a short time and the Rebels lost hardly any men. I don't know if my friend, James, survived, because I was captured and led off before I had a chance to look for him."

"I'm sorry about your friend. When the war is over perhaps you can search for him. But for now, we need to do all we can to bring this terrible war to an end."

Mary Bowser looked around President Davis' office and smiled to herself. I'm so honored that I can help Miss van Lew and her Mother in their work. I'd never been able to have an education if it weren't for them. After the war I'll go back to Boston and finish and then I'll be a nurse and can help my people. Until then I'm a spy.

Tonight Ben will call on me and take what I've written to his friend who will get it to Miss van Lew. Not only am I able to take information off his desk, but sometimes when President Davis is in a room, talking with his generals, I'll bring them glasses of water. Then I'll just stand in a corner as if waiting for further orders. Often they would continue to talk about their plans. The President and most white people in the south think all Negroes are stupid so they can't imagine that I'm able to read and pass information onto the Union. They are the stupid ones.

Mary peeked out the door of President Davis' office and looked up and down the hall. No one was coming. Now she could get to work. She began to dust his desk and then dropped all pretense and began to look through his papers, committing to memory the ones that showed troop movements. The door opened and she had the presence of mind to hold the papers in one hand and pretend to dust under where they'd been. "What are you doing, Mary?" President Davis entered and walked toward her.

"Jes dusting yer desk, President Davis." She put the papers down upside down and looked up at him.

"Fine, but you need to leave now. I have work to do." He waved a hand toward her in a gesture of dismissal.

That was close. Mary sighed with relief.

Rose O'Neal Greenhow shielded her eyes and peered out at the seemingly unending sea. She thought she could finally see some shoreline. It was September 18· and the blockade runner she was on, the Condor, was getting close to the North Carolina shoreline. She could hardly wait to get home.

The Captain came up to her. "Miss Greenhow, we've been spotted by a Union gunboat, but you needn't worry. These blockade-runners are built to outrun the gunboats."

"Where are we, Captain?"

"We're just off the coast near Wilmington, North Carolina. I've given the order to go up the Cape Fear river because I believe it will increase our chance of escape."

Rose Greenhow clasped her hands together and looked up at the Captain. "We must escape! I can't be captured by the Union. I don't know what they'd do to me this time."

Just then someone called out for the Captain, he excused himself and returned to his post. Miss Greenhow's eyes followed him, a worried expression on her usually pleasant face. If I'm captured they'll put me in a Union prison and I may not get out. Henry Wilson will be in Washington, far away from a Union prison down South, so he may not be too concerned about what I might say. And the Union will take away the gold I earned from my memoirs. I can't have that happen!

Passengers on the Condor watched as the blockade runner left the ocean waters and began to travel full speed on the Cape Fear river. They could see the union gunboat following at a distance. Suddenly there was a crash and they were thrown violently onto the deck. The ship had stopped and shipmates were running everywhere, trying to discover what was wrong. Rose heard someone yell out, "We've hit a sandbar. We're grounded."

The Captain came onto the deck and people gathered around him. "I'm sorry, but we can't get the ship off the sandbar. The Union gunboat will be here soon so I advise you to collect your things and wait for the soldiers to board."

"Where will they take us, Captain?" a woman passenger asked in a trembling voice. Her husband put his arm around her.

"I imagine we'll be taken to a nearby Union prison. You passengers shouldn't have to worry. It will be me and my crew who they'll be interested in. Now, go and get yourselves ready to debark."

Rose Greenhow waited until most of the passengers had left for their rooms. "Captain, I must not be captured. Is there any way I can get to shore?" Two passengers stopped to listen.

"Miss Greenhow, we have a lifeboat, but I'd advise against it. The waters are very choppy and it would be extremely dangerous."

"I don't care. It's better than staying here, knowing I'll go to prison. Please get the lifeboat ready for me. Do you think any others would like to go as well?"

One of the two passengers spoke up. "We prefer not to be captured. We'll go with you."

Soon the three had gathered their belongings and, against the advice of the Captain, who again warned them about the rough waters, had been helped into the lifeboat. Two of the crew members went with them. They soon discovered the Captain was right. The little lifeboat tossed and turned on the waves and they made little progress toward shore. The oars were useless so all they could do was to hang on and hope the wind would soon die down. When Rose looked back she could see soldiers climbing over the sides of the blockade runner. At least they can't get my gold. Just then a huge wave picked up the small boat and tossed it into the air. Rose, the two passengers, and the crew members were thrown into the rough water. Rose struggled, but her gold was heavy and it pulled her down. Within moments it was over.

The next morning a fisherman walked along the shore, looking for a good fishing spot. What's that? Looks like a body. He bent over, seeing that it was a woman who had drowned. Something around her neck sparkled in the sunlight. Gold pieces! He checked further and found several more hidden in her underwear. Hannah warned me I'd better come back with fish for tonight. I don't think she'll mind if I bring these back instead. He put the gold in his pocket, turned around and headed home, a very happy expression on his face.

"President Davis, Miss Rose O'Neal Greenhow has been found dead on a beach near Wilmington, N. C. She was trying to escape capture by a Union gunboat and her lifeboat overturned."

"I want you to make arrangements for a military funeral. She did so much for the Confederacy that she deserves that."

A military funeral was held on October 1, 1864, in Wilmington, NC. Miss Rose O'Neal Greenhow was laid out in state, a confederate flag for a shroud.

December 25, 1864
Dear Margaret,
I'm certain you've heard that Atlanta was captured by Sherman's Army on September 2. That helped President Lincoln get reelected and put us much closer to winning this awful war. Sherman then began a March to the Sea, destroying everything in a 300 mile long

path of destruction, 60 miles wide. When he reached Savannah he telegraphed President Lincoln offering him Savannah as a Christmas present. Also, in December, Hood's Rebel Army was crushed at Nashville by Federals, including some Negro troops. The tide of the war is definitely turning.

General Lee's numbers of soldiers is rapidly diminishing, through death, capture and desertion. Our gunboats are keeping out the blockade runners with their supplies. The Rebels are running out of food. I don't think it'll be long now. This will be the last Christmas without you, and I am happy about that.
See you soon.
Fondest Regards,
James

Chapter 18

1865

Henry rushed into the main room of Margaret and James' home, waving a newspaper. "It's happened! On January 31, 1865, Congress approved an Amendment to the Constitution, abolishing slavery. Now it's not just in the States that were in the Confederacy—it's all the States. And the war is almost over from what James and the newspapers tell us. Soon James will be home!"

Elizabeth van Lew knocked and, after hearing a "Come in," poked her head in her Mother's room. "Mother, I need to talk with you."

"What is it, dear?"

"As you know, the Confederates have taken or killed all our cows, chickens, and mules and horses from our farm except for one horse, which I've kept hidden in the smoke-house. However, it's no longer safe there. I need to save that horse in case I have to use it to pass on a message. I understand the Rebels are so desperate for food they are eating all the mules. And they can get a high price in town for a horse as the military have most of the horses now." Elizabeth paused and looked her Mother in the eye. "I'm proposing that we stable our last horse in the study."

"What?! You want to keep the horse in the house? What are you thinking?"

"It won't be for long, Mother. It's the first of March and people are saying the war is almost over. Then the soldiers will be going home and there won't be a need for horses for the war effort. Joe is going to help me put down straw in the study so if the horse stomps he won't be heard. And the study is in the back of the house so people won't be able to hear him from the street. Joe will clean out the room early every morning. Besides, the towns people call me 'Crazy Bet' now so if they find out I'm keeping a horse in the house they'll just say, 'That's just Crazy Bet.'" She smiled at her Mother.

"Oh, what does it matter? Just try to keep him quiet and don't let him get loose and run through the house." Mrs. van Lew shook her head in disbelief.

"Thank you, Mother."

Three weeks later Elizabeth was in her nightclothes and brushing her long brown hair when she heard sounds coming from outside her window. What's that? Sounds like men's voices. She peered out her window and saw several men standing there, holding torches. Suddenly there was a loud pounding on their heavy wooden door. She ran down the stairs, fervently hoping her Mother wouldn't wake up. As she opened the door one of the men stepped forward. "We want you and your Mother and the servants to leave the house immediately. We are going to burn it down because we don't want traitors like you in our town. You'll have to go somewhere else because you're not wanted here." There was a murmured "Yes" from the men.

Elizabeth's heart was beating rapidly, but she spoke in a firm, clear voice. "Is that right? You know, don't you, that the war has almost ended. The Union soldiers are advancing on Petersburg and soon after that they'll be marching into Richmond. General Grant happens to know me and I know each and every one of you. Believe me when I say that if you burn down my house General Grant will receive a list of all your names and where you live and you'll find your homes burned to the ground too. I don't think the soldiers will worry if people are in them when they burn either." The men heard in her firm, steely voice that she meant what she said and, grumbling to themselves, took their departure.

April 9, 1865
Dear Margaret,
This terrible, killing war is finally over! On April 2, we began a general advance and broke through Lee's lines at Petersburg. Lee was forced to evacuate. The Confederate Capital of Richmond was next. We entered after the Rebels evacuated, and raised the Stars and Stripes. Today General Lee surrendered to General Grant.

I was able to accompany General Ulysses S. Grant to the the village of Appomattox Court House in Virginia, where he accepted General Robert E. Lee's surrender. I must say General Grant was exceedingly generous, allowing the Rebel officers to keep their sidearms and permitting soldiers to keep their horses and mules. I heard Lee convinced Grant to let the officers keep their horses because they'd need them to plant spring crops. After the papers were signed, General Lee, mounted his horse, Traveller, and addressed the troops who were with him, saying, "After four years of arduous service marked by unsurpassed courage and fortitude the Army of Northern Virginia has been compelled to yield to overwhelming numbers and resources."

I supposed you heard President Lincoln's Inaugural Address. He doesn't want revenge on the poor southerners. He said, "With malice toward none; with charity for all..." I agree that forgiveness is needed to heal our Nation and help us move forward.

Your family and my family have suffered enough, Margaret. Since I am in Virginia, I'm going to visit both families before I return home. I can't wait to take you in my arms, but I need to check on our families to see if they are alright. I'll be home as soon as I can, never to leave you again.
Fondest Regards,
James

James waited outside Libby Prison. He'd learned that Ned was in there and knew the prisoners were to be released that day. Several soldiers were present to escort the prisoners to a Union camp where they would be able to have a good meal, receive new clothes and clean up. They're coming out now. Oh, I see him! "Ned! Ned!" Ned turned, recognized him, and greeted him with a big smile.

"James, it's so good to see you! I didn't know if you were still alive or not." His voice caught. "So many of our friends aren't."

"Yes, but I'm glad we both are. Now let's go to camp where you can eat as much as you want. You look very thin." He looked down at Ned's clothes. "And you certainly could use a change of clothing."

"I wouldn't be alive today except for an angel named Miss van Lew, who, I heard, spent her entire fortune feeding us prisoners and bringing us books."

Ned joined James later that evening. "It's the first time I've had a full stomach in almost a year. And I no longer smell!"

"I have something for you." James handed over Ned's knapsack. "I found this after the Battle of Cold Harbor, but I couldn't find you. I could only conclude that you may have been taken prisoner. That's why I started checking the prisons as soon as the war was over. I also collected your mail for you. Here it is."

James gave four packets to Ned, whose eyes lit up. "These are from my Father. Remember, I told you he was so angry I was fighting for the Union and said I was a traitor to the South." Ned quickly tore open the first packet. "Oh, James, he wants me to come home. He misses me."

"That's wonderful news, Ned. You are due back pay, which should get you to Maryland. We'll celebrate tonight and I'll see you off tomorrow before I leave to see my Mother and Father."

Lewis tied up his horse to a broken down fence in front of the home where he'd been told Elizabeth lived with her Father. He could see the barn had almost been burned to the ground, the lawn was overgrown, and everything was too quiet. He knocked on the door and an elderly Negro with curly gray hair answered. He asked if he could speak to Mr. Wells and his daughter, and was escorted into a parlor containing nothing but a faded sofa and two worn chairs. He noticed there were two paintings on the wall but otherwise the room was quite barren. He dreaded what he had to do, but there was no way of escaping it. He stood up straight and waited until they were in the room.

"Mr. Wells and Miss Wells, my name is Lewis Burns. I was a good friend of John Ramsey during the war."

"Oh, Mr. Burns, have you brought news of him? Will he be coming soon?", Elizabeth patted her hair and straightened her dress, a broad smile on her face. Lewis could see that Mr. Wells had an idea why he was there, but Elizabeth apparently didn't. Mr. Wells motioned for him to sit down. Elizabeth sat next to him and turned toward him, waiting for a reply.

"I'm sorry, but John was killed in Gettysburg. He asked me to get a letter to you. After the battle I looked for him but couldn't find him or his knapsack." Lewis paused as Elizabeth began crying. "He often talked of you and couldn't wait to get back to you." He hesitated. "John was worried about something else and explained about it in a letter. Since I don't have the letter I thought I should tell you what that something is."

Elizabeth and her Father listened as John told about Robert Jones being their Captain and how he seemed to deliberately put John in harm's way. Mr. Wells spoke up. "That doesn't surprise me. He seemed to be a very wicked man."

"Do you mean that John might have survived if it hadn't been for Robert putting him in the battle front?"

"I don't know that for certain, but Captain Jones' orders certainly increased his chances of being hit. The reason I'm telling you this is that Captain Jones told John once that he was going to get you back, Elizabeth, and that John wouldn't be able to stop him. John thought if he was killed that Captain Jones would return here and want to court you again."

Elizabeth's eyes blazed. "I'll have nothing to do with that murderer!"

"You certainly won't, Elizabeth. He won't come near you!" Mr. Wells walked over to the sofa and shook Lewis' hand. "Thank you for bringing us this news. You are invited to stay for dinner, and if you have a long way to travel tomorrow, you are welcome to stay here tonight."

"Thank you. I'd like that."

The next morning after breakfast Lewis caught Elizabeth by herself. "I know this is too soon, because you just lost your fiance' and John was a good man. I enjoyed our talk last night and would like to get to know you better. Would it be alright if I begin to call on you?"

Elizabeth smiled up at him. "I'd like that, Lewis. I, too, enjoyed our talk."

"I need to go home and spend some time with my family, but I could return two weeks from today if that would be alright with you and your Father."

"It's fine with me, but you had probably better speak to my Father. He's in the library. She smiled at Lewis' anxious expression. "Don't worry, Lewis. He told me last night that he likes you."

James rode away from camp on an old brown horse he was able to buy off a Union cavalry soldier who now had other transportation. When he reached the plantation of Thomas Wells, he hesitated. It's good I'm not in Union uniform. Elizabeth and her Father and Margaret's Father and Mother wouldn't appreciate seeing a Union officer now-or ever, he added to himself. I don't know if Mr. Wells will even remember me. They came to some of the balls, but quit coming after Elizabeth's Mother died. He dismounted, tied his horse to the fence, walked to the door and knocked. An elderly Negro took his name and then led him to the parlor.

Soon Mr. Wells appeared. "James, it's good to see you after all these years. Elizabeth will be down shortly. What have you been doing?"

"I married Margaret Ramsey. We have a boy and a girl, and we live in Canada now."

"Canada! Why did you go there? Have you been in the war?"

"Yes I have. I'm on my way to see my Mother and Father before returning to Canada."

"Glad you survived the war. So many of our Southern soldiers didn't. We should have won, but the North had more soldiers and more resources. That's what General Lee said anyway. Here's Elizabeth." Since Mr. Wells was assuming he fought for the Confederates, James was glad the conversation could now turn to Elizabeth and the purpose for which he had come.

"Hello Elizabeth. I'm James. I haven't seen you since you were about eleven. You've grown into a beautiful woman."

"Let's sit down." Mr. Wells motioned, and he and Elizabeth sat on the sofa. James looked at both of them and then handed John's letter to Elizabeth.

"I don't know if you've heard that John is dead." He paused as Elizabeth bowed her head slowly in acknowledgment. "I found him after the battle. He was still alive and insisted I get his letters out of his knapsack and get them to you, his Mother and Father, and his sister."

Elizabeth tore the envelope open and began to read. Tears coursed down her cheeks. She looked up at her Father. "He's saying he loves me and he's also warning me about Robert Jones." She turned to James. "Lewis, a friend of John's, stopped by a few days ago. He told us about John's death and said he was to deliver the letter to us, but couldn't find the knapsack, so delivered the message in person. He also warned us about Robert Jones and how Robert would deliberately put John in the front line, trying to get him killed so he could court me again. As if I'd see that wicked, terrible man!"

"I remember how he treated my wife and how John rescued her. You will do well to stay away from him."

"James, can you stay for supper and then stay overnight? We'd love to have you."

"Thank you, but I'm not too far from Margaret's Mother and Father, and I need to tell them about John as well."

"By the way James? Where's your uniform?"

"James? Would you like another drink? You look too warm," Elizabeth added in concern.

Beads of sweat began to run down James's forehead. He glanced out the window, toward his horse."Ah, well. You see, Mr. Wells, I'm saving it for a different occasion." James turned slowly, avoiding Mr. Well's eyes.

"What's with that odd look, my boy? No need to be ashamed of your service, son! We very nearly won the war!" Mr. Wells patted him on the back.

James gave a quick bow, rose, said his good-byes and rode off, thankful that Elizabeth and her Father hadn't discovered he was a Union soldier. Unfortunately, Margaret's Mother and Father would know.

"James! Come in." Bella held the door wide open and reached out to envelop him in her plump arms. "Mistress will be so glads ter see yer. Come wid me." Bella led James to the parlor where his Mother-in-law was sewing in a corner of the room and his Father-in-law appeared to be passed out on the sofa, a whiskey bottle on the floor next to him.

"James!" Lillian Ramsey dropped her sewing and came running toward him, giving him a big hug. "Are Margaret and the children with you?"

"No, they're in Canada. The war is over so I can finally go home to them. I wanted to drop by and see how you're doing."

"Did you hear John was killed?" Lillian wiped a tear from her eye.

"So you know? I found him after the battle and he was still alive. He asked me to give you this." James handed the envelope to her as she sat down in the chair. When she opened it she began to cry.

"He says he loves us and that he hopes he'll be home to work on the plantation because he's discovered he loves the land. He wants to marry Elizabeth and have several children." She looked at James. "What are we going to do, James? We counted on John coming home and taking over for his Father. Look at him." Lillian pointed to her husband. "He's not good for anything anymore. All he does is drink. Bella and George run the plantation. I can't do anything because of my delicate condition. I don't know what we'll do." She put her head in her hands and burst into tears.

"Margaret and I think you, Charles, Bella and George should come to Canada with me. The house needs a lot of repair and you can't farm with so little help. You can leave the land to the Negroes who are still with you. George and Bella can't keep on running everything here, but they might enjoy helping us run our farms in Canada. What to you think? We'd love to have you with us." He leaned forward and looked intently at Lillian.

"I'm not going anywhere. This is my home and I intend to die here. And don't take Bella and George with you. I need them!" Lillian folded her arms and gave James a determined look.

Later James sneaked out of the house and walked down the hill to Bella and George's cabin. What shall I say to them? We planned to invite them to Canada too, but how would Margaret's Mother survive without them?

George opened the door. "James, come in. Bella done tells me yer here. Her be in de garden, but her comes now."

"Good to see you, George."

Bella came bustling in and soon they were catching up on the news. "George and Bella, you should see your great grandson, Sam. He's doing very well in school and loves to write stories. He lives with Henry, who loves him and treats him as his own son. They work together on their farm. Sam is really good with horses, like you, George." George rewarded James with a big smile. "Now Henry has found himself a wonderful woman and they will soon be married. They are waiting until I return to be in the wedding. Sam really likes Mary and already thinks of her as his Mother. He knows about his real Mother and is proud of what she did for him. Margaret says he's writing a story about it."

"I'd sure likes ter see him," exclaimed Bella.

James hesitated. "That's one reason I'm here. Margaret and
I would like her Mother and Father and you and George to come to
Canada to live with us. George, we have two farms and 4 horses
and we could use your help. Bella, Margaret could use some
assistance with the home and the children. We have a school for
both Negroes and white children and she'd like to teach more, but
can't get away with little Rose to look after."

Bella glanced at George and then at James. "What do de
Mistress says 'bout dis?"

"She says she's staying here, but..."

"But?" Bella prompted curiously.

"I think if you two go she'll have to leave. She and Charles
can't stay here by themselves. They could be persuaded to come
with us. "

Bella shook her head. "Us'n kaint leaves. I done took care
ob de Mistress since her a little girl. Her won't go and I's kaint
leaves her behind." George nodded in agreement.

The next day James said good-bye and rode off to see his
Father and Mother. He was worried. I certainly hope they are
doing better than Margaret's Mother and Father!

"I'd like to see Miss Elizabeth Wells, please."

"May I say who is calling?" the gray haired Negro asked,
blocking the entrance.

"My name is Captain Robert Jones, and I have news of her
fiance'."

"Just a minute, please." The servant, who had been warned
about Captain Jones, went to tell Miss Elizabeth.

"I was afraid he'd come. Go find Father. I think he's out in
the barn. Tell him to bring his gun. I don't expect trouble, but he's a
wicked man, we know that."

Elizabeth stayed in the library while the servant left to fetch
her Father. Robert Jones saw the servant leave, and suspecting
something was amiss, opened the door to the library and entered.

Elizabeth managed to remain calm, although her heart was beating faster.

"Please excuse my unannounced entrance, Elizabeth, but I didn't feel like waiting for your servant to announce me, especially since he seems to have left the house."

"That's alright, Robert, please come in. My servant is just running an errand for me. Why are you here?"

"I bring you news of John Ramsey, your fiance'. It saddens me to tell you that he was killed in one of the battles. He fought bravely." John moved over to the sofa where Elizabeth was sitting and sat down beside her.

"Yes, I've heard he fought bravely, even though you persisted in trying to kill him off by putting him in the front line. I would like you to leave now." Elizabeth stood up, frowning, her arms crossed.

Robert stood and glared at her. "I was going to ask you if I could court you now that you are no longer engaged, but I can see that someone has poisoned you against me. If I can't marry you, I'm going to have you now. I haven't been with a woman for a very, very long time and you'll just have to do." Robert pulled his gun out of its holster and aimed it at Elizabeth's chest. "Now take your clothes off, and hurry!"

Elizabeth, with trembling hands, started to undress. Robert, who couldn't wait, begin to rip off the dress and the petticoats. Then he threw her onto the sofa, pulled down his trousers, and started to mount her. Elizabeth saw the manic look in his eyes and realized with horror that she was the sole target of his focus. At that moment Mr. Wells burst into the room and pointed a rifle at Robert. "Get off her," he growled. Robert stood up, his trousers at his ankles. Elizabeth quickly covered herself with an afghan.

"You wouldn't kill me, Mr. Wells. Nothing happened. Here, give that to me." He pulled up his trousers and started toward Mr. Wells, arm outstretched for the rifle.

"Stop right there or I'll shoot."

"You couldn't kill anyone, old man." Robert laughed and continued to walk toward him.

"I warn you—one more step..." Robert lunged for the rifle, but Mr. Wells had his finger on the trigger and pulled it. The gun went off. Robert jolted, and with a surprised look on his face, sank to the floor.

"Oh, what did I do? I didn't mean to kill him!" Mr. Wells stared at the bleeding body and dropped the gun as the servant ran into the room. The three of them looked down at Robert, no one saying anything. Finally Elizabeth spoke up. "Could you avert your eyes so I can run to my room and get dressed? Then I guess we'd better figure out what to do with the body." Elizabeth made it to her room, sat down on her bed, and began to shake. I can't be like this. I need to be strong for Father. He's so upset about killing a man. After all, Robert didn't do anything to me except undress me. Still, I feel so dirty, so embarrassed.

After Elizabeth returned to the library she sat at a table with her Father, Abram, the gray haired servant, standing nearby. Elizabeth still felt embarrassed that her Father and their servant had seen her with nothing covering her but an afghan. I'm just glad Father came in before...She stopped. It was unthinkable what could have happened.

Elizabeth's Father spoke. "I think we could bury him down by the river. The ground is softer there and Abram and I could dig a big enough hole. No one need know he was ever here." He looked at Abram, who nodded.

"Yes, we could do that." Elizabeth paused. "I just keep thinking of Robert's Father and Mother, who would never know what happened to him."

"You're right. We know the Jones family and his Father and Mother are good people. They would want to bury him on their plantation. We must take his body to them."

"If we wait a little, Father, Lewis said he'd be returning today. He could help us move the body and take it to Robert's Mother and Father."

It wasn't long before Lewis rode in and helped to build a wooden coffin. After the coffin was loaded onto the wagon Mr. Wells, Elizabeth and Lewis set out to do the difficult task of delivering a dead son to a Mother and Father. When they arrived Mr. and Mrs. Jones welcomed them and invited them into the parlor. Elizabeth, her voice catching, explained what led to their son's death, with Mr. Wells saying more than once that he didn't mean to shoot Robert. Mrs. Jones sobbed while Mr. Jones just looked serious and listened. When she finished, Elizabeth and her Father waited anxiously. Finally, Mr. Jones, looking at Mr. Wells and Elizabeth, said, "We want you to know we don't blame you. We've known something was wrong with Robert since he was a little boy."

Mrs. Jones wiped her eyes and looked up. "Yes, he was always very mean to his little sister and seemed to enjoy torturing animals. He even lit a fire one time..."

"While we loved him it's almost a relief that he's died. He can't hurt anyone anymore." Mr. Jones looked at Lewis, Elizabeth and her Father. "Now, can I ask you if you could help us bury our son?"

James stopped his horse before the front gates and looked with fondness at the home where he'd grown up. He noticed the grass was longer and the house could use some paint, but nothing had burned down at least. When he rode his horse to the home and dismounted his Father came around the corner of the house, paused to look, and then ran towards him, shouting his name. After hugs and a big welcome by his Father, he was led into the house where his Mother hugged him, amidst tears. A servant brought coffee and they sat down in the parlor to catch up on the last ten years. James was glad to see that his Mama and Papa, while having acquired gray hair and a few wrinkles, still seemed to be in good health. A squeal brought his attention to the door where a beautiful, young girl was running toward him. He stood and was wrapped in her arms as she exclaimed, "Oh James, I've missed you so much!"

James pushed her away at arms length and looked her up and down. "Who is this beautiful young woman who is attacking me? I have no idea who this could be." He pretended to be perplexed.

"James, I'm your sister, Sarah. Don't pretend you don't know who I am."

"Not my little sister! She only came up to the top of my leg when I left. You can't be her."

"You left ten years ago when I was only six. Did you think I'd stay a six year old all this time?"

James laughed. "No, I guess not. But I had no idea you'd turn into such a beautiful woman." He turned to his Father. "Do you have to keep many men away from her?"

"   Yes, all the time. She has so many suitors sometimes they are lined up at the door."

After the evening meal James and his Father discussed the plantation. Mr. Graydon explained that fifteen of the Negroes stayed on and he'd given them land and paid them what he could. That way he'd been able to keep a large garden and have some of the land in tobacco. They were doing better than many of their neighbors, including Margaret's parents. He knew about John being killed in the war and wondered how they would manage, especially with Mr. Ramsey's drinking.

"Yes, I'm worried about that too. I don't know what to tell Margaret. I tried to get them to go to Canada with me, but Lillian won't go and Charles is in no condition to make a decision. Bella and George are running the plantation and won't leave the Ramseys, but I wonder how long they can keep it up."

"That is a concern, James, but there's not much you and Margaret can do from Canada. It's late now, and I guess we'd better go to bed. It's so good to have you home! Good night." James' Father got up and headed for the stairs.

"Good night, Father."

It had been difficult to say good-bye to his family after only two weeks, but James knew Margaret would be expecting him. He found it slightly amusing that he'd felt somewhat protective of Sarah when suitors came to the house. He was relieved to discover that they all seemed to be nice young men. And he soon realized that Sarah was a strong, independent woman who could take care of herself.

Then there had been the long trip to Canada, some of the way by horse and the rest by train. A neighbor had been passing the train station and had insisted on giving him a ride to the farm. Here he was, but something didn't seem right. The trees around the house were burnt, and the house seemed different. Yes, it was facing a slightly different direction for one thing. He approached slowly, looking around him as he went.

Margaret opened the door upon hearing his knock. "James!" She looked at him, mouth open, then ran into his arms. "We didn't know you were coming." She self consciously pushed back her hair. "Come in. Come in. Would you like some coffee?"

"Hello, Margaret! Yes, coffee would be good. Where are the children?"

"Ben and Sam are working in the barn with Henry. Rose is playing with..." She paused, looking uncomfortable. "Let me make the coffee and then I'll tell you about a few things that have happened since you've been gone."

Soon they were sitting at the table and James was waiting expectantly. "I guess you noticed the burned trees and that the house is slightly different." James nodded. "We had a fire and Henry saw it from his place. He and Sam brought us to the neighbors in town, along with some of our animals. They saved our lives. Everything was gone though. Henry, Joe, the boys, and our neighbors rebuilt the barn and the house. Joe made most of the furniture and the neighbors contributed some. Henry and Sam stayed with us for a few weeks until their house could be built after the planting season.

"When did all this happen?"

"It was the middle of April, 1864, shortly after Henry returned from the war."

"Is there anything else you neglected to tell me, Margaret?"

Margaret looked down at her lap. "Yes, Henry lost an arm in the war." James looked shocked. "Oh, and you were gone so long that Mary and Henry couldn't wait so they had a nice wedding in the Methodist Church. Mary and Henry and Sam are living in their rebuilt house and are very happy."

Just then a little blond girl and a small brown haired boy ran into the room from the bedroom, yelling "Mama". Margaret bent down to give each of them a hug. "You can see Rose has grown since you left. She was just two then and she's six now. Rose, this is your Papa." Rose immediately hid behind Margaret's chair while Robert James crawled onto her lap. "I guess she doesn't remember you." Margaret looked down. "This little boy is your son, Robert James. I knew I was having a baby when you left, but you wanted to join the Union Army. I didn't want to keep you from that so I didn't tell you."

James, a very angry expression on his face, exclaimed, "You didn't tell me you were having a baby! What happened after that? This little boy is, what, over three years old? Why didn't you let me know sometime during those three years? Didn't you think I'd like to know I had a son?" He stood up and walked to the door. Turning toward Margaret, he said, "I'm going out to the barn to see Henry and the boys."

Ben, Sam and Henry rushed to James as he entered the barn door, hugging him and all talking at once. They sat on haystacks and talked until Henry spoke up, "Boys, get back to work. James and I are going to walk around so I can show him the improvements we've made." As they set out, Henry turned to James. "I can see you're upset. Want to tell me about it?"

James burst out, "Yes, I'm upset! Margaret hid everything from me. I didn't know about the fire, your arm, your marriage and, most of all, she didn't even tell me I had a son. How can I forgive her for that? He may not even be my child!"

"James, I know he's your child. I came in one day shortly after you left and she was sick. When I asked her what was wrong, she said she was having your baby, but didn't tell you because you'd think you had to stay. She knew you wanted to join the Union army."

"What about after that? She had a lot of time to tell me and just didn't do it."

"Yes, I know. Mary and I both urged her to write you, but she'd let so much time go by she thought you'd be angry with her and it might make it harder for you in the army. She convinced herself that it would be easier if she waited until your return and you saw your son."

"It doesn't make it easier. I missed out on three years of my son's life, not even reading about how he was growing up. I don't feel like he's my son. He's a stranger. He could belong to anyone else and it wouldn't matter to me."

"Don't say that, James. Robert James is a smart, loving little boy. It won't take you long to love him just as you do Ben and Rose."

"I don't think so."

A few weeks later Mary and Margaret were in the kitchen getting the meal. "What's wrong, Margaret? You seem preoccupied. Is James settling in? I know he was gone a long time and the Army changed Henry at first. We had some adjustments to make when he returned."

"Oh, Mary, I don't know what to do. James pushes us all away. Rose wants hugs and he just gives her stiff ones and won't let her sit on his lap. Robert James puts his hand on James' knee and James just takes his hand off and pushes him away. Robert James will look up at James and then take his toy to a corner of the room and just sit and watch him. James doesn't say he loves me or put his arm around me like he used to, and if he does want me in bed it is quick and almost rough. He hasn't forgiven me for not telling him about Robert James. Then, he sometimes yells out during the night and really scares me. Occasionally he'll sit up and yell. When I ask him about it, he just turns over and doesn't answer. The other day I dropped a pan and he jumped and looked so frightened. We can't go on like this!"

"I'm so sorry. All I can tell you is about the yelling and the loud noises. Henry yelled during the night and jumped if there was a loud noise when he first came back. He still occasionally does it. He finally was able to tell me a little about his war experiences and that the loud noises made him relive the cannons and guns and the noise they made. The yelling at night was from the bad war experiences, seeing so many wounded and dying, the guns going off, the marches, the lack of food, and, of course, with Henry, having his arm cut off. I don't think they will ever truly be the same. They went through an awful time. Henry still can't talk about it. We just have to be patient and love them."

"Thank you. I suppose it helps to understand that, but I don't know what to do about his being so angry with me. I hate to see Rose and Robert James looking puzzled when their Father pushes them away. He's better with Ben and Sam, but is somewhat distant around them too. He seems like a different person than the husband and father who left here four years ago. How do I get the man I love back again?" Margaret wiped away a tear and looked sorrowfully at Mary.

"Perhaps Henry could talk to him. He can explain to James about having the night yelling and the reaction to loud noises so James doesn't think it's just him. I don't know if he can do anything about James being angry with you and pushing away the children. That may take time. It may help when he gets back to the farm work with Henry and the boys. He may gradually just get over the anger."

"And if he doesn't?"

"James, you've been home two months now. I understand about your yelling at night and your reaction to loud noises—that they are related to your war experiences, which must be more horrible than Mary and I can ever imagine. What I don't understand is how you can push away your children. They didn't do anything to you and all they want is for you to love them. I know you haven't forgiven me, but please don't take it out on the children." Margaret stood, looking up at him. She'd kept this in a long time and it was a relief to finally say it.

"I don't know if I can ever forgive you. I just don't feel close to the children anymore, especially Robert James, who is like a stranger to me. And the others have grown so much since I last saw them. Rose was only two. I just can't seem to adjust to all the changes. Perhaps I should just go away for awhile since I seem to upset you and the children. I could stay with Joe and Liza."

Margaret looked down at her feet. "Do you really think that would help? I would think it would make matters worse— especially with the children. You are gone for four years and then go away again for no reason." She looked up. "Please consider what you are doing if you want us to be a family again." She turned and went into the kitchen.

James left the house and walked over to Henry and Mary's. "Come in, James. Have a seat. Mary's in town, visiting her Mother and Father, and she has Sam with her. I believe Ben is in the barn with the children, looking at the new colt. What's wrong?"

"I just told Margaret I didn't know if I could ever forgive her and suggested I go to stay with Joe and Liza for awhile. She thinks I'm upsetting the children since I can't seem to get close to them, and I guess she's right. I have no feeling for Robert James and I don't want him near me. I can't hug him or let him climb on my lap. I'm not even comfortable hugging little Rose. I don't know what's happened to me," James exclaimed, his hand clasped to his forehead.

"I don't know how you can work this through, James, except to give it time. I don't think it would help at all by leaving. Please stay and keep trying. This is no time to walk off. You won the battle down south; now fight the battle with yourself here. "

It was three weeks later when James looked up from reading the newspaper, noticing that Margaret was rushing back and forth to the boys' bedroom, carrying a wet cloth in her hand. "What's wrong?"

"Robert James is still coughing and is now running a high fever. The doctor came today when you were working in the field and gave him some medicine for the cough and for the fever, but it doesn't seem to be helping. Could you get Mary to come over, please?"

James immediately left and soon returned with Mary. He saw Mary and Margaret coming periodically to the kitchen for more cool water and rushing back into Robert James' room. He could hear Robert James continuously coughing, while giving occasional little weak cries. Hours later Mary came out. "I'm having Ben and Rose stay another night with Henry and me because we don't want them to be exposed. I'll go home for a few hours sleep and then come back and relieve Margaret. She's had hardly any sleep for the last two nights, with Robert James coughing, and she won't leave him. James, your little boy is very ill and the doctor said today he may not make it through the night. He has pneumonia." She shook her head and quietly walked out the door.

Oh no, not that! What will Margaret and the children do if Robert James dies? They love him so much. And he is such a loving little boy. He and Ben are especially close. They sleep in the same room and I know Robert James crawls in bed with Ben almost every night. Ben will be so sad.

James got up and entered the bedroom where Margaret was sitting next to Robert James' bed, applying cold cloths to his forehead. "Let me do that for awhile. You need to get something to eat and rest."

Margaret looked up and yawned. "If you would, James. I couldn't ask Mary to stay longer, but if you could put cool cloths on his forehead and wrap him in a cool, wet blanket, I'll get something to eat. Thank you."

"Take a nap too. You haven't slept much for the last two nights. You won't be any good to Robert James if you get overtired and become ill as well. I can watch him for a few hours."

"Perhaps I'll take a half hour nap on the sofa. Thank you, James."

James wet the cloth from the pot filled with cool water and applied it to Robert James' forehead. His skin is so hot. James wet the already damp blanket lying nearby and wrapped him in it. Robert James moaned and didn't open his eyes. He's so little to be this sick. His hair is brown like mine, not blond like Margaret, Ben and Rose. I never noticed but his nose is shaped like mine as well and I know his eyes are brown. In fact, I definitely couldn't deny he's my son. He looks more like me than either Ben or Rose. James looked up at the ceiling. "Oh, dear God, don't let my son die!"

I noticed Margaret was talking to him while she nursed him. I wonder if it would help if he heard my voice—not that he's heard it much since I've been home. James grimaced. I know. Ben and Sam and Rose used to love my stories, especially the ones about Brer Rabbit. I'll tell him a story. And when he's well I'm going to start telling him and Rose a lot of stories. James bent over Robert James. "Do you hear that, my son? I'm going to read and tell you and your sister stories, so you need to get well to hear them because you'll love my stories."

It was four hours later when James noticed Robert James' skin felt cooler to the touch. Soon after, Robert James opened his eyes, raised his arm toward his Father and said, "Papa." He then closed his eyes and fell into a deep, normal slumber. James couldn't help the tears coursing down his cheeks.

Mary crept into the room an hour later and whispered, "I notice Margaret is asleep on the sofa. How is Robert James? She bent over him, then turned toward James. "His fever is gone and he's sleeping normally. He's going to be alright! When did this happen, James?"

"About an hour ago. He woke up and said, 'Papa'. I didn't even know he knew I was his Papa." James smiled. "He's a bright little one. I'm looking forward to telling him stories."

Mary smiled back. "Do you think we should wake Margaret and tell her or let her sleep?"

"I think she'd like to know and then she can really sleep. Let me wake her." Mary nodded and James slipped out of the room.

James leaned over Margaret and shook her arm slightly. "Margaret, dear, wake up."

"Robert James! Is he alright?" Margaret sat up, looking worried.

"Yes, Margaret, our son is fine. His fever is gone and he's sleeping normally."

"I must see him. It's more than a half hour. Why did you let me sleep so long?" She walked quickly to the bedroom and tiptoed inside. After bending over Robert James and feeling his forehead she straightened up and smiled. "You're right, James. Our son is fine."

James took her in his arms and they held each other. "Yes, my dear wife, everything is fine."

It was a month later and everything on the Graydon farm really was much better, Margaret thought. Rose and Robert James loved sitting next to their Papa on the sofa and hearing his stories before they went to bed. James was working hard with Henry, Ben and Sam on the two farms, and she and James once again were showing their love for each other. James had told her he wished she'd written him about Robert James, but forgave her and that was now in the past. She'd said she was sorry and she'd never hide anything from him again. James was still yelling out in his sleep and jumping at loud noises, but it wasn't happening as often and it wasn't upsetting the family as much. James had explained to the children and all but Robert James were able to realize that it was a result of the war and wasn't about them.

"Margaret, I need to talk to you." Margaret looked up from her sewing and waited. "I never mentioned about how our parents were doing because there was so much else going on when I came home, but now I think we need to talk about it. When I visited your parents I discovered your Mother just sits in her chair, sewing, while a servant waits on her. Your Father is usually lying drunk on the sofa. Bella and George are running the plantation, with the help of six other Negroes. Bella supervises the household staff with the cooking and cleaning while George supervises the work in the garden and with the animals. They persuaded your Mother to give the Negroes some land and that's why they stayed. However, Bella and George are getting older and can't continue indefinitely."

"When I went to my family's plantation, the situation was better. My Father is still able to work and Mother manages the household servants. Father gave each of the Negroes a piece of land and pays them what he can afford after the tobacco is sold, so they have a large garden and a small tobacco crop. However, they are getting older, too, and can't continue forever. My sister will be marrying as soon as she makes up her mind which suitor she wants." James smiled. "She will probably leave and live at his or his Father's plantation. What I'm trying to say, Margaret, is I think we need to go back."

"Go back? Now?" Margaret caught her breath.

"I've been thinking about it a lot lately. Henry, Mary and Sam can live on your Father's plantation and work with Bella and George. I'm certain your Mother would agree to giving them part ownership in the plantation. Then you and I can live with my Mother and Father as they are planting tobacco and Father needs a lot more help with that. We'll live close enough that we can see each other often. What do you think?" James looked anxiously at Margaret.

"James, I don't know what to say. It's a big decision to make and I think I'll need to consider it. I do know one thing. If Henry, Mary and Sam get part of the plantation, then Bella and George deserve a part as well. They have been running the plantation by themselves for years now." She looked at James. "We are settled here in Canada, have nice farms, many friends, and our children are doing well. I hate to leave all that. Have you discussed it with Henry?"

"No, I'm waiting for you to decide, because I wouldn't go ahead without you."

"Thank you for that. How about if I think about it today and give you my decision in the morning?"

"James, I thought about it yesterday and last night. The only conclusion I can come to is that it is our duty to return to Virginia and help out your Mother and Father and my Mother and Father."

James put his arms around her. "Thank you, Margaret. That's the only decision I could come to as well. I'll talk to Henry and then we'll tell the children. We'll need to start making arrangements to sell the farms. They should bring a good price because of all the work we've put into them. I don't imagine we'll be leaving for two or three months."

"Henry, I've told you about the terrible shape the plantation of Margaret's Father and Mother is in. Bella and George are running it and can't do that very much longer. My parents are managing now, but eventually they'll need my help. I've decided, and Margaret agrees with me, that we need to return to Virginia. You and Mary and Sam will take over the Ramsey plantation and I'm certain Lillian will give you part ownership, as well as Bella and George. Margaret and I and the children will live with my Father and Mother and take on a lot of the work on their plantation." He paused and looked at Henry. "I know this is sudden, but it will take time to sell both farms and make all the arrangements, so we won't be leaving right away." James suddenly noticed Henry was just sitting there stiffly, saying nothing. "You'll need to talk to Mary and Sam about this."

Henry looked at him rather strangely, stood up and said, "Yes", and made his departure.

A day later Henry approached James in his barn. "James." He hesitated. "Mary, Sam and I would like to visit Joe and Liza and the children for a few days. Would you mind looking after our animals until we return?"

"No, of course not. Since they are Sam's family I suppose you want them to know what we're planning. Sam is going to miss his uncle, aunt, and cousins."

"Thank you, James. We'll leave early tomorrow morning."

"Glad you're back, Henry. The children missed Sam and we missed you and Mary. Five days was a long time. Did you have a good visit?" James, bent over while milking a cow, looked up and smiled at Henry.

"Yes, we did. The children are catching up and Margaret and Mary are as well. Do you have time for a talk?"

"Would you mind going with me while I check on the fence? I'm done here. Two of my cows escaped and I'm wondering how. A neighbor brought them back."

Henry cleared his throat. "I don't know how to say this, James, but Mary, Sam and I aren't going back to Virginia with you."

"What? Why?"

"We talked about it after you told me we were going and decided we want to stay in Canada. The three of us would have less prejudice here. Joe and Liza are Sam's family and are like Mary's and my family now too. Mary grew up in Canada and her Mother and Father live here. Joe has found us a property near him and we are planning to buy it when we sell our farm. It has much more land and already has a big barn. We'll stay with Joe and Liza until we build our house. Sam is thrilled he'll be living next to his cousins. We can't leave Canada, James. I'm sorry."

"I'm sorry too, and very surprised." James walked over to a large oak tree and sat down under it, Henry following his lead. "We've always been together and I guess I thought we always would. I just can't imagine my life without you. Are you certain about this, Henry?"

"Yes, we are. I wonder if you realize the difference between when we lived in Virginia and now. In Virginia, we were always together because I was your slave and had to go with you wherever you went. Here Mary, Sam and I are free and we can choose where we go. Do you realize that you didn't even ask me if I wanted to move back to Virginia, you just assumed I would—like I was still your slave?"

208

James sat there in silence for awhile, looking down at the grass. Finally he lifted his head. "You're right of course. I had no idea I still thought of you as my slave; but I must because I never did ask you. And I asked Margaret. I really did just assume you and your family would come along, without having a say in the decision." James had a stricken look on his face. "Henry, I'm so sorry! Can you forgive me for, after all these years, thinking you are still my slave?"

"Of course I forgive you. I'm not your slave, but I'm your friend, and I'll really miss you."

Three months later Mary, Henry and Sam were at the train station saying good-bye to James and Margaret, Ben, Rose and Robert James. Rose was hugging her special friend, Sam. Ben was trying not to cry about losing Sam, and Robert James was clinging to his Father in all the confusion. Margaret and Mary were hugging each other and didn't even try to stop the tears. James and Henry hugged. "Maybe we'll get back for a visit someday, Henry, or you can visit us."

"Yes, and in the meantime, we'll write and let each other know what is happening with our families."

"There's the train. It's time to board." James took Rose's hand and held Robert James while Ben shook hands with Sam and promised to write.

"Wait a minute. I have something for you." Sam handed Margaret a small package. "You told me all about my Mother, Rose--how she had such courage and sacrificed her life for you and James and Henry and me. I've always wanted to write her story and I finally did. I'm giving a copy to you and to Joe and there's an extra copy in the package for Bella and George. I don't want our families to forget what she did—how she helped us make it to freedom."

"Thank you, Sam. We'll always treasure this."

Margaret sat down on the train seat, Ben beside her. She glanced over at her oldest son and saw how unhappy he looked.

Ben was the only one who objected to leaving Canada and she'd overheard him say to Sam that he'd return someday. He might, she thought to herself. Ben's best friend all his life has been a Negro. How will he be when he encounters all the prejudice in Virginia? I would miss him, but he might be happier when he's older if he did return to Canada.

She smiled as she looked at James sitting across from her. Robert James was asleep, his head resting against his Papa. James was looking down on him, a loving expression on his face. Ever since Robert James was so sick they'd been close. Robert James followed his Papa around the house and the farm and loved to sit on his lap in the evenings, listening to stories of Brer Rabbit. Rose was sitting on the opposite side of James, staring out the window and occasionally telling her Papa to look at something, although when he'd look out, whatever Rose had seen had passed by. Rose would be alright in Virginia. She was a flexible child and could adapt wherever she went. Robert James, of course, was young enough that the plantation would quickly become his home. Margaret passed an eye over her husband again. She admired him for doing what he thought he should do, despite the hardships he would face trying to run two plantations with little help and not much money. She'd do what she could, but she'd be busy with the little ones. It would be an adjustment for both of them, but they loved each other and that would help them face any difficulty.

Margaret picked up Sam's small book and began to read. When she closed the book she wiped a tear from her eye and looked at James. "Oh, James, this is so wonderful! After reading his book I can see much of Rose in Sam—his intelligence, his eye for detail, and his writing talent. Rose used to like to write stories and she'd read them to me."

Margaret looked down at the book in her lap. "Sam not only writes about Rose, but he talked to Joe about his experiences as a pirate and has written all about that. He wrote about our escape to Canada and our life on our farms. And he's written about you and Henry serving in the Civil War. I wondered why he was always asking so many questions. The book shows how, throughout this difficult period of slavery and Civil War, our families managed to have friendships, despite our different skin color." Margaret handed the book across to James. "Sam has written our entire family history. It's something we'll always treasure and it should be passed on to Ben, to his children, and to his children's children.

PART III

THE CIVIL RIGHTS MOVEMENT

"Love is the only force capable of transforming an enemy into a friend."

Dr. Martin Luther King, Jr.

Chapter 19

1960

Daniel Craig Edwards sat in his chair, staring straight ahead,
seeing nothing. Michael had been pacing back and forth for the last
half hour, but pacing had never worked for him. It didn't matter.
Nothing mattered now that their Mother had only hours to live.
She'd survived 5 years with cancer, but this time—this time—Doc
said she wouldn't. Dad was in with her now, but they would have
their turn. What could he say to let her know what she meant to
them—to him? She was the glue that held the family together.
She'd encouraged him through his four years of University and
through his first year of law school. He could always come to her
with his problems and she'd listen. She wouldn't give advice, but
would help him work it through. That was a rare quality and one
he'd never found in anyone else.

Oh, here's Dad. He looks so old, so haggard. His parents,
Tom and Helen. They were still in love, even after 25 years of
marriage. I hope someday I have a marriage like theirs. I wonder
how he'll manage without her.

"Dan, your Mother would like to see you next, then
Michael. She wouldn't take the pain medication because she wants
to be alert when she talks with each of you, so realize that she'll be
in a lot of pain, and don't stay too long." As his Father walked
away, Dan noticed him wiping his eyes with his sleeve.

Dan approached the bed, looking down at the thin, pale
woman who had her arms outstretched toward him. He hugged her
gently and then pulled a chair next to her.

"Dan, I was so proud to attend your University graduation
and hear your speech as Valedictorian. I'd hoped I'd be here to see
you get your law degree, but it looks as if God has other plans. Just

know I'll be there in spirit." She drew her breath and Dan could see she was struggling for air. "Can you reach that box there on the dresser? That's right. Now open it. That tiny book inside is our family history. It goes back to the 1800's and was written by a fourteen year old black boy named Sam who lived in Canada at the time. It has been passed down to the oldest child in our family from generation to generation. As you know, my maiden name is Ramsey." She started coughing.

"Mom, perhaps we should stop."

"No, Dan, this is important. Since the book is so fragile I made three copies of it so we wouldn't have to handle the original. It's my understanding that other members of what was the Ramsey side of the family—our side, and the Graydon side were given copies as well. Apparently, because of masters getting slaves pregnant, there are black and white persons in both the Ramsey and Graydon families. I'd always intended to trace the ones who are alive today, but never got around to it. Would you do that for me, Dan?" She lay back on her pillow and drew her breath.

Dan nodded. "Of course I will."

She squeezed his hand feebly. "You've always been strong and centered, knowing what you wanted in life and going after it. You have other wonderful qualities as well--your intelligence and your sensitivity to the needs of others. When I'd drag you and Michael along to help out in soup kitchens, you were always the one who, after everyone had been served, would sit down with people and listen to what they had to say. I remember how both men and women would want you to sit next to them. The smell and the way they sometimes ate wouldn't bother you like it would Michael and your Father. You do take life a little too seriously though, and need to get out more and have fun while you're young—not always have your nose in a book." She paused a moment and looked Dan in the eye.

"Because you are the strong one, Dan, I have another request. I want you to look after your Father and brother. I think I've told you that Tom, after we were married, took an additional job so I could finish college. He said at the time that he was happy as a postman, but I'd always wanted to be a teacher. He thought if I couldn't reach that goal I might resent him some day. So it is because of him I've spent many happy years as an elementary school teacher. Then, years later, he took another second job to raise extra money for your college expenses. Even though you had a scholarship to put you through, you needed money for clothes and other things. He's always been there for the 3 of us—camping trips where he taught you and Michael how to fish, volunteering at my school after his postman rounds were finished, helping at the soup kitchen and at our church. You boys and me, we've been everything to him." She paused. "I'm afraid he might have a difficult time with my death and I want you to be there for him. Can you do that?"

Dan nodded, afraid that if he tried to speak he'd break down.

"Michael will need you too, Dan. While your Father may withdraw from the world for awhile, Michael will probably act out. He already has a tendency to get into trouble at high school, and has chosen some questionable friends this, his freshman year. Michael was a surprise, because we'd been told we couldn't have another child, yet he came along 8 years after you. You know he doesn't like school and has, in the past, tried to play hookey on occasion. You've always been the academic one and Michael likes to create, to build with his hands. I don't want him, in his grief, to become angry and act out. Please, Dan, keep an eye on him and be there for him if he needs support and encouragement, because Tom may not be in any shape to do that for at least a little while." She paused and looked at him. "I'm asking a lot of you, Dan. Can you do it?"

Dan nodded, and then couldn't help saying, "What about me, Mom? Whose going to comfort me when you're gone?"

Helen had a stricken look on her face. "Oh, Dan, you're right. Even the strong need someone at certain times. You have good friends, and there is always the pastor at our Church. Please seek someone out that you can talk to. I love you so much, Dan. You and I could always talk about anything and everything, and I

215

know you'll miss that. I hope and pray you'll find someone who can support you through this time while you'll be supporting Tom and Michael. Now, could you ask Michael to come in?"

Dan gave his Mother one last hug, told her he loved her, and went to get his brother.

"Mike, are you ready? It's almost time to go to the Church." Dan entered his brother's room, finding him sprawled out across his bed, dressed in clothing he'd worn the day before. He turned him over and shook him. "You're drunk and it's almost time for Mom's funeral. Did you stay out all night, drinking?"

Mike groaned. "Not all night. Got in a 5 AM, brother dear. Go away."

"Oh no you don't. I'm helping you to the shower and then you'll get dressed and attend our Mother's funeral. Everyone will be expecting you there."

"No can do, bro. No shape to go. Tell 'em I'm sick or something." He turned over and put the pillow over his head.

Dan grabbed the pillow and shook Mike again. "Guess it's too late for you to make the funeral, but you WILL get up now, shower, and help the church ladies who are coming over to fix food for after the funeral. Now GET UP!" Dan then forcefully escorted Mike to the shower before he left for the funeral.

Tom worked his way through the crowded house until he reached Michael. "Where were you at the funeral? The Church was packed, but I still would've seen you."

"I was sick, Dad, so I stayed home and helped the church ladies get the food ready."

"You should have been at your Mother's funeral, son." Tom shook his head and walked away.

"Dad, I just got a call from Michael's school. The counselor wants to talk to you. There's an appointment with her for 5 PM tomorrow night." Tom sat in the recliner, staring at the TV screen, watching "My Three Sons", so Dan repeated what he'd said.

"I can't go, Dan. I'll write a note that you are representing me. I just can't face people."

"Dad, you need to start getting out. Mike needs you. He's drinking and getting into trouble at school. How about if I go with you?"

Tom shook his head. "No, son, I just can't."

"Dad, the counselor looked at the note you wrote and talked with me, but said you need to see her. Michael is skipping school and has let his grades slide so he's been suspended from the basketball team. You know he's always loved basketball. If he shows up at all for school he's late and disheveled looking. He may fail the year and have to repeat. She says he's hanging around boys who often get into trouble and has dropped his former friends. She knows about Mom and wonders if family counseling would help us." Dan didn't mention that he'd told her how depressed their Dad was— that he just went to work and when home he sat in his chair in front of the TV, not speaking unless spoken to, and then just answering their questions with a "Yes" or a "No".

"Dad, will you go and speak to her about Michael?" Tom just shook his head and continued to watch TV.

"Sarah, you're not going and that's final!"

"Oh yes, I am. Just 'cuz you're my big brother doesn't mean you have the right to boss me around. I'm attending Howard "U" now, just like you, and I'm entitled to take part in the sit-ins too." Sarah put her hands on her hips and looked up defiantly at her 6'2" brother. "Well, Richard, whether you approve or not, I want to help our people, not just leave it to you. Ever since Rosa Parks refused to give up her seat to that white man in Montgomery, Alabama, back in '55 and started the Montgomery Bus Boycott, things are starting to happen for us around the country. Who could believe at the time that the buses in a southern city would be integrated and that a high school in Little Rock, Arkansas, would have to integrate in 1957? And now, because of four colored men sitting at a lunch counter of Woolworth in Greensboro, North Carolina, in February, sit-ins are taking place in eleven cities, including ours. I want to be a part of this. Please, Richard." She looked up at him, a pleading look in her soft brown eyes.

"I'm a member of CORE. You know what that is, don't you, Sarah?" Sarah shook her head. "Well, it stands for Congress of Racial Equality, and they practice Gandhi's ethics of non violence. CORE believes that, when taking part in a sit-in, you can't respond when hit, kicked, spit upon, and whatever else whites want to do to you at the time. If you were with me at a sit-in I'd just have to watch them possibly do some of those things to you. I wouldn't be able to protect you, my little sister."

"I'm a big girl now and I can take care of myself."

"Sarah, when Mom and Dad died in that car crash two years ago I promised myself I'd look after you. We have their house, all paid for, and they'd even set a little money aside for our education. They both worked so hard at low paying jobs to have enough to pay off the house. Mom and Dad believed the only way black people would get ahead is by being educated. They had no idea of the sit-ins back then, but I remember how excited they were about Rosa Parks and the Bus Boycott back in '55. I'm sure they would've gotten involved in what's happening now." Richard frowned. "I'm tired of arguing with you about this. I don't like it but I guess I can't forbid your taking part."

Sarah watched, wide eyed, as neatly dressed Negroes stood outside the local Woolworth, moving to and from the lunch counter in orderly shifts. Finally it was Richard's and her turn to take a seat at the counter. White men and women stood behind them, taunting them. A middle aged, balding man put his face next to hers. "What you doing here, Nigger? How 'bout comin' home with me and givin' me a rub down?" He reached up and pulled her head back by her hair. Then he took his hand away. "Naw, I don't want no dirty little Nigger girl." He laughed, spit in her face and walked away.

Richard had risen from his counter stool, hands clenched. Another member of CORE saw he was losing control and put his hand on Richard's shoulder. "Alright Richard, it's my turn at the counter now. You can go outside for some fresh air." Richard slowly walked towards the door, turning to see if Sarah was coming.

"Hi. I'm Thomas. You must be Richard's sister, Sarah. You OK? Do you want to join your brother?"

"No, I'd like to finish out my time. I'm OK." She wiped the spit off her face, and, with a determined look, stared straight ahead.

"Roy, are you ready to fill out the membership application, in front of these witnesses, to become a member of the Ku Klux Klan?" Roy nodded and looked up at Jimmy York. "Alright, Roy, read off the application and then sign and date it."

" I, Roy Ramsey, of Birmingham, Alabama, believe in the ideals of Western, Christian Civilization and Culture and in the great people that created them, in the Constitution of the United States. I am a White person of gentile descent. I believe in the aims and objectives of the Knights of the Ku Klux Klan...I swear that I will keep secret and confidential any information I receive in quest of membership." Roy leaned over the table and affixed his signature and the date, February 1, 1960.

"Now, Roy, put your address, phone number, birth date and your occupation as service station owner next to your photograph. You know this is just the first of four stages you go through before you can become a full fledged Klan member." Roy nodded. "You know, too, that the Klan demands loyalty, secrecy and cooperation from you." Roy nodded again.

"Congratulations, Roy, you are now an official member of the Ku Klux Klan." Jimmy smiled and shook his hand.

Roy walked in the door of his shabby two bedroom home and called to his wife and son. "I've just become a member of the

Ku Klux Klan, like my Father before me, and like you will be, Bobby Joe, when you're old enough. We swear to pertect the southern way of life from white folk from the Nawth and Niggers who are trying to change things." He slammed his fist down on the table and both Betty Lou and Bobby Joe jumped. "We'll keep it the way God intended, with the man out workin', the woman in the kitchen, boys workin' with their Fathers in their business, and the Niggers in their place, workin' for the white people. Niggers ain't as smart as Whites, and were meant to always be slaves, and still would be, except for those Nawtherners interferin' in our way of life." He looked down at his son. "Bobby Joe, you're only eight, but you're already helping in my service station. Some day it will be yours and mine. You'll join me in that and in the pertection of our South from evil outsiders who are tryin' to destroy it. Now, woman, don't you have a meal to git on the table?"

Roy crowded into the back of the truck, trying to see through the eye slits in his Klan hood. His heart pounded fast with the excitement of his first cross burning. Jimmy York told him that he'd show him what to do. And Roy knew Jimmy had lots of experience. He knew Jimmy and others beat up a young Nigger woman with belts and handmade clubs back in '56. Then, in '57, Jimmy and a few other Klan members were arrested for bombing the First Baptist Church, Colored, and a white jury found them not guilty, even after a couple of them had confessed. Jimmy bragged that they could do anything because a white jury would never convict a white person for doing something to a Nigger.

Tonight they were going to a Nigger's house who acts "uppity." He worked at the steel mill with a few of the Klan men and the word was that he tried to make other workers look bad because he was always working, never took unscheduled breaks, and tried to learn all the jobs, not just his own.

Soon they piled out of the pickup in front of a tiny white painted home and pounded the cross into the ground in the middle of the small front yard. Roy could see two black faces peering out of the front window. The match was lit and the Klan members stood in a circle around the cross. Soon the flames were shooting skyward. Jimmy and another Klan member pounded on the front door, but no one answered. Jimmy yelled out, "Nigger, this is a warnin' for actin' 'uppity'. Remember, you are a Nigger, nothin' more, and if you act like you are, we'll do somethin' much worse to you next time."

Roy reached his home and fumbled with the knob. Finally, he pounded on the door and Betty Lou let him in. "What took you so long, wife?" He drew back his hand and slapped her across the face, hard. "Where's my supper?"

Betty Lou trembled. "It's 2 AM. I thought you ate out with your friends so there's no food left."

"What?! You and the brat ate my supper?" His fist hit her again and again—in the face, in the stomach and in the shoulder. "Next time you'll know to save me some food, no matter what time I come in." Then Roy stumbled up the steps to his room.

Mary knocked on her neighbor's door after she saw Roy leave for work. Betty Lou slowly opened it, but turned her face away. "I heard noise early this morning. Let me see what damage he did this time, Betty Lou," Mary said grimly. Betty Lou slowly turned toward her and Mary did a quick intake of breath. "You need some ice for the swelling and some meat for those black eyes. I'll be right back." Soon she returned, brushed her gray hair back out of her eyes, and started applying the ice and meat to Betty Lou's face, something she had done more than once in the past.

Dan entered the police station and there was Michael sitting on a bench with another boy. "What have you done now, Michael? I don't appreciate getting calls from the police."

Michael looked up sullenly. "I guess I'm not important enough to Dad that he'd come. It's always you, my big brother." He looked down at the floor.

A policeman approached. Are you Daniel Edwards?" When Dan nodded, the policemen continued. "These two were caught shoplifting at Woolworth. Both of them laughed and gave false names when they were caught. This is not a laughing matter." He frowned as he looked at the two boys. "We realize this is Michael's first arrest and won't book him, but if it happens again..." The policeman walked back to the desk, not finishing his sentence.

Later, at home, Dan looked upward. "Mom, you gave me an impossible job. It's been four months and Dad is still depressed. Michael is really angry at the world and acting out. Neither of them will talk with me or with anyone else. I don't know what to do."

"Sit down, Mike. I need to talk with you." Dan waited until Mike was sitting in a chair near their Father and then turned off the TV. Tom looked up at Dan and frowned. "Sorry Dad, but I need to talk with both of you. It's been six months since Mom died and all you do is go to work and then come home and watch TV. You never speak to either Michael or me. And, Mike, you're hanging out with some trouble makers, coming home drunk, your grades have slipped and you are off the basketball team, not to mention being caught shoplifting. It looks as if you are going to fail the year and have to repeat. I've put my life on hold these past six months, trying to keep this family together. What do you think Mom would think if she could see you now?"

"Well, I'm finished worrying about the both of you. I've joined a group of students called The Student Non Violent Coordinating Committee. They call themselves just 'SNICC'. Some of the law students are participating in sit-ins at Woolworth and other stores; and I'm going to join them and do my bit to help break down segregation. Promise me you'll shape up this summer. I won't be around to baby-sit either of you."

Chapter 20

1961

Dan glanced across at his Dad and Michael, sitting together on sofa and looking at him expectantly. He could just hear what they were thinking—another stupid family meeting. What is it this time?

"Thank you for joining me. Tomorrow, May 4th, I leave for Washington, D.C., with a couple of other law students, to join the Freedom Riders. We intend to ride in an integrated Greyhound bus and a Trailways bus through the South. It's to test the Supreme Court's decision, ruling that segregation on vehicles traveling states is unlawful because it violates the Interstate Commerce Act."

"I'm not sure how long I'll be gone. Since we're traveling through Birmingham, Alabama, I might get off there and try to track down some very distant relatives of ours, dating back to the 1800's and a plantation in VA. I told you how Mom shared the family's book with me and asked me to do that. Then I'll try to catch up to the Freedom Riders. I'll fill you in when I get back if I'm able to see these relatives. In the meantime, Michael, good luck with your summer job at the grocery store and, Dad, I'll be thinking of you doing your postman rounds. I'll try to keep in touch."

"Hi. It's Dan, isn't it?" A smiling, very pretty girl with long brown hair and blue eyes sat beside him on the Trailways bus. "I see you at Georgetown Law Center, but I'm a first year law student and you are in second year, so we don't have the same classes. I'm Laura Evans."

"Hello Laura. So you are a Freedom Rider as well. Perhaps we can get better acquainted as we travel through the South. Should be an interesting time."

"An interesting time?" She smiled. "That's why I'm here."

A serious young black man tapped her on the shoulder, "Couldn't help overhearing, Miss. Please don't just ride if all you want is an interesting time. These Freedom Riders," he gestured to a tense group of black and white men and women, "and myself, do not wish it, but we are headed south. What I'm saying is, we have to be aware that we could die on this trip."

Laura glanced at Dan and then back to the small group of men and women sitting behind them. "I'm sure it won't come to that, will it? They don't expect major resistance, do they?"

"Even so, Laura," Dan's eyes grew large, his face grave like the men and women behind them. "We must be ready; we shall not be moved."

Laura dropped her head. The group was silent. "No one talked this way at my meetings. I'm not sure. I'm a law student because it's interesting. We're on the frontier of something great. What's the point of living if your life is dull? But I must admit, I want to settle down and have a family some day. I'm just not sure." She shook her head.

Dan sighed and looked Laura in the eye. "My mother always wanted me to take care of my brother, you know, keep him out of trouble. So, yeah, family is important. If I die they'd really struggle. I haven't come to terms with that fact either. But this just seems too important. How can I practice law and not make a stand for justice? You know, you can always signal the driver and get off."

Laura looked at the small group of people around her, then squeezed Dan's arm. "Just stay with me. Can you do that?"

Dan patted her on the shoulder and smiled. "Sure, I'll stay with you, but you have to understand this could get ugly."

Laura smiled and leaned on him, but her brow began to furrow and her face tighten with worry as she gazed down the road to the South. She fidgeted, and sweat beaded on her forehead in the increasingly humid air. The group was silent again.

Sarah glanced at her brother's face as they settled in the Greyhound bus seats, noticing his frown and the tightly crossed arms. "Look, I know you aren't happy I came along on this Freedom Ride, but I want to do this. You know I was able to handle the sit-ins, and I can handle this trip across the South. I think it's good we are doing this together." Getting no response, she opened a book and began to read.

Undercover plainclothes agents, Corporal Cowley and Corporal Harry Sims looked around from their seats in the back of the bus. Only 14 on board, counting them. Corporal Cowley patted the microphone in his pocket. He was supposed to gather information on the Riders and their plans for Governor Patterson, and his boss, the Director of the Alabama Highway Dept.

Corporal Cowley leaned over, whispering into Sims' ear, "You watch that side, I'll observe these here nigger-lovers over this way. Don't miss a word. We'll get 'em."

Sims looked around and smiled nervously. He shifted in his seat, adjusting the bulge on his hip. He looked at Cowley's side, then his own. Un-tucking his shirt a little, he made sure his gun wasn't as obvious.

"There's the sign, 'Anniston city limits'" Sarah smiled at her brother. Low murmurs and gasps spread through the bus. "What's that? Richard! Look!"

Richard reluctantly looked up from his book. His mouth fell open. "Looks like about 200 men out there. Stay close to me, Sarah. Get away from the window! I knew I shouldn't have let you come." Richard gazed at the crowd. They were still some distance away. It was a loose, dispersed group of white men, but there were a lot of them. As the bus approached the station each head in the mob turned and followed them in unison. Turning down an alleyway by the station the bus jerked to a halt. Richard grasped

Sarah as she was thrown forward. The engines died, revealing a small collection of angry voices outside.

"Niggers!"

"Nigger-lovers!"

"Yeah, show yourselves, you communists!"

The bus driver shouted out his window. "I'm just doing my job! Get that man out from under the front tire! He can't lay down there; he might get hurt! Move out of the way, all of you!" He spun around in his seat. "Ladies and gentlemen, the crowd out there is becoming too thick. I'll get another driver to ease us through and you'll be on your way." The driver hurriedly stepped out.

"Come on then! Come on out! We dare you nigger-lovers! Come on out and integrate Alabama!"

"Yeah! Not on our watch you ain't!"

"You hear us in there, Niggers?! This is the Anniston Ku Klux Klan!"

Richard looked down at Sarah and felt in his pockets. "I wish I'd brought a knife or something now."

No, Richard!" Sarah shook his shoulders. "We have to stay non-violent!"

"They won't harm a hair on your head. They won't even touch you. 'Til my last breath I won't let them." He sat in silence, arm around his sister, fists clenched.

Cowley leaned over and hoarsely whispered into Sims' ear, "Did you get anything from the Governor about this Klan business? Huh? Don't they know we're in here?"

Sims shook his head, smiled nervously and looked around, gripping his gun.

"An incident is the last thing we want! The governor will have my hide! Let the new driver get us outta' this crowd."

Scraape! The bus shuddered. Cowley's eyes widened as he looked out the back window. "They've slashed the tires!" The walls of the alley cast a shadow over the passengers as the crowd gathered closer. The bus began to tremble with the beating of hundreds of hands. Thwump, ump, ump, ump!

The bus started again. Richard bit his lip as it inched forward through the crowd. They pulled away from the bus station. The riders sighed and stretched their legs. Some even laughed. "Sure glad that's done with," grunted a white man behind them.

"Do you smell burnt rubber? Maybe it's that escort of cars behind us?" asked Sarah. Richard gritted his teeth. "Those cars behind us aren't no escort."

The bus swerved as a blue shape darted in front of them. The bus swerved again and the blue car swerved with them. Back and forth, the bus driver looked for an opening and honked the horn. Cowley groaned, "Great. Now one of them's trying to block us. Better get ready, Sims." Richard grimaced as he heard the flapping of the bus's tires going flat. They were riding on the rims. He leaned against the window and held his breath; another crowd was waiting for them along the road. The bus pulled over to the side and came to a stop.

"Well. I-I guess I'd better go out now and check on the tires," called the bus driver halfheartedly as he crept out the door.

"He's leaving! Look! He's just leaving us," Sarah whispered to Richard, pointing out the window. The driver had turned his back on them and was marching stiffly away from the bus.

A young black woman in front of them turned back to face Richard. "Sit straight and don't react!"

"Crash!" The sharp, rusted edge of a crowbar burst through the back window. Richard put his hand over Sarah's face as glass sprayed past them. He touched his forehead and felt blood. Passengers ducked down in their seats.

The crowd chanted in unison, "Throw it in! Throw it in! Throw it in! Throw it in!"

Sarah looked up at Richard, her face pale, "Throw what in?"

"Somebody get the gas!" yelled another man outside.

Something glass smashed at the back of the bus. The thick smell of gasoline grew. Sarah yanked away Richard's arm and peered behind them. A flash of flame swallowed all sound and sight. Thick smoke replaced it and all of a sudden everyone was heaving and choking. In the smoky darkness something flew past them. There was a rattling at the front of the bus, a man was wheezing, "Let us out!"

"Burn them niggers!"

"Burn them niggers!"

"Burn them niggers alive!"

Corporal Cowling pried open the door. Pulling out his gun he shouted, "I'm a plain clothes investigator. Get back and let these people off, or some of you are going to die."

Black smoke billowed out across the fields. The air burned with the stench of cooked rubber and upholstery. Yet, the grass was still green and the sky was still blue.

"Sarah!" Richard croaked weakly.

"He's alright! I think he's okay!" called a voice.

"Thank you," Richard coughed. He saw the blue sky and smiled at the figures above him. He asked, "Where's my sister, Sarah?"

A man slammed a pipe into his side. "Yeah, I'm glad you're okay too, nigger. Now we can beat you some more."

"Bobby Joe, you're goin' ta get a treat. The Klan says it's OK that you watch today when we meet the Freedom Riders at the Trail ways bus station. You're goin' ta see some real action." Roy rubbed his hands together and smiled.

Dan and Laura looked at each other. Something was really wrong. First, when they were lined up to get their bus tickets in Atlanta, a group of men approached people and then a lot of people left the line. Those same men boarded the bus with them. As soon as they left the Atlanta terminal the men started making threatening remarks. "You niggers will be taken care of once you get in Alabama." Later, when two black Freedom Riders wouldn't go to the back of the bus where the group of white men said they belonged, they were attacked. And when James Peck, the leader of the Freedom Riders, and Walter Bergman rushed forward to protest, they were attacked so viciously that they were both soon unconscious. The men dragged the four of them to the back of the bus and then sat in the middle of the bus to prevent any further attempt to break the color line. Laura shivered when she heard, "You're going to get what's coming to you when we get to Birmingham."

It was after 4:00 PM when they arrived at the Birmingham bus terminal. Dan looked around him when they stepped off the bus. There was a group waiting, but he didn't see any weapons. Laura muttered in Dan's ear, "Our leaders were horribly beaten alright, but the worst seems to be over. We may not get served in the cafe' though. It was all just intimidation." She smiled weakly, but clung to his arm.

"Laura, I think you're right." Dan smiled back. He looked down at her nervous quivering lips, her fingers gripping his arm. "Don't worry, I said I won't leave you and I won't."

Laura relaxed her grip, sighed, and began to stroll, casually swinging her arms. "I'm glad. On the bus I realized I've still got so much I want to do with my life."

James Peck, their leader, walked into the white waiting room with Person, who was black. Both had been badly beaten and had been unconscious for some time while on the bus. Peck could hardly walk. Dan and Laura and the rest of the Riders started to follow them into the waiting room. Peck and Person were dragged from there into a dimly lit corridor where Dan could see they were being attacked. He grabbed Laura's hand and pulled her out the door, thinking it was definitely time to leave. Other riders were disappearing into the crowd and one was getting on a city bus. Perhaps they could catch a bus. As he headed for the direction of the street he was stopped by three burly men. "Where do you think you're going?"

The next few moments were a blur. Suddenly they and other riders were met by a mob of men who called out "Nigger Lover" and "Sieg Heil" as they kicked them and hit them with pipes, clubs, and fists. Dan tried to see where Laura was, but couldn't because of the mob. He raised his arms to protect his face, but a pipe hit him forcibly alongside his head. Everything began to spin around him. A fist hit his nose and the blood started squirting out. Two men swore at him, calling him 'Nigger Lover', and one of them punched him in the stomach. I'm going to die here, he thought, and Laura will die here with me. She'll never start the family she wanted.

He heard someone say, "Get the boys out of here. I'm ready to give the signal for the police to move in." A man kicked him hard in the knee, laughed as he fell to the ground, and then left. Dan called out "Laura," and then all was dark.

"Dan. Wake up!" As he opened his eyes he saw Laura leaning over him. "The police finally came and the men are gone. I think they were members of the Klan." She helped him sit up. He gingerly felt the side of his head and noticed that his hand then had blood on it. "How do you feel? Do you want to go to the hospital?"

His head, ribs and knee hurt, and he was bleeding a little from a cut on his head, but nothing seemed to be broken. He shook his head and looked up. "Laura, what did they do to you?"

"They tore my blouse nearly off and gave me a bruise under my eye and on one arm, but I'm one of the lucky ones. They're taking a few off to the hospital. The police commissioner, the so-called 'Bull' Connor, is over there. I heard he's called 'Bull' because of his strong voice." She pointed to her right at a man who was talking to a couple of policemen. "He's ordered his police to take the ones who are continuing the Freedom Rides to the Birmingham Jail under 'protective custody'. The police were very slow to respond." She shook her head.

"Another thing, Dan. The Greyhound bus that was ahead of us...we just learned they were attacked by a mob outside of Anniston, and barely escaped with their lives. These attacks were planned, I'm sure of it."

"What are you going to do now, Laura?"

"I'm going home on the first plane out of here. I don't mind saying that this scared the living daylights out of me. These people are crazy with hate, totally irrational. What are you going to do?"

"I have some people to see, so I'll probably stay in town a day or two."

"Be careful. Don't let anyone know you're a Freedom Rider, and get out as soon as you can." Dan nodded. "I guess I'll see you in school next Fall then, Dan." She felt her black eye, hung her head and turned to go.

Dan winced as he tried to move. "Laura!"

Laura turned and folded her arms. "I thought we could do this safely. It was supposed to be a completely different experience. I can't forget this. Together we should be able to rise above anything, but..."

"Look. I'm sorry we got separated and that this happened, but I don't want to wait for school. Would it be OK if I called you when I get back? Perhaps we can get a bite to eat."

Laura's eyes shone. "I'd really like that. Here, let me give you my number." She took out a piece of paper from her purse, wrote on it and handed it to Dan. "I'll look forward to hearing from you. 'Bye for now."

Dan painfully rose and looked around him. The area was clearing of wounded Riders. The Trailways bus, with his suitcase, was nowhere to be seen. He looked ruefully down at his shirt, drenched in blood. Well, he obviously wasn't going to see distant relatives looking like this. He touched his right pocket and was relieved to feel his billfold. He stumbled, but caught himself against a building. A couple of men followed him. He began to walk faster. I've had enough, he thought, but justice is justice. Swinging around to face his followers he let out a yell, "Look! You have no right to..."

"Whoa! Easy there, son!" One of them laughed, his hands up.

"Yeah. We just came to ask if you wanted a ride to the hospital."

Dan looked them both in the eye and noticed the car parked behind them. Their arms and legs had red stains on them.

"I'm fine."

One of the men grabbed his arm. "I'm no doctor, but that gash on your head looks pretty bad there, boy. If you don't get it looked at you might be..."

"I said I'm fine!", Dan pulled away and ran around a corner.

"They'll get ya sooner or later, son, if you walk around like that," he heard one of them call after him.

Limping down the street he came upon a department store, entered, and soon found the men's section. "May I help you, Sir?", asked a clerk who, although he pursed his lips, managed not to comment on Dan's appearance.

"Yes, I'd like a couple shirts, a pair of jeans, underwear and socks, please."

The clerk paused, one hand on a shelf of underwear, one pressed firmly on the front counter. "You look like an agitator. Are you an agitator, Sir?"

Dan threw down twice the amount of money for the clothes. "That's right. A rich northern agitator and a good customer."

The clerk smiled and pocketed the money, "I think I can arrange something special for you, Sir, for a little more of course."

Soon Dan left the store with clothing, toiletries, and a small suitcase to put it all in. He headed in the direction where he'd been told there was a nice, inexpensive hotel. A shower will feel good. Guess it's too late to look up these people now. I'll do it in the morning.

Mary opened her door when she heard a timid knock. Bobby Joe stood on the porch, tears streaming down his face. "Honey, what's wrong?" She held out her arms and Bobby Joe flew into them. Soon he was sitting on her lap, his face hidden in her plump shoulder, sobbing. After the sobs subsided she again gently asked him what was wrong.

"Pa had me go see the Freedom Riders come in on the bus. Him and a lot of the Klan attacked them and it was awful." He sniffed and looked up at her. "They hit them and hit them with pipes and everything. Blood was all over on them and on the ground. One man was hit so hard on his head I thought he was dead, but he wasn't. Why does Pa and the Klan do that to people? What awful things did they do?"

Mary sat for awhile in silence. How do I explain prejudice and hatred to an eight year old? "Bobby Joe, do you remember when my husband was alive and you were five when you moved in next door? You loved to come over for milk and cookies and then you'd sit on Joe's lap and he'd tell you stories. Well, I want to tell you a story about Joe. I learned from my Mom and Dad to hate Negroes because they had a different skin color than me. When I married Joe he taught me that we are all human and all have the same parts of the body—a heart, a mind and a soul. We all love our children and we all want basically the same things--a home, a family, food, jobs and enough money to live on. Negroes can't help that they were born with a darker skin color than us. Joe worked with Negroes at the steel mill and he said the ones he met were just as honest and hard working as any white man."

"Your Father and other Klan members grew up with all that hate just like I did, but they still have that hate inside them. They want to see the Negro kept in what they call "his place". They want Negroes to have separate restrooms, separate drinking fountains and separate restaurants. The people from the North and many whites and Negroes in the South don't think that's right and want to change things. The Klan want to stop that change. Do you understand, Bobby Joe?"

"I think so. Does my Mommy hate like my Pa does?"

"No, I'm sure she doesn't. She probably just doesn't say anything because she knows it'll upset your Pa. Some day, when he isn't around, perhaps you can ask her."

Bobby Joe slid off her lap, then reached up and hugged her. "Thanks, Aunt Mary.

Dan walked up to the home where his distant relatives apparently resided. The home next to theirs was painted white, the grass was cut and a few flowers were planted along the sidewalk. Their home was in striking contrast. It desperately needed a coat of paint, the yard was full of weeds, and the steps were unpainted and planks were missing. From his research he knew a man, woman and a little boy lived there. He walked up to the door and knocked. A thin woman with stringy blond hair answered the door. Dan introduced himself and was invited in and asked to sit down on a faded, ripped chair. A young boy, wearing jeans too short for him, no shoes, and a ragged looking shirt, peeked out at him from behind his Mother. A plump gray haired lady sat on a faded, lumpy sofa and, after introductions and a refusal of coffee, Betty Lou and Bobby Joe sat down next to Mary.

The three of them were fascinated with what Dan had to say about Sam, who lived in Canada so many years ago and had written a book about their family way back then. They thought it amazing that the book had traveled through so much time to the descendants who live today. "I believe Roy told me about having a book that showed his family was rich and had a plantation in Virginia. He said we'd be sitting pretty if it hadn't been for Lincoln and the Niggers."

Dan smiled. "Yes, the plantation was lost because after the war the family couldn't keep it up when they didn't have free labor, and it was sold to a carpet bagger." Dan looked down and felt in his pocket. "Oh, Bobby Joe, I have something for you." He pulled out a little red pickup truck and reached over to hand it to him. "Saw this in a store and thought you might like it."

Bobby Joe's eyes lit up. "Thanks!" He immediately got on the floor and started to move the truck back and forth. Mary and Betty Lou smiled. Dan couldn't help but notice furniture was sparse and he guessed that toys weren't plentiful either.

Later in the conversation Dan mentioned, "I live in Maryland and we have excellent schools there. If you want to send Bobby Joe to us for high school he could stay with my Dad, brother and me. We'd be happy to have him. He could help around the house for his keep."

"Thank you, Dan, we'll keep that in mind." Suddenly Betty Lou glanced at the clock. "It's 11 AM. Roy doesn't usually come home until noon, but sometimes he shows up earlier. It's just a guess, but you said you're from Maryland and you arrived about the time as the Freedom Riders. Are you one of them?"

"Yes."

"Go, Mr. Dan! My Pa'll beat you up if he comes home. He beat up a lot of riders yesterday." Bobby Joe took Dan's hand and tried to pull him out of the chair.

"Wait a moment, Bobby Joe. I want to give you and your Mom my card. Feel free to contact me anytime." As he reached in his pocket, Betty Lou happened to look out the window. There was Roy coming up the sidewalk.

"Quick, Dan—into the closet." She shoved him in and closed the door almost all the way just as Mary scooped up the toy truck and stuck it in her knitting bag under the yarn. Bobby Joe froze, eyes widened.

"Hi Roy. You're home for lunch early."

"That's 'cuz I got a lot to tell you." He looked over at Mary as she stood up to leave. "You can stay, Mary, so you can hear about our success too. He looked at his wife and son. "I didn't get a chance to tell you about what our Klan did to those interferin' Nawthern Nigger Lovers because we went out to celebrate afterward and you were both in bed when I got home."

Dan peeked out the crack and saw a short man with a receding hairline sitting down in the chair he'd just vacated.

"Bobby Joe, did you see what happened at the bus terminal?" Bobby Joe nodded. "Well, you don't know what went on before that. First of all, a Greyhound bus with so-called Freedom Riders were met outside of Anniston by Klan and other concerned citizens wantin' ta pertect our Southern way of life. Their bus was burned, but they escaped. Then the Trailways bus came into our terminal and we were ready for them. The FBI had notified the police to expect the Freedom Riders and the police notified the Klan. In fact, our Klan leaders had a meetin' the night before and planned our attack. Our Commissioner of Public Safety, 'Bull' Connor, told the Klan they'd have fifteen minutes to beat the Riders until they 'looked like a bulldog got hold of them.' And we did." Roy smirked and rubbed his hands together.

"They came off the bus and a white and a Nigger tried to enter the white waiting room together. They were dragged into a corridor where some Klan members were waitin' and beat them with lead pipes and oversized key rings and their fists. I stayed outside and me and other Klan members tore into some other riders. A few got away, but not many. I had a lead pipe and managed to hit one of the riders upside the head while another Klan member kicked him really hard in a knee. Then the fun was over because a plain clothes man gave a prearranged signal that the police were goin' ta arrive and we had to clear out. We sent some of the riders to the hospital though. I think the white man I hit was unconscious or dead. I hope he's dead. It was a success, and Imperial Wizard Shelton even came by and congratulated a few of our Klan for a job well done. We went over to a Klan member's house ta celebrate. Those interfering Nawtherners have no right ta come down here ta stir up our Niggers and try ta ruin our Southern way of life. And we won't let them either!"

Dan drew in his breath slowly. Here was the man who'd hit him on the head and wished he was dead. He was still getting headaches from that lead pipe and might even have a concussion. And this was the distant relative he'd wanted to meet.

Roy went into the kitchen, grabbed a sandwich and said he had to get back to the station as he had a car to repair that afternoon. When he'd left Betty Lou let Dan out of the closet. "You see what we mean?"

"I wish you wouldn't keep following me on these Freedom Rides, Sarah. CORE stopped doing them because they were so dangerous. Now SNCC is running them and has called for people to join the ride from Birmingham. We were supposed to leave yesterday, but the Greyhound bus drivers were too scared to drive us. We're leaving today, because the Kennedys intervened, but I wish you'd return home. I'll worry about you the whole time we're on the ride. We had a narrow escape when they burned our bus, and who knows what these white supremacists have in store for us along the way."

"You know I'm going, Richard, so just accept it. Oh, we're boarding."

"Richard, we are going awfully fast. I bet it's about 90 mph. And there's a contingent of Alabama Highway Police following us. I heard that was arranged to protect us."

"Looks like we are finally pulling into the Montgomery bus station, Sarah. The highway police left us at the Montgomery border and I see a crowd by the station. Hope there are some police there too. Stay in back of me when we get off the bus."

Richard looked around and saw no police. He noticed the mob attacking the journalists and photographers first and destroying their cameras. I guess that's because they've gotten such negative publicity across the nation and even overseas. A white woman is yelling, "Get them niggers. Get them niggers." Oh oh! Now they're coming for us. How will I keep Sarah safe? "Run, Sarah, run!" He pushed her away from the crowd. Then he was pummeled with fists, kicked, and hit with a baseball bat until he fell to the ground. A kick in the stomach knocked the wind out of him. He put his arms around his head and curled into a ball to protect himself. After his attackers were satisfied they'd done enough damage, they left him and went to attack another.

Several moments later the area cleared. Someone called the ambulances, but when they came the drivers refused to take the riders to the hospital. Local blacks stepped in and gave them rides. Sarah found Richard when he was waiting to be examined. She'd run for it and hid in an alley until the mob left. By then a black man had given Richard a ride to the hospital.

"Looks as if I'll live." Richard grimaced as he got off the bed. "Let's get out of here."

"Richard, if you're OK, I'd like to stay for the meeting tomorrow night at Reverend Abernathy's First Baptist Church. It's to honor the Freedom Riders."

"Someone said there are more than 1500 people packed into this Church, Richard. Reverend King, Reverend Shuttlesworth, and James Farmer are speaking."

"They'd better be good because I don't think we're getting out of here any time soon. I heard there's an angry mob of more than 3000 whites outside. Oh no! They're breaking the windows with rocks and setting off gas canisters."

The next morning Richard was relieved to see the Alabama National Guard arrive to disperse the crowd and lead them to safety.

"I heard President Kennedy threatened Governor Patterson that if he couldn't control the situation he'd send in federal troops, Richard."

"Well, whatever works. The President didn't do much in the beginning of the Movement, but he's taking more action now that we're in the papers and on TV. He's feeling public pressure from across the country and even from other world leaders. He's had no choice but to get involved, despite his efforts to stay out of it."

Mary came to her door and found Betty Lou there, holding her arm. "I fell and hurt my arm. Do you have aspirin?"

"Let's take a look." Betty Lou cried out in pain when Mary barely touched her. "Alright, Mary, what really happened? Your arm may be broken."

Betty Lou sat down and started to cry. "Roy twisted it this morning. I had to show him Bobby Joe's report card and it said he has to repeat third grade next year. He's only reading at a second grade level and can't do simple add and subtract. Roy says if his son is stupid it's from my side of the family. I think it's because

Roy has him stay out of school and help at the station—even though he is only eight. He's missed a lot of school."

"Come on, let's get you to the hospital. We'll talk about Bobby Joe later."

When they got back to Mary's house she settled Betty Lou, her left arm in a cast, into a comfortable chair and brought her a sandwich. "Now, I think I have a solution. School is almost out for the summer so Bobby Joe can come over here every day and I can work with him on his reading and arithmetic." She held up her hand as Betty Lou started to protest. "I'll enjoy it. I always wanted to be a teacher and you know I love Bobby Joe. Maybe, if he catches up by high school, he can go to school in Maryland and stay with that nice young man, Dan Edwards."

"Thank you, Mary." Betty Lou looked down, tears in her eyes. "There's something else. I'm pregnant."

"Oh no!"

"Usually Roy comes home too drunk for sex, but 3 months ago he came home one night a little earlier than usual. He tore off my clothes and forced me to..." Betty Lou looked up. "Mary, I can't bring another child of Roy's into this world. Roy's drinking more than ever and we barely have money for food because Roy spends almost all his earnings on beer. I send Bobby Joe over to the station when we run out and Roy gives him a little money out of the cash register. It's never enough and Bobby Joe goes to school hungry. He told me once his teacher sometimes says she brought too much lunch to school and asks him to share. The children call him "stupid" because he's behind in school. His jeans and shirt are too short. He has a hole in the bottom of one shoe and I put cardboard in the shoe. The shoes are too tight and I don't know if I can get him another pair by Fall. How can I have another child go through what Bobby Joe goes through? He gets nothing for Christmas and the only toy he has is that little truck that man, Dan, gave him."

The worst of it is that this child will also have Roy, a Klan member, as his Father. He'll learn to hate, just like Roy. Bobby Joe hasn't, and I think it's because he's sensitive, like me, and has you to talk to. What if the next one is a little Roy? I just can't bear it." Betty Lou put her head down and burst into tears. "I thought of ending my life and the baby's, but what would happen to Bobby Joe? I couldn't leave him with such a wicked Father."

Mary leaned over and put her arm around Betty Lou. "Don't you have an older sister in Georgia? Why don't you just leave and go stay with her?"

"Because Roy would just follow me there and make me come back. Also...," Betty Lou hesitated. "My sister was dead set against me marrying Roy. I was in tenth grade, rather pretty, and had two guys asking me out. The other one was steady and rather bookish and my sister liked him and kept pushing him on me. Roy was more exciting and, when he asked me to marry him, we eloped and then we both quit school. My sister never forgave me. She didn't even send a card when I wrote her about Bobby Joe arriving a year later. No," Betty Lou shook her head decidedly. "I can't go back there."

"Then it looks like you have only one choice. I think I can find someone who will do it and I'll pay the cost. Will you?" Betty Lou nodded. "They have pills now to prevent pregnancy and you need to get on them after..."

Mary knocked on Betty Lou's door. It was the first of August and her plump figure was dripping wet with perspiration. "Come on in and have a nice, cool drink, Mary."

"Thank you. I just left Bobby Joe next door, doing an arithmetic test. He's to bring it over here when he's done. You know, that little one is smart. His reading has definitely improved and he's doing well on the arithmetic. I think the school will be very surprised, come Fall."

"I really appreciate what you've done, Mary. I've been thinking that somehow I have to leave Roy so that Bobby Joe can have a future. I'd like to get a job, but I was fired from the last one I had because I missed so many days. I couldn't go to work with black eyes and bruises. That would still be a problem. Also, Roy would look through my things and take any money I had for booze. He sold my Mother's necklace she'd given me and my wedding ring. Even if I could bring in some money he'd take it all."

"Hmm. Let me think about this a moment." Mary leaned back in her chair and was silent. Finally she looked at Betty Lou, a big smile on her face. "I got it! You are a really good seamstress and there are several wealthy women in the community and, in fact, in my Church, who would probably hire you to sew for them. You can sew at my house after Roy leaves for work. The answer to the other part of the problem is that I could keep your money for you at my house until you and Bobby Joe have enough saved for a couple of bus tickets. Where would you go?"

"Anywhere that isn't in the South. I was thinking of going west or east. I even thought of Maryland because perhaps Dan would help me get a job cleaning houses. He seemed like such a kind man."

"Wonderful idea! Let's get you started raising that money."

"I'm so glad you're back, Dan! How long were you in that Jackson, Mississippi, prison?" Laura reached across the cafe table and clasped Dan's hand in hers.

"Was it bad?" Laura asked, a concerned expression on her face.

"Do you really want to hear about it?" Dan continued after seeing Laura nod. "First a bit of background—Attorney General Robert Kennedy negotiated a deal with officials in Jackson that the Freedom Riders couldn't be hurt but could be arrested, so when Riders reached Jackson, Mississippi, and tried to integrate the bus station waiting room they were immediately arrested. The strategy then became to keep the Freedom Rides going and fill the jails. At one time Jackson, Mississippi, had over 300 Freedom Riders in their prisons. I imagine that affected their budget." Dan leaned back and smiled. "Most of us ended up in the Mississippi State Penitentiary, also known as Parchman Farm, where they put hardened criminals."

Dan paused and looked at Laura. "Yes, it was bad. When we arrived they did a strip search and then all we were given was a tee shirt and underwear. The guards always tried to intimidate us. We had to work on a chain gang and the rest of the time we spent in our tiny cells with nothing to do—no books, no paper and pencils. All we were given was a Bible, an aluminum cup and a toothbrush. We had one shower per week and weren't allowed to get mail. The lights were on 24 hours a day."

The Riders started singing freedom songs almost nonstop because that kept up our spirits and our solidarity. Also, we soon found out it irritated the hell out of the guards." Dan grinned. "When we refused to stop they took away our mattresses and bug screens. We finally got our mattresses back just before an inspection tour of officials from Minnesota who were coming to check on the condition of the Freedom Riders. Quite a coincidence, huh?"

"Did you get enough to eat?"

"Well, we didn't starve. We got mighty tired of the same thing day after day. For breakfast we got black coffee, grits, biscuits and black strap molasses. Lunch was usually beans or black-eyed peas with pork gristle and with cornbread. Supper was the same as lunch. I couldn't wait to get home and have a big piece of steak with mashed potatoes and gravy! You know, we survived, and the Riders got a lot of publicity over the summer, which certainly helped our cause. I'm just glad I got out in time to register for Fall classes."

"I'm glad, too, and that you're safe. I missed you."

"I missed you too, honey. I was surprised that my Dad and brother had been so worried about me. By the way, I told the them about you, and Dad asked me to invite you to dinner on Sunday. Would you mind? I should warn you that my Dad likes to tease."

"I'd love to come."

Dan turned in his driver's seat to face Laura. "When you invited me to your parents' home for dinner I didn't realize they live in a mansion. What does your Father do?"

" He's a cardiac surgeon and my Mom's a CEO."

Dan laughed. "My Dad's a postman."

"That doesn't matter. My Mom and Dad will like you, I know, and they won't care what your Dad does for a living. I've told them all about you and your family and they can't wait to meet you." Laura smiled. "Let's go in. I promise—they don't bite."

Richard sat on the sofa, reading the newspaper and relaxing. "Sarah, I don't know about you, but I'm glad it's September and the Freedom Rides and sit-ins are done for awhile. I start my new job tomorrow and will only be going to classes part time this year. I should still get an engineering degree in a couple of years. What about you?"

"Well, I'm in my second year toward a journalism degree. I volunteer for the school newspaper and am starting to work in the library part time. Richard, do you think we really accomplished something with the Freedom Rides and sit-ins?"

"I remember when the Kennedys called for a 'cooling off period' and condemned the Rides as unpatriotic because they embarrassed the nation on the world stage at the height of the Cold War. The Soviet Union had criticized the US for its racism and the attacks on the riders."

"Yes, and James Farmer, head of CORE, had an answer for them. He said 'We have been cooling off for 350 years, and if we cooled off any more, we'd be in a deep freeze.' I thought that was a great answer."

Richard grinned. "CORE, SNCC and the SCLC took no notice of the so-called 'cooling off period' and kept the Rides going all summer long. There were over 60 different Freedom Rides going through the South and a lot of them ended up in Jackson where every rider was arrested. The rides, the attacks, and the arrests were all shown on TV with photos and articles in newspapers across the Country. The President had tried to avoid taking action so as not to offend the Dixicrats, but ended up having to because of all that publicity. Yes, Sarah, I think we accomplished a lot."

Chapter 21

1963

Bobby Joe skipped down the path to the river. School would be out in a month and this Saturday he was going to catch some fish. Aunt Mary had told him about her husband fishing at Cahaba River and catching bass they'd eat for supper. She'd even given him a couple of fish hooks and told him how he could put a worm on it. He'd made a pole out of long stick and some string. Pa thought he was stupid and couldn't do anything right, but he'd change his mind once he saw the fish Bobby Joe would bring home for their supper.

There's a good rock to sit on...now to put the worm on the hook. Gee, the stupid worm keeps wiggling. There! Now to catch some fish.

A couple hours later and still no fish. When Bobby Joe looked at the hook he knew why—the worm was gone. This happened time and time again and Bobby Joe was getting restless. He got up to stretch and notice a Negro boy about his age up the river a ways from him. As he watched the boy caught two good sized fish. Bobby Joe cautiously approached him. "How'd you catch those fish? I can't catch any."

"Let me see your hook. Oh, the hook's too small for the fish we catch here. I have an extra hook. Let me put it on your line." The boy sat on a rock and began to thread the hook. Then he took one of his worms and put it on the hook. Bobby Joe watched, fascinated. A small white dog with two black spots on its back came up, sniffed Bobby Joe's hand and wagged his tail.

"That your dog?"

The boy nodded. "His name's Spot. He likes you."

"I want a dog, but my Pa won't let me have one. I had a kitten once, but my Pa kicked it across the room and killed it."

The boy looked at Bobby Joe, surprised. "We have cats too, but my Dad would never kick 'em." He handed Bobby Joe his line. "There, I think this'll work. The fishing is better here, if you want to fish next to me."

"Thanks. What's your name? I'm Bobby Joe. Can I play with Spot too?"
The boy nodded. "I'm Tom."

The rest of that Saturday morning was spent fishing, playing with Spot and sharing the sandwich Tom had with him. Bobby Joe, with Tom's help, caught four good sized bass. "I've got to go now. Do you fish here on Saturday?"

"Yeah, I'm usually here about seven so if you want to come next Saturday we can fish together."

"OK, see you then. 'Bye." Bobby Joe took off, running. He'd almost forgotten he was supposed to help his Pa at the gas station that afternoon.

"Richard, guess what!" Sarah's eyes were shining and she was practically jumping up and down.

"I can't guess, what?"

"I've been chosen for a journalism internship to go with the Washington Post reporters and photographers to Birmingham, or, as we journalists say, "Bombingham," because of the number of unsolved bombings. Martin Luther King has said that Birmingham is the most thoroughly segregated city in the United States. Word is out that Martin Luther King and the SCLC are going to have a demonstration of some sort and I get to help cover it."

Richard looked worried. "Be careful. Those Civil Rights demonstrations can be violent."

This was more than Sarah expected. They were calling it the D Day campaign and children from elementary and high school were attempting to march from the churches to the Birmingham City Hall. "Bull" Connor, the Commissioner of Public Safety, who was always saying 'Segregation at all cost', was arresting the children and putting them in jail. She'd heard that more than 600 children, from ages eight to eighteen, were now in the Birmingham Jail, which brought the number of protesters up to 1200 in a jail that had a capacity of 900. Sarah smiled. The Washington Post was getting some good coverage and she'd been able to interview a few protesters. The children's march was supposed to continue tomorrow.

Sarah pressed herself against a building and watched as "Bull" Connor ordered the fire department to turn the high pressure water jets on the 1000 children who were marching. The police used attack dogs on the children and other demonstrators and bystanders. Sarah watched as a photographer took a photo of a police dog biting a high school student. The fire hoses knocked down the school children and even ripped off boys' shirts. She saw a young woman pushed over the top of a car by the force of the water.

Sarah was glad to be home. The Washington Post had printed a photo of the water jets on three students. And the New York Times had a vivid photo of the student she'd seen being attacked by a police dog. This Children's Crusade was televised nationally and received worldwide attention. By May 7th, over 3000 demonstrators had been jailed. President Kennedy had been quoted as saying that the New York Times photo made him sick. Three days later, the Birmingham City businesses had agreed to desegregation, the upgrading and hiring of blacks, and releasing all jailed demonstrators.

"Richard, people are saying that Bull Connor has helped the Civil Rights movement by calling attention to the segregation of the South and what goes on there. How about that—an avowed racist actually helping the Movement. Bet that gets his goat!"

Laura sat down next to Dan in the Law Library. "Let's go get a cup of coffee, my treat." A little later they were sitting at a cafe on the Georgetown Law Center campus. "What are you doing this summer?"

"I'll take a couple of classes, work part time in the law library, and I've promised to help out in the SNCC office if any law issues come up. You know, Birmingham has jailed 1000 more Negroes. Danville, Virginia, had one of the most brutal attacks by police ever, with 48 out of 65 demonstrators being injured. Then after President Kennedy's speech endorsing the Civil Rights Movement and announcing he would propose meaningful legislation to Congress, someone shot Medgar Evers, the Mississippi field secretary for NAACP, right in front of his home. Alabama's Governor George Wallace has said, '...Segregation now! Segregation tomorrow! Segregation forever!' He's followed that up by blocking the doorway at the University of Alabama so Negroes couldn't enter. He only backed down when Kennedy nationalized the Alabama Guard. Dan shook his head. "It's not over yet—not by a long shot. I want to help bring about real change, real equality, for the Negroes." Dan paused. "What are you doing this summer?"

"I'm taking an internship out in California and I'll finish my degree there. The internship will pay for my last year and also give me experience. I couldn't afford to pass this up."

"What about us, Laura? We've been together two years now and I thought that would continue. California is clear across the country and my work is here..."

Laura looked down at her lap. "I think we need to take a break from each other. This last year I've hardly seen you because of both of us studying and you working on the Movement. All you ever talk about is Civil Rights. It's as if you're obsessed. I'm not sure how I feel about you anymore."

"I thought we loved each other."

Laura shook her head and stood up. "I think we should say good-bye now. I wish you the best."

Dan just sat there, a stunned expression on his face.

"Damn key won't go in lock," Dan muttered to himself, and then began to bang on the door.

"What's going on?" Michael opened the door and stared at his brother. "Hey, big bro, you're smashed. I've never seen you drunk before. Here, let me help you."

"Laura dumped me... Thought we'd get married. She..." He leaned on Michael and, with difficulty, they made it to Dan's bedroom where Michael lowered him onto the bed and removed his shoes.

"You're not going to feel too good in the morning. I know from experience. Glad to know you're human, big bro."

"Come in, Bobby Joe. Would you like some milk and cookies?"

Bobby Joe nodded and sat down on a kitchen chair. "Aunt Mary, I have a friend and we fish every Saturday and play with his dog. We even have a secret hole in a tree where we can leave notes to each other."

"That's wonderful, honey. I'm glad you have a friend. You brought me those two fish last Saturday and they were delicious. Thank you. Would you like me to make chocolate chip cookies for you and your friend for next Saturday?"

The KKK meeting was over and people were gathered in small groups, talking. Usually the talk was about beating up niggers, but this time the discussion was about bringing in more members. Roy stretched to his full 5'6", puffed out his chest, and looked up at the group. "My Father was a KKK member, I'm a member and my boy will be a member as soon as he's old enough."

"Not if he keeps playing with nigger boys he won't."

The man called Buddy looked at Roy and smirked. "My boy and his friend saw your boy down at the river, fishing and playing with a nigger and his dog. They saw him the next Saturday too, but your boy didn't see them. He was too busy playing with his nigger."

249

"That's not true. My boy would never be seen with a Nigger. Your son confused him with someone else."

Buddy shook his head. "Go home and ask him, but he'll probably lie about it. The Klan isn't going to let him in if he has nigger friends. Looks like the Klan membership stops with you." Once again Buddy smirked, and a couple of others in the group laughed.

Roy stomped into the house. "Where's Bobby Joe? I want to see him RIGHT NOW!"

"Here I am, Pa." Bobby Joe came from his room and approached his Father, only to have his arm grabbed roughly. He was then pulled back into his room and flung onto his bed.

"Do you have a nigger friend?" Bobby Joe looked up, terrified, at his Father and nodded.

"How could you shame me in front of my Klan friends? Well, you are going to learn that you don't hang with niggers and embarrass your Father, a Klan member. Get your shirt and pants off."

While Bobby Joe, shaking, stripped down, Roy took off his belt and flexed it. "Lie on your stomach," Roy demanded grimly. Soon Betty Lou, locked out of the room and standing in the hallway, crying, could hear the sound of the belt hitting the back of her son again and again. She could hear his screams. She pounded and pounded on the door, yelling, "Beat me, Roy! Beat me! He's just a little boy. He didn't mean to shame you. He won't do it again. Let me in! Please, beat me instead!"

Roy ignored her and continued to whip his son until, finally, he decided he'd done enough to teach Bobby Joe a lesson. He unlocked the door, walked past his wife, and out the front door.

Bobby Joe had been whipped from his neck down to the soles of his feet. Some of the skin had been ripped off and there were deep cuts across his back. Blood was leaking from the cuts. Bobby Joe didn't move but would occasionally whimper. Mary looked at Betty Lou. "Can you send for his doctor?"

Betty Lou looked down at her feet. "We don't have a doctor—can't afford one."

"Then I'll send for mine."

Dr. James glanced up at the two women as he leaned over Bobby. "I've given him a shot for pain so that should help him sleep. Here's a prescription for pain medication and an ointment to put on his wounds. He'll need to sleep on his stomach and won't be able to sit for awhile. It's going to really hurt to put the ointment on, but it'll prevent infection and help him heal. Give him the pain medication before putting on the ointment." The Doctor shook his head. "I understand your husband did this, Mrs. Ramsey. I am going to have to call the police and report it. I hope going to jail for a couple days will keep him from doing something this awful again." He again shook his head and then let himself out.

"I hear you almost went to jail, Roy." The Klan member looked down at Roy and grinned.

"Yeah, well, I didn't. Commissioner Bull Connor just gave me a warning."

"You're lucky he's a friend of the Klan. He's not a member, but he agrees with what we are trying to do—keep the South the way it is. He always says, 'Segregation at all costs.' You know who the Father is of that nigger boy, don't you?" Roy shook his head. "It's that uppity nigger where we had the cross burning. We said if he did anything else we'd make it worse for him. Well, I think him encouraging his son to make friends with a white boy is a lot worse, don't you? I think we should teach him a lesson so's he don't ever do that again. Why should your boy get punished and the niggers get off scot-free?" The Klan member looked around the room. "Hey guys. We got a nigger beating tonight."

Klan members piled out of the truck and Jimmy went up to the door and knocked. When the man answered, a gun in his ribs forced him and Tom out of the house. A Klan member held onto Tom while three other members dragged the Father to a small tree in the yard. A little dog rushed out of the house, ran up to the Klan member holding the Father, and bit him in the leg. Roy, who was standing nearby, drew his leg back and kicked the dog with all his might, sending him flying. Spot lay motionless on the ground.

"OK, we'll tie his arms around that tree. That's what masters did with their slaves." Jimmy glared at the man. "Strip down, Nigger. We'll teach you that you don't let your nigger kids play with white children."

"Since it was your kid that was defiled by that nigger boy, you get to hit first, Roy. I got a bull whip here that'll make some good cuts. The masters used to give 100 lashes to their slaves so, with five of us, I reckon we each get 20 lashes apiece." Jimmy handed the whip to Roy. "Give it to him good!"

Roy stepped up to the tree, holding the whip. A surge of anger poured through him. Because of this man and his son he'd had to punish Bobby Joe and now his wife and kid hadn't talked to him in three weeks. Well, he'd get his revenge alright. Roy struck with all his force and fury. The Klan counted, "One, two, three..."

"No! Don't hit him. It's my fault. Hit me! Hit me!" Tom struggled to get loose from his captor.

Klan members looked at him and laughed. "I reckon you'll get punished enough just watching your Pa get beaten. I reckon you'll never try to play with a white boy again." The Klan member, Buddy, smirked beneath his hood.

Finally it was over. Each Klan member had gotten in their 20 licks. The Klan member holding the door so the wife and two little girls couldn't come out, released them, and the wife ran to her husband, sobbing loudly. Tom and she began to untie the rope around his wrists while the five Klan members piled into the pickup truck, laughing and waving good-bye.

"Come in, Betty Lou. What's the matter?" Mary noticed Betty Lou looked about to cry.

"I've got to send Bobby Joe away. I can't protect him from Roy. Now that he's started on Bobby Joe he'll be beating both of us—not just me. Do I have enough money saved for one bus ticket to Maryland?"

Mary went to her desk, pulled out a small drawer, and then gave Betty Lou its contents. After a few moments, Betty Lou looked up in relief. "Yes, there's enough for one ticket. I'll write a letter asking Dan Edwards and his family to keep him and then I'll keep working until I have enough to join him. I'm sure Dan will help me find a job when I get there and then Bobby Joe and I can be together again. Until then, at least I'll know he's safe."

"Can I send Dan your address and phone number so perhaps Bobby Joe can write me here? Dan may want to call to work out a legal guardianship. Although I'm giving him permission in my letter that may not be enough. I'll tell them I'll pay them back for Bobby Joe's care when I get there and get a job."

"Of course you can use my address and phone number. Are you sure about this? You don't really know this Dan and you've never met the Father and brother?"

"I know Dan is kind and I'm sure the Father would be too. The worst they can do is send him back, but I'm counting on, once they read what Bobby Joe is going through, they'll decide to keep him. I have to do this. Anywhere is better than here for Bobby now. And he's family..."

Mary shook her head and looked at her feet.

"Please Mary, help me do this."

Mary turned away and started pacing, biting her lip. "If they send him back Roy'll make things even harder for the both of you."

"Things will get worse if he stays anyway."

"I wish I could think of another solution, but I can't. When are you going to put him on a bus?" Mary sat down next to Betty Lou and put her arm around her.

"I was thinking next week some time. Would you be able to drive him to another town? I won't be able to go because someone might recognize me. I thought perhaps we could dye his hair black and get him away without anyone noticing."

"What will you tell Roy?"

"I'll tell him Bobby Joe must've run away because of the beating. Did you know they also beat that little Negro boy's Father, for letting him play with Bobby Joe? They gave him 100 lashes last night. Roy was bragging about it. He kicked the boy's dog too. The man must be in terrible shape. And all this because two little boys wanted to play together."

"That's awful! Say, Betty Lou, is Bobby Joe done with the medication from the doctor?" Betty Lou nodded.

"Could I take the leftover medication out to Tom's Mother so she can doctor her husband?"

"Yes, but be careful."

"I'm not worried. I'll go in the middle of the day. The men will be at work."

Mary approached the Jones home and knocked on the door. A Negro woman opened the door a tiny bit and peered out. "Hello, I'm Mary Davis. I don't know if you heard that the boy your Tom played with was badly beaten by his Father for playing with Tom. We got some medicine from a doctor. That was three weeks ago and Bobby Joe is done with the medicine. We thought maybe your husband could use it." Mary held out a paper bag. The woman hesitated so Mary withdrew her arm.

"There are some pretty strong pain pills which helped Bobby Joe sleep. Also, there's ointment to spread on the wounds. That'll keep your husband from getting an infection and will help heal the wounds."

The woman reached out for the bag and whispered a thank you. As Mary started to walk away she asked, "Is the boy OK?"

"Yes, he's OK now. He wanted to know if Spot is OK."

"You tell him that Spot is sore on the one side, but is walking around a little."

"Mrs. Jones, I'm so sorry this has happened. I'm sorry that our two little boys can't be friends because of all this hate." Mary shook her head and departed.

Bobby Joe wrapped his arms around Betty Lou, tears in his eyes. "I don't want to go, Mama."

Betty Lou knelt down beside him. "Aunt Mary and I have explained why you have to. I'll work hard so I can join you, I promise. In the meantime, you be a good boy and mind your cousin, Dan. When you get there be sure to give him the envelope right away. You can write me any time and I'll answer you. I love you so much!" Betty hugged her little boy and then watched tearfully as Mary placed a little boy with black hair under a blanket in her car and drove away.

"He's on his way, Betty Lou. I told him not to talk to anyone and to just read his little book and look out the window."

"I asked Dan to let us know when he arrives. I'm sure he'll want to talk to me about all this."

"Well, Betty Lou, now we'll see how good an actress you are."

"What do you mean, Bobby Joe didn't come home for supper? Where is he? Is he at a friend's?"

"He doesn't have any friends, Roy. I've looked around the neighborhood and even checked down by the river. I don't know where he could be." Betty Lou put her face in her hands. It wasn't hard for her to be sad and upset she discovered. She was sad and upset. Bobby Joe was gone.

Betty Lou was surprised at the turnout. A lot of them were from the Baptist Church they sometimes attended, but a few, she knew, were from the Klavern Roy was in. They divided into groups with some groups combing the downtown area and others looking along the Cahaba River. Mary and she went down to the river, calling Bobby Joe's name. She heard someone say, "Maybe he tripped and fell into the river and drowned." Another shushed her, saying, "His Mother is right over there." Only at nightfall did they stop, vowing to pick up the search the next day. Many of the searchers came up to her and expressed their concern and support.

Bobby Joe stepped out of the taxi and watched it drive away. The long bus ride was over. It hadn't been too bad, except when that old man sat next to him and started touching him. That was weird. But then, at the next rest stop, a woman across from them had treated him to a snack and asked him to sit with her. She was nice. When they got to the station the woman helped him get a cab and gave the driver the note his Mother had given him with the address on it. She had even paid the driver. Now he was here. He squared his shoulders, walked to the front door and knocked. He tucked in more of his shirt and carefully patted down his hair. Everything about him had to look perfect. If it didn't they might not take him. And if they didn't take him his Dad would... He flicked a hand across his face to catch a tear before the door opened.

Bobby Joe recognized the man he'd seen at his house two years ago and handed him the envelope. "I'm Bobby Joe and my Mama wants you to read this."

Dan looked puzzled. "I thought you had blond hair."

My Mama and Aunt Mary dyed it so Pa wouldn't find me. I can change it back if you don't like it."

"Well, Bobby Joe, you had better come in. Sit down while I read this." As he read a frown appeared. Bobby Joe held his breath and grasped at the material on the knees of his jeans. "Please," he whispered under his breath. Finally Dan looked up at Bobby Joe. "I guess you're hungry and tired after that long trip. Let's go in the kitchen and get you some food and then you can lie down for a little while. Does that sound OK to you?" Bobby Joe nodded and Dan put his arm on his shoulder and led him into the kitchen.

"Well, Dad, you've met Bobby Joe and read the letter from his Mother. I talked with her and her neighbor on the phone and they both think this is the only way to keep Bobby Joe safe from his Father until she can get away and join him here in Baltimore. She begged us to keep him. It's highly unusual, but..." Dan gave his Father a questioning look.

"Poor little tyke. Nothing but skin and bones. What did you tell her?"

"I said I'd talk to you and Michael and let her know. Then, if we kept him, we'd have to have legal guardianship. She said she'd sign the papers."

"I don't think it would hurt us to have a little one around the house."

"I just wonder what Michael will say—especially since Bobby Joe will have to be in his bedroom. It's the only one with 2 beds in it. That was so when he was younger his friends could sleep over. The so-called friends he has these days just drink and then they crash at their own homes."

"What about Michael's drinking? He's only 16, yet he's out drinking with friends. Nothing I do or say makes any difference. If Bobby Joe's Father is an alcoholic, won't that bother him, when Michael comes home under the weather? It looks like this might not work."

"I thought of that. Michael is drinking a lot less than he did just after Mom died. Also, he'd never admit it, but he has a big heart. Perhaps he'll agree to go to a friend's and stay there overnight if he's had too much to drink. We'll just have to see—if he even agrees to this arrangement."

Michael sneered. "Not another family meeting! What did I do now?"

"Nothing, son. We just have an unscheduled guest. Here, read this." Tom handed Michael the letter.
Michael looked up after quickly reading it. "I don't understand. Where is the boy? What does this have to do with us?"

"He's in your room sleeping. Remember me telling you two about the Mother and her eight year old son I met two years ago when I was in Alabama and searching for the very distant relations on Mom's side of the family? These are the people I went to see. They hid me in their closet when her husband came home because he's a Klan member and can be very violent. He'd just been involved in beating up the Freedom Riders, including me, as it turned out. Recently he beat his son badly because Bobby Joe had a Negro friend, and he and other Klan members beat the Father of the boy for letting his son play with a white boy. Mrs. Ramsey, the Mother, is afraid for her son's life."

Michael shook his head. "Doesn't make sense. Why didn't she come too?"

"Ramsey would've gone looking for them. This way they all searched the area, especially down by the river. The story most seem to believe is that Bobby Joe fell in and drowned. Mrs. Ramsey will stay there a few more months, earn some money, and then sneak away and join Bobby Joe here."

"A few months! I'm not having that kid in my room a few months! I have a life, you know!"

"OK, OK. Could you put up with him for a week or two? I'll move things around and find another place for him. I really think he needs to be with someone now because he'll be missing his Mom and everything here is strange to him." Michael nodded reluctantly, a scowl on his face.

"Oh, and Michael, that means when you've had too much to drink you'll need to crash at a friend's. Bobby Joe's Father is a mean drunk and we don't want to scare the little guy. Remember, not a word of this to anyone. His father might come looking for him. We know how you get when drunk."

"Oh yeah and what's that supposed to mean?" Michael moved in on Dan, staring him in the face, their noses almost touching.

"Back off. You're just a little too chatty when you're buzzed, that's all. Think of Bobby Joe's safety, okay?"

"Find somewhere else for him. Or I will." Michael stepped back, muttered a few more things under his breath, and walked up the stairs to his room.

As Michael came into the room, followed by his dog, Bobby Joe sat up and rubbed his eyes. "Are you Michael?"

"Yeah, you Bobby Joe?"

Just then Bobby Joe saw the dog and his eyes brightened. "That your dog? What's his name?"

"His name is Scruffy because he's a terrier mix and his rough gray-brown fur kinda' sticks out all over the place. You want to pet him?" Michael reached down, picked up the dog, and put him on the bed with Bobby Joe. The dog immediately licked

Bobby Joe's hand. "I like his pointy ears and waggedy tail." Bobby Joe looked up at Michael. "I always wanted a dog, but my Pa wouldn't let me. Had a kitten once, but Pa kicked it across the room and killed it." Bobby Joe hugged Scruffy. "Prob'ly good I didn't have a dog 'cuz he woulda' killed it too. He kicked my friend's dog and hurt it real bad." Bobby Joe looked up at Michael again. "Can I play with Scruffy while I'm here?"

Michael nodded, then noticed Bobby Joe had been sleeping in his tee shirt and jeans. "Don't you want to get into your pajamas?"

"Don't have any. I can sleep in these."

Michael went to a drawer and pulled out one of his undershirts. "Here, you can wear this." When he saw Bobby Joe struggling to get his tee shirt off, Michael reached over to help him. That's when he saw Bobby Joe's back. It made him sick to see the red scars and the areas of the back that were still raw from the beating. What that little boy must've been through! "Here, let me tuck you in. My Mom used to tuck me in when I was a kid. Sleep tight, Bobby Joe."

"NO! NO! DON'T HIT ME! I WON'T DO IT AGAIN! DON'T HIT MAMA!" Michael looked over at Bobby Joe, who was sitting up in bed, eyes wide with terror. He went over and put his arms around Bobby Joe.

"It's alright, Bobby Joe. You're having a nightmare. You're safe here. Your Pa can't get you." Michael slowly pushed Bobby Joe down, patted his face, and covered him with the blanket.

"I want my Mommy!" Bobby Joe began sobbing. Scruffy jumped up on the bed and licked his hand. Bobby Joe put his face in Scruffy's fur and began to cry softly, still calling for his Mommy. Michael sat on the edge of the bed until the crying stopped and eventually Bobby Joe went back to sleep. When Michael returned to his own bed he noticed Scruffy had stayed behind, curled up next to Bobby Joe.

Michael walked into the family room, closing the door behind him. "He's asleep. We can have our family meeting now." He plopped his lanky frame into a stuffed chair, placing one long leg over a chair arm.

Dan noticed Michael was actually smiling—not his usual reaction to a family meeting. "It's the end of July and Bobby Joe's been with us a month now. I thought it was time we met as a family to talk about how things are going. Michael, you know him best so why don't you start first?"

Michael looked surprised. He'd never been asked to lead a family meeting before. He paused. "Well, the nightmares are rare now, but he still cries most nights for his Mama. I go sit with him until the sobbing stops, but Scruffy curls up closer and Bobby Joe puts his face in Scruffy's fur and cries his little heart out. Poor little guy. We know what it's like to lose your Mother." He glanced down at his hands and then continued. "By the way, Bobby Joe has asked to be called Bobby from now on. He's noticed that people up North don't use their middle name. Guess that's it for me. How about you, Dad?"

Tom cleared his throat. "I've been helping Bobby read his letters from his Mama and write to her. He really struggles with both reading and writing. He said he doesn't like to read so a couple weeks ago I started reading <u>Tom Sawyer</u> with him. I'll keep it up until school starts and then help him with his homework. He told me he had to stay home from school a lot to help his Pa at the service station. I think that's why he's so far behind. He doesn't like school and wants to quit when he reaches high school. His Pa was planning to take him out when he was twelve to work full time at the station."

"I think he's bright, Dad. I taught him checkers and now he occasionally beats me at it. He hasn't had a lot of experiences other boys his age have had."

"Yeah, Dan. I've been shooting hoops with him and he told me he's never seen a basketball game." Michael looked away, embarrassed. "I know I told you I was going to get a job in the Fall and not go back to school. I've changed my mind. What's another year out of my life? Who knows—maybe a high school diploma could actually help get me a job." He hesitated. "I might try out for the basketball team again. Saw coach in town the other day and he said he'd put me back on the team if I got my grades up."

"That'll be terrific, Michael. Bobby will really enjoy watching you play. We will too, of course," Tom added. "Along the line of not many experiences, I was wondering if we could plan a camping and fishing trip like what we did when you two were younger."

Michael leaned forward in his chair. "Hey, that's a great idea, Dad. You know how we used to plan them together in family meetings? Maybe we could have one with Bobby and plan the camping trip. It might be kinda' fun taking a kid camping and teaching him how to fish."

Tom looked at his sons—so different from each other. Michael tall for his age and into sports while his older brother was more studious and more serious about life. Yet both, right now, were totally in sync, accepting a little boy with a difficult life into their lives. He smiled.

After the meeting was over Michael went upstairs and Tom and Dan adjourned to the kitchen for a cup of coffee. "Dad, have you noticed how, when Michael walks through the house, Bobby is often two steps behind him and Scruffy is right behind Bobby. It's like a little parade. You know, Dad, I think Michael is really helping Bobby, but the reverse is also true. Bobby is helping Michael."

Dan looked over at Bobby, sitting next to Michael at the supper table. "Bobby, when you lived down South you only knew about segregation and prejudice. I've told you about Civil Rights and how a lot of us in the North and in the South are working to get it so blacks and whites are equal. On August 28th, in one week, there's to be a March on Washington. I'm going to be there and I'd like to take you with me so you can see white people and black people working together for equal rights. Would you go with me?" Bobby nodded.

"Hey, bro, I'd like to go too. I hear you yakking on about the Civil Rights Movement all the time so I'd kinda' like to see it for myself."

"I'd like to go too, son. I read that one young black man is roller skating all the way from Chicago and an eighty-two year old is bicycling from Ohio. I guess we can make the distance of a one hour drive." Tom sat up in his chair, raised his chin and gave a quick smile to Bobby and his two sons. He patted Bobby on the shoulder.

"My friend, Will, and his daughter, want to meet us at the Law Center Library. It's about a mile walk from there, but at least there'll be parking. I think his daughter, Rachel, is about your age, Bobby. Will is a teacher. He and I volunteer at the SNCC office. By the way, they are expecting some celebrities coming to the March—Harry Belafonte, James Garner, Dianne Carroll, Joan Baez, Bob Dylan, Peter, Paul and Mary, and a couple of others I believe. Some buses and trains have been hired to bring people in. They're coming from all over."

"I like Peter, Paul and Mary. Will they sing, 'Puff the Magic Dragon'?"

Michael laughed. "Probably not, Bobby. A more likely song would be 'If I had a Hammer'."

"There they are, waving at us." Dan waved back.

Bobby pulled on Michael's sleeve and he leaned down. "Michael, the little girl is a Negro."

"So...that's what happens when a black man and a black woman have a child."

"I can't be friends with a black girl. Someone might beat me up."

Michael crouched down beside Bobby and looked him in the eye. "No one here will beat you up. If you two become friends, she can come to the house and eat with us. She will be welcome. Now, let's catch up to Dan and Dad and meet them. OK?"

"OK. Things are really different here than in Alabama. It's kinda' weird." Bobby fell behind the group a little and kept his distance. Dan rubbed his chin and watched Bobby walking by himself and looking over his shoulder. Michael grabbed Bobby's hand and moved him along as the crowd got thicker. Bobby's eyes got huge. "C'mon, Bobby! Stop messing around! Keep up!"

"Okay everyone. Back to the car," Dan commanded. Silently, they meandered down the pavement. That is, silent, until Bobby piped up, "Peter, Paul and Mary didn't sing my favorite, 'Puff the Magic Dragon', but the hammer song was good."

I liked 'Blowin' in the Wind', didn't you, Dad?"

"Yes, Rachel, I liked the songs Mahalia Jackson, Joan Baez and Bob Dylan sang too. I 'spose you two weren't too interested in the speakers." Turning to Dan, Will asked, "What did you think of John Lewis from SNCC saying '...we want our freedom and we want it now.'? I understand he had to revise his speech because some of the Civil Rights leaders thought it was too inflammatory. In fact, the archbishop wasn't going to appear if he didn't change some of it."

"It still was pretty strong though. I liked Martin Luther King, Jr., quoting the Negro spiritual, 'Free at last, free at last. Thank God Almighty, we are free at last.' Oh, if that were only so!"

Bobby kept looking around him and then back at Rachel. He peeked around Michael and called out, "Rachel, what do you like to do best?"

Rachel thought for a moment, then replied, "I guess read. How about you? What do you like to do?"

"Go camping and fishing, definitely. We go to a favorite spot on the river, put up our tents, and then fish. At supper we build a fire and cook the fish and eat them. Then we roast marshmallows. It's so much fun."

"I've never been camping. Dad, why haven't we ever gone camping?"

"Oh oh. Now I'm in for it. Rachel will go on about how she's a deprived child. I've never been camping and don't know the first thing about it."

Tom smiled. "Perhaps we can remedy that." He looked at Dan, Michael and Bobby. "How about we plan a camping trip before school starts and invite these two deprived people?" Dan and Michael nodded. Rachael jumped up and down.

Bobby looked around, moved out from Michael's shadow, and did a quick little jig. "How about next weekend?"

Sarah came into the room, excitement written all over her face. "Richard, you should have gone. What a crowd! Wow! People everywhere, so close you could barely move. Every spot of ground was taken!" Sarah waved her arms around in great exaggerated circles. "The whole place was packed from the Lincoln Memorial out to the Washington monument beyond the reflecting pool. Every inch of the lawns were filled with people too! Heads and shoulders as far as you could see in all directions. But it was all so peaceful. The buses just kept coming, scores of them every hour. I thought we were going to be crushed or there'd be some kind of riot, but everyone was so patient. You missed hearing a great speech by Martin Luther King, Jr., and fantastic music by people like Mahalia Jackson and Bob Dylan. People raised their arms in the air and joined hands, moving side to side with the music. Laughing and singing! And they were black and white, next to each other. You know, the March wasn't just about ending segregation in the South, it was so that all races had access to jobs, quality education, and affordable housing. And we sang 'We Shall Overcome' at the end. I'll never see anything like that again as long as I live. Oh, Richard, it was such a positive step in the Movement." Sarah stood, eyes shining and hands clasped together.

"I wonder how long that will last. I agree with Malcolm X." Richard snorted. "He calls it the 'Farce on Washington'."

Sarah glared at him, mouth open and arms spread, "How can you say that?"

"It's presenting an inaccurate picture of racial harmony." Richard pointed his finger at her. "You'll see, Sarah, it won't make a bit of lasting difference in the Civil Rights Movement. I've tried it your way and all I got was beat up. We need to take real action. Enough is enough."

"You're wrong, Richard. If only you saw the crowd. You have to be wrong."

"Come on, Rachel. I'll show you how we set up our tents." Bobby pulled a canvas bag with a tarp, tent and pegs in it and they began setting up one of the tents on a grassy spot overlooking the river. Dan, Michael and Tom got their tents and showed Will how to set up his and one for Rachel. Will was inside his tent when a car drove up and a middle aged couple with 2 teen age girls got out.

"Howdy neighbors. Mind if we set up over here?"

Tom looked up and waved. "No, that's fine with us." Just then Will came out of his tent.

"Hey, wait a minute. Is that Negro with you?" Bobby and Rachel ran up from the river, holding hands. "That's disgusting. A white boy holding hands with a Negro. Dorothy, we can't stay here. Get back in the car, children."

After they drove away Tom told Michael to take Rachel and Bobby into the woods to gather branches for a fire. "I'm so sorry, Will."

Will looked down at his feet. "This is a week after the March on Washington and it hasn't really changed things, has it? I can shield my daughter from some things, but not prejudice and hate. She'll encounter that all her life, wherever she lives."

"You can see how it perpetuates, can't you? Those 2 girls have learned prejudice from their parents and when they get married they'll pass it onto their kids, and so on. I don't know how we break that cycle." Dan shook his head. "Look at our two. They were so natural with each other, but when they heard that man say how disgusting it was that they were holding hands, they immediately dropped their hands to their sides. I'll bet they don't hold hands the rest of this weekend."

"We aren't going to let those idiots spoil our camping trip. We came to have fun and we're gonna' have fun. A pox on them!" Tom pounded his fist in his other hand to illustrate how he felt. "Now, let's go fishin'."

Bobby looked up from his wood gathering chore and saw that Rachel was ahead of them. "Michael? You told me it was safe here! It's not much different here than down South, is it? People here don't like blacks either, do they?"

Michael paused, thinking what to say. "There's prejudice, people hating people who are different from them, all over the country, Bobby. I guess in the South they're just more blatant, more in the open with their hate. We can't let their prejudice affect us though. We know prejudice is wrong and we need to take a stand against it, like Dan does. This weekend we'll have fun and enjoy each other as friends and not be influenced by people who hate. We're all still safe here. OK, Bobby?"

"OK."

Richard, stretched out on the sofa, reading the paper, looked up at Sarah as she walked by on her way to the kitchen. "Didn't I tell you that the March on Washington wouldn't make a difference? It's been less than a month and Alabama's Governor Wallace used his state troopers to try to keep blacks out of the schools. He had to allow integration when President Kennedy federalized the Alabama National Guard and the black students were escorted into schools. That touched off some racist violence--a couple of bombings and rallies by the Ku Klux Klan. And yesterday a bomb ripped through the Sixteenth Street Baptist Church in Birmingham, killing 4 teen-age girls. A 13 year old boy was shot and killed too. Just ask the parents of those girls and that 13 year old boy if they think the March did much good."

Roy listened intently as the speaker at their Birmingham Klavern was introduced and began his talk by saying that the terrorists who bombed the Sixteenth Street Baptist Church deserved medals. "The 4 little girls weren't children. Children are little people, little human beings, and that means white people...They're just little niggers...and if there's 4 less niggers tonight, then I say, Good for whoever planted the bomb." Roy and the other Klan members nodded and clapped. Roy thought to himself, I'm pretty sure it was the man they call Dynamite Bob and other Klansmen from the Eastview Klavern 13. Well, good.

"Dad, what's wrong?" Dan entered the living room on November 22nd to find his Father sitting on the sofa, tears running down his face. Tom just pointed at the TV. There was the President's car going down a street in Dallas. Suddenly shots rang out and the President appeared to fall over onto Jackie's shoulder. It dawned on Dan what had happened. President Kennedy, our President, has been shot. What's going to happen to this country now? Later Dan sat with Tom in the living room. "I can't believe this," Dan moaned.

"That's not the half of it," Tom answered slowly. "What do you think the Russians are going to do now? What's going to happened to the stability of this country? We should prepare." Jimmy York stopped by Roy's service station. "Hey, Roy, did you hear the news? President Kennedy's been shot. Johnson is an 'ole southern boy from Texas so maybe he'll stop this integration crap and help us preserve the south."

Sarah was watching TV and crying. Richard put his arm around her, trying to comfort her. "I know you really liked and admired President Kennedy. I must admit that, despite a slow start, he was supporting the Civil Rights Movement and was trying to get the Civil Rights Act through Congress. I wonder what President Johnson will do with the Act."

"Dad and Dan, I'm taking this opportunity to call a family meeting while Bobby is asleep, since any of us can call a family meeting." Michael looked at both of them. "We haven't had a Christmas since Mom died, but I'm wondering if we should have one this year for Bobby. He's never had a Christmas. He said Santa never found his house. When I told him about gift exchanges he wondered if he could send his Mama a gift. He wants to use the allowance money he gets from doing chores to buy something special so it will be just from him. I told him I'd take him shopping and help him wrap it."

"So, Michael, are you suggesting we do as we used to—pick out a Christmas tree, attend the Christmas service at the Church and exchange gifts?" asked Tom, slowly rubbing his chin.

"Good idea, Michael. Can't you just see Bobby's face Christmas morning? By the way, are you planning to get that cheer leader a gift too?" Dan smirked as Michael's face turned red. His brother had become very popular with the girls—one in particular--since he'd become a high school basketball star. Bobby loved attending the games and now hero worshiped Michael even more.

"Let's go to a tree lot next week and Bobby can help pick out our tree and help decorate it. We'll show him what a family Christmas is all about." Tom stood up, smiling. "It will be good to celebrate Christmas again."

"Bobby, it's only 5:30 AM." Michael put his pillow over his head and turned away.

"But Santa's come and I saw lots of presents under the tree."

Michael groaned and sat up. He was remembering the many early Christmas mornings when he and Dan did this to their parents. I guess this is payback. "OK, let's wake up Dad and Dan."

Wrapping paper was strewn all over the living room floor. Bobby had quit exclaiming about everything and was now playing quietly with his erector set. Dan smiled at how excited Bobby had been. The kid can always lift your mood, he admitted to himself and smiled. He sat back and drummed on the arm of his chair, eyes wandering around the room until he noticed the pile of Christmas cards. Might as well go through them while I'm sitting here. He ripped open an envelope and looked at a photo card of friends of theirs. Judy is sure growing up. She must be about 5 now. This one is addressed to me, with no return address. He ripped open the envelope and read:

"Dear Dan, We know about you and your ongoing activities in support of the civil rights movement. Just want you to know that the KKK is alive and well in the North too. We have a Klan here in Maryland and have selected you as someone who needs to be educated about the Klan and what we do to people who push integration on us. If you continue your involvement in civil rights you or your family members, including little Bobby, may suffer. We will be watching you. Yours truly, KKK"

Chapter 22

1964

Dan, a worried expression on his face, spread the papers out on police sergeant Miller's desk. "I've been getting threatening letters once a month since Christmas. The first came in a Christmas card. The March one came yesterday. They all say if I continue my Civil Rights work a member of my family might get hurt. I can't stop my volunteer work with SNCC and I'm planning to participate in the Freedom Summer to help get Negroes registered to vote. I'll be leaving in June for Mississippi. But how can I leave if my leaving might put them in jeopardy?"

"Have you told any of your family members about this?"

"No, but I'm thinking of telling my brother, Michael. I don't want to worry my Dad and little Bobby, but someone in the family should know, just so there's two of us keeping an eye on things."

"Good idea." The sergeant stroked his chin. "Have you had any thoughts as to who could be doing this? Friends? Neighbors?"

"I've been trying to think. It's someone who obviously knows about our family so it could be friends or neighbors or even church friends. I've tried to think of someone I know spouting off extreme statements or prejudicial comments, but I can't think of anyone."

"I'm sorry, Mr. Edwards, we don't have enough here to go on, but please let us know if you get any more threatening letters or have any idea of who it might be."

Dan put his face in his hands. "I don't know what to do. The police don't have enough to go on and the threats get stranger and stranger; 'Flames of white pride will punish you.' 'Traitors will burn.' and 'Things will get hot for you and your family if you don't stop.' or this one, 'We'll come when you're asleep.'"

"Wow, Dan! Who do you think could be sending these?" Michael looked over the letters, one by one, shaking his head as he did so.

"I don't know, but we need to take them seriously. I'm worried something might happen when I leave for Mississippi in June, or even before then. That's why I'm asking you to help me keep an eye on Dad and Bobby."

"We've got to get Dad involved; the two of us can't keep watch all the time. It's not possible. Something will happen. Dad will be furious if we keep this from him."

Dan shook his head slowly in a great arc, "No. It's too late. He'd already be furious anyway if he found out what I've been hiding. There's no need to worry him. No. Just you and I keep watch."

"Woof!" agreed Scruffy, sneaking in between their legs.

"And Scruffy too," grinned Dan. "Together we'll catch this before it starts."

"Woof! Woof! Woof!" Scruffy was barking excitedly into the darkness of the front picture window.

"There's someone out there!" Michael whispered.

Dan responded in a normal tone. "Don't get excited. You know how Scruff gets when he hears any sound outside."

"I know my own dog, Dan. This bark is different!" Michael grabbed his jacket and ran to the door.

"Together, remember! Don't just go out by yourself," Dan yelled back. He was tired and slow. The nights of worrying and studying dragged his body down. As he swung open the front door a stinging chemical scent burned his nostrils. Was it acid? No. He'd smelled that before in chemistry class and this scent was different. He flipped the switch for the outside light. Nothing happened. He flipped it again. A flickering light dimly lit the outdoor stoop; it was not from the outside light. Dan craned his neck as he fumbled in the dim light. Now he recognized the smell. It was kerosene. "Michael!" coughed Dan. There was no response. A loud crackling sound filled his ears. He took a deep breath and leaped out into the front yard.

"Dan, come here. See that?" Michael pointed to a wooden cross, 5' in height, that was on fire in their yard.

"Keep your voice down! Don't wake Dad or Bobby! We don't want this to turn into a bigger problem," Dan whispered.

Another light, this one much stronger, shone from inside the house. "What's going on out there?" Tom came out onto the porch, dressed in his robe, and saw Dan and Michael putting out a small fire. "What?"

Michael groaned, "Come inside, Dad, and we'll fill you in." After they'd settled in the family room Dan handed Tom the letters, including the latest one for April. "I've called the police about the cross burning. They should be here soon."

Tom looked at both of them. "And when were you planning to tell me about these?" Tom's eyes darted from Dan to Michael and back again, his face bright red. "This is my house and you are my family. Don't you think I have a right to know what's going on?"

"Sorry, Dad. I had no right to keep it from you. Now that you know we can work together to protect Bobby and each other and try to figure out who would send these letters. Are you okay?"

"Of course I'm not okay!" snapped Tom.

"This shouldn't have been such a shock for you. I'm sorry. I should have shown you and Michael the letters from the beginning. We all need to be part of this."

"Hey, listen ta this." Roy held up a newspaper. "It's the Cavalier, a college newspaper from the University of Virginia. My cousin sent it to me 'cuz he thought I'd be innerested. It has a quote in it from the Imperial Wizard Shelton." Roy looked around to make certain he had the Klan members' attention and then read: "'Our aim is to educate the people to the conspiracy between Jews, niggers and communists to take over the government. We all know the nigger ain't smart enough to manipulate the moves he's makin'. It is the Jews who are back of this.'"

As Richard and Sarah sat down at the kitchen table for supper, Sarah helped herself to the potatoes. "Next month, June 5th, I'm leaving for Mississippi to help with the Freedom Summer. Along with registering people to vote and perhaps teaching at the Freedom Schools, I'll be sending back articles for the Washington Post. Do you want to come along?"

"No, Sarah, I can't. I have to work this summer to have enough for tuition in the Fall. You'd better be very careful. Why, Cambridge, Maryland, just had a demonstration where demonstrators were sprayed with pepper gas. If that can happen here, just think what the Klan in Mississippi might do to disrupt the Freedom Summer. I wish you wouldn't go. I'll worry about you."

Sarah smiled. "When will you realize I'm a grown up now? We'll always travel in twos and threes and take care of each other."

It was late summer in downtown Baltimore. Flowers bloomed and birds sang. His theater was always in winter though, Jim thought, as he shifted nervously on his cold wooden stool. It was the same feeling the day his father left when he was five. The cold returned just before his mother gave up caring about whether he existed.

Maybe he and Michael could party and he could forget—for awhile. Michael was a pretty laid back guy and was a warm dude. He'd do his best, maybe he could prove himself to Michael. He took out a paper, licked it, rolled up the best pot he could find, careful not to separate out the stems and seed for his new friend.

"Tell me about that great family of yours, man. Are you guys doin' anything this weekend?"

Michael looked at him with a raised eyebrow and a half smile showing through his stubble. "Wait man! I know it's a slow day, and hey, you're cool and all, but you know I just can't get high right now, man." He grabbed his mop awkwardly and looked around. "I got work to do."

Jim scrunched up his nose and snorted. Abandoned again. "I guess you have to concentrate on work more these days to try to help out Bobby with all those school supplies and things. I know I'd be grateful if I had a brother like you," he muttered in a strange tone of voice.

"Why yes. That- That is exactly what I'm concerned with right now. Heck, man. Sometimes you know more about my family than I do!"

"Maybe I should come around and show you boys how to fish properly."

Michael straightened up. "Look, I told you Jim. I'm sorry, but the fishing trip is strictly family. You can't come."

Jim frowned. "Well- yeah. Yeah. I guess I understand how things are. Family is important. You have to know who you stand with, and that Bobby sounds like a cool kid. Aren't you afraid Dan's kinda' a bad agitating influence on him?"

Michael laughed, "Dan? Maybe you've not been listening as closely as I thought. You don't know my family that well if you think Dan is a bad influence. I think he's trying for President Goody-Goody of Squares Ville. He's annoying and boring, but Bobby should look up to him."

Jim frowned and he dropped the joint.

"Whoa! Watch what you're doing! This is a gas station you know. What's wrong? You look like something stung you, man!"

Jim stood up."It's nothing. I hope you and Bobby have a good time on your little family trip. 'Bye, Michael."

"Hey! Don't take off like that! You gotta' help me close up. Hey!" Michael gazed out the window, scratching his head for a moment. Looking down, he noticed the joint. Dang it, leav'n the joint on the floor in a gas station! He's gonna' cause a fire some day, the blockhead! Michael muttered as he stomped out the joint.

Scruffy stood in Bobby's bed, barking and barking. Bobby rolled over, told him to shut up, put the pillow over his head and tried to get back to sleep. Scruffy then began to lick his face and pull on his pj top. "Hey! Scruffy, Michael and Dan, and Tom told me it'll all be okay here in the north. We don't have really bad guys here. I don't wanna sit up at night anymore, I'm tired of that. Go away before you get Tom mad at me!" He drifted off to sleep. Then jolted awake again. Scruff had barked in his ear and scratched his arm. "What?" Bobby sat up. This is when he noticed the red glow outside his bedroom door.

Tom turned over in bed. "Bobby, I told you to go to sleep. Tell Scruff to go to sleep too." His eyes rolled around in his head. Thoughts broke into fragments. Tom felt as if he was rising out of his bed and looking around his room. This was far stranger though; instead of the north wall of his house there was something grey and wispy. It was like the fog you see in early morning when hunting. How he wished he'd shared more of these things with his sons. But this fog seemed to fill everything now. His heart, mind, his life was lived in a fog. I don't want to remember. My pain helps no one. I want the fog, he shouted in his mind. He dreamed he was opening his arms and the fog of those exciting, carefree morning hunts was enveloping him. Those foggy mornings before he lost his wife; when his kids were younger. He saw Dan's face, ten years old, happily holding up the antlers of a deer on a foggy morning. Next it was Michael, holding up a fish by a misty lake. This fog was great; he could stay here now where he'd been staying anyway since his wife died. Wait. What happens to Dan and Michael if I stay here? Tom asked, watching as the smiling Michael aged before his eyes and his memories. That's right. Michael wasn't here, neither was Dan. Right now they were so much older and out with girls or something. Who was the young one who stood in the mist here right now. The fog got darker and sinister. The boy's smile faded and his face changed. It was Bobby! He couldn't stay in this fog in his memories; Bobby needed him. Bobby needed all his help growing up: he had to stay. Bobby needed him. Bobby was talking to him now, but he couldn't hear. His throat burned. That's not fog. It's smoke! Must-get-Bobby-outside! His brain's thoughts gasped with his breathing in the thick smoke.

"Wake up! Tom! Fire!"yelled Bobby, shaking Tom's shoulders. "Don't be dead, Tom! I need your help! Don't be dead!" Bobby screamed again, shaking Tom by the shoulders, trying to pull him out of his bed. A roaring cough came from somewhere inside Tom and he stumbled to his feet. Without a word Tom grabbed Bobby in one arm and Scruffy in another and marched dazedly toward the stairs. Bobby held his breath as the smoke got thicker and hoped the stairs were down there somewhere under Tom's feet.

Stairs! Got to get through! I'll hold my breath so I can get down to the front door. Tom marched downstairs and out the door. He marched through smoke like a single minded machine, half asleep, half adrenaline. Tom tripped on something and fell face first into the grass and passed out.

A hand with an oxygen mask swept down to Bobby's face from somewhere. His eyes grew large. There was a fire truck and their neighbor, Mrs. Parling, was barely recognizable in her strange night robe and curlers. She picked her way across the lawn in her thin slippers. "Oh Bobby, are you okay?" She rushed toward him.

"Aah!" Bobby exclaimed.

"I called the fire department. Another man was here in your yard earlier. Was he a guest of yours? Is he still in the house? Where are your brothers, Bobby?"

Bobby, still holding Scruffy, put him on the ground and noticed that it looked like Scruffy wasn't breathing. Bobby started crying. A fireman came over, knelt by Scruffy and put the oxygen mask over his head. Soon Scruffy started moving, stood up, and wobbled over to Bobby, wagging his tail. Bobby hugged him and told the fireman, "Thank you."

Just then Dan and Michael arrived home and, when they heard how Scruffy had saved Bobby and their Father, Michael promised Scruffy the biggest bone he could find in the butcher shop. "Scruffy is a hero, Bobby, and you are too, for waking Tom up." Bobby beamed, and Scruffy was passed around and hugged.

"Our neighbors have invited us to spend the night, but I think we should just go to a motel and be by ourselves after all this trauma. What do you think?"

Police Sergeant Miller looked at Tom, Dan and Michael sitting across the desk from him. "Well, it looks as if you had a narrow escape. Can someone fill me in?"

Dan glanced at the others, hesitated and then began. "We had planned a fishing trip for this weekend, but then Bobby was running a slight fever so we postponed it. Dad said he'd stay home with Bobby Saturday night because my brother, Michael, here, said he could get us a couple of hot dates. We'd taken the weekend off from work so wanted to do something. When we arrived home we saw Dad and Bobby being treated for smoke inhalation." Dan paused, looking at the sergeant. "We would have lost both of them if it hadn't been for our dog, Scruffy, waking Bobby and Bobby waking Dad."

"It's official." The Sergeant looked serious. "The fire department discovered oily rags next to the back of the house, below the kitchen window. Whoever did this wasn't trying to hide that it was done on purpose, although, unfortunately, there weren't any other clues. The shoes had been apparently wrapped in plastic bags and there were no prints. We'll certainly be looking for the person or persons who set the fire and who probably also sent those threatening letters."

The house had been thoroughly cleaned and the water from the hoses sucked up from the carpets and the floors dried. Tom, Dan and Michael were sitting at the kitchen table drinking coffee and eating doughnuts. "At least there wasn't too much damage to the house and our insurance will take care of most of the cost." Tom looked away for a moment. Turning around he revealed a frighteningly dark expression. He leaned back in his seat and relaxed his body, but his hands gripped the arms of the chair. "I hope I never meet the guys who did this. I don't know what I'd..."

"That's not the point, Dad. You and Bobby could have died in that fire. We have got to get this bastard locked up or none of us will rest easy."

Michael looked thoughtful. "Come to think of it, I have an idea who this bastard might be." He paused, then continued. "There's this new guy, Jim Snider, working at the gas station and a lot of times he works weekends, when I'm working there part time. He's always asking me about my family. His Father took off with another woman and his Mother had to work all the time to put food on the table, so he didn't have much of a home life. When I was telling him about Bobby's first Christmas he told me he'd never had one since his father left when he was about five. He was interested in what each of us was doing, so I did tell him about you and your work with the Civil Rights Movement, Dan. Oh man, I hope..."

Dan stood, leaned forward, and held his finger in the air. "Did he ever make any comment that could have indicated some involvement with the KKK?"

"No. man."

"Stop that! I'm not 'man', I'm your brother! What's with your bad English lately?"

"Okay, brother," Michael smirked. "Anyways, not that I can recall. Oh, I almost forgot. I was telling him about our fishing trip and so he knew we were planning to be gone all weekend."

"So, he could have thought the house would be empty Saturday night."

"If it was him, he was planning to burn down the house, but not kill anyone. I'm going to call the Sergeant. I think he needs to check out this man." Dan got up and went to the phone.

In a dark room with abrasive light green walls, Jim Snider sat, muttering, at his feet. A policeman slammed his hand on a cracked white desk. "A boy, Bobby, the boy you say you so admire, almost died! Is that nothing to you?"

Jim looked up, tears in his eyes, "Bobby? Then me, too," he whispered harshly.

The policeman opened a small metal door and tapped on the wall. "Get a psychiatrist in here..."

It was a couple days later when Dan came into the family room and sat next to Michael on the sofa. "Well, Michael, you were right. That was Sergeant Miller on the phone. He interrogated that fellow, Jim Snider, and he caved and confessed to setting the fire. He thought no one would be at home because of the fishing trip. He became very upset when he thought he could have killed

Bobby. The Sergeant said there was some involvement with the KKK, but another part of it was that this Jim became emotionally involved in the story of our family and didn't think I should leave the family, especially Bobby, and go to Mississippi. Apparently, he was identifying with Bobby and trying to place himself in our family. The Sergeant said they've ordered a psychiatric assessment. I'm feeling greatly relieved because now I can go to Mississippi and not worry about you three."

"I'm so proud of you, Dan—4 years to get your B.S. Degree and then another 3 years to get your JD, your law degree." Tom gave his son a hug. "And we enjoyed your graduation ceremony, didn't we, guys?" Michael and Bobby nodded. "Now, sit down and tell us your plans for this summer. We know you're going to Mississippi, but give us more details."

After everyone was situated in the family room, Dan looked at the others. "I've taken a job with COFO, the Council of Federated Organizations—a federation of all the national Civil Rights organizations in Mississippi. It also includes local political and action groups and some other organizations. This summer it's running a Freedom Summer, helping Negroes register to vote, because in Mississippi only 6.7% are registered. There will also be Freedom Schools. Charles Cobb, SNCC field secretary, says the overall theme of the school would be 'the students a force for social change in Mississippi'. My job will be to work on any legal issues that may arise. I'll be leaving in a couple of weeks, but I'll keep in touch."

"Michael, you can have my room this summer while I'm gone. In the Fall some friends are going to help me build a small apt. over the garage so then each of us can have our own space." Dan looked at Tom, Michael and Bobby. "I'll miss you."

Michael looked away into the distance.

"What is it, Michael?"

"I dunno. Just with you leaving its not gonna' be the same, man. Gotta stick around for Bobby. I know I act like I don't give a... Well, you know. But with you hitting the road, it's not a good time for me to leave."

"What?! You know you can't do that, especially now! And what about high school?"

"Yeah. I know, man. Don't worry. I'm just getting restless, that's all"

It was June 21st when Sarah poked her head inside the Meridian COFO headquarters. "May I come in?"

Three men looked up at her, smiling. "Of course. I'm Michael Schwerner. The gentlemen to my right are James Chaney and Andrew Goodman."

"I'm Sarah Graydon from Baltimore, and I'm reporting for duty," said Sarah, smiling back.
"Well, Sarah, Andrew and I are from New York and James is from here. James and I spoke to the congregation of the Mount Zion Methodist Church in Longdale, Mississippi, about setting up a Freedom School in the Church. I also urged them to register to vote." Michael frowned. "Since then members of the congregation have been beaten and the church has been burned to the ground. We're just heading out for Longdale to investigate. We plan to be back by 4:00 PM, so perhaps we'll see you then."

The three got up, said their good-byes, and left for Longdale. They never returned.

July 11, 1964
Dear Richard,
I know you've heard about the three missing Civil Rights workers. It's all over the news. Some of the Negroes here think it's getting so much publicity because two of the workers are white and that's why the FBI has become involved. I don't know about that. I'm sure you think that's the case. As for me, I've been too involved with individual people to become cynical. I know we are all grieving here. It's been three weeks and most people now are

certain they've been murdered. They found their burned out car. The FBI and the Navy haven't found the Civil Rights workers but they did find the bodies of eight Negro men. We hope for the best, but you should understand that we are not naive. Mary scolded Frank and Jeanie for going out without good cause. I agree with her and have started asking more questions when my friends decide go anywhere. Every day at lunch I stop by the office and try to call everyone. I'm being careful, but I have to check in on my friends or I'd not be able to sleep at night.

I met Michael, Andrew and James my first day at the COFO headquarters and they were very nice to me. They were such wonderful persons. We discussed their lives in journalism class today. A few in class didn't want to say anything about them, but others thought everything should be discussed no matter how painful. Some say the outrage over their disappearance and murder helped President Johnson and the Civil Rights activists bring about the passage of the Civil Rights Act of 1964. I'm glad the Act passed, but am sorry if it took the murders of three civil rights workers to pass it. I'd rather have Michael, Andrew and James back with us. I know it's too early (I mean it just passed!), but I don't see a piece of paper changing things quickly enough for any of us. I guess I can understand a little why you think the way you do. Peace is still the way, however, because we can't risk being drawn down into this kind of sickness with those who oppose us.

I know we've all heard rumors about MLK from the other freedom riders. Yet you know, as I do, that he was needed elsewhere. Besides that doesn't change the truth of his words. If all people in this country could only experience life through our eyes, especially the dreadful pain experienced by our southern brothers and sisters. We've had it hard, you know, but it's nothing compared to how these people suffer down here. Mary's husband just got beaten within an inch of his life a month before I arrived for 'looking at a white girl'. Such terrible nonsense! Those hateful minds will not change with guns and laws--they must see what we see.

Now for some happier news. When I arrived in June I worked on helping to register Negroes to vote, but when the Freedom Schools opened during the first week of July, I was asked to teach. It's so exciting to see such a solid change happening in our new friends' lives every day! Education is the key, Richard. All of us need to learn and become stronger in voice. We need to encourage our brothers and sisters of the South to bear witness to their suffering. I'm now at the Ruleville Freedom School. Our curriculum is the following:

9-9:15 AM Civil Rights songs
9:30-10:30 Core classes: Negro history and citizenship curriculum (I help teach Negro history.)
10:30-11:30 Choice of dance, drama, art, auto mechanics, guitar and folksinging or sports (I teach drama. It's lots of fun!)
12-2 PM School closed.
2-4 Classes in French, religion, craft, music, play writing, journalism (I teach journalism.)
4 PM Seminar on non violence

We have small children up to the elderly with the average age being 15. The evening school is popular with adults who work in the fields and the kitchens and teens who are working during the day. You wouldn't be as skeptical about our movement if you saw the skills and the power these people are grasping. This will really change things. I know it! But everything takes a long time, even what you're proposing. You should at least include free education in your grand plans. It will change the future forever. There's an elderly gentleman taking classes who has had such a hard life. It gives me hope to hear how he's lived through beatings, poverty and discrimination and stayed strong. He has such a kind, noble attitude. Now, because of our training, he's writing his story for everyone to read. I hope as many white people as possible down here read it. Many others are following his example. Education has brought so much hope to all of us, worker and resident alike, in Mississippi. For the sake of Michael, Andrew and James' families, I hope they find them quickly. Regardless of the outcome, their stories need to be told too.

I know you worry about me and have heard that there have been beatings, arson and false arrests, but we don't go anywhere alone and we never ride in a car that has both whites and blacks, because that is just asking for trouble. The KKK is just too sneaky. Those sickos use any bit of personal information about a person against him or her. Now that we know this all too well, we don't talk to strangers about where we're going. We don't even share names or photos with some people.

The schools close in August so I'll see you then.

Love,
Sarah

"Oh look, Mary. Bobby Joe's included a photo of him with their dog, Scruffy, in his letter. That's the dog that saved his and Dan's Father's lives when they had the fire. Oh my, how Bobby Joe has grown." Betty Lou passed the photo to Mary and when it was returned to her she placed it in her pocket.

"Aren't you going to leave it here with the letters, Betty Lou? I thought you were afraid of Roy finding anything from Bobby Joe."

"Oh, Mary, I just have to have this photo to look at every day. It's of my boy, and I miss him so much. Besides, since you keep all the money I've earned from sewing Roy has given up looking in my purse and around the house because he never finds any money. I don't have to worry about that anymore. It's taking me longer to save for a bus ticket because I have to buy the groceries with the money I earn. Roy doesn't make much at the station and what he does earn he spends on booze. Oh well, I should have the money in another few months and then I'm on my way. In the meantime I can look at the photo of my boy and dream of the time we'll be together." Betty Lou smiled. "Now that I'm here I might as well finish the dress I've been working on."

"OK, but first let's have a cup of coffee and some fresh baked cookies. Remember how Bobby Joe used to love my cookies?"

"Richard, it's so good to be home!", Sarah exclaimed, as she put down her suitcase and threw herself on her brother, giving him a big hug. "Let me make us some coffee and then I have so much to tell you. Can you believe it's already August and the summer is almost over? It really went by quickly for me down in Mississippi."

Once they were settled at the kitchen table and sipping their coffee Sarah continued. "First of all, I really enjoyed teaching. Attendance varied because it wasn't compulsory, but the adults especially seemed to like the classes. We did notice a difference in their attitude at the end of the summer. Perhaps they will be more likely to push for social change now."

"Good. Let them push for social change and you stay here, like a sane person," Richard exclaimed.

Sarah became serious. "You've heard they just found the bodies of the three civil rights workers August Fourth. An informant told the FBI where to find them, and well, it's not good."

Richard shook his head, "This is not convincing me that you're going to be any safer out there. You know that, right?"

"They were buried at an earthen dam a few miles south of Philadelphia, Mississippi. I have friends; people to think of down there! And they take good care of me too. I made it back didn't I? Everyone looks out for us. We know more about what's happening than most. Well, we who were in Mississippi probably heard some things that didn't get in the papers. When everyone was looking for them, Neshobe County Sheriff Rainey said they were probably just hiding and trying to cause a lot of bad publicity for that part of the state. Turns out he was one of the men involved in the murders."

"I knew all the time they were dead. Those dumb kids." Richard sighed.

"What do you mean, 'those dumb kids?' This was planned. Listen, there's nothing they could have done. The burning of the Church was to lure the CORE workers to Neshoba County. Chaney was arrested for speeding on the way back to headquarters. The other two were held to be investigated. They were released from the Neshoba County jail around 10 PM and were followed by

Deputy Sheriff Price. The lynch mob members were notified which highway the three were taking and they caught them and drove them to a secluded area called Rock Cut Road."

"This is the horrible part, Richard. A man named Alton Roberts, who had been dishonorably discharged from the US Marines, he... he." Sarah looked down at her coffee cup and wiped a tear from her eye.

"He what? What, Sarah?" Richard tensed up his body and flattened his palm on the table, searching her eyes.

"He asked Michael and Andrew both, 'Are you that Nigger lover?' and then he took his gun out and shot them each in the heart!"

"Poor bastards." Richard patted Sarah on the shoulder. "I guess they didn't get Roberts."

"No. No. Not exactly, Richard. I think the FBI knows who they are because the informant named them all. He wanted to plea bargain for a lighter sentence. They haven't rounded them up yet, but there are several involved. But there's more."

"What happened to James Chaney?"

"They beat him, really, really badly, Richard, and then two men shot him."

"Dang!"

"They took the bodies to an earthen dam on a farm owned by one of the White Knights Klan members. Their bodies were buried by a bulldozer. They never would've been found if it hadn't been for that informant. Apparently the Klan member who recruited and organized the lynch mob is a Baptist minister named Edgar Ray Killen."

"After the men were murdered, Deputy Sheriff Price told the lynch mob they'd done a good job and that they'd struck a blow for the white man. Price also said that Mississippi could be proud of them. He warned them that the man who talked would be 'dead, dead, dead.'" Suddenly Sarah put her head down on the kitchen table and began to sob. Richard reached over and put his arm around her. After a couple minutes she lifted her head and wiped away her tears. "I'm sorry, Richard. I thought I was handling what happened this summer, but I can't seem to get it out of my head what Negroes down there go through. They have to be totally submissive to the whites or they can lose their jobs, be beaten, or end up dead like the eight Negroes the FBI found. We volunteers helping to register voters or teaching in the schools risked arson, beatings, false arrest, and in the case of the three Civil Rights Workers, murder; but Negroes in the South have to live with the threat of that every day of their lives."

"Well, you're not going down there again. And you're not associating with any whites again either."

"You should meet some of these white men and women I worked with, then you'd see. They're not all bad. But we're so lucky to live here."

"Lucky? Okay, Sarah. We don't live in the South, but you still can't trust the police and you know everything is still rigged against us, North or South. Come join us with my neighborhood group. We're focusing more on self defense now. More realistic. We could use you."

"It's hard, but I just don't want to give up the more peaceful way. Two of these men who died were white. With what they gave up why shouldn't white people be involved in Civil Rights?"

"Because it's not their fight and so they can't be trusted!"

"If I accepted the view of those revolutionary papers you're always reading I'd lose everything I'd worked toward as a journalist--truth, peace- everything about myself. I've learned it with black people and white people. They are a part of me. I'd be frightened of what I'd become if I started shutting whites out of the movement like you want to do. This involves both of us, black and white, and it has to be solved by both peoples together."

"You're not based in reality! How well do you really know these white 'friends' of yours anyway?"

"It's more than some unrealistic idea. It's who I am. True, I've never known white people that well. Maybe, if I met a white person I had something more in common with I would understand them better. I love you, Richard, but I can't give up. I can't see things your way."

"Every day the white devil pulls something. Just more inhumanity, beatings and murder. You'll see. And you'll change too, for the better." Richard poured her another cup of coffee and kissed her forehead.

Oh, Betty Lou's gone somewhere. She's not expecting me until this evening. I wonder if she has any money left. She always seems to have money for food and I don't give her that much. I can sure use a drink! Roy begins to search through her drawers. What's this? A photo of a boy and a dog. Wait a minute—is that Bobby Joe? It sure looks like him, but he's a lot bigger. How would Betty Lou have a photo of Bobby Joe? She's sure got some explaining to do!

"Alright, where have you hidden my son?" Roy asked in a belligerent tone as he thrust the photo in his wife's face. "Tell me now!"

Betty Lou stood in front of him, shaking, a terrified look on her face, saying nothing.

Roy brought his fist back and punched her hard in the face, knocking her into the kitchen wall. "You had no right to take my son away from me and you will pay for this. Oh, you will really pay for this! Tell me, where is Bobby Joe?" Betty Lou put her hands over her face and scrunched over as she usually did when Roy beat on her. Roy, his face bright red and eyes glowering, looked around the kitchen, found a frying pan and hit Betty Lou over the head with it. She fell to the ground and didn't move. Roy hit and kicked her as she lay there, continually screaming, "Where's my son?"

"Betty Lou, are you all right? I heard Roy screaming at you and just saw him leave. Has he beaten you up again?" Mary cautiously opened the door and looked around, seeing nothing. She walked into the kitchen. "Oh no!"

"Hello. May I speak to Dan Edwards, please? Oh, hello, Mr. Edwards. This is Mary Davis from Alabama, Betty Lou's neighbor. I'm calling because Betty Lou is in the hospital in a coma and the doctor doesn't know if she'll come out of it. I thought you should know." Mary listened to Dan. "No, it wasn't a car accident. Her husband beat her badly because he found the photo of Bobby Joe." She listened again. "Yes, it might bring her out of the coma if she saw Bobby Joe. If you come let me know when and I'll pick you up at the airport. Good-bye."

Bobby got off the plane and ran into Mary's arms, tears running down his face. "Is my Mama dead?"

"No, Bobby Joe, she's very much alive and can't wait to see you." Mary looked at Dan. "Betty Lou woke up last night and I told her you were coming. She is really excited Bobby Joe is here.

Bobby Joe, your Mama has some bruises on her face, she's sore, and her arm is broken, but she's going to be OK. Now, let's go to the hospital."

Dan walked into Sheriff 'Bull' Connor's office and introduced himself. "I'm here to make certain Roy Ramsey is put in jail for beating up his wife so badly that she's now in the hospital."

"I'm sorry you came down here from up North for nothing, Sir. I've talked with Roy Ramsey and he said he wasn't home at the time and someone must have broken in and beat her up." "Bull" Connor smirked as he looked at Dan.

"Betty Lou said you'd say that. Apparently you said the same thing one other time he put her in the hospital. If you don't do anything I guess I'll have to go higher up to get some action. I'm not leaving until that bastard is in jail."

Dan walked into the hospital room smiling. "Betty Lou, I had our Maryland governor contact your governor, who contacted that awful sheriff of yours, Bull Connor. He quickly backed down under pressure and Roy is in jail. Now, I have a proposition for you. Fly back with us. We want you to stay in our home until you can get an apartment of your own. Bobby needs you and you certainly can't stay with Roy after this."

Betty Lou shook her head. "Oh, I couldn't impose. I have nothing to pay for rent."

"You could help us around the house like Bobby does. Can you cook?" Betty Lou nodded. "Then you'd be more than welcome. Come now, say you'll join the mad Edwards men. You can probably find a job and then can save for a place of your own."

Betty Lou hesitated. "Are you sure it's all right with your Father and brother?"

"I talked with them on the phone this morning and they can't wait to meet you. They love Bobby and I'm sure they'll love you—especially if you can cook." Dan grinned. "By the way, we just finished building an apartment over the garage that will be perfect for you and Bobby."

Bobby burst into the room. "Mama, Dan just told me you're coming home with us. It'll be December in one month and I can't wait to show you what our Christmas is like. You're gonna' love living up North."

Richard, newspaper in hand, walked into the kitchen while Sarah was preparing the evening meal. "Listen to this, Sarah. In late November, the FBI accused twenty-one Mississippi men of engineering a conspiracy to injure, oppress, threaten and intimidate Chaney, Goodman and Schwerner. Most of the offenders were just recently apprehended by the FBI. The state of Alabama refuses to charge the men with murder so the FBI is going after them with other charges."

Sarah, a bitter expression on her face, said, "I hope they all go to prison for life. At least now I can try to put it all behind me." She brightened. "After all, it's almost Christmas—a time for peace on earth, good will toward men."

Chapter 23

1965

"Didn't I tell you Christmas is wonderful here?" Bobby snuggled up to his Mama, who was sitting on the couch in their apartment above the Edwards' garage.

"Yes, and it was so nice of Tom, Dan and Michael to give me the present of a dress a little early so I could wear it when we went to the Christmas Cantata at their Church. I met so many friendly people there and I loved the music. One lady who sat beside me heard me singing and suggested I join the choir."

"You should, Mama. You've always loved to sing."

"I don't know, Bobby Joe. I need to look for a job before I do anything else. I need to start paying the family rent for this lovely apartment."

"Oh, and Mama, now that we are up North you need to just call me Bobby and you should go by Betty. People here don't usually use their middle names. And I should probably start calling you Mom instead of Mama."

"Sarah, it's a tragedy, a national tragedy, that Malcolm X was killed this February. He said, 'There's no such thing as a non violent revolution.' and I think he's right."

"I don't agree. Martin Luther King, Jr., and his followers practice non-violence and look what they've accomplished."

"Yeah, and look at all the beatings and the murders that have occurred because we practiced non-violence. Malcolm X also said, 'I don't even call it violence when it's in self defense; I call it intelligence.'"

"Well, I call it stupidity!" Sarah stood up from the kitchen table and crossed her arms. "A lot of people support us because they see in the news how we are persecuted and don't defend ourselves. That's how we got the Civil Rights Act, don't forget."

"Oh, and Richard, the paper is sending me and John, my photographer, to Alabama to cover the March that is going to go from Selma to Montgomery, Alabama, to appeal to Governor Wallace to stop police brutality and also to call attention to the struggle for suffrage. James Bevel of SCLC suggested it after that army vet, Jimmy Lee Jackson, was shot by a state trooper while trying to protect his mother from blows during a march. This march is supposed to be on Sunday, March 7th. I'll tell you about it when I return."

"Alright, but it won't accomplish anything. None of the marches do these days. Martin Luther King and his non-violence is old, gone and over."

"Well, John, Martin Luther King has flown to Washington to get permission for the march because Governor Wallace wouldn't give his permission. The people don't want to wait for King to get back and are going ahead with the march today. So let's get ready."

John stretched out his arms. "I'm just glad to take some photographs outside for a change."

"That last report we did on the Baltimore jail was a little stifling." Sarah tensed her shoulders and shivered, "I knew my brother wouldn't want to help with that one since he's so afraid of small rooms, but now I guess he's genuinely not interested in the movement anymore."

"No, probably just fed up like a lot of us. I'd like to meet him." Sarah saw John's face redden a little as he looked away.

Sarah laughed. "Well you'll get plenty of fresh air this time. We've got a march of fifty-four miles from Selma to Montgomery. It's good I have comfortable shoes."

"Look, Sarah. We'd better be careful crossing the Edmund Pettus Bridge. There's a wall of troopers going clear across the bridge. They're not going to let us pass. Poor old woman! They're hitting her. They're moving this way. Can you see from down there? They've started shoving marchers already. Knocking them down, looks like. I'm getting some pretty powerful photos."

Sarah bounced on her toes. "Oh! I wish I wasn't so short! I should witness this!"

The crowd rippled like a whip. Sarah saw a trooper rise up before her, with no chance to get out of his way. Suddenly she felt a sharp pain in her shoulder and she was pushed to the ground. Ah! Her shoulder really hurt. Wonder if it's dislocated. Where's John? They'd become separated. John was trying to get some action shots; he'd floated away in the currents of the crowd. She was drowning under people's feet. There he is—on the ground. She recognized the blue shirt. Slowly, painfully, she stood up. She tried to move her left arm to no avail.

"John, are you alright? Oh no, you're bleeding!"

"My camera! Where's my camera?"

"I have it here. It's OK."

"A trooper on horseback hit me with his whip. The horse knocked me over. I can't believe I was hit by a horse. When does that ever happen?" He looked around, noticing several demonstrators on the ground, some writhing in pain. "I need to take more photos. This is unreal." He took his camera from Sarah. With a strength that surprised her, he raised his tall, lanky frame from the ground and limped over to another bloodied lump. It was a 12 year old girl. She had a broken leg.

"Help! Help me!" she cried.

"Snap, snap, snap.", John methodically examined every angle of her with the camera.

"Help! Please!"

"Why don't you put down that stupid camera and help her? Here!"A stocky Negro burst out of the crowd, two other men following him. His angry dark eyes looked at John, then at the girl lying on the ground in obvious pain. Her screams of agony pierced right through him as they slipped a cloth under her and whisked her away. John looked at the camera in his hand, then down at his feet. "Help! Please help!", another voice called out from the crowd. John let his camera swing to his side and moved quickly toward the sound.

"Look at this Sarah. I got a photo of John Lewis, the march leader, being beaten. His skull fractured. What figures were you quoted? I was told about 600 people marched. Is that right? I got photos of troopers attacking demonstrators with billy clubs, tear gas, fire hoses and dogs. I heard they used rubber tubing wrapped in barbed wire. And the men on horseback used bull whips." John winced and gingerly pulled his shirt away from his back. "I've never felt pain like this. Let's see, my sources say fifty-six marchers were hospitalized, eighteen seriously injured. Look at the photos of the ones who are lying on the ground, bleeding."

"We're not going home yet. There's to be another Selma to Montgomery march on Tuesday, March 9th, and Martin Luther King should be in it. Sunday's march is now being called 'Bloody Sunday'. The paper picked up my article and a couple of your photos so you're stuck with me a little longer." John gave her an unusually warm smile.

"Apparently the American public are horrified with what happened. Get your camera and your marching shoes on, John."

"Well, that was disappointing. King and the others marched 2500 demonstrators to the bridge and it looked like the troopers were going to let us by. But then King just turned everyone around and marched us back the way we came. Some people were upset, especially members of SNCC, and thought he should have defied the restraining order from Judge Johnson, saying no marching until he held a hearing. I just don't know."

"Listen, did you just hear what was said on the radio?" John turned up the sound. "Something about three white ministers who were here for the march that were attacked by four white supremacists and badly beaten."

"There's talk about there being another march after the hearing, so we may be back. I want to see this march to Montgomery through to the end."

"See, I told you we'd be back. Our paper was happy with our work and they want to see it to the finish too. Since Judge Johnson granted an order on March 17th, authorizing the march, we march again on March 21st, this time under full protection of 2000 National Guard troops and federal marshals. By the way, did you hear that one of those three ministers died from being so badly beaten?"

"Yeah, I'm fed up with this," John growled.

"Sarah, it's March 25th, the final day, and we've grown from around 8000 demonstrators to they say around 25,000 are now in front of the capitol. We made it—all fifty-four miles! And no one got hurt." John pulled Sarah to her, reached down and kissed her.

"Wha?" Sarah pulled away, then seemed to change her mind and leaned in to John, putting her head back. After a longer kiss this time, John smiled down at Sarah. "I've wanted to do that for quite a while. Didn't think I could go on working with you every day and not tell you how I feel. Do you care a little for me as well?"

"Yes, John, I do. When we return to Baltimore you can come over for dinner. If our relationship survives your meeting my brother, well, then, we'll see where this goes."

"I'm home again, Richard. This march was wonderful. No one hurt this time. I've got so much to tell you." Sarah gave her brother a big hug.

"I've something to tell you, too. You probably didn't hear because you were traveling. The night the march ended a woman from Detroit, Viola Gregg Luizzo, was ferrying demonstrators back to Selma from Montgomery. She was killed because some Klansmen were angry that she had a young black man seated in the front seat next to her. Thought you'd want to know."

Sarah smiled as she cleared the table. Richard and John were in the living room, ranting and raving about politics. She could see Richard pounding his fists on the coffee table and he was saying something about Johnson not moving on the voting rights bill. She couldn't tell if they were agreeing or disagreeing.

After John left, she came out of the kitchen and approached her brother. "Stop keeping me in suspense. Do you approve or don't you?" Someone had to meet her brother's expectations. He hadn't thrown him out; that was a good sign wasn't it?

Richard began to shake his head.

"No! You can't be like this with everyone. Please! What's wrong this time?"

Richard paused, looking up. His fist lay on the arm of the chair. As he thought, he slowly dragged the fist to his side and loosened his hand. He looked down, then up into her eyes."Okay," he grunted.

"I don't get it, Richard. You've never approved of the guys I've brought home. There was always something wrong with them. Why do you like John?"

"Well, Sarah, you finally found a man who is smart, well mannered and knows how to debate. So, yeah, I approve of John."

"Congratulations, Michael. You graduated. And you looked smart up there in your cap and gown. Did Judy enjoy going out to dinner with us to celebrate?"

"Yes, Dad, she did."

"Good to see you're settling down. I must admit I was afraid you might become some kind of vagabond, especially with those hippie friends of yours. Tom slapped Michael on the back.

Michael sheepishly looked away. "Actually, Dad, plans change, but I wouldn't do that unless..."

"Let's all go into the family room and have a family meeting. We haven't had one for a long time." Tom turned to Betty. "Please join us, Betty. You're a member of the family now."

After they'd settled on the sofa and in a couple of chairs, Tom asked, "Betty, you've been here over seven months now. Is everything going okay? Do you like your apartment?"

Betty smiled. "I love it here." She hugged Bobby, sitting next to her on the sofa. "It's such a joy to be with my son, living in a lovely apartment, and being included in your family events. I'm enjoying singing in the choir of the Methodist Church too. People there have been so kind."

"I see a man walking you home from choir practice every Wednesday night."

Betty blushed. "That's Bill Richards. He's just a friend. I told him I'm still married." Betty looked so uncomfortable Tom went on. "I see you with a couple of women from the church too. One is the Pastor's wife."

Betty's eyes brightened. "Do you know, when I moved here I only had two old, faded dresses. Then you gave me a beautiful dress for Christmas. Somehow, a few ladies in your church heard about me. The pastor's wife came over with dresses that looked like new. She said people had outgrown them, but they might fit me. She mentioned, because of my situation, she knew I had to get out quickly and didn't have time to pack anything. Anyway, a couple of other ladies visited me and said they heard I could sew and they needed some sewing done. Next thing I know I was offered cleaning jobs." She hesitated. "If you need the apartment I can now look for something else for Bobby and me."

Michael, Dan and Tom protested simultaneously. Betty smiled. They were hospitable, true, but they also loved her cooking. "Thank you." Bobby breathed a sigh of relief. "We'd love to stay here, but I'm going to start paying a little more rent now that I'm steadily employed. I can never repay you for what you've done for Bobby. He's a happy boy. You helped him catch up on his studies and he has friends." She wiped tears from her eyes. "He has a family." She added, "and I have one too."

"OK, Michael, now it's your turn. What are you going to do now that you are a high school graduate?"

Michael looked thoughtful. "Well, I've been given a basketball scholarship, but it's out of state. I think I'll start at the community college in the Fall. They have a team too. Then maybe I'll transfer in a couple of years. What about you, Dan?" turning to his brother.

"Apparently, a few people in Washington heard about the legal work I did for the Civil Rights Movement and I've been offered a job working for a senator. I'll be handling legal work for him, doing some research, and going over his speeches. I start next month. Should be interesting."

"That's great, son. But I wish you'd give the Civil Rights cause a rest. There are other people who can take up the cause. You're starting to worry me."

"But this is my passion; it drives my career. Besides, realistically, it's probably only about as dangerous as Michael's basketball games."

"Oh no, man! Don't drag me into this one. You guys finish this amongst yourselves. Oh, one more thing." Michael looked at each of them. "I'm taking an auto mechanics course at the community college this summer and Dad's given me permission to buy a '55 Chevy convertible and rebuild it." He turned to Bobby. "How would you like to be my assistant and then, when you can drive, I'll let you borrow my car? We'll make it so cool that all the girls will want to ride in it." They laughed as Bobby bounced on the sofa.

Roy hunched over and gave the group of men across the bar a squinting stare. He sauntered clumsily over to their place at the counter and landed on a chair. Light glared off the glasses behind the bar. He held his head, scratched the stubble on his face and screwed up his eyes at the bartender. "Get me a beer, nah, make that two."

A fat man hunched next to him stretched out his large arm in front of Roy and coughed. "He'll have a soda." He and the others gave Roy an odd look and turned their backs.

"You got it, George," murmured the bartender.

"How come I'm never told about cross burnings and nigger beatings anymore? You had a nigger beating last week and I just heard about it at the meeting tonight." Roy, a belligerent look on his face, stared up at the small group of Klan men gathered together, drinking beers.

The men looked at each other and George spoke up. "It's because we can't trust you, Roy. Most of the time you're so drunk you can hardly stand up. You may go into a bar like this and start talking about what the Klan has done, hell, you just did. Your station has lost business because you're drinking so much. You need to get your act together, Roy."

The other men nodded. A small man in spectacles moved off his chair and leaned into Roy's space. "You must understand. Our organization, as you know, has a heritage of professionalism. All the services we do for the white community. The beatings, lynchings, cross burnings- see we're a respectable organization. We can't have no drunks making us look bad, especially after all that work we do. You're just too irrational and dangerous for the Klan, Roy, with all this drinking. We're a family oriented group and we want to set a good example. You understand, right?"

"Well, I ben' thinking of getting a change of scenery. I got some family matters to get sorted. I'll figure out somethin'." Roy grunted and stumbled out the door.

When John knocked on the door Sarah answered it and gave him a big hug. "John, President Johnson just signed the Civil Rights Act today. It outlaws those terrible literacy tests and the poll taxes that kept blacks from voting and provides nationwide protection for voting rights. It also regulates the administration of elections. And do you know what else?"

"No, what?"

"They are giving credit to the marches from Selma to Montgomery for helping to get it passed." Sarah grinned. "I've been rubbing it into Richard because he said the marches didn't do anything to help the movement. Come on in and help me rub it in a little more."

"Not until you give me a big kiss, darlin'."

What do I do now? Roy looked around his house, a bewildered look on his face. He drew the curtains and slid sideways onto his bed. I can only stay here another month and then the buyer wants me out. He hardly paid me anything for the house and the service station. I was screwed, but I need the money. Well, I want ta leave this punk town anyway. Maybe I'll go ta Georgia or Virginia and work at a service station 'til I get enough money ta buy a service station of my own. Wish Bobby Joe was here. We'd make a lot more money if there was two of us workin'. Wish I knew where he was at.

That's it! Roy sat straight up in bed. Mary would know where Bobby Joe and Betty Lou are. She and Betty Lou were good friends. I'll bet Mary was in on sending Bobby Joe away. Why didn't I think of this before? Tomorrow I'll get it out of her. Yeah, I'll get it out of her—one way or another.

"You're goin' ta tell me where my wife and Bobby Joe are and you're goin' ta tell me now!" Roy pushed open the door and shoved Mary backward.

"Roy, leave my house. You've been drinking. Come back when you can be more rational and we'll talk."

Roy reached out and shoved her again. "We'll talk now!"

"What makes you think she kept up with me after she left Birmingham? She's been gone a long time and I..." Roy punched Mary hard in the face and she fell back against a coffee table. Pushing herself up, Mary ran for the kitchen, trying to make it to the back door. Roy followed, shouting obscenities. Reaching her as she was turning the knob, trying to open the door, he pulled her toward him, turned her around and punched her in the stomach.

"Tell me. Where's my son?" Mary, bending over in pain, just shook her head.

Roy, his face red with rage, looked around the kitchen. Finding a long knife, he held it in front of her. "Tell me or I'll cut you with this. How'd ya like to lose a finger?" Mary again shook her head, then tried to make it to the door.

"Oh no you don't. You're not going anywhere 'til you tell me—where's my wife and son?" He waited and when she said nothing he made a swipe with the knife, making a deep cut in her arm." Mary screamed in pain, holding her arm. "Now you know I mean business. Tell me and I'll let you go."

Mary bent over, holding her arm. "Nothing to tell you."

Enraged, Roy pushed the knife toward Mary, then backed up in horror as she fell to the ground. Gotta' get out of here before...She might have the address in one of her drawers. He tried the two drawers in the desk in her living room. Nothing. Running into the bedroom he began dumping everything from the drawers onto the floor. Nothing. Oh wait, here's a letter. And its from Betty Lou with a return address on the envelope. He opened the letter, quickly glanced at it, dropped the letter, and thrust the envelope into his pocket. Looking down, he noticed his shirt, jeans and shoes were spattered with blood. Can't leave like this. Must change. Roy stumbled next door. I need clothes! But I gotta git goin'! Undressing, he threw his bloody clothes up in the attic. Grabbing the nearest things he could find in a closet he charged out the door. He scrambled into his truck and thrust some extra clothing into the seat next to him. That'll do. Baltimore here I come!

Dorothy peeked her head in the front door. "Mary, I've come to pick you up for choir practice. I've been knocking, but you must not hear me. Mary?" Dorothy moved into the living room. Still no Mary. Guess she's gone out back to her garden and forgot about the time. I'll have to get her or we'll be late. She went through to the kitchen. "Oh NO!"

Brr! Baltimore's a lot colder than Birmingham, and it's only September. Roy pulled a blanket around him and took another swig of whiskey. I've been sitting in my truck for two days now. Roy ground the truck to life, punched it into gear and took another short drive around the block.

Betty Lou is normally home at about 4:00 PM and Bobby Joe is back from school by then. A man shows up about 5:00 PM. Guess today at 4:00 PM will be the time. Blast!

A police cruiser had slipped behind him and was flashing its lights. Roy whipped his head around and tossed the whiskey bottle into the pile of clothes beside him on the passenger seat.

"Can I help you off-offisher?" Roy asked as innocently as possible.

"You were drift'n a bit there, buddy." The police officer peered into the truck and noticed Roy smelled of whiskey.

"Well now," the officer smiled, "Look Sir, drive yourself right home. It's not safe to stay driving when you've been drinking, you know. I'll let you off this time."

"Yep. I mean, thank you, officer." Roy sighed with relief as the officer drove away. That was close! Alls' I gotta' do now is be ready. Four o'clock is the time!

"Someone's at the door, Bobby. Can you get it?"

"Sure, Mom." Bobby opened the door and stared.

"What's the matter, son? Aren't you glad to see me?" Roy pushed his way in. Betty came into the room, a shocked look on her face.

"Well, Betty Lou, you're looking good. Never went all out like that for me. Who's the guy you're fixin' up for, slut?" Roy turned to Bobby, waving his gun. "Get a bag. You're coming with me."

Bobby stood, transfixed. "Get goin'!"

"Okay, slut, I've got about an hour before that man shows up so you might as well pack a lunch for Bobby Joe and me. We'll check on how Bobby Joe is doing with his packing and then we'll go to the kitchen."

"All packed, Bobby Joe? Let's all go to the kitchen where your Ma is gonna' make us a nice lunch for the road."

Betty turned to Roy. "Where are you taking him?"

"None of your business, slut."

"Take me instead."

"Now, why on earth would I want you? Bobby Joe can earn money for me. What could you do, Slut? You're getting too old to earn much on the street." He shook his head. "No, Slut, you're no use to me."

"Bobby Joe, grab the lunch and let's get out of here." Bobby stood, not moving. "I said, move it!" Still Bobby didn't move. Roy, losing patience, grabbed Bobby around the neck and pulled him toward the front door. Just then Scruffy went into action, biting Roy in the leg. "Ow!" Roy kicked the dog across the room, aimed his gun and pulled the trigger. Scruffy lay there, bleeding.

"You shot my dog!" Bobby kicked Roy in the leg and began to pound on him until Roy aimed the gun at Betty.

"Bobby Joe, stop, or I'll kill your Ma." He glowered at Bobby. "I mean it!" Bobby pulled back, terrified. Roy yanked the telephone from the wall, then pushed Betty into a chair. "You just sit in that chair and don't move." He tossed a rope to Bobby. "Tie up your Ma to that chair and tie it tight 'cuz I'll be checking it." Once the rope was secure Roy placed a rag in Betty Lou's mouth. "There, that oughta' hold you until the man shows up. By then we'll be long gone."

"Betty!" Dan dropped the bag of groceries he was carrying, took the rag out of Betty's mouth and began to untie her, noticing Scruffy lying nearby, bleeding.

"It's Roy. He's taken Bobby! He tore out the phone. Call the police! I'll untie myself." Dan rushed out.

Soon he was back. "I called the police and called Bill to come stay with you. I'll take Scruffy to the vet. Don't worry, Betty. We'll find Bobby."

The police searched Mary's house, but didn't move her swollen body. "Hmm. There's a letter here from someone inviting Mrs. Davis to move to Baltimore and stay with her. Does the neighbor, uh, Mrs. Dorothy, know anything about this?"

"That would be Betty Lou Ramsey," called out Dorothy, trying not to look at the blood. "Mary helped Betty Lou out a lot when her husband, Roy, beat her and the son. All the ladies in the neighborhood knew about that, but we kept our mouths shut on account of poor Betty Lou." Dorothy picked up her bag and choir robe. "I can't go to choir practice today, but I can't go home...Guess I'll stay at a friend's."

"Just let us know where you'll be. And if you remember anything, let myself or officer Smith know," added the detective absently. He busily examined the back windows and checked the drawers of a dresser.

"Wait! They moved to Baltimore to be with a cousin named Dan Edwards and escape from Roy. Oh, I wonder if Roy was trying to find out where they are. I don't think Mary would have told Roy. And he might have killed her when she didn't tell him. Please catch Roy quickly. For as long as we've known him, he's only gotten worse. He's been so-so desperate lately. What if he kills someone else?"

The detective dismissively waved his hand. "We'll contact the Baltimore police force and check it out. You've been very helpful."

"Shouldn't you contact them now?"

"For now we need to concentrate on the scene of the crime. Besides, we're not sure of his involvement."

"Listen, We know Roy; he's a dangerous man. I should have said something before."

"Now don't you worry about that. This just doesn't fit what our department knows about his character. Especially, since we know of his involvement in a highly reputable social organization. It could have been a break and enter. Probably a Negro."

Dorothy stood in the doorway, her mouth wide open. She turned to leave, and then lifted her eyes in thought for a moment.

"Oh... Uh... I thought I heard also that some reputable social organization was wanting to know where he was on account of him leaving that organization and betraying the southern way of life."

A policeman took a step towards her. "I thought he was just a drunk."

"Oh yes, he was! Didn't your Mama ever tell you traitorous men always drink? Rumor is he aligned himself with those troublesome northern agitators. Like the group his wife was involved with."

The policemen all looked up at once. The detective strode over to her with a serious look on his face. "The Kla... uh, an organization is looking for him too, eh? Well, maybe we should check this lead first. Let's git 'em, boys."

"Scruffy has a bullet wound in the back leg and he's lost a lot of blood. I don't know if I can save him, but I'll do my best. We'll know more in the morning." The vet nodded at Dan, then bent over Scruffy.

Dan entered the room. Bill had his arm around Betty, who was crying, comforting her. "Any news?"

"Betty just got a call from the Baltimore police who had heard from the Birmingham police department. Apparently they suspect that Roy just killed his next door neighbor, Mary Davis. The police want you to call them."

"Roy's headed West. I asked if I could ride along with the police. I think Bobby would be less traumatized if I'm there when they rescue him. Is that okay, Betty?"

Betty nodded and uttered a weak "Thank you".

"This is officer Rick Johnson. It looks as if the suspect is going speed limit so as not to attract attention. Shouldn't take too long to catch up." Rick yelled into his radio, picking up speed. "Hey Buddy," he turned to Dan in the passenger seat and then back to the road. "You know, he'll probably have to stop somewhere for the night, unless he forces the boy to drive." Dan sat there, saying nothing.

It was two AM when they pulled into the parking lot of a run -down motel in Indianapolis, behind two other unmarked police cars. Rick got out to talk to the policemen and Dan followed. "Hi Rick. They got here a couple hours ago. I don't think we'll see any action until morning when the suspect might come out and we can get a bead on him. We don't want to storm the room. The boy might get hurt. Might as well take turns getting some shut eye."

Dan nudged Rick, waking him. "Look, there he is—and Bobby's not with him."

"Perfect." Rick and Dan opened their car doors, bent over, and quietly moved toward the other policemen. "Dan, you be ready to go into the motel room when we give the signal." Dan nodded.

The police crouched beside their unmarked cars and one of them yelled out, "Police! Drop your gun!" Roy quickly turned and began firing. His first shot hit a policeman who had stood up. He ducked behind a car, continuing to answer the volley of shots headed toward him with a volley of his own. Roy emptied his gun. Rick lifted his head from behind a car. "I think he's out of bullets."

Roy pulled out another gun from his belt and continued shooting. "You'll never get me, you pigs. I'm a crack shot."

Rick yelled as a bullet grazed his ear and another landed near his foot. Finally the shooting ceased. "Yes, there he is—trying to escape." Rick took off after Roy, who had run behind the motel. "Stop or I'll shoot!" When Roy kept running, Rick took aim. Roy fell to the ground and stopped moving. Rick leaned over him, withdrew a key from Roy's pocket and gave it to Dan. "Go and get your boy."

Bobby was handcuffed to the bedpost, a look of terror on his face. "Bobby, you're safe. Your Pa is dead. He can't hurt you or your Mother any longer." Dan gave Bobby a quick hug, then tried to get the handcuffs off. "I need the handcuff key. Do you know where your Pa put it?" Bobby motioned toward a bag. Dan found the key, unlocked the cuffs, and Bobby fell into his arms.

"Is it true? Is my Pa really dead?" Dan nodded. Bobby put his head down. "I peed on myself."

Dan reached down, his arms on Bobby's shoulders. "Bobby, I would've shit in my pants if I'd gone through what you've gone through. Get some clothes out and take a shower. Then this nice policeman, you and I will have breakfast before we head for home. How does that sound?" Bobby nodded, a half smile on his face.

Bobby ran up the steps, into the apartment, and into his Mother's waiting arms. "Pa's dead." Betty gave Bobby a hug, then wiped her tears away. "Oh darling, I know."

"Bobby, you and I have some place to go." Dan winked at Betty. "We'll be back soon."

Dan pulled up in front of the vet's. "Come on in, Bobby. I've something to show you." They walked to a room in the back where Scruffy was lying in a kennel. As soon as he saw Bobby he wagged his tail and attempted to get up.

"Scruffy, I thought you were dead!" Bobby reached in and Scruffy licked his hand. "When can he come home?"

"Now. That's why we're here. He'll have to be quiet for a day or two and then he should be back to normal."

"Dan, this is the best day ever. Scruffy is alive and I never, ever have to be afraid of my Pa again."

Chapter 24

1966

Michael walked in the front door, dropping his suitcase and taking off his jacket. Bobby ran towards him. "Welcome back. How was the New York rally?"

"Great! There were 50,000 anti-Vietnam protesters there on March 25th and 26th. Some burned their draft cards. Most of us swear we aren't going to 'Nam. It's a civil war and we shouldn't be involved. Some men are leaving for Canada and some are faking disabilities."

Bobby looked up at his hero. I sure wish Mom would let me grow my hair to shoulder length like Mike's. Guess I'm too young for a beard yet, but someday I'll have one.

"Hey, Mike," Dan yelled. "We're in the kitchen. Come and tell us all about it."

"Join me, Dan." Tom smiled and motioned to the armchair across from him. "I'm so proud of you. Imagine, my son, the Congressman."

"Wait a minute, Dad. The election isn't until November 8 and I have stiff competition." He shook his head. "I still can't believe this is happening. When the Senator had me writing his speeches and then going on the campaign trail I saw that perhaps politics was a faster way to get things done in Civil Rights than working as a lawyer. However, I wasn't prepared for the Party, with the Senator's recommendation, to support me in a run for Congress. Guess they were desperate." He smiled.

"They weren't desperate. I read an article on you which mentioned your speaking ability, your sensitivity to people's needs and your great potential. I wish your Mom was alive to see you become a member of Congress."

"Hey, Dad. Don't count your chickens. I haven't been elected yet."

"You will, my son. Nothing's in your way. Just be careful in your private life. I've spent enough time watching television to know that the press loves a scandal."

"Marry me." John stood in front of Sarah, his arms outstretched. "I love you and you say you love me. We've been going together for a year now. Your brother approves of me and thinks we should get married. This is my fourth proposal. I can't understand why you keep turning me down." John frowned.

"I don't know, John. I guess I'm just not ready and need some more time." Sarah smiled up at him. "When I am ready, you'll be the first to know. Now, however, we need to get down to Mississippi for our next assignment. Since James Meredith was shot on his one man 'walk against fear' June 6, our paper wants us to cover King's and Carmichael's continuing the Meredith March. It starts tomorrow. I've got the airline tickets and we need to get going."

"Do you hear the rumbling, John? Stokely Carmichael wants the march to be black only and King wants whites and blacks to march. Well, so far, looks like King's won out."

John came running over to Sarah as she tried to pitch her tent for the night. "Guess what. The police are saying we can't put up our tents at this Stone Street Negro Elementary School here in Greenwood. Stokely Carmichael started to argue with them and got arrested for trespassing on public property. We're going to have to move."

Sarah sighed, then brightened her expression. "Well we know we have their attention now, don't we? I hope Carmichael's okay." Sarah took out her notepad and scanned the crowd.

"Well, John, they just released Carmichael and he's going to the speaker platform. He looks angry."

"Did you hear that, Sarah? He said, 'This is the 27th time I have been arrested, and I ain't going to jail no more!' And you don't want to miss this quote. He said, 'We want black power', and he said it five times. Soon the marchers were yelling 'Black Power!' How did you miss that?" John asked excitedly.

Sarah laughed. "I just can't catch anything through this crowd. I'm too short. You'll have to be my eyes and ears."

In a triumphant voice, John exclaimed, "That's what we blacks need—Black Power!"

"Can you hear me down here? John? Are you listening?"

"What's the date? The 23rd? Oh! Look out! Here we go again. The patrolmen won't let us camp and they're using tear gas and impounding our tents. Gotta' get some photos, Sarah. Stay out of the way of the tear gas!"

"I'm glad it's over, John. I'm tired. How wonderful it'll be to sleep in my bed again!"

"We're back, Richard." Sarah ran into the house, John following.

"Come into the kitchen and I'll make some coffee while you two tell me all about it."

"It was great! Carmichael gave a speech where he used the words, 'Black Power'. Soon the marchers were shouting it and a lot of the marchers used it during the rest of the march." John looked at Sarah. "Didn't you think that was exciting?"

"No, I didn't. And I didn't like the way it ended with a division between King and Carmichael—King's followers are advocating non-violence with their cry of 'Freedom Now!' and Carmichael's are advocating violence and separatism with the cry, 'Black Power'."

"It's just a short slogan, Sarah. Besides, Carmichael doesn't want violence, just basic self defense. Don't let white journalism slant your view."

"Yes, but everything's so sensitive right now!"

"If not now, when?" Richard jumped in. "I think John's right."

"But we've accomplished so much in the Civil Rights Movement with non-violence, and the white people have always had a part in the movement. Now Stokely Carmichael wants to change all that. I think he'll hurt the movement."

"Well, I don't. I think it's time we blacks go it alone and non-violence isn't working. Look at all the people who have been beaten, gassed, and killed over the years. Sometimes we need to fight back. We have a right to defend ourselves. I'm exercising that right whenever, wherever, I get the chance, regardless."

Richard slapped him on the back, "Right on! Sarah, I love this guy!"

"Hi John. Come on in and sit down. I'm almost finished typing this and then we can go see that movie. Can you believe it's almost Christmas? Pretty soon we'll be looking at 1967. I wonder what the new year will bring to the movement." John continued standing, looking uncomfortable. Sarah looked up and frowned. "Okay, out with it. Something's obviously bothering you."

"Sarah, you know how you became really upset with Richard and me when we agreed SNCC and CORE made the right move in October, in asking the whites to leave the organizations."

"Kicking them out, you mean."

"You've said Richard and I have more in common than you and me. We seem to fight all the time about the Movement." Sarah nodded. "Richard and I are excited about Black Power and the formation of the Black Panther for Self Defense. Huey Newton and Bobby Seale have really made something new and incredible out there in Oakland this October. You still think they're too militant and separatist?"

"What are you trying to say, John?"

John looked down at his feet. "I got a call from a buddy of mine who now lives in Oakland and is trying to help the Panthers get off the ground. They're starting a newspaper and want me to take the photos and write articles."

"Oh, John, what? Leaving? What about your job here?"

John reached out and grabbed Sarah's hand. "It's just something I have to do, Sarah."

"Well, I'll miss you, but if this is something you feel you should do..."

"That's not all, Sarah. Richard is curious about the Black Panthers too. He's going with me. We leave in a week."

"What? My brother is joining the Black Panthers! I don't believe this!" Sarah paused for a moment, then looked up at John. "And what about you and me?"

"I no longer think there is a you and me, Sarah. I love you, but I don't think you feel the same way about me."

"Oh... That's not...," Sarah began, and then paused in thought.

"See? I can't go on the way we've been, so I'm saying good-bye. I wish you well, and I'll always love you, but I need to get on with my life. Good-bye, Sarah."

Chapter 25

1967

John leaned over and looked in the full length mirror, adjusting his black beret, then slowly turning around, admiring his new Black Panther uniform of black pants, blue shirt and black leather jacket. He reached in his holster and removed his handgun, holding it up to the light. Richard, lying on the bed across from him, exclaimed, "Hey, watch it. You might shoot someone, namely me, with that thing."

"OK, but we need these guns when we shadow the pigs, policing them so they don't do anything against our people or us. The open-carry gun laws permit us to carry a loaded rifle or shotgun as long as it isn't pointed at anyone. And don't the police hate it though, when we shout, 'The Revolution has come, it's time to pick up the gun. Off the pigs!'" John snickered, then put the gun back in its holster.

"Look at you. You've really changed, man. And you gave up my sister to be here."

"You sore?"

"No, I'm proud."

"Thanks, Mom."

"You ready to maybe give up your freedom for this?"

"Are you?"

"Well," Richard looked out the window at the sunrise. His eyes found a pair of black boys walking to school, looking over their shoulder through an ominously narrow alleyway. "Yes, but I don't know how well I'd really deal with that. I never liked being closed in. I'd rather die."

John chuckled and slapped Richard on the back. "Don't worry. Together we're unstoppable."

Richard smiled confidently. "I got you more than covered, man."

"Well, we did it, Richard. We published an issue of the 'Black Panther Party Black Community News Service' on April 25th. I think our headline, 'Why was Denzil Dowell Killed?' a good one. The police shooting and killing of a black unarmed twenty-two year old has got people up in arms. Maybe our paper can raise awareness in the black community. At least we can publish our Ten Point Program calling for 'Land, Bread, Housing, Education, Clothing, Justice and Peace' and our other demands. It explains 'What we want. What we believe'."

"Yeah, and I like the ten points that tell how we reach our goals—especially number 7, the end to police brutality and murder of black people."

John looked up and down the street where they stood in a black neighborhood. "No police. No harassment. Maybe it's working better than we think? Maybe Denzil will be the last martyr. Can't treat us like dogs forever. I tell you, the revolution is changing things. Beatings and murders of black youth by the police are already becoming a thing of the past. They'll be gone within five years."

Richard scratched his chin. "Can I get that in writing?"

A week later Richard was driving down a familiar street. His sharp eyes fixed on a point a few cars ahead of them. Something was wrong. It was hidden in the glare of California sun and traffic. The whites drove by unaware, but he lived here and studied life here. To him it was as clear as a slap in the face. "John, look at those policemen stopping that car."

"That's a pointless stop if ever I saw one," remarked John

" For sure. The man wasn't speeding or doing anything wrong. Here we go." John and Richard got out of their car, holding their guns facing downward. John started walking fast, nervously overtaking Richard, who firmly held up his left hand. He raised his head high and began to walk slowly towards the officers. "Let me do the talking on this one, John," he murmured. Richard waited until one of the officers noticed him.

"What seems to be the trouble, officer?"

"None of your business. This is just between us and him." The officer looked Richard in the eye, then back at John. "Maybe we should just arrest you instead, for carrying guns."

"Afraid you can't do that, officer. California law says we have a right to carry a loaded gun as long as it's not pointed at anyone. If you arrest us we'll be happy to take you to court for violating our constitutional rights. We were behind you and saw the man you stopped was doing nothing against the law, so we'll be witnesses if you arrest him."

The officer grunted, looked at Richard and then at the black man. "We was just checking for drugs. You can go now." The officer waved a dismissal to the man; then he and his partner got into their police car and drove away.

Richard and John were thanked by the man and then got into their car. "Incidents of police brutality have really decreased since the Panthers started showing up with guns. The pigs aren't so tough now." John smiled.

"Well, here we are, John, at the California State Assembly. Wouldn't you know they'd come up with the "Mulford Act" to make our carrying loaded firearms in public illegal. Seale wants all thirty or so of us to march in with our guns. The media's been contacted. This will get us some publicity, if nothing else."

"I've been itching for an arrest since I started here. Maybe I'll finally get one."

"Whoa! I've created a monster! Why so eager?" Richard snorted.

John looked several men around them in the eye and said loudly enough for them to hear, "Rather be arrested for havin' a gun in my hand now then be arrested for just being black later!"

Several men echoed with "Right on!" and "Black power!"

Not long after, Richard woke to find himself alone in a cell. At the time he couldn't even remember why he was there. He twitched as he sat curled up in his cell bunk and things started to go dark. He forgot where he was, just that the walls were moving in on him. Feeling around the floor he searched for something with which to attack a guard or knock himself out. He couldn't stay here any longer. His mind was so lost he couldn't even remember where 'here' was. That gave him an idea. He squinted. The walls became the sides of buildings. A single light bulb in the ceiling of his cell was the sun. The hallway nearby was the alleyway. He squinted more and thought he could just see those two black boys he'd seen walking down the alley outside when he first came to California. Those boys, their future, was why he was here. And he was back in his apartment at that first hopeful moment, looking out his window to his new neighborhood home on the outside. And he was talking to someone now about the movement. It was John- John was looking at the sunset out the apartment window with him.

"Richard! Are you okay? I feared the worst, man! I didn't know what you'd do. C'mon, let's get you outta here."

"Thanks for getting me out of jail, John. Don't know why they picked me and four others, along with Seale, to arrest."

"Yeah, and they didn't arrest me and I was standing right next to you. You look terrible. Wish they'd arrested me instead."

"Let's get something to eat. Prison food leaves a lot to be desired." Richard smiled and put his arm around John's shoulder.

Michael sneered. "What? No family meeting to discuss my faults, big brother?"

Dan looked at him sternly. "I thought you'd like to discuss your using drugs with just me rather than in front of Dad, Betty and Bobby."

"Who's saying I'm using drugs?"

"Bobby for one. He said you came home last night and you were acting weird and the black part of your eye was big. He also said you smelled funny. You know Bobby looks up to you and imitates what you do. Do you want him to get into drugs too?"

"I do if he'll share with me, man." Michael rolled his eyes and began to saunter out of the room.

"He's only fifteen years old, Michael. You've just recently dropped out of college and now he's wondering if he needs to go to college."

"I'll talk to him." Michael put up his hand. "But he could have gotten that idea from anywhere."

"He's already saying he wants to grow his hair long like yours and be a hippie too."

"Groovy. Always wanted a stunt double for those days when I don't wanna get out of bed. Look, I can't help it if he imitates me. He needs to make up his own mind about things and not be such a copy cat."

"But this is such an important time in his life!"

"What? Why is three thirty so special? Personally, I like four twenty, but I'm not that particular."

"Grow up Michael!"

"Okay. Let's be straight. You gotta be fair with me, man. I can't be something I'm not just to be a blinkin' example for 'lil ole' Bobby, for Pete's sake! He should take after my wonderful, do no wrong, Congressman brother. I'll leave, and then he'll only have you as a model. Will that suit you, brother dear?" Michael sneered again, then left the room.

"Bobby, some friends and I have decided to drive to Height Ashbury, California, where there's a summer of love happening. I want you to take good care of Scruffy and my car for me. Just think, you can get your driver's permit this year. Maybe Dan can teach you to drive—only not in my convertible. I'll let you drive it when I return. Hey, what's this?" Bobby put his arms around Michael and clung to him.

"Can't I go with you? It's summer and I'm out of school."

Michael slowly pulled away. "Sorry, champ, but no go. You stay here with Tom, your Mom and Dan and I'll tell you all about the love-in when I return. Peace."

"What's do people do at a love-in, Michael?"

Michael smiled and glanced over his shoulder, "Ask Dan. He'd love to tell you all about it."

"Bobby is really missing Michael. He's coming over and sleeping in Michael's bed at night instead of sleeping in our apartment. And he's ignoring Bill, even though Bill is trying to be a good father to him. We're going to be married soon, and I don't know if Bobby will ever accept Bill." Betty looked up at Tom and sighed. "I don't know what to do."

"Do nothing, Betty. Give Bobby some time. He's grieving for Michael, but he'll get over it. Dan can't help because he's traveling so much as a congressman, but I can maybe do something. I know Bobby wants to learn to drive so I'll teach him. Perhaps I can take him fishing this summer too. Maybe Bill can come along and then Bobby will get to know him better. Don't worry, he'll be OK."

Richard slammed the newspaper down on the table. "Damn! The California State Legislation passed an anti-gun law on July 26th. It prevents us carrying firearms in any public place or street. That effectively outlaws our police patrols, John."

John raised his hands in front of him. "The Panthers are everything. I left Sarah for this. Then these shifty little honkeys pull this one. You're not leaving, are you?"

"Well, you know how I love jail cells, but don't worry, man. I still got your back."

"Thanks. Don't know what I'd do without you".

"Yeah," Richard answered. Poring over a thick stack of manila folders with a calculator he rubbed his temple and sighed.

"We are fighting the worst injustice since the founding of this country."

John pounded a fist on the counter."That's why we need to stick together."

"Yeah, but where is everyone else? What's the rest of our generation doing?"

Michael stretched out on the filthy, littered floor and looked around him. Hmm. Only eight here tonight, but it's just 10:00 PM. Probably more will show up later. As he turned toward Judy, she reached for him. Still stoned. No thanks, he didn't want any more free love tonight. When he rolled over, facing the other direction, she got up and walked to the other side of the room. Oh, she's gonna' get some from Ron. She's always amorous when stoned.

What's the matter with me? I've been in Height Ashbury for only two months and I'm getting tired of playing guitar at Golden Gate Park, giving the peace sign, saying "peace". Even the "afternoon delights" and "trips" are losing appeal. Never thought that would happen. Mike smiled to himself. And I'm almost out of money. Oh sure, we can get free food and drugs down at the park, and some hippie dude will always let us crash in his pad, but this is all getting old.

"Hey, Mike. Looks like Judy found someone else for the night. I saw the disgusted look on your face after she left. Don't worry, there's always plenty more wanting free love." Steve plopped down beside him. "Say, I'm going to drop acid tonight. Want to join me?"

"No, I'm getting tired of it all—the drugs, the free love, everything. I've tried acid twice. The first time was groovy—saw moving geometric patterns and bright colors and I could see the music. The second trip wasn't that great. I don't agree with Timothy Leary that it's a mind expanding experience. I prefer pot. Anyway, I'm thinking of thumbing my way home tomorrow."

"Not a bad idea. I was gonna' have to leave in two weeks anyway, 'cuz university starts then. Might as well go now 'cuz it'll take a couple of weeks for me to butter up my folks so they'll pay my fall tuition. They weren't too happy when I came to California for a Love In instead of earning money for school. You can ride back with me. Do you think Judy'll want to go with us?"

"Nah, she seems to prefer California over Maryland, and I don't think she's finished with the free love. I have just enough money to help you with gas for your van. Let's leave tomorrow, if that's all right with you. Guess I'd better get home and enroll at the college or the draft board will be contacting me. I ain't goin' to 'Nam regardless what they tell me. Or my stupid brother, Mr. Congress, tells me."

"Oh yeah! You're the one with connections, man. That's rough, dude."

"I'm nervous about this war, about what my brother's gonna' expect of me now."

"Screw their war, man. Don't take his government lies. Yeah. Peace! Fine, man. I'll skip the acid tonight and we can make an early start."

"Michael, you're home!" Bobby dropped his school bag and ran to give Michael a hug. Scruffy was jumping up, trying to get his attention.

Yeah, it's good to be home. Guess I'll stick around for awhile. Even Dan and Dad seemed glad to see me. "Good to see you, too, Bob. How are the driving lessons coming along?"

Tom entered the room. "He's doing great. You'll have to let him take you for a drive."

"Guess it's time you try out the convertible." Seeing the rapt expression on Bobby's face, he added, "if you are very, very careful."

"Hello. Edwards residence. Dan speaking."

"Hello, Dan. This is Laura. I'm back in Baltimore and I wonder if we could get together for lunch. I'd like to talk with you."

Dan hesitated. "Yes, I guess I could find the time for lunch next week. How about Monday? We could meet at my office and then find a restaurant. One o'clock okay?"

"Fine. See you then. 'Bye."

Laura rushed up to Dan and reached out to hug him, but drew back when he stiffened. Later, they made small talk until they were settled at their table at the restaurant and the waiter had taken their order. Then Laura leaned toward Dan. "I'm so sorry I hurt you. I just wasn't ready for a serious relationship back then. Guess I had to get far away from Mommy and Daddy in order to grow up." She looked across the table at Dan. "I never forgot you. None of the guys I dated ever measured up to you. Can you forgive me?"

Dan ignored the question. "So, are you here in Baltimore for awhile?"

"Yes, Father helped me get a good position at a law firm. I think they wanted me closer." She paused and took a drink of her coffee. "I know you don't trust me, but we had something once and perhaps it might still be there. We could go slowly..." Laura held Dan's eyes with hers. "Would you give me another chance?"

"I don't know, Laura. That was a long time ago. We've both changed. Also, I'm busy with my duties as a congressman. I don't really have time to go out." Seeing Laura's disappointed face, he hesitated. "I guess it wouldn't hurt to spend some time together just to see. However, I really don't expect there's still anything between us."

"Mail call." Tom handed Michael an envelope, a concerned expression on his face.

"Oh no!" Michael saw the return address, just as Tom had. He slit open the envelope and read the letter, then dropped it on his lap. "Dad, it's from the draft board. I have to report." He put his face in his hands, then looked up at his Father. "I've only been home two weeks."

"Bobby, wake up." whispered a gentle voice.

"Wha?" Bobby glanced at his clock, then rubbed his eyes. "It's only 5 AM."

A hand slid across Bobby's mouth. "Don't say a word, Bobby. Okay?"

Michael sat on the edge of the bed. "I'm going to Canada and want to say goodbye." Michael continued, his voice breaking. "I told you before that I wouldn't go to 'Nam, and now it looks as if I'll be drafted. A- A buddy and I are heading out to Canada now. D- Don't let Dad and Dan know until we are gone for several hours. I know I can trust you not to say anything."

Bobby sat up and put his arms around Michael. "Don't go! You just got home. I haven't even had a chance to take you for a ride in your car."

"I know, Bobby, I know. I don't want to leave, but I have no choice. I just can't stand the thought of killing people. And I don't like the idea of being shot at much either. If it was defending our own country I could do it, but not fighting another country's civil war." He looked down at Bobby. "I'll keep in touch. Scruffy is yours now, so take good care of him. Perhaps Dad will take you out in my convertible a couple of times. Tell him I said it would be okay." Michael gave Bobby a big hug. He crept off the bed and grabbed his suitcase. Leaning over, he accidentally banged his guitar with his foot. A hollow twang reverberated into the floorboards. Michael stiffened. Slowly, he cracked open the door and peered down the hall. No one. Soon he was silently waiting in the front drive. A car cruised quietly up to the curb.

"Honk!" The driver slammed on the horn. "Canada here we come, eh buddy?"

"Shut up, Ron!" Michael waved his arm and whispered. "Are you stupid?" He felt a tear in the corner of his eye as he heard Scruffy begin to bark. Something moved inside the house behind him. The engine revved. He took a deep breath, grabbed the door handle and jumped into the front seat with his luggage on top of his lap.

"Drive," he said, looking back at the still dark windows of his former home. A light flickered inside somewhere. He thought he saw his Dad, half asleep, scratching his head, squinting out the door. The face disappeared inside. A light flicked out again. Michael exhaled slowly.

Tom and Dan sat at the kitchen table, drinking coffee. Mike had been gone two months now and they still hadn't heard from him. "I'm worried, Dan. I have no idea where Mike would be in Canada and if he's alright. Canada's a big country."

"Dad, you know Mike can take care of himself. He's gone off on his own before and always manages to find his way home, safe and sound.

"Only this time he can't come home or he goes to prison." Tom glanced down at his coffee cup.

Dan's expression was cold. He huffed and put his arms by his side, "Well, maybe we should go get him. He's breaking the law. Shirking his duty. Perhaps he should go to prison for a while. He needs to straighten out."

"Quit the lawyer act, Dan," Tom snapped. "You know he's my son. And your brother!"

"They say the war will be over soon anyway. Bobby sure misses him," Dan added.

Tom looked up. "Yep. I'd hoped he'd turn to Bill for comfort now that Betty and Bill are married, but he hasn't seemed to have done that. Bill's a good man too. Bobby spends all his spare time in our home and is still sleeping in Michel's room. I guess we'll just have to give him more time."

Tom turned, facing Dan. "By the way, how's it going with Laura? You've been out with her quite a bit lately."

"I don't know, Dad. She's a beautiful woman. She's smart, sensitive, fun, and we seem to be able to talk about anything and everything. We have so much in common. She really understands when I talk about politics and encourages and supports me in what I'm doing. Trouble is, I don't trust her and I don't feel any kind of spark or connection. I'm beginning to wonder if I ever did. She's had me at her parents' home for dinner and they seem really pleased to see us back together. You like her. I know I could do a lot worse, but something just seems to be missing..."

"Dad, I wonder if Mike saw this in a Canadian newspaper. It says that on October 6th a mock funeral was held, entitled 'The Death of the Hippie'. The message from the organizer, a Mary Kasper, was to stay where you are, bring the revolution to where you live and don't come here because it's over and done with.' Guess the people of Height Ashbury and San Francisco got a little tired of all those lawless hippies and their Love In." Dan grinned.

"Hey, Richard, there's a "Free Huey" movement on, protesting Huey Newton's arrest for allegedly killing that police officer on October 28th. It's really taking off. There are 'Free Huey' buttons and posters and protest meetings going on all over the country. Wonder if it'll do any good."

"We're Panthers. If we care about our freedom we should check it out."

Chapter 26

1968

Dan glanced around the fancy ballroom, his eyes taking in the men
in their tuxedos and the women in their beautiful shimmering
gowns of all colors, shapes and sizes. This was a room full of
intense political power—he could almost feel it. It reverberated
with their voices off the carved marble around them, and
throughout the capital. The world they'd created. He'd seen some
of them use power badly, usually when they were threatened or not
getting their way. Chipping away and sculpting the country to the
form of their will. A few seeking harmony and stability in their art.
Right now, however, these politically powerful men and women
and their spouses had their eyes riveted to the huge screen where
the Times Square Ball Drop was about to occur. Laura was
hanging on his arm and her blue eyes were bright and following
the ball as it started to drop. One. Two. Three. He wondered what
power she held, if she was chipping away and sculpting him, or
was she just a carving tool? Would their relationship be different if
she wasn't so well connected? She was especially beautiful tonight
in her blue full length gown, which matched the blue of her eyes.
She'd told him she bought it for him because he'd told her he liked
the color blue. Oh, it's almost up to ten. Laura will be waiting for a
kiss. "Ten!" "Happy New Year!" He pulled her to him, reached
down, and planted a firm kiss on her waiting, desirable mouth.

Sarah looked in the mirror and saw her eyes were red and swollen.
Today, April 4, 1968, would go down in history as the day a great
man was assassinated. I can hardly believe the TV—showing
Martin Luther King being shot while standing on a balcony. I

know he was in Memphis to lead a march on behalf of the striking Memphis sanitation workers. Who is going to carry on his work? I need to talk with some SCLC people. She put on her coat, grabbed her purse and headed out the door.

A few days later Sarah was sitting around a table with a few SCLC members, all of them trying to get a grip on what was happening. Besides dealing with their grief they were coping with the knowledge that King's death had resulted in an outbreak of racial violence, causing 40 deaths nationwide and property damage in over 100 cities. The question on everyone's minds was how do we go on without our leader—without Martin Luther King?

"Richard, have you read Mao's "Red Book" yet? After selling it to students to raise money for guns it's now required reading for every member of the Party. Must say, I don't understand all of it and how it applies to us. I wonder why Cleaver has us waiting in this house. Are we having a meeting or something?"

"I don't know, John. We weren't told much."

"See anything out the window?"

"Oh, man! Yeah! Some pigs are coming to the door!" Richard backed up slowly. "I think... I think we need to get away from the windows."

"Why?"

"No! John! Are they insane? They're shooting the Oakland police at the door. The pigs are shooting back! Duck! I think a bullet just came through the window. We've gotta' get out of here. I'm not going down for killing a cop! Try the back door." Richard and John bent over and headed for the kitchen.

Shots rang in their ears. Objects fell and broke around them. An eerie silence grew as they approached the back door. John cautiously cracked it open and peered out. "Can't see anyone. This is the only chance we have. Let's make a run for the alley. Go!"

John went first. Richard could see him looking back at him as he ran and motioning. He hesitated, then burst into the alley.

Was that someone yelling behind him? Richard turned to see a blur of police uniforms rushing towards the building. Police were rounding the corner to the other side of the building and didn't see him. Richard ran until he could run no more, then bent over, gasping for air. He'd never forget this experience.

"Richard, what are you doing?"

"As you can see, I'm packing. I've had it! Little Bobby Hutton was killed because of that shoot out, and he was just a kid—only seventeen. The Panthers are claiming the police ambushed them, but I've heard it from some Party members that Cleaver led the Panther group, including you and me, on a deliberate ambush of the police officers set for today, provoking the shoot out. If so, then Cleaver's the one responsible for Hutton's death. Supposedly he did it because of Martin Luther King's assassination. Two police officers were seriously wounded with multiple gunshot wounds. Just listen to the radio, will you?"

"Yeah, I heard Hutton and Cleaver surrendered ninety minutes after we left when the police tear gassed the building. Cleaver said the pigs shot Bobby more than twelve times after he had surrendered and had stripped down to his underwear to show he was unarmed."

Richard shook his head. "I can't take it anymore. I'm leaving."

"Don't you believe in the ten point program—what the Panthers are trying to do?"

"Yeah, John, I do. More now than I did before. However, there is so much corruption. I help with the books on occasion. I know the leaders are skimming off the top of the donations coming in. Last week I learned some even condone robberies as long as they get a percentage of what's taken. I'm no fan of King's methods anymore, but he never did this."

"Richard, you know that a lot of these men were on the streets before they signed up to be Panthers. All they knew was stealing, drugs and violence. They aren't going to change overnight."

Richard sighed. "I know that, but they'll never learn if the leaders are condoning their behavior as long as they get in on the profits. John, since being here I've been in jail and I've been shot at. If they can't at least keep it clean and fully back me up on the street I'm going home. There are Black Panther groups forming all over the country. There's gotta be a better group with better leaders. Might as well check out the Baltimore Panthers and see if I can do any good there. I'm sorry, John."

"What about you and me? What about always having my back?" John furrowed his forehead. For a moment he looked betrayed. "You just don't understand them."

"You're right. I don't. Just think, man, and be careful."

"Hey man, I'm gonna' miss you."

"And I'll miss you. Still think my sister made a big mistake in not marrying you."

John smiled. "Me too. Give her a hug for me."

"Package for you, Bob. And it appears to have a Canadian stamp on it." Dan teasingly held it out of Bobby's reach as Bobby grabbed for it. "Oh, you want it, do you?" He grinned and finally handed it over. Bobby immediately ripped off the brown paper.

"Look, there's a small book on Canada and a little box wrapped in birthday paper." Bobby looked up at Tom and Dan. "I guess he didn't forget I have a May birthday. And there's a letter here too." Bobby ripped the paper off the box, removed the cover, and gasped. "It's a key to his car. Maybe he's gonna' let me drive it sometime."

"What does the letter say, Bob? Does he say where he is?" Tom looked up from his armchair.

"It says, 'Dear Bob, Happy Birthday! You are now sixteen and can legally drive without another driver, assuming you've passed the driving test. Since it looks like I may not be able to return to the States for a very long time I've decided to give you my car. After all, you helped me build the thing and so it was half yours anyway. Take good care of it, and if I do return, perhaps we can go for a drive.

Tell the family that life in Canada isn't half bad. There are several of us so-called draft dodgers here and a few of us get together occasionally and talk about our families, where we're from, and what's happening in the US. We try to keep up on what's going on. I've had a few jobs, but have kinda' settled in as a mechanic and work for a good boss.

Hey, Bob, there are some good looking Canadian chicks here. Perhaps someday you can visit and I'll introduce you to a few.

I miss all of you and really hope to see you again. In the meantime, I'll try to stay in touch. Sorry I can't have you write me. We're all kinda' paranoid as to whether or not they're actively looking for us so, for now, the correspondence will be going only one way.
Love, Mike.'"

Bobby quickly wiped away a tear. All was silent and then Tom spoke up. "Well, at least now we know he's okay."

Later in the evening Tom noticed that Bobby was sitting silently on the couch, staring at Mike's letter and rubbing the car key between his thumb and forefinger. Tom moved over to the couch next to him. "Bob, we need to talk. I know you miss Mike and we do too. However, he won't be back, maybe for years. In the meantime, you are ignoring Bill, a very kind man who wants you, your Mom and him to be a family." Bob looked down at his lap and didn't reply. "I wonder if you're afraid to trust Bill, thinking he may turn out to be like your Father. You've never known a kind Father, but, believe me, Bill could be that to you. Won't you at least give him a chance?" Bob nodded, then stood up and left the room.

"Dad, I haven't finished what Mom asked me to do. I tracked down the Ramsey side of the family, Mom's side, but haven't looked up the Graydon side, and our family tree has the name Graydon in it. Apparently there is a Graydon brother and sister living here in Baltimore. I'm going to visit them soon."

"I know it's one of your mother's wishes, but write them first. You don't know these people. We don't want to meet another Roy Ramsey. Make sure they're friendly."

"I did write them, but never got a reply, so now I'll just have to pay them a visit."

Dan walked up the sidewalk and entered the yard through a small gate to a white picket fence. The Graydon home appeared to have been freshly painted in white with a dark green trim. The grass was mowed, flowers of different colors were planted in front of the house. He nodded approvingly. There was pride of ownership here, as in the other homes in this lower middle class neighborhood of mostly black people. He knocked on the door. A large black man who was at least 6'2" opened the door and scowled at him.

"Hello. My name is Dan Edwards." Dan held out his hand, which the large black man ignored. Dan quickly took his hand away. "I have information that we may have ancestors in common back in the 1800's and I'd like to talk with you and your sister about it." Dan could see a young woman peering around a corner, listening to him.

"My sister and I ain't related to no honky. Get lost!" The door slammed in Dan's face.

Dan turned away and retraced his steps back to his car. "Wait, please wait!" He turned around and saw the young woman from the house running after him. When she reached him she held out her hand. "I'm sorry for the rude behavior of my brother, Richard. I'm Sarah, and I'm very interested in finding out about how we are related. Could we go somewhere and talk? I'll treat you to a cup of coffee and a doughnut." She smiled. "There's a cafe not far from here."

Dan shook her hand and smiled back. "I'd like that. Hop in." He opened the passenger door for her.

Two hours later Dan looked at his watch and exclaimed about the time. "Sarah, I've really enjoyed talking to you, and I have a feeling there's a lot more we could explore about our families. Would you be willing to meet here next week, same day and time?"

"I'd love to! I can't believe that young boy, Sam, recorded our family history and it has passed from generation to generation. Thank you for giving me one of the copies your Mother had made. I'll have to check to see if my brother has an original. It's so interesting, finding out about our genealogy. I wonder why my parents or brother didn't mention this before? I'll look forward to next week."

The following week, after they sat down at the cafe table and ordered, Sarah opened the conversation. "I talked with my brother about the book Sam wrote. He admitted he had a copy, but said we shouldn't be proud of our history since the reason we are related to whites is that the masters of the plantation and the overseers raped the slave women and got them pregnant. That's why there are so many black people with mixed blood. He's a Black Panther and is into black power, so doesn't want to admit we have mixed blood." She looked down at her hands. "I don't feel the same way. I feel proud I had an ancestor like Rose, who died to save her son, a white couple and her fiance'. I want to learn as much as I can about them. Could we read through what Sam wrote and stop to discuss it as we go?"

Dan nodded, took out the book, and they began to read, taking turns.

As they read and talked Dan noticed Sarah's eyes were a deep brown and her skin was a smooth, beautiful, milk chocolate color. Her hair curled around her oval face and she was tiny— probably about 5'3 to his 5'10. He liked the way she looked directly into his eyes and her laugh was infectious. After two hours they set a time to meet again and said good-bye. Dan realized he could hardly wait until the next time they'd get together.

"Hi Dan. It's Laura. I haven't heard from you in awhile."

"Oh, hi Laura. Yes. I've been pretty busy."

"Mom and Dad were wondering if you could come for dinner next Sunday afternoon about one o' clock."

"Yes, that should be good. Thank your parents for me and tell them I'm looking forward to seeing them again."

"I hope that includes seeing me again as well."

"Yes, of course. See you then."

Dan stood by the phone, thinking, after he'd hung up. He hadn't called Laura during the last two weeks and had ignored a couple of her calls. What did that mean anyway? He was confused. Laura was so good for him. The public was used to seeing them together. They'd been in the newspaper, standing arm in arm, had been seen together at parties, and she'd been with him, supporting him, when he'd given speeches at various gatherings. Everyone expected...He shook his head. Can't think of all that now.

"Sarah, after we have our coffee, do you think we could walk to the park? It's a beautiful day."

"I think that's a wonderful idea."

They sat on a park bench and Sarah began talking about the research she'd been doing on the slavery period, trying to place their ancestors in what was happening then. He had a hard time concentrating on what she was saying, so entranced was he with watching her animated facial expressions and the way her hands moved around as she talked.

"Dan, where are you?" Sarah was smiling. "Are you back in the 1800's? I don't think you heard what I just said."

Dan shook his head. "Sorry. Guess I was away for a bit there. And it wasn't because what you said wasn't interesting."

"We'd probably better say good-bye now anyway. It's been at least two hours again. Same time and place for next week?"

Dan nodded and, as they stood up, Sarah impulsively reached up and gave him a hug. Dan held on, not wanting to let her go, and they looked deep into each other's eyes before they reluctantly pulled apart. They were silent as they walked back to their cars, neither knowing what to say.

"Dan, welcome!" Laura reached up and planted a kiss on his mouth. She was dressed in a green, low cut dress and looked as beautiful as always. She took him into the living room where he presented her Mother with a bouquet of roses and shook hands with her Father. When they sat down at the dining room table a servant dished up the soup. Conversation began with what was happening politically in Washington and, by the end of the evening, became more personal. Dr. Evans mentioned he'd read recently that Dan is the shining star of the Party and plans were to have him run for a Senate seat at the next Congressional election. Had he considered that it might be time to get a home of his own and settle down? He looked meaningfully at both Dan and his daughter. Dan squirmed and mentioned the run for Senate was not decided as yet. He commented on how delicious the dinner was and avoided looking at Laura.

When he was ready to leave he thanked Dr. and Mrs. Evans for the wonderful meal and Laura walked him to his car. She reached up and kissed him. "I love you, Dan." Dan reached down and kissed her, then said good-bye and got into his car.

Now, why couldn't I say I love her? I used to think I did. I know she's perfect for me and would be a great help in my career as a politician. Her parents are influential people with a great deal of money and would support me as well. My family likes her. What is stopping me from making a commitment? I do care about her only...

"Gather in the family room, everyone. We have another letter from Michael." Dan, Bob, Betty and Bill found their seats while Tom opened the letter.

'Hi family, it's July, and I'm going to try to write at least every two months. Wonder if Bob has tried out his new car yet.

Drive carefully, Bob. I've read about you, Dan, in the papers. They cover a lot of US news here, and you are a hot topic right now as a upcoming party favorite in the US. I'm proud to be your little brother. Don't think I said congratulations to you and Bill, Betty. You got a good man there and, of course, Bill, you married a wonderful woman. Dad, I miss you trying to keep me on the straight and narrow. Want you to know, though, that you've influenced me after all. I gave up drinking and other stuff and am working hard. And I've met a terrific woman who seems to think I'm okay too. Am thinking of proposing. Hope that isn't too much of a shock for your heart, Dad. I'll let you all know if I actually do it and don't chicken out. Guess that's all for now. Wish I could hear from you. Perhaps someday. Please know I think of you often. Keep safe and happy. All my love, Mike.'

"Mike getting married! That IS a shock! Wonder what kind of a woman would marry my brother." Dan grinned.

Tom looked down at the letter again. Sounds as if he's gotten himself straightened out. Sure wish I could be at that wedding. He watched as Bob got up and left the room without saying anything. Guess I'd better talk to him and see how he's feeling. Glad he has a closer relationship with Bill now, but I know he still misses Michael.

"Dad, I told you I was going to see the descendants of the Graydon family and I did. The man isn't interested in meeting us, but his sister is. Her name is Sarah. I wonder if I could invite her to dinner next Sunday."

"Of course, son. It'll be interesting to have people from the Ramsey family and the Graydon family, all descendants from families in the 1800's and all under the same roof. I only wish your Mom was here."

"I do too, Dad. I do too."

"I don't know, Dan. What if your family doesn't like me?" Sarah turned on the bench to face him, a worried expression on her face.

"Of course they'll like you. How could they not? You're terrific!" Dan couldn't help himself. He leaned over and pulled her close, kissing her gently on the lips. She moved in and pressed against him, arms around his neck.

Sarah pulled away. "I'm sorry. I shouldn't have done that." She started to rise, but Dan pulled her down next to him and held her tight.

"Sarah, we both feel something. Let's not try to deny it."

Introductions were made and Sarah was led into the dining room. She was placed next to Bob who kept her entertained with stories about building his car and his fishing and camping trips. Dan was in the kitchen most of the time, as he had cooked his famous spaghetti and meatballs to impress her with his cooking prowess. After dinner they retired to the family room where card tables were set up for Scrabble, Clue and Yahtzee. The conversation was lively, interspersed with lots of laughter.

Much later, Sarah thanked the family, said good-bye and promised Bob a rematch with Clue and Scrabble. Dan walked her to her car and, thinking someone might see them, said good-night without a kiss.

Dan went into the kitchen to get a drink and found Tom sitting at the kitchen table. "Sit down, son. I really like your friend, Sarah."

Dan brightened. "Yeah, she's a wonderful person."

"I noticed the way the two of you looked at each other this evening—not unlike the way your Mom and I used to look at each other as two people very much in love." Tom saw Dan's face reddening. "You don't need to tell me anything. You know we have no problem with the color of her skin. I just want the two of you, before this goes any further, to take a good hard look at the ramifications—how other people will treat you and your children, how it will affect your career, will your love be strong enough to rise above all the problems you will face with an interracial marriage? Just know that I will support you in any decision you make. Good-night, son." Tom stood and headed toward his bedroom, leaving Dan sitting there, deep in thought.

"I like your family, Dan."

"Yes, and they like you. Bob was really taken with you and wants you to come again and play board games with him."

"They didn't seem to think it was a problem that I'm black." She hesitated. "They don't know that we are more than friends though. That might make a difference."

"I know my Dad and the others would support us if they knew we had feelings for each other. My Dad and Mom were never prejudiced."

"I wish my brother was like that. He hates the white people—whom he calls 'honky'. It got worse after he went to Oakland and joined the Black Panthers. He'd have a fit if he knew I cared about a white man."

"He'll have to know sooner or later, Darling, because I'm not going to give you up. I'm falling in love with you."

"Hello Laura, it's Dan."

"Hi. I was wondering if you'd disappeared off the face of the earth. Haven't seen or heard from you in ages. Is anything the matter?"

"I'd just like to get together and talk. Could you meet me at our favorite restaurant on Saturday night about seven?"

"Of course, Darling. I can't wait to see you."

Laura rushed up to Dan and reached up to kiss him. He put his arm behind her back and led her into the restaurant and to their table. After ordering, Laura talked about her job and asked about his family. Finally, she said, "Okay, Dan, something's wrong. I can feel it. Don't keep me in suspense. Is everything going well with your job as a congressman?"

"It's not that. It's about us," Dan began.

"Oh it's okay! I know I was distant with you before."

"Wait," Dan held up his hand.

"No, let me say this first. I'm sure it'll answer your concerns. From the beginning I wasn't as interested as you in Civil Rights. See, after that experience on the bus I was so frightened. I had to admit I wasn't as committed to the cause as you. I'm still not. I thought this meant we couldn't be together. I was just too afraid of what being with you would mean. But these past few weeks when we haven't seen each other very often, I missed you and did some thinking. I may not be ready to die for this cause, but I am ready to live for you. That was the struggle, the part of me I held back from you for so long. But I love you, Dan, and I think that's enough."

Dan turned pale.

Laura smiled and grabbed his hand, "Whew! Such a relief to get that off my chest! It's okay, dear. You can trust me completely. What did you want to say?"

This is it, Dan thought. There is no way of saying it without hurting her. "Laura, I'm in love with another woman."

Laura looked stunned, and for a moment just stared at him, saying nothing. "I don't understand. I thought we had something. I love you and I thought you loved me."

"I thought I did too, but recently I met someone else and we just..." He stopped, not knowing what else to say.

Laura rose. "Good-bye, Dan." She grabbed her coat and was out the door before he knew what was happening.

"We have to do something besides meeting at this cafe and going to the park. It's the beginning of September and it will be getting cold soon. How about I take you out for dinner at a nice restaurant and then we go to a movie?"

"Someone might see us and I don't think we're ready for that."

"OK, we'll wear disguises. I'll put on dark rimmed glasses and pull a hat down over my head and you wear glasses and a wig."

Sarah laughed. "That could be fun."

The next week Dan and Sarah were back at the cafe. "Thanks for the dinner and movie last week. I enjoyed going in disguise." She smiled.

"Sarah, we need to think about how we are going to deal with going out in public. Sometimes people recognize me and the word may spread that we are going together."

"What about the woman you've been dating? Can't you just continue seeing her in public and we keep our relationship private for the time being? Wouldn't that be best for your career?"

"Too late for that, my dear. I didn't think it was fair to Laura to lead her on, so I broke it off last week. No, we need to face that our relationship might cause us some problems, but I think our love is strong enough to handle those problems together. How about you, Darling? Are you ready to face what we'll face as an interracial couple?"

Sarah squared her shoulders and looked Dan straight in the eye. "I'm ready if you are."

Dan reached across the table and took her hand, noticing as he did so a woman at the next table pointing at them and frowning. It was not going to be easy.

"Dad, thought I should tell you that I broke it off with Laura. Sarah and I have decided to go public soon about our relationship."

"I assume you've talked about it and you know this could really affect your career as a politician."

"There are more and more interracial couples these days and I think my constituents will accept Sarah and me. There might be an initial reaction, but eventually..."

"Dan, I don't think you are looking at the hard, cold reality of the situation. The few interracial couples you read about aren't in politics. Interracial marriages are illegal in many states. It will probably be the end of your political career, and you say that politics is the way you can do the most for the Civil Rights Movement. Are you prepared to give all that up?"

"Yes, Dad. Sarah means more to me than a career in politics. I'll go back to practicing law if I have to."

Sarah and Dan sat down at their usual table at the cafe and gave their order. "You were going to talk with your Dad about us. How did he take it?"

"He said he'd support us."

Sarah leaned forward. "Come on, Dan. What else did he say?"

Dan hesitated. "He mentioned it would probably affect my career in politics and that our marriage would be illegal in several states. I told him I didn't care. I could always practice law."

"Oh, Dan. You love politics. I can't have you give that up for me. That's too great a sacrifice."

"Darling, I'd give up much more than politics for you. You are worth everything to me."

The meal came and they ate in silence. There didn't seem to be anything else to be said.

When they stood up and put on their coats, Sarah spoke up. "Dan, I think we should each really think about how this will affect you and me in the future. We need to talk about it." Dan nodded.

As they walked toward the cafe door, Sarah looked out the window and stopped in horror. "Richard's out there!"

Dan glanced out the window, noticing a very tall, muscular black man standing near the door. His arms were folded, legs apart, and he wore a glowering expression.

"Dan, go out the back door. Go!" She pushed him in the direction of the back of the cafe.

"No, Sarah. I have to face up to him sooner or later. Now is as good a time as any." He took Sarah's arm, led her to the door and opened it for her.

As soon as they were outside, Sarah went to her brother. "Richard, you met Dan before." Richard pushed her aside and punched Dan hard. Dan fell to the ground, blood gushing from his nose. Richard bent over him. "If you ever try to see my sister again, you'll get more than this next time." He grabbed Sarah's arm and pulled her away, taking her to his car where he pushed her, crying, into the passenger side and then drove off.

Dr. Stephen Evans sat down on the sofa next to his wife. "Our little gal is still crying over that bastard, Daniel Edwards. How could he prefer another woman to our Laura? So far she hasn't been seen in public with him. I'd sure like to know who she is. That's it!" He punched the sofa. "I'll hire a detective to follow Dan and learn about this woman. Maybe there's a chance it won't last and he'll come back to Laura. I'd always figured they'd get together. He just needs to wake up. Dan is going places in the party and Laura could help him get there. They are so well suited to each other."

"Thank you for the information, Mr. Jones. Send the photos and the written report to me as soon as you can and I'll give you your check then." Dr. Evans hung up the phone, looked at his wife and smiled. "Well, that relationship can't last. Dan is involved with a Negro girl. It's obviously a passing fancy, connected with all his Civil Rights work. He must know how this would affect his political career. No wonder they're keeping it quiet. I'm going to see Tim Martin"

"Who is that dear?" asked his wife.

"That's the party leader. He might be interested in what his bright and shining star may be doing to his political career."

"Thank you for bringing this to my attention, Dr. Evans. You are absolutely right—this relationship would damage Dan's career."

"I certainly hope you can knock some sense into him. I know he has a bright future, but not if he continues to see this girl." Dr. Evans shook hand and said good-bye.

Tim Martin sat at his desk and looked at the report and photos Dr. Evans had just given him. This report on Sarah Graydon is helpful. She's a fairly well known journalist and I've read some of her writings. Her articles over the years on the Civil Rights Movement show her to be a bright, sensitive person. I may have more luck getting through to her than to Daniel. It's worth a try. That naive young man doesn't know what he's getting himself into. If they continue, he can kiss his public life, well, life as he knows it, good-bye—that would be a shame.

Tim Martin entered the cafe and looked around, immediately spotting Sarah in a back booth. He introduced himself, sat down, and they both ordered coffee. "I guess you are wondering why I asked to talk to you."

"Not really, Mr. Martin. The relationship I have with Dan Edwards could end his political career. He and I are both aware that could happen. He says, if it does, he could always go back to being a lawyer. What I don't understand is why you, a leader of the party, are taking such a personal interest."

She is bright, Tim Martin thought to himself. "I'll be honest with you. We've made a lot of progress in Civil Rights and you've been a part of that. So has Dan. However, we haven't gotten to the place that the general public is accepting of interracial relationships. Interracial marriages are illegal in several states. The US is not ready to accept the two of you and it may be years before it is."

Tim Martin took a drink of coffee. "Sarah, Dan's work on Civil Rights is not finished. He is a great orator, and when he speaks, people listen. More than that—he is sensitive to their needs and they somehow realize that. People are becoming aware of him and he has the potential to be more than a great politician. He has the makings of a great statesman. The Party is planning to have him run as a senator and are even thinking that someday, if he keeps on the way he's going, he may have presidential potential. Some are already likening him to John F. Kennedy. Could you imagine what he could do for Civil Rights then?" Tim smiled. "Now, I'm not saying he'll eventually be our president. What I am saying is that he is showing the potential to be a great leader in our country." He paused. "That is, if he's given the opportunity. If he continues to see you, that opportunity will be lost. Period." He looked into Sarah's eyes and sighed. "I know you love him and he loves you. This is a difficult thing to ask, but are you willing to sacrifice his career and the potential good he can do our country for this love?"

Sarah wiped her eyes and looked down, shaking her head. "I'll talk with him."

Dan walked in the cafe door, saw Sarah in the back booth, and waved at her. He came up to her, leaned over and kissed her, then sat down. "Hello darling. I thought we weren't going to meet at our cafe anymore because of your brother."

"No problem today, because he's working. Let's order. I'm so glad my brother didn't seriously injure you. He didn't break your nose, did he?" Dan shook his head. The coffee and food came and they were quiet for awhile.

"Dan, I don't think my brother will ever accept you."

"Don't worry, Sarah. "I'll work on him. Eventually, he won't be able to resist my charming personality." He grinned.

"It's more than Richard, Dan." She hesitated. "It's the prejudice you and I and our children would face throughout our lives. I don't think I could deal with it." She looked him in the eyes. "And, most of all, our being together would ruin your political career. Mr. Martin, came to see me yesterday and he presented a powerful case."

"What? Tim had no right to do that!"

"He spelled out what I already knew—that you have great potential as a leader in the Party and that a relationship with me would ruin that."

"I already said I'd give up a political career and go back to being a lawyer."

"Yes, but is that what you really want? You might come to resent me for your having to give up politics, and I would surely feel guilty for your having to make that choice."

"I'm going to have a talk with Tim. He had no right!" Dan raised his pointer finger in the air.

"I'm glad he did. It helped me see things more clearly. Did you know the Party thinks you have the makings of not just a great politician, but a great statesman? Mr. Martin said people listen to you and you understand their needs. He thinks you can help the Party make headway in the Civil Rights movement. Did you know he mentioned some people are already comparing you to John F. Kennedy? There's even talk that, if you keep on the way you are going, you could eventually become President of the United States." Sarah leaned forward and looked into Dan's eyes. "Much as I love you and know you love me, I cannot, will not, come between you and a promising political career. I am saying good-bye now, Dan, and I don't want you to ever contact me again." Sarah stood up, looked at him, a determined expression on her face, and walked out of the cafe.

Dan sat there, stunned. She can't mean it. We love each other. That should count for more than anything else—right? Did she really say that some people are comparing me with Kennedy? And the Party thinks I could help make some positive changes in the Civil Rights Movement. I'm sure someone else could do it if I can't. But who? I'm already making talks around the state and have a following, plus I do have a lot of experience in working in Civil Rights. And I know the Party wants me to run for senator next time.

I just can't go on without her. I think of her the first thing when I wake up in the morning and the last thing at night, plus a lot of time in between. I imagine her and me in a nice home with a couple of kids running around the family room and Dad playing Grandpa. He smiled to himself. How can I give that up? But then, Sarah, with Tim Martin's assistance, has pointed out what my political career could mean to people—especially black people, if we get laws passed to help them. And I know how to write bills.

I should run after her. But then...What a decision this is! It's way too big a decision to make on the spur of the moment. I'll go home and sleep on it.

Made in the USA
San Bernardino, CA
04 June 2016